Embers of Shadow

Praise Page

Unpredictable and gape-worthy…the entire Ages of Malice series is worth devouring every word.

— RACHEL DEHNING, *READER VIEWS*

Jeffries gives as good as a reader can possibly get. Themes that **explode off the page**…very highly recommended.

— JAMIE MICHELE, *READERS' FAVORITE*

Spectacular…fascinating characters, unexpected twists and turns, and **an ending that will blow you away even as you beg for more**…I honestly **read the book in one sitting**.

— *FEATHERED QUILL* BOOK REVIEWS

Gripping…an **extremely fast-paced adrenalin-pumping ride!** This high-tension thriller is **masterfully composed**.

— TRACY TRAYNOR, *READERS' FAVORITE*

This book **will nearly overwhelm your senses. The gifted work by this author continues unabated…incredibly well-crafted. I can't recommend this enough.**

— *NN Light's Book Heaven*

Is as believable as it is **thought-provoking.** Has all the ingredients to become **a massive hit with readers**.

— Essien Asian, *Readers' Favorite*

After reading the first two in the series, I found **Embers of Shadow to be an incredible novel.** Lloyd Jeffries is a **master storyteller**…I am a huge fan…and he never disappoints. You hardly ever come across supernatural thrillers of this quality. I only have praise for this **magnificent story**!

— Rabia Tanveer, *Readers' Favorite*

Cinematic, and as one reads the novel, it is almost **like one is watching a movie.**

— *The US Review of Books*

The **series' trademark unpredictability is maintained**, with **a masterful narrative that shatters preconceived notions** and keeps readers on the edge of their seats.

— Miche Ardennes, *Readers' Favorite*

A wonderfully complex fantasy thriller with **a BLAST of an ending!** Pick up a copy of all three novels now! **Trust me; you won't regret it.**

— *The Wishing Shelf Book Awards*

Gold Award, Feathered Quill
Silver Award, Feathered Quill
Bronze Award, Reader Views

Finalist, IAN Book of the Year Awards
Finalist, The Wishing Shelf Book Awards
Finalist, Chanticleer Int'l Book Awards

Notable 100 Shelf Unbound Best Indie Competition

Semi-finalist, BookLife Prize
by Publisher's Weekly

BookLife Elite Author

Bronze Award, Readers' Favorite
Gold Award, Literary Titan

"Unpredictable and gape-worthy"
"Fresh and exciting"
"Cinematic…like one is watching a movie"
"Masterfully written"

Follow Lloyd at www.lloydjeffries.com

Embers of Shadow

Ages of Malice, Book III

Lloyd Jeffries

Library of Congress Control Number: 2023915798
ISBN 979-8-9855269-8-1 (paperback)
ISBN 979-8-9855269-7-4 (ebook)
ISBN 979-8-9855269-9-8 (hardcover)

Cover design by Design for Writers
Inkslinger Editing

For permissions, contact
Buckminster Publishing
Info@lloydjeffries.com

For Goat

PROLOGUE

MARYLAND, UNITED STATES

Bill nods and stifles a yawn.

The pastor's face is red; spit flies as he shouts.

Bill likes church. The dynamics, the music, the things he learns. The problem with church is you can only take so much.

The dude's mostly wrong about everything.

"The end is coming!" the preacher screams.

Comments follow. "Amen!" "Preach!"

Then dude asks for money, lists a litany of reasons to give. "It's your duty as a Christian." "God's work costs." "Cast your bread upon the water. Soon it will come back with every wave."

Bill thinks of bread, thinks of seagulls, thinks of PB&J's. The offering plate comes and he passes it along. He has no need for money and carries none. He doesn't notice the looks from those around him.

Finally, the service ends, and Bill moves through the parishioners. "Hi, Bill," a man says. "Come for dinner?" Bill shakes his head, anxious to be home with his books. The sanctuary is hot from the relentless heat of the past week. He unbuttons his suit, runs a hand through shoulder-length hair.

He squeezes through parishioners. Hears talk about pies baked, prayers granted.

Wishes, he thinks, supplications. Foolishness.

Do these people know anything about God?

Have they ever considered their fates lie in their own hands?

Have they taken the time to research, to gain knowledge, to learn what exists is based on everything that existed prior? "No man is an island," Hemingway said, "but a part of the main."

People think history started the day they were born but give no consideration to its end. Never a thought to the vastness of time, the fullness of humanity and its time on this planet. No thought given to what's come before, how that shapes events today.

Too self-centered, he thinks. Too interested in pie and supplication.

Outside, he turns from the concrete walkway, then moves across a quaint, manicured lawn. Children play here, try to climb a broad oak while boosting each other and chasing in circles.

"Hi, Bill." Priscilla, a tiny girl with dark curls, smiles as other children gather behind her. "Can you do your trick?"

Bill rubs a dry eye. "Does anyone else want to see it?"

"Yes!" they cry.

"I haven't done it in a while," he says. "Hope it works."

Kneeling by the tree, he holds out his hand and makes kissing sounds. He spins a walnut, glances up as children beam with expectation.

A squirrel chatters, then scampers down the tree and up his arm. Its tail swishes like a feather as it snatches the nut. Shell shavings fall as it gnaws.

The children cheer, move close.

"Careful," he says. "Don't scare him."

They quiet, move around the tree, take turns stroking the rodent's ample fur.

The squirrel gnaws unphased. It swishes its tail, makes a small squeak. Another scampers down and soon four squirrels happily munch walnuts while kids pet and coo.

"How many nuts do you have?" Priscilla asks.

"None."

"How many did you bring?"

"None."

She looks at him for a long moment, then something dawns in her eyes. "*You're* a nut, Bill."

Bill leans close and whispers, "We all are, sweet Priscilla."

A drop of sweat drips from his forehead. Then, the toot of a horn as a limo pulls in front of the broad, white church.

"Be nice to these animals or next week they won't come back."

The children nod, solemn expressions on innocent faces.

Priscilla gives him a hug. "See you next week?"

"Of course."

He moves through the grass, down a sidewalk to the waiting car.

The driver smiles and hands him a joint. "We have to go, Bill. Cain called, said it's urgent. Said no stops, no lunch. Said, 'Just get him here ASAP.'"

Bill sparks the joint, then puffs a white cloud into the day's sun. "May as well," he says, then snickers. "That dude's always panicking about something."

As the limo pulls off, he doesn't notice the contemptuous stares from the gathered parishioners.

———

INCOMING…

The word blinks as electric turquoise floods his wrinkled face in a dusky jade glow. Above, a fluorescent light flickers, makes his head ache.

This contract should provide the money to disappear forever.

On the screen, pixelated letters: HIGH PRIORITY. FEMALE, 34, MURDER, TREASON, ESPIONAGE. LAST SEEN HEADING NORTHWEST FROM D.C. APPROACH WITH CAUTION. ARMED AND EXTREMELY DANGEROUS. APPREHEND ALIVE.

An icon appears, gets clicked. Then, an image starts to form.

He props his feet on the cheap desk, feels it shift under the weight. Panel walls surround, an arsenal on dust-covered ivory. Three Glocks, two shotguns, assault rifles, flashbangs, hand grenades, knives, tactical flashlights, body armor.

Think I'll take the big boy.

The rifle feels heavy, solid, deadly. He pulls the bolt; clean, dry and serviceable. Smooth. Ready. The sniper's choice, Barrett M82, made to reach out and ruin your day.

This should be fun, if the demons stay away.

Let's see: ammo, cold weather gear, silencer, poncho, double Glocks, MRE's; what the hell, a shotgun never hurts. His chuckle sounds joyless. His mouth feels dry. The computer's fan thrums at high speed. The room's hot. *Need to install that vent.* He sighs, glances at the computer.

Her image fills the outdated screen.

Auburn hair cascades. Her smile twinkles like she's up to something.

And those eyes. Like a cat's, glowing, feminine emeralds holding a tint of mischief, a touch of mystery.

High priority.

Apprehend alive.

This *will* be fun.

———

16 A.D.

Misthli (Modern Day Turkey)

He races the wind, sweat streaming from dark locks.

She wasn't home, wasn't in the marketplace.

She'd never leave without saying goodbye.

He thinks of his father as strong legs propel him up the winding road. The glade is the only place left. Their secret, the only other place he can think of.

He veers down a rugged path through tall grasslands.

A spear whistles by, misses by a foot. He twists his head to find his pursuers. Gwenna's father, Dorman. His own father, Archelaus. Sephus, the miserable liar and his sly deeds, never good with a spear or at pankration.

Longinus pushes beyond his limit, forces his body forward, past exhaustion, head spinning as the sun scorches.

Galloping horses grow close.

He plunges into the wood, too thick for the horses. They'll have to dismount to catch him. Doesn't matter now that they'll know of the secret glade.

All that matters is Gwenna.

Branches scratch as sunlight splinters maple, sycamore, laurel.

Then, the broad trunk with the dark knot, as big as his torso.

Glancing over his shoulder, he stoops, stumbles through thorny branch and bramble.

Gwenna lies waiting.

He races to her, lifts her head, feels something tickle his skin.

"Gwenna! Gwenna?"

Blood covers his arm.

A dagger drops from her hand.

Lifeless eyes bore into him.

His head buzzes. Breath catches as he presses lips to her forehead. "No, no, no." The word drips from his mouth, razes heart and hopes to burnt husks.

His father moves close, then kneels beside him and lays a hand on his shoulder. "She's taken her own life."

Dorman, her father, drops beside, pries her from Longinus's grip. Eyes flare rage as a dark beard twitches. "This was you!"

Longinus stands, faces them, fists clenched.

Then Sephus stands before him, sixteen years old, same as Longinus.

A spear presses Longinus's chest. "It be the gallows for ye."

Despair rends his heart. He moves without thought.

Then Sephus lies, spear rising from his chest.

Dorman lunges, is intercepted by Archelaus.

The grunts of struggle, prized bulls doing battle.

Then Dorman lies, huge hands having choked his life.

Archelaus spins and grasps his shoulders. "Run, boy! Toward Rome. To return is death!"

He hears the sounds, other pursuers searching the wood.

Strong arms enwrap and hold him close. "You're strong and brave. I'll find you in Rome. Go now!"

Longinus glances toward the wood, hears voices close.

"Go!" Archelaus whispers. "Be silent. Don't come back. I'll find you."

Their eyes meet, then his father slips a dagger from his sheath and kneels beside the dead men.

Longinus stalks away. He knows these woods like his father's face.

Tears flow. Hands tremble.

Gwenna.

My love.

CHAPTER 1

MOUNT TABOR, ISRAEL

Church of the Transfiguration

As Longinus sleeps, I take the time to explore the grounds. And fix up, of course. The church seems no worse for wear as I stare from an ancient stone sidewalk and relive the prior day's events.

Even if I wrote an article for the *Times*, no one would believe me. A junkie reporter has-been making up stories to garner the good graces of the HR department and notoriously picky editors.

But the events happened, and I was at their center.

I just can't wrap my mind around them.

To my left, tall trees offer charred trunks and crackled leaves to the burning sun as if hoping to gain a semblance of healing.

What happened here was epic, lending new meaning to the term *of biblical proportions*.

Longinus was transformed before my eyes. Or, to stick with the theme of this place, he'd transfigured. Had become his giant self to wield the spear and decimate an army the likes of which, I'm certain, has never before been seen on the planet. Enormous, fantastical, awesome.

Again, I think *biblical*.

The use of such cliches sends my mind wandering, the familiar struggle to find the right word and express that which I witnessed and survived. Only cliches remain these days, language kidnapped by younger generations, then beaten into the ground like the proverbial plowshare. Now, all words are overused, lack impact. No longer have the ability to describe a scene that's truly awe inspiring.

But at least the rain's stopped, replaced by a sweltering heat uncommon for this time of year. Sweat drips from my hair, makes my shirt sticky and transparent. White's a bad color for days like this.

I move toward the church, look for someone from the Franciscan order. I'd seen one of them earlier, moving quickly, too far away to catch. I try to think of the appropriate term. Father, padre, senõr, brother, all equal possibilities, and all probably wrong. I hope not to offend when I finally gain an audience.

It's not like they can be *that* busy today. The road up here has been sealed off by Israeli security forces, and if I have to guess, I'd say Cain is probably responsible for the whole debacle. I'll wager he probably put the wheels in motion in order to bring some plan to fruition.

But why the attack? The airplanes bore emblems of different nations, only one of which I recognized: Russia.

I'm sure once I speak to Cain, all these things will be explained as he's too vain to *not* take credit. Too vain to *not* tell me how he's engineered it all.

All serve at the pleasure of the gloved man, words truer now than when I'd first heard them.

I close my eyes, inhale, try to will my body cool. A voice behind me breaks my thoughts. "Hot today."

I turn to find the subject of my search, Father Papadopoulos, the priest we'd encountered when we'd first set foot up here. The padre that seemed so bothered by my inability to become a mountain goat and traverse the church's roof.

Intelligence burns through blue eyes, portrays depths of thought both wise and inquisitive. Long brown robes flow to the ground as open-toed sandals jut from beneath.

"Too hot for me." I shake his hand. "I thought I was in Israel, not Africa."

He laughs, glances around the place. "How are you feeling after all of that?"

I consider the question, survey my mind and body. "No worse for wear it seems. Mostly lucky to be alive."

He steps close, lowers his head. "You think luck had some sway in your fate. Interesting." He casts a glance to the sky as if expecting another swarm of enemy aircraft. Then, he chuckles, as if I don't get something. "I fear you're mixed up in an apocalypse," he says. "Thought I'd ask if you know that already."

I try to look pleasant as his gaze burns into me, as I try to guess his connection to Cain. "I'm starting to get a clue," I say. "If you have the time, Father, I have a few questions."

"Friar," he says, "or Brother, whichever you prefer. Although I'm called Father frequently, I'm not, well, anymore."

I like the man, straightforward, his tone gentle, as if speaking to a child and guiding them to enlightenment.

"Of course," I say, "my apologies."

He waves a hand. "Come, let's get out of the heat. Beneath these robes is a tsunami of sweat, and I fear if we tarry, we'll both be swept away."

I laugh, then follow as he turns down the path toward the L-shaped building to my right. I remember passing this building on my way to the church, remember thinking it probably held dorm rooms or offices.

A painted door opens on greased hinges, and he motions me through. The place is shielded from the day's heat but only partially. There's no cool caress of conditioned air as we enter. The place seems to lack such an appliance, or it was destroyed in the attack. Still, it's cooler in here and feels good.

He moves up a long hall adorned with crucifixes and pictures of the members of his order. Beneath each is a caption announcing their names and from where they hail.

"We'll talk in my quarters," he says. "I hope that's comfortable for you." He opens another door, and we enter a small room, void of décor.

A single cot presses against a whitewashed wall. A pitcher of water drips condensation on a small end stand. Next to that, a small white basin made of some sort of metal, chipped in places, well-used. There's a single chair to my left. Nothing fancy, just four legs and a back rest, no cushion.

He moves to the cot, sits, slides his sandals off. "I hope you don't mind. Lately, they've been a nuisance."

I grin. "How does one pronounce your name again?"

Eyes twinkle as he regards me. "It doesn't matter. Most people just call me Pappy."

"Pappy?"

"Yes, short for Papadopoulos. Greek. You'd think I'd be Greek orthodox." He chuckles, runs a hand over the sweat on his temple, through thinning salt-and-pepper hair. He holds my eyes, examines them for a moment, then rises and moves to the pitcher where he pours water into a red plastic cup and offers it to me. "Thirsty?"

"Yes, thank you." I accept the liquid, feel the coolness slide over my tongue and down my throat. It's as if I can feel the furnace in my body lower a few degrees. "I really needed that."

"My pleasure," he says. "You've been through a lot."

I glance out the room's lone window. It's small, rectangular, makes the room appear more prison cell than the living quarters of a holy man. "Father," I say, "er, I mean, Brother, um, Pappy, I was hoping perhaps you could explain to me just what the…" I start to say *hell* but correct myself. "What in the world happened? I can't wrap my mind around it. It's just, it's just too, um, superhero. Too action movie. Too hyperbolic, I guess, to really absorb with any type of intelligent thought."

"Yes, my son, a lot to digest." He raises a finger, then glances at the room's small window. "I'm reminded of a saying: *There's no such thing as extraordinary men. Only ordinary men, made extraordinary by circumstance.* Have you ever heard that?"

I glance at my empty cup. "I haven't."

"It's been on my mind the last few weeks as I see God's hand in recent events. The times are hardly normal, and I fear extraordinary people are needed." He stares at his bare feet. "But for what purpose? That's the real mystery. It's obvious God's with us in a special way. There's no greater evidence than your friend, who not only saved all of us, but the entire country. If Cain wouldn't have sent him, I'm afraid we'd all be dead."

"About that," I say, "what's your relationship to Cain? How do you know him?"

"He's a parishioner, one of my flock. Comes here quite often and sits in the third row. Just shows up, sits in quiet meditation. Never attends services, though. No matter how many times I ask, his response is always the same…"

"That is well beneath me."

His laugh reminds me of Santa Claus, hearty, full, loud. "Exactly!" He points a finger at me. "That's what he always says. I see you know him quite well."

It's my turn to laugh. "I'm afraid I don't. He's the original enigma. Just when you think you know him, he changes to something else."

I think to tell him my true thoughts. Think to speak my belief that Cain is evil incarnate. That the malice dwelling in his soul can't be contained or channeled. That the man cares nothing for anyone. Has proven time and again that he cares not at all for humanity or its plight, cares very little for Earth's inhabitants whether human, animal, or plant. I think to tell him how the man has his own agenda and works for nothing save that.

Brother Pappy regards me patiently, so unlike the man I'd first encountered up here.

"In truth," I finally say, "I've concluded nothing about Cain."

Pappy leans forward and props his elbows on his knees. "He's been a generous benefactor for our order, but I get the feeling he's a man with other, let's say, frustrations. Like he carries a weight far greater than what an ordinary man can manage. My instincts tell me he has an important role to play. One I fear will be to the detriment of the faithful and to the world as a whole."

I press my lips shut. I've barely met this friar and have no idea if I'm being baited or if what I say will return to Cain's ears.

He doesn't seem to notice as he rises, refills my cup, and returns to the cot where he leans back and clasps his hands behind his head. His next words are spoken in a sigh, spoken with a detached tone as if just an off-hand statement. "I fear the end times have found us."

His eyes flick up, a look that says he's assessing my current level of sanity.

"You don't seem surprised?" he says.

"I've heard worse," I say. Unlike Pappy, I have the advantage of knowing his reasoning is completely accurate. That Cain is, indeed, singularly focused on clanging the chimes that call the apocalypse to dinner. I'm hit by an urge to tell him the truth, seized with the notion to just spill my guts and tell all I know.

The man before me is pious. Judging by the way he lives, the way he serves, the possessions in his room: Bible, water pitcher, ewer, plastic cups, robes and sandals. The man certainly lives his oath of poverty.

He grasps his Bible from the small table, caresses it with his hand, then opens and flips through the pages.

"You mentioned you have a theory," I say. "Care to share?"

He searches my eyes once more, his face solemn, sizing me up, probably making the same calculations about how much he can say and what I'll tell Cain. He glances toward the door, then the window, and I wonder if he thinks Spiderman's out there eavesdropping.

He waves a hand. "You're just humoring an old man."

"No sir. I'm a reporter. Asking questions and exploring people's thoughts are part of my DNA."

His expression is serious as he considers my words. "You might not be able to handle it," he says. "But I have compelling evidence."

"Do tell."

He waits a few seconds, glances at his Bible, then sighs. "As you wish."

He clears his throat before he starts, slides a hand through thinning hair. "I believe the attack your friend repelled is the opening of Revelation's second seal." He speaks like telling a secret, hushed and low. "This belief is *not* popular with my order."

What his order considers popular is the least of my concerns. The words he'd just spoke, the second seal of Revelation, has my mind spinning. I feel a bit embarrassed as I realize I know very little about Revelation and its interpretations, despite having actually met the work's author, John the Apostle.

"What?" is all I can manage. Not very reporter-like, but as always, my brain's a bit distracted by the chemicals I'd injected earlier.

"I can prove it," he whispers and leans forward. "Revelation speaks of the opening of the second seal. Something John saw while exiled on Patmos. A divine vision, inspired, prophetic." He holds up the Bible. "*This* is a road map. Look no further than this and it's all right in front of you. For centuries people have guessed at it, assigned certain major world events as the start of the end times. The Black Plague, the World Wars, Hiroshima. Fact is, they've made mistakes and, to a person, have been wrong. You see, they've always taken things literally or failed to connect clues in a sensible way. Throughout history a dizzying number of men have been called the antichrist. Endless volumes exist on Revelation's interpretation and true meaning." He nods as he talks, becomes animated, voice rising above a whisper. "Fools, the lot of them. They read the work and see only the words but never consider the *mind* of God, God's true intent. Hmm? It's not so difficult to comprehend if one's willing to spend the thought energy."

"Know the mind of God," I say. "So, you must have it figured out?"

"Hardly!" His laughter rises to a drop ceiling flecked with red. "But when you think about it, I think it comes into view. Just as God intended.

"He created us, knows what we're capable of understanding, what we're capable of working out. He also knows that people will claim some divine knowledge of His plan for no other reason than to gain glory for themselves. I mean, who could know human nature better than the creator of humans?"

He looks at me for two ticks, then stands and starts to pace, talking to himself, expressing thoughts as they go through his head. "I saw the army attack, grander than anything I've ever seen. Today should be

Israel's first day in history's waste basket. Another failed civilization wiped away by its enemies. Yet, here we are. Yet, standing we remain. Our attackers are decimated, utterly defeated. By your friend. Using a relic of Biblical power. Don't you see the miracle? The road sign pointing to the next destination? It's so obvious, it might as well be flashing neon. No other explanation is possible. The second seal has been opened in accordance with Revelation's sixth chapter. *Peace will be taken from the Earth.* The red horse of the apocalypse." He raises a finger. "People think an actual red horse is going to gallop through the heavens, shouting words to all on the Earth.

"But they're wrong. You see, John saw the vision in a certain way. God used symbolism John could understand to make His point. I mean, can you imagine looking up and seeing a huge red horse sprinting across the sky, its rider waving a giant sword in the air? Does anyone believe God works like that? We were made in God's image, an intelligent creation. *Oh, what a piece of work is man. How noble in reason, how infinite in faculty.* Shakespeare got it, wrote it down. That's how God made us, smart enough to put two and two together." Bright eyes regard me and flare beneath unkempt eyebrows. "No, yesterday was more than an attack, my boy, and if I'm right, and the second seal is opened, we're all in big trouble."

I watch the friar. Each sentence causes a torrent of questions to flood my mind, scores of them. I start to speak, but become tongue tied as my brain struggles between the effects of my drugs and which question to ask first.

Then my vision fills with the friar's face, six inches from mine. Bright eyes gleam beneath a hedge of eyebrow. Passionate eyes, full of knowledge, worry, even indignation. They radiate intelligence, decry the speed at which Brother Pappy's intellect operates.

His next words halt the tumult in my head, render me silent as if I've lost my voice box.

"I believe our friend Cain is the Antichrist."

Chapter 2

Mount Tabor, Israel

"I've surprised you, haven't I?" He stops staring and affects a calm demeanor. "I find one needs to enjoy surprises when they happen."

I chuckle. "Things that surprise *me* are mostly horrific anymore."

I stare at the monk, think about Cain as Antichrist. It sounds otherworldly, fictitious, even crazy. As if Frodo Baggins and Samwise Gamgee just flew in on eagles to take lunch in a meadow by the church.

I push away my paradigms and examine the facts. Certainly, Cain's a bad seed, but is he really worse than any other great madman of history? But Pappy has a point, and I'm sure has tested his theories through many days of solitary study in this room.

Time to appear intelligent, I think, to show the friar I can operate on his level. My thoughts flash to the back of the SUV we'd driven up here, the place I keep my fix kit. The vehicle had sustained some damage during the attack, but to my colossal relief, my fix kit remained unharmed. Of all the blessings I have to count, I can think of none of which I'm more grateful. I want to go there now. Want to plunge the needle and let all this madness occur without my interference or attention. I feel Frodo's eagles pick me up as a torrent of flotsam surrounds and sweeps toward inevitable doom.

I choose my next words carefully, try to avoid cliched speech as I search the rolling fog of my drug haze for original thought. My hope is for eloquence and coherence. I manage only: "The Antichrist?"

He stops, regards me again. Does he notice the subtle glaze in my eyes? A sure sign of the chemicals that course through my system. I fidget beneath the stare; think how long it's been since I injected the demons. "If you have some time, I'd love to explain," he says.

I nod, feel relieved, drain my cup, and glance at the water pitcher.

"Please, forgive my indulgence," he says. "For many years I've had only myself to bounce these thoughts off. A solo game of ping pong, if you will, each ball bouncing away to never return. If I bore you, or if you just aren't up for conversation after such a traumatic ordeal, I understand. Simply let me know."

He stops again, looks at me for what seems minutes.

Of course, the drugs are in full swing now, and I stare at him not from a sense of stupefaction, but because the visions rending my mind are terrifying.

Any junkie will tell you that visions are as common as a skin abscess and generally caused by a bad batch of the active chemical and whatever the cartel's chemists have cut them with. Any junkie knows the way to cope with them is to lie somewhere and just, well, let the demons have you. Let them rend and tear, howl, skewer, shred and shriek through every wrinkle of your addled brain. All junkies know the horrors will eventually stop, that the drugs will be slowly processed through whatever systems make them inert.

Any junkie will tell you those things. What they won't tell you is that the ride can be the worst possible thing ever visited upon a human. You see, the mind has an infinite capacity for creativity, can create anything you desire. Monsters, demons, supernatural creatures with scaled wings and razor claws. Aided by drugs, it has the capacity to dream up images you could never imagine while sober. Images that petrify, horrors so real they stand before you, in the flesh, threatening, drooling, intent to rend and maim.

And so it is with me as the visions flow and the demons howl. Cain, rising above the Earth, immense in his proportions, a single step sowing him leagues across the landscape. A fanged nightmare with broad, green head, and scaled body. A dragon of sorts, scooping up humans and stuffing them in his mouth by the handful. Their screams mean nothing as he chomps, and I watch as they're vividly devoured, bones crunching, wails silenced mid-scream. I see children, running, crying, searching for parents that no longer live. The beast is ravenous, his appetite unquenchable. He strides, scoops, crunches, repeats.

Then I see Rhyme. Auburn hair adrift on a gentle breeze, surrounded by great, fiery pillars that stretch into the atmosphere and make her hair stand on end. Flames rush toward her as she turns to me, reaches for me. I hear Cain rasp through his mouthfuls. "Come to me, wife." Her eyes fill with tears, then she steps toward the monster and offers herself. A sacrifice. I raise my hands, try to rush to her, find I lack the ability to move. Then Cain glares down at me, speaks truth through bloody fangs, his voice clanging through my skull. "Coward."

I wake with a start, lying on the cot.

Father Pappy sits at the table, reading his Bible, occasionally looking out the window of this room slash prison cell. Cain's gone. Rhyme's gone. I stare at Pappy and expect him to transform into another vivid nightmare.

He closes the Bible. "I see you're beset by demons of a different kind."

His eyes hold empathy. A slight smile comforts. He helps me to sit, then hands me the plastic cup.

I drink like I haven't had water in six months, then upend the cup and shake every last drop over my parched tongue.

The sound of my voice recalls the rasping croak of the Cain monster. "Forgive me, Father," I say. "Must be the heat."

He knows I'm lying; I can tell by his expression. An expression that says he knows of my deception but need not bother with it.

Yes, Friar, the demons are my own. The drugs my respite. Have you any alcohol? Now, where were we, oh yes, Cain as Antichrist. Do forgive me, it seems my constitution is such that I wilt in extreme heat.

Drugs, you say? Oh no, not me, Father. I'm actually a bit shocked at the question. You see, I effect this facade to bullshit everyone around me. Everyone who ignores my addictions, my cries for help. I mean, and I've never really thought about it, understand, but I mean, now that I do think about it, a snort of chemicals from time to time is probably just the thing for some in society. I mean, who could hold them to account when our world is plagued with nightmare disasters, human decay, indecency on a colossal level? No one could blame them for using such devices to attain a wee bit of happiness, a small oasis in a vast and malicious desert. All quite normal, if you ask me, and please accept this diatribe of rationalization as a proper excuse, an accounting by me on their behalf. What's that you say? You're concerned for me. Oh, how very compassionate of you, but don't worry over me, I've become adept at crafting excuses and shoveling heaps of horse shit.

Pappy fills my cup again, hands me a plate of food. Dates, thin strips of lamb, boiled potatoes. At first, I refuse, but within minutes the plate is empty and I perk up a bit. My senses clear like thunderheads on a steel wind, moving off to reveal a sun both happy and pleasant. After doing its worst, my high is wearing off. I immediately think of my fix kit. Count the excuses to abandon the room and plunge the needle once more.

Pappy watches me eat, takes the plate when I'm done.

"Thank you, Father," I say.

He doesn't correct me. "Don't mention it. Feeling better?"

I run my hands through my hair. "Yes." Then I double down on my bullshit. "The heat is stifling, must've been that. Thank you for looking after me. Again, I apologize."

He continues to watch, says nothing.

"Um, we were talking about the Antichrist," I say. "Specifically, your theory as it applies to Cain."

"Perhaps later, my son. I'm not sure you're up for it."

My mind yearns for the fix kit in the SUV. "I assure you I am," I say, and although I'm certain the friar is correct, that I may not be up for it, I need this conversation. Need something to keep my mind occupied, off the constant and ever-present thoughts of the next fix. That endless longing, endless running, the true demons of addiction.

I search his expression, wonder if he's buying my shtick. I know he's not, but, in the end, what I'm really doing is counting on the man's kindness. His compassion. Using it against him to serve my own ends. A junkie's ploy, I tell myself, but all for the greater good.

He nods, opens the Bible. "As you wish."

"Thanks, Pappy." I grin. The food is working wonders. The water, continually refilled by the friar, nourishes my come-down with astonishing speed. I wonder if Longinus ever feels this way. Perhaps someday he and I can exchange tips on how to manage a bad high.

My mind turns to the friar's accusation. Cain as Antichrist. "Care to explain your theory, Padre?"

"Of course, Emery. Are you certain you're up for it?"

"I am."

"Very well," he says. "Now, the first thing to consider is the prophecy as outlined in Revelation. It can get confusing and, I believe, uses symbolism to make some of its points grander than needed. A bit of Biblical hyperbole, if one thinks about it, but no less valid or believable."

"It's a false document." I speak before I think, and he looks at me as if expecting I'll pass out again.

He shakes his head. "False? Tsk, it's the Bible, my boy. The direct word of God."

"I'm sorry, Pappy, and I don't mean to offend. You've been very kind and that means a lot. But if you're going to consider these theories, then you must have all the facts—and you don't have all the facts. Revelation is false. Cain isn't who he appears to be. The stories in your book are made up."

The friar is subdued, concentrating. A credit to the man not to discount my words because they don't match his paradigm. "Care to explain?" he says.

I think it over. I've babbled too much already. It's a risk telling him all I know, especially without Cain's permission. I may be signing his death warrant. Or mine.

"Okay," I sigh. "Here goes." I tell him everything. From the moment I pressed Mr. Sig to my head, all the way through the events on the church's roof. I leave nothing out.

It feels good, cathartic even, to confess the horrors in which I've taken part. My relationship with John the Apostle, the other immortals, Cain's fulfillment of prophecy, his disappearance after he entered the Temple, his magnificent return at the peace treaty signing in Jerusalem.

The friar listens, appears dumbfounded, opens his mouth to speak three or four times before he snaps it closed. He reaches for a plastic cup, fills it with water, takes a long drink, looks at me, refills the cup, takes another long drink.

"Astonishing," he says.

I'd expected him to mimic my own thoughts when Cain first told me his tale. I expect him to look at me and just say, "Bullshit."

But he doesn't. He sits with his hands clasped in the basket of the robe's stretched fabric between his knees. I can see his mind racing, adding to the tale I've told, snapping puzzle pieces into place.

He wags his head a couple of times but doesn't let up in his thought experiment.

Finally, he says, "It's all true," and a grand smile stretches his face. "My son, do you know what you've done?"

"Of course, I do," I say. "That's why the drugs."

"No, not that. You've just tied up all my loose ends. You see, all holy men suffer a crisis of faith now and then, but you've just solidified all I believe. Yes, the story is unbelievable, but at the same time not unbelievable at all. When one considers the evidence without preconceived beliefs, it all adds up. God *is* in control." He emphasizes the word *is*, as if the Messiah has come and explained everything.

He stands. "Come, we have work to do. Much more to explore and explain."

He moves to the door, then returns and helps me stand. "Are you alright?"

My legs feel strong, my body re-energized. I'm surprised to realize I haven't thought about my drugs in the last half hour. Even thinking about them now, their call is diminished, the urge to run to them lessened.

"I'm fine, Pappy," I say. "Let's go."

Chapter 3

West Virginia, United States

"Should we wait?"

"No, fuck them."

"They won't like it."

"I don't care. By the time they get here, she'll be dead. Which is what they want, right?"

"I think they wanted *catch and interrogate.*"

"Who is she anyway?"

"Who knows? Some lady that ran afoul of the government. A high priority target." Sam makes finger quotes as he speaks.

Anton rolls his eyes. "Another one? You'd think these guys could get their shit together."

"Yeah. You'd think."

Anton rubs his eyes, blinks into the darkness. "Think she's in there?"

"Yep."

"Think she's sleeping?"

Sam stares at the old Bronco, the piece-of-shit camper attached to it. Gray and white, faded, rusted. "Hard to say. No lights are on, but then she didn't hook it up to anything, either."

"Probably afraid it'll explode."

Sam chuckles. "We're not that lucky." He glances into the darkness. "Should be an easy enough approach. You ready?"

"We should call."

Sam's sigh is long, loud, and theatrical. "You're not gonna get off it, are you? They had their chance in Carter's Glen. We've been on this chick for sixteen hours, including the time it took her to buy that hunk of shit RV. It's simple. The librarian called X'chasei, who called the FBI, who fucked it up. Should've been easy for them but wasn't. So, either there's more to this woman than meets the eye, or they're idiots. Either way, I'm tired, hungry, my butt hurts, and I'm sick of waiting. I'm going in. You can call if you want, but I'll be back before you even get off the line."

Anton stares at his partner, waits for more quibbling. "Okay, okay, I'm hungry, too, but you don't hear me whining. If we go take care of her, what are we gonna tell the G-men?"

Sam smirks. "We'll torch it when we're done. They think they're such hot shots. They can look for her in the ashes. C'mon."

"Wait, I have an idea." Anton gets on his knees, leans into the back seat, rustles with something on the floorboard.

"So help me God, if you don't quit messin'…"

Anton's smile is broad as he offers his prize. "This will help."

Sam grins. "We'll be at IHOP in no time."

CHAPTER 4

WEST VIRGINIA, UNITED STATES

Having driven all day and most of the night, far away now from Carter's Glen, Rhyme Carter suppresses a groan as she applies antiseptic to the wound from the agent's gun. It's not bad, a slice really, although knitting it closed with a pocket sewing kit hadn't been the most fun.

If there's a good thing about being shot at close range, it's that the bleeding is generally minimal provided the bullet didn't go through. Lucky, she thinks. Another few inches and that would've been the end. She sighs, grins although she knows she shouldn't. The gamble was foolish but had allowed her escape. Crispy *would not* agree with her methods or the risks taken.

Desperate times and all that, she thinks, then presses the gauze to the bottle of Isopropyl as a sharp odor fills the camper. She lays it on the laceration on her right arm, grimaces against the sting.

Pain keeps you alert, Crispy once said, and if by *alert* he meant teeth clenched and tears streaming, then she's as alert as she can possibly be.

I'm rusty, making mistakes. Should've anticipated the FBI. Should've assumed the library was wired, if not recently, then certainly monitored by Cain and his X'chasei associates.

She thinks it over, can think of nothing she'd missed or even a close guess as to how they'd found her.

Bet their bells are still ringing. Bet they're mad as hell. She thinks of the agents, waking, handcuffed ankle to wrist. She giggles, yawns again. Crispy always warned about taking care of herself, warned how sluggish and dull one gets without appropriate rest.

And he's right. Her body aches; her mind is dull. Hell, even her vision rebels. She looks at the interior of her new home on wheels. She'd passed it on a country road in front of a rundown farmhouse. A hand-written sign scrawled on an Amazon box flap. 4 SALE-FITEEN HUNDRET.

She'd immediately stopped and purchased the thing for a thousand cash without even peering inside.

Might not have been the best decision.

Cobwebs hang in dusty wisps over formerly beige walls that appear yellow in the dark confines. She doesn't want to know what the bed looks like. Maybe she'll sleep in the Bronco, re-evaluate in the morning.

The Jet-boil hisses, starts to bubble as she opens a pack of ramen and dumps the dried noodle-brick into the pot. A few minutes more and she'll be eating. Should help the pain, help to clear her head, help sleep, help heal. Nothing but the best in Rhyme's Diner, ramen noodles and a Twix bar she'd picked up at her last stop.

She glances at the cobwebs; wonders how fast they'll ignite if exposed to the proper source. Tomorrow she'll find a broom, but first, sleep.

The packet crinkles as she dumps the SECRET SEASONING. She looks around, realizes she doesn't have a spoon. A quick search of the little camper's kitchen produces a spork, rusty and bent as if someone used it as a screwdriver. She holds it close to the light, tries to find a way to use the thing despite thoughts like *tetanus shot* and *flesh-eating bacteria.*

Just then, there's a sound from the caravan's back bedroom. Sig appears in her hand without conscious thought. Maybe not so rusty.

The Petzl headlamp casts a narrow beam at the bedroom's

accordion door. She stands as quietly as possible. The door glows yellow from dirt. She steps close, grasps the cheap handle, slides it open.

A throaty growl comes from the darkness.

She scans right to left, sees the dusky outline of an animal. Too big to be a raccoon, something dark that blends easily in the shadows.

She steps in, gun leveled. *I've already been shot, I'm not getting rabies.*

The growl comes low and steady as her vision adjusts. Long white teeth glow through the darkness.

It's a dog, a Doberman, teeth bared, hackles raised. Crouched and cornered.

"Easy, fella," she says, keeping her voice lyrical, calm.

Crispy always said dogs were great companions but never taught her what to do in a situation like this. She squats, lowers the gun a bit, speaks softly. "Hey, big fella, what's your name?"

The bark splits her ears, rattles her head. The dog disappears.

A real Houdini, that animal.

Rhyme moves through a mass of cobwebs, deeper into the room. *Maybe RV life isn't for me.*

There's a three-foot hole where the bed should be. Leaning forward, she shines the light, sees nothing but dirt and darkness.

Her sigh is audible, disappointed. *Guess it'll be the Bronco's back seat after all.*

There's a clunk from the front of the caravan. *Maybe the dog's circled around, re-entered through another hole up front.*

She steps into the main area, glances at her boiling ramen.

The next sound is hard, metallic, something weighted.

She scans the filthy floor.

The thing wobbles, dark, cylindrical. A rodent maybe. The Petzl focuses. Not a mouse, it's black, looks like a can of WD-40.

It spins, then sits very still.

Grenade.

CHAPTER 5

MOUNT TABOR, ISRAEL

The phone rings but no one answers. I can only assume the lines are down from the attack. I think of Rhyme in Washington and wonder if she's holding her own. I wish I was with her, there to protect her.

Pappy and I exit the dorm and proceed to the church. From the valley, lines of smoke rise like skeleton fingers, too numerous to count. As if millions of bonfires were ignited in celebration of the victory over the invading force. Naïve, I think, given the carnage below. The death toll *must* be beyond imagination, the people, struggling to subsist, those still alive, wondering how such a thing could befall them.

Pappy moves ahead, robes swishing in the sweltering heat. I follow, feeling no worse for wear, amazed at the still-sheltering buzz from my fix.

We approach the church, and I see no signs of damage. It's pristine, ancient, just as it was when Longinus and I entered. I wonder if he still sleeps and think to go check on him. The relic certainly gave as good as it got, and the Roman's rest seems to know no end.

The church is cool. Dust coats the floor, shaken from the rafters above. We stamp our footprints into it as we move down the main aisle and under dark braces that support the ceiling. Under the arch and past the altar, we move left down a short hall, where Pappy produces a key and unlocks the door.

The room is small, square, lined with shelves surrounding an old desk stacked with papers. Sticky notes are everywhere. Yellow, pink, blue, some barely legible, others printed in a careful, slanted script. I note the absence of anything personal. No pictures hang or sit framed on the desk. There are no tokens of friendship or mementos to be found. Poverty, I think; this friar takes the vow seriously.

He moves behind the desk. Motions me to sit in the single chair on the other side.

"What do you suppose your role is in all of this?" he asks.

I shrug. "I don't know. Up until now it's been to do what Cain tells me." The chair creaks as I lean back. "I'm afraid I'm in too deep. Even when I've tried to escape, I've been returned to his side. I guess my role is to record events as they transpire. I mean, that's why I was hired."

He nods a single time, "Uh huh. Just blown on the breeze to follow the Antichrist?"

I chuckle. "No, no. You have it wrong. I'm in control of my own destiny, and just as soon as I finish my contract, I'll be doing very well."

His stare is deadpan. "Without your wife?" he says. "Made numb by all the drugs you can take? A False Prophet spreading the gospel of the Antichrist?"

The words pierce my gut as surely as Longinus's sword. I finger the scar through my shirt, remember the feel as the steel pierced my body. I've been solely focused, mostly horrified, but solely focused on holding to the belief that I fill only the role of observer and biographer, nothing else.

I realize then the depths of my delusion. The fact I've used my tasking as an excuse despite everything I've witnessed.

But everything's changed. Everything I've known, pushed to the periphery as I traverse this rabbit hole like Carroll's *Alice*. I've been deluding myself, glugging drugs and booze to keep my horror at bay.

I've lost my wife, my job, my status, have drifted farther and farther down a road littered with empty syringes and fifths of brown liquor.

I think back, realize the only emotions of which I'm now capable are disgust and detachment, using the excuse *it's just my job* to avoid sinking too deep.

But self-delusion isn't so easily discarded, so I reach for the last card in my deck. My tone makes me proud, one of certainty and confidence. *"I control my own fate."*

"Do you?" His expression unmasks the darkness of my philosophy. His eyes, blue, deep, expose my failings without statement. I squirm in my chair. "And if you don't mind sharing," he says. "What are your plans?"

This is an easy one. "Well, I plan to finish this project, get paid, then, um, get my wife back."

His stare is unwavering. "You realize none of that's possible."

I blink, caught off-guard. I've had no such realization. "How's that?" I say as my cheeks flush.

"Because the man who employs you is the Antichrist," he says. "Because even with the *slight changes* Cain made to the Bible, there's no denying the end times are on us. Do you think you'll get your money and your wife, then spend your days relaxing by a pool, drink in hand, white dust on your nose?"

I start to protest but can't. He's exposed my bullshit in a deft way. Has refocused my delusions as if through a grand telescope. My task is folly, and the only truth I know is that I'm trapped with these madmen.

I'm transported to the day I'd entered the room holding Blake's *Vision of the Last Judgment* on its door. I remember saying, "How bad can it be?" Remember Cain's smile as the door swung wide to drench me in terror, murder and mayhem.

Pappy pushes a stack of papers to the corner of his desk, reveals a grand and ancient Bible: thick, bound in tooled leather, etched in swirled spirals with images of saints. He points at it. "This is the map, my son. All we need is here.

"I'm going to wax soothsayer," he says, flipping pages. "I'm going to become prophetic and foresee what shall come to pass. You see, I believe God has it well in hand. I also believe, even with Cain's changes, this book remains inspired by divine providence." He gives me an ominous stare, dead serious. "Never doubt God, Emery. If there's anything to give you hope, it's that." He raises a finger, wears an expression of dour determination. "The road ahead will be hard, but things will work out."

I nod but don't know why. Perhaps it's his certainty, combined with his tone and intelligence. Perhaps some remnant of the drugs continues to dull my mind.

"Billions will die, of course," he says, "and the planet will never be the same." He looks down, flips a few more pages. "So, there's that."

I slouch in my chair, his words sapping my energy.

"But take heart," he says, "I believe you have a role to play here. That you are, in fact, in charge of your own destiny. That's if you can figure out what it is."

I wave a hand. "If I haven't by now…" I let the thought trail off.

"You must have some thoughts."

I sigh, slouch lower, cross my arms over my chest, wonder what became of Vince and Lenny. "Nope." I pop the final P in the word like I'm spitting.

"Well, let's see if we can figure it out. We'll start by examining what we know." Pages rustle as they turn. "The legend of Cain, the Earth's first murderer. Kills his brother in a fit of rage, then tries to deceive God. Gets cast out and made immortal as punishment." He pulls eyeglasses from a drawer and props them on his face. "In my opinion, the most horrible punishment imaginable. I'm impressed he's still sane."

"Barely," I chime in. "If one examines the data."

"I disagree. Don't you see, the evidence of destiny, of providence? The man endures despite everything, which, to me, is proof that God's ordained these things and allows them to happen."

I snort, but don't mean to. I guess I meant to tsk, which is still better than my urge to blow a huge raspberry over his theory. Then I think about it, hear Cain's words float back to me. *God prefers blood.*

He glances up. "What?"

"Something Cain likes to say, *God prefers blood*. Says it's the only thing anyone need know concerning God. If one examines the evidence, it's hard to refute his theory. We've received no reports from the valley, but I expect the carnage to be mind-boggling. Add to that, the length of time Cain's endured. I mean the guy's sort of an expert on humanity and its atrocities." I look at a crucifix on the wall, think of Cain watching that spectacle. "But you're going to tell me it's all the devil's fault and that God *allows* all of this to happen. But wouldn't you say *He's* complicit? That if God truly cared—even a little—He wouldn't allow such things to befall us? The Earth's an inescapable nightmare. Worse by exponents the longer one dwells on it. And God has all this power but does nothing to stop this suffering?

"I haven't the faith, Pappy, not after all of this, all I've been through. I think Cain's right, God does prefer blood."

I sit back, look at the floor, diatribe complete. A master's thesis on God, written and performed by a junkie. If I'm honest with myself, I feel a bit embarrassed. This is a good man, a faithful, penitent man. A man who lives his convictions while seeking only to understand them. He's been kind to me, helpful, even compassionate. He doesn't deserve my rhetoric or my attitude.

Pappy sits back too, takes his time, sizes me up. "Cain may indeed be correct," he says. "God *may* prefer blood. But that changes nothing. Whatever we know, or think we know, whatever evidence we collect and examine, the pieces we snap together, changes nothing about the fact that we're here now and have choices to make."

Here it comes, I think and roll my eyes. "You're going to say we have to choose between good and evil."

He looks surprised by my mind-reading. "No. Our choices are much simpler. To live well, or not live well. Everything else will proceed as ordained whether you believe that or not.

"But make no mistake, this is the crisis of our times. I'm certain generations before us thought the same. Events like the Napoleonic wars, the Holocaust, the volcano of Pompeii, those people must've been scared witless, certain God had abandoned them.

"Think about it, you're a lowly peasant who works in the fields all day, then some super-storm or," he makes finger quotes, *"act of God* comes along and completely decimates everything. You have no idea where it came from or even how it formed. You blame yourself, think you're not living right, that you've somehow angered God by your action or inaction. You think and think but, in the end, find your only choice is to live on.

"You see, man's corrupted everything. The more knowledge at our fingertips, the more insane we become." He jots something on a sticky note, sticks it atop a dozen others on the wall beside him. "What we *think* changes nothing. We stand teetering on a world-shattering precipice, and like the peasants of old, despite our knowledge and pride, we're no better off. No better informed. We have the same choices. Endure or die. It's really that simple."

He holds my eyes, lets his words hang for a moment.

"Let's examine our position," he continues. "We sit atop a mountain in a land savaged by war. We have evidence that makes us believe we know the identity of the Antichrist. We have a book that outlines what will happen in the times ahead. Do we close the book, put in on a shelf, and go have tea? Or do we choose to move forward armed with only our faith in ourselves."

"I knew it'd come to this," I say.

"Faith?"

"Yes."

Pappy steals the words from my mind. "You have trouble believing without proof?"

"Precisely."

"That's good news because no one expects you to believe a thing. You're not dumb, judge the evidence for yourself. Whether God prefers blood or doesn't is irrelevant. What matters is how will you choose to serve humanity and those you love? That's the real question."

"I'm not *following* the Antichrist, if that's what you mean."

"But you serve Cain."

"I *work* for Cain. There's a difference."

"Is there?" He stares at me with laser eyes. "I suppose you're correct. If Satan employs you, it's still just a job."

My sigh is audible. "You're impossible."

"But not incorrect."

I nod at the Bible. "Okay, let's see where this road map leads."

"Excellent."

Chapter 6

Mount Tabor, Israel

Afternoon gives way to smoky evening, casts a shadow across the wallpaper of sticky notes and the friar's thinning hair. He's been reading while I repeatedly glance at my phone and wonder when Rhyme will call.

"Okay," he says. "Let's start with the presupposition that the end times are upon us and that Cain is indeed the Antichrist."

"That's going to be tough to source," I say. "What evidence do you have to support that?"

He waves a hand. "Easy. Prophecy is pretty specific about certain things. One is that the Antichrist will recover from a mortal wound to his head."

"When Drake was assassinated."

"Precisely. You saw the whole thing. In fact, most of the living world saw the whole thing. Now, who could've survived that? No mortal to be sure. Only Cain, made immortal by God to pay for his sins. At least that's what Cain thinks, but he's failing to see the bigger picture. So, we've checked our first box.

"Now, let's consider Cain as Constantine the Great. He'd pursued that path thinking, even then, that he'd conquer the world and offer it as a trade for release from his punishment. Then, seeing the impossibility of the task, the vastness of the planet, the limits in technology, he realizes he can attain better control by infiltrating the faith. And what better way to do that than to create the very book that all the faithful take as truth? He'd read John's original writings, knows what's omitted and what's added. What he didn't count on was God. When his plan to wipe away religion failed, he adapted, just as God wanted. Played right into God's hands, as it were. After that, he tries again and again to subdue the planet and fulfill the prophecy, but always fails. Did he fail because he wasn't prepared? Because he isn't intelligent or motivated enough to bend events to his will?" He shakes his head. "No, he failed because God hadn't yet ordained the time for his success."

I listen, rather amazed. So far, he hasn't said anything that doesn't ring true.

"Now onto the other immortals. You say Longinus was a Roman centurion, made immortal after killing Christ with his spear."

"No, he drank His blood. Apparently made a spectacle of it at the Crucifixion. Or at least that's the story they told me. After that, Cain had only to convince him of his immortality. Longinus joined Cain directly and seems to follow his orders without question."

The friar nods, scribbles on a yellow sticky note.

"Longinus admits he saw the advantages of that shift in his life," I say. "He relishes the power, basks in its possibilities. He's really nothing more than a psychopathic child but, still, a child you don't want to cross."

"And of this Igneus?"

"Well, he's a different sort entirely. He lacks the stomach for violence, and his story is one of reluctance. I haven't seen him in a while but the last time I did, it was at the Temple. He'd changed, was bold and fearless. He was the one always arguing with Cain, always opposed to his next ghastly step. I've no idea what's become of him."

The friar handles the old Bible gently, turns each page with care. "What a puzzle. Why would God give Cain two henchman?"

"I've no idea. Haven't really thought of it in that way. Igneus has a genius-level intellect, is a whiz with finances, is responsible for creating a one-world currency."

"One-world currency? How do you mean that?"

I chuckle. "I wish I could explain it back to you. But suffice it to say that Igneus said it's done. And if he said it, I believe him."

Pappy frowns. "Can't be right. There hasn't been new money."

"Precisely. Igneus said the beauty of the world currency was that it required no change in any nation's money."

His eyes light up. "So Igneus's role was to fulfill the prophecy of a world currency? Makes perfect sense."

"Does it?" I say. "That's Igneus's entire purpose? Sounds like… crap. Couldn't God just have raised up a modern-day accountant or something? Why make Igneus immortal?"

"Good question. I'm not sure. You see, no one can comprehend the mind of God."

"You sound like him."

"Really?"

"Yeah, Igneus says that all the time."

He scribbles something on a sticky, then stares at it for a few seconds. "Interesting," he mumbles, then looks at me. "Why Longinus, do you think? Why has God provided Cain with an ally like Longinus?"

I shrug. "No idea. Not even a good guess. Before yesterday, I've *never* seen Longinus do anything that wasn't evil. If he's a tool of God, then God needs a hardware store gift card."

Pappy laughs his hearty laugh, leans back. "You may be right, but still, there has to be some reason those two are around. You mentioned the Apostle John. Where is he?"

"Heaven, I suppose. I saw him taken up." I gulp as my mind fills with visions from the Temple. The scene as I lay bleeding, watching the Apostle rise. "If he were still on this planet, I'm sure he would've found me by now." Pappy makes another note. "Perhaps he was God's counter to Cain and the others," I say, "although he didn't seem too effective and would never admit he actively worked against Cain. He'd only say he'd been charged by Christ to perform a specific task. He told me he'd know when it's time. You know, he's the one who ordered Cain's assassination. Then, he helped us fight Longinus and we entered the Temple together to stop Cain. Long story short, Cain returned, John didn't."

"So, Cain can kill immortals?"

"Not that I know of. The only thing I can think is that John fulfilled his task and was removed from the Earth by God." Even as the words leave my mouth, I sound like a crackpot. God removed the Apostle, I'd just said. Then He'd stayed for dinner, watched some football, played some poker.

"What was John's task?"

"I never found out. He didn't know himself. My guess is his task required him to stop Cain from doing something in the Temple."

"Did he do it?" He raises a hand before I can answer. "You've told me already, you don't know. But you say he ordered Cain's assassination. Perhaps that was his task, to fulfill the prophecy of the Antichrist's critical head wound."

I hadn't thought of this before. "Possible," I say. "Although I was taken aback by an Apostle of Christ ordering a mafioso-style hit."

"Yes." Bushy eyebrows crinkle as his word trails off. "Are there any more immortals?"

"Not that I know of, but who knows?"

"Okay," Pappy says, "we have three immortals besides Cain, two of them with whereabouts unknown."

"Yep."

He leans back, looks out the room's tiny window. The orange glow of twilight has fled before the black of night, a few stars twinkle against the backdrop of space. "The tough part is knowing what's real." He writes the question on a sticky, then posts it on the wall atop the others. "We have to take Revelation with a grain of salt, which makes our efforts decidedly more difficult. And dangerous," he adds. "We can't stay on our back foot through this. If we can figure it out, we can predict, despite knowing Revelation's been tampered with. The last place we need to find ourselves is providing historical context *after* events occur. That serves us nothing."

He swivels in his chair. Eyes dart over the hundreds of notes stuck to the walls. I'm struck with the image of him doing this for hours, losing track of time, connecting dots, solving mysteries.

"Let's stick with facts and hope for guidance," he says.

"Another way of saying, let's hope and pray."

He chuckles, produces another sticky note and writes. "We know the Antichrist has some prophecies to fulfill. One is to recover from a critical head wound. Check. Two, bring about world peace." He looks up, eyes darting back and forth, face tense. "Well, Cain certainly accomplished that, at least for a time. Seems it didn't last long."

"Does it count, then? I mean, was a few weeks of world peace enough to count as prophecy fulfilled?"

"Who knows? I'm not the judge here. No man can comprehend the mind of God and that's what we're trying to do."

"Seems like a hot topic." I'm thinking of Igneus and our ride to Damascus. Running from the madmen and the events at Sundamir's mansion. "We better be able to comprehend something."

"You're right. Perhaps we start with what prophecies have been fulfilled."

"Okay, does your book tell you that?"

His laugh echoes from the stone to brighten the darkness. "It tells me everything I've ever needed!" He flips some pages, pulls a pad of sticky notes close. "Let's see, other prophecies fulfilled. Temple rebuilt; check. One-world currency. I'll give the benefit of the doubt on that one; check. World peace, maybe, maybe not. After recent events, I'm going with not. Uncheck. Antichrist needs to recover from a head wound; check. First seal is the appearance of the pale rider, the white horse." He flips some pages, starts to read. *"And behold a white horse: and he that sat on him had a bow; and a crown was given unto him; and he went forth conquering, and to conquer."* He sits back, spins to look at his sticky notes, mumbles to himself, "conquering and to conquer. A crown given." He turns to me. "Perhaps more fulfilled prophecy here. He certainly conquered the invading force, but as far as I know there's been no crown given, no authority."

I find myself leaning forward, hanging on his words. He's like a hound on a scent, and I'm anxious to see what we'll discover.

"The Antichrist," he mumbles. "Christ's opposite. Christ's foil. The UN-Christ." Then his eyes widen, and I watch him have a eureka moment. "I'm struck by the fact Cain decided to enter Jerusalem, riding a white horse, on Easter Sunday during Passover. Not exactly like Christ, who entered Jerusalem to great fanfare a week before his crucifixion. That was also during Passover." He flips more pages, turns to glance at his wall of stickies. "There are similarities though. Cain enters Jerusalem on Easter Sunday during Passover. Easter's significant because that's when we celebrate Christ's resurrection. Cain enters Jerusalem to commemorate his own resurrection. The first time he's seen in public after the world thinks him dead. A resurrection celebration to be sure, and, if one thinks about it, the opposite of Christ."

I'm having a eureka moment of my own. I think he's spot on. Things are falling into place. Cain as martyr, Cain as persecuted, Cain as persecutor. Cain, condemned to wander, cast out again and again. Cain surviving assassination, entering the Temple, a Temple built solely by his influence and single-minded pursuit. Then assassinated only to re-emerge on Easter Sunday. And on a white horse, no less. What the friar says makes sense, adds up like an accountant's ledger. Cain's proclaimed himself God, said it was his destiny. Then he'd mixed his own blood with the remnant of Christ's on Longinus's spear and the weapon came alive. Was it the combination of good and evil? A secret recipe for superhero relics? Either way, Cain knew how to use the spear when he needed it. A fact that can't be ignored.

As I'm thinking, the friar continues. "Second seal is the red horse, the rider of war; check. Antichrist arranges peace deal with Israel; check. Third seal, black horse of famine; uncheck. Israel attacked; check."

"The attack was prophecy?"

He looks up, puts a pen to the corner of his mouth. "Oh yes. A well-known prophecy, in fact. Ezekiel, 38, I think." Pages ruffle as he looks for the reference. I want to laugh at the way he mumbles.

"Gog...Magog...young lions...Israel dwelleth safely... Ah! Here it is. And thou shalt come from the North parts, and many people with thee, a great company, a mighty army. Thou shalt come up against my people of Israel as a cloud to cover the land."

"Nailed it," I sing the words in falsetto.

He doesn't laugh, just glances at me. "You should read this. It's really fascinating. It basically says God's going to crush any attackers who come against Israel."

"But Longinus crushed Israel's attackers, and believe me, he's the furthest thing from a tool of the Almighty."

Bushy eyebrows flutter. "Doesn't mean God didn't use him."

"Doesn't mean He did?" I feel like a child bantering like this. "You're telling me God made Longinus immortal all those centuries ago, just so he could defend *this* church yesterday?"

"I'm telling you that this is more proof of providence, more proof that God's will is being done. That God allows this to happen, that God..."

"Prefers blood?"

He becomes silent, clears his throat, flips the page of the ancient tome. "Perhaps. Looks that way. But no less provident. The centurion killed the Messiah with a spear, then uses the same spear, centuries later, to defend Israel from a multi-nation attack."

"Thor must've been filming his next movie."

He looks at me. "Thor? Are you being sarcastic?"

"Kind of," I say, "although what I saw reminded me of Thor. Or Zeus."

"Yes, he did look rather other-worldly."

"You saw?"

"Oh yes, as soon as I realized I was safe in that purple haze, I watched from the bell tower. Quite magnificent."

Magnificent, I think; another watered-down cliché. "I'm not sure I'd choose the same word."

"Yes, well," he says, "I don't deal in words. I think magnificent sums it up quite, well, magnificently."

"My point exactly." I decide to move on. "Is there any prophecy about Longinus's spear?"

"Not that I'm aware of, but I'll be sure to study up on it." He looks down here, removes his glasses, rubs his eyes. "I can think of no other weapon that could perform such a feat. Maybe a nuclear warhead, but nothing else that could crush such a force as the one that attacked us. A force *like a cloud to cover the land,* as Ezekiel said. The prophecy was right about that. If I hadn't seen it myself, I'd never believe it. Israel, defended by an immortal with a spear."

He stares out the window for a few moments, then nods as if coming to a decision in his mind. "There can be no doubt that this is God's plan and has been from the time of the Earth's first inhabitants. You have to admit it's rather brilliant, how he's used Cain to bring it all about."

"It makes sense. Something Cain always complained about was the fact that he was so harshly punished for his crime. How it wasn't fair for him to suffer such a fate, especially after he'd spent centuries being penitent and performing good works. Then, he's cast out again by Christ. Said, after that, he entirely changed, no longer cared about redemption. He used the words, *set free.*"

Pappy smiles. "Providence, lad, it's everywhere. One need only look with different eyes. Cain thinks he controls the situation, thinks he's God's equal. All he's planned has come to pass by his own hand. Or so he thinks." He points his glasses at me. "But I see a different reality. I see God's hand at work. Like everyone, Cain serves God's plan while thinking he serves himself."

He spins again to face the sticky notes. I stifle a yawn. The day's been exhausting. Surviving the attack has exhausted me. I wonder if Longinus has risen yet, then glance at my phone and think about Rhyme.

"Two things," Pappy says. "First, we can't forget the crown prophecy. At some point Cain will claim his throne. That should be a solid sign we're on the right track."

"And second?"

"The spear's power is unequaled. If Cain has it, all is lost. At least until the final battle."

"Battle?" I say. "Didn't we just endure one of those?"

"Oh yes, my son, but the one of which I speak is the final battle. At Armageddon. Not far from here, in fact."

"Splendid," I say, not trying to hide my sarcasm. "And what of Longinus? What's prophecy say about his role?"

Pappy flips some pages, glances at the wall of stickies, at me, back to the book. "It seems we don't know," he says. "Remains to be seen. A mystery without a clue. Why the metamorphosis? Why the duality? More to research." There's a certain twinkle in his eye as he says *research,* as if he loves nothing more than sitting in this small room, surrounded by sticky notes, combing through ancient texts.

I suppress a yawn. "I need some rest. Seems current events and the heat are catching up to me."

"Yes," he says, not looking up. "Sleep well, my son. Who knows what tomorrow holds?"

He returns to his musings, to his Bible and the wallpaper of stickies.

I exit through the church, cold and dark, and into the humid blanket that holds the night.

CHAPTER 7

BEIRUT, LEBANON

Sundamir's mansion
Weeks earlier

Longinus steps forward, plucks one of Sundamir's daughters from the clutch of her sisters. It's Sima, the pianist. The girl is frail with delicate hands and a round mouth. She's like a porcelain doll in the Roman's grip.

Sundamir doesn't move, only sobs pleas at deaf ears.

Longinus pushes the girl down, rears back, sword poised. He looks at Drake.

Drake turns to Emery. "You may go."

Emery sprints from the room.

Drake nods and Longinus starts to plunge the sword.

"Wait!" the girl screams.

Longinus stops. There's something familiar here, some long dead feeling stirs. He pauses, Drake forgotten, surrounding screams fade to muffled sobs he doesn't notice.

She's delicate, beautiful. His mind speeds to the days of his youth, time spent in pankration and study. Stealing away at dusk to spend precious minutes with Gwenna.

He stares into eyes as dark as a mountain tunnel. Fragile hands, elegant chin, a rose for a mouth.

"Let me," she says.

"Aye?"

"Please. They make me suffer. He—" She points at her father, "does unspeakable things. In the night. No one helps. No one listens. I hate them all."

Longinus relaxes his grip, glances at Drake.

Sima's eyes burn like embers of shadow. She grasps the sword, twists it from his hand.

The Roman steps back, grins a bit.

Sima smiles, a mix of anticipation and glee. She licks her lips, steps toward the fat Arab, Pavel Sundamir, her father.

"Through long nights I've waited." She raises the sword. "With every thought, every breath, every tear and invasion, I've thought of this moment. Every time you touched me, had servants hold me down, each time, each second, I dreamed of the day I'd have my chance."

"Sima! No! You can't— I'm sorry! Please!" Tears roll over plump cheeks.

She takes another step.

Bloated cheeks flutter. Sundamir raises his hands, closes his eyes.

The sword drops.

Again, and again, and again.

Jerusalem, Israel
Weeks earlier

"She's a little demon."

"Aye."

"And she used your sword."

"Aye."

48

"Seemed to enjoy it."

"Aye."

"You can't keep her, you know?"

"Why non?"

"She's an unknown, aligned with factions that can delay and jeopardize our plans."

"I do non seek ye'r leave."

Drake blinks at the comment, sighs. "Can you tell me why?"

"Non."

"How old is she, anyway?"

"Perhaps twenty-two, anon and agin."

"Young compared to your lifetimes."

Longinus keeps silent, looks rather glum.

Drake places a hand on his shoulder and holds his eyes. "You've served us well, dear Longinus, and have been my greatest general through all these lives. We've accomplished much and stand poised on the brink of all we seek." He shakes his head. "I can't risk that for a girl, even one as soulless as Sima. I like her, she handles herself well, has quite a mean streak, all very endearing. But find another plaything. You'll forget about her soon enough."

Longinus thinks of his father, Archelaus, and the things he said about Gwenna. "She's only a girl. Unimportant. A plaything. A distraction." He'd dismissed their love, threw it asunder for personal gain, for family riches. Longinus won't let that happen again, no matter who it is.

"Non," he says. "We shall non part."

"Does she want to be here? Are you sure she's not just humoring you?"

"Aye."

Drake sighs. "Okay, dear Longinus, but find a way to make her useful. We have much to do, and I don't have time to babysit an enemy's daughter."

The Roman's smile catches Drake off-guard, true joy. He blinks at the grin, unsure if he's ever seen Longinus wear the expression. Is he really in love? And if so, from where in the vast, gaping universe has that come? Drake never considered him a man with a heart, let alone a capacity for deeper emotions like love. He'll need to be watched; love does odd things to men.

Sima enters the room. Small, delicate, brimming with youth's radiance.

"Dear Sima, what a pleasure."

Sima smiles, flips a dark braid from one shoulder to the other. She wears a summer dress, blue with yellow flowers, plunging neckline over small breasts and tiny frame. Not Longinus's type at all.

Drake nods at the room's grand piano. "Care to play us something, dear Sima?"

She moves to Longinus, looks in his eyes. A huge hand wraps her waist as she melts into his side.

Longinus beams, stares at the girl, looks hypnotized. He nods at the piano, smiles. Sima moves to it. Its size enhances her frailty. She looks like a doll propped on a bench. Slim fingers work the keys. The music haunts, sad and slow. She plays beautifully, fingers the keys with perfect pressure, produces music both complex and dark. Rachmaninov's *Rhapsody,* if Drake recalls.

Drake stands watching as Longinus smiles next to him.

Sima's eyes are closed, her body swaying as she plays. Petite fingers lift off, hover above each note, then barely touch down pressing just enough to make the instrument sing. It's an extension of her, a happy place, a true oasis. Her hands remind him of butterflies flitting from flower to flower, note to note, leaving no trace.

Drake slaps Longinus on the shoulder and exits the room.

Chapter 8

Mount Tabor, Israel

Present Day

Sunlight streams through a small, high window onto his feet. Before his very eyes, they shrink to inadequate appendages.

The cot, just moments before too small, feels cavernous.

Foreign hands grip his head, new hands, too small, off-putting, out of place.

He rises, plucks a rough robe from the door's peg.

The sleep did him good, but still need more.

The door cracks. "Longinus, you ready?" The reporter doesn't look like much, but there's more to him than a scruffy exterior and constant addiction. Perhaps that's why Cain chose him, perhaps he knows something about him that isn't readily apparent. The lad had certainly showed his quality on the church's roof. He'd risked his own death and faced the onslaught. He even did it with bravery and courage.

He would've done well in the Legion.

"Aye," Longinus says, "I'll be out in a minute."

The door closes quietly, like the reporter thinks the sound will be too harsh for his tiny ears.

Elegant hands grasp a chipped pitcher in white tin. Water pours, then flows down his throat to fill his stomach. He stares at the plastic cup, can't believe a single drink sated his thirst.

Through the centuries he's endured many things, witnessed manifold amazements, but the events on the church's precipice tops them all. Cain's plan grows a strong stalk, although the extent of what it blooms remains largely unknown.

Like Drake and Constantine, Cain has it well in hand. Always has.

He refills the cup halfway, then sets it on a stand of skimpy wood.

He shakes off the dream, memories of Gwenna. Then grins and licks his lips when he thinks of Sima.

She'll be surprised at his changes, at his *smallness.*

He's enamored, he knows. The word *love* even floats through his mind from time to time. There's something about her. Something about this new body. This new life. Something about Cain's changes: the hair, the eyes, the power and confidence. Something about his own changes: now elegant to a fault, now a worthy partner in Cain's ambitions.

A smile blooms, feels different on this new face.

He glances down. Feels astonished such small feet can bear his weight.

Trust in Cain.

Be worthy. Show your quality.

Always and forever.

So sayeth the Father.

Chapter 9

West Virginia, United States

Grenade!

Rhyme dives for the hole in the back bedroom.

The rapport deafens; the explosion blinds.

She hits the camper's rear wall and falls as the sharp thwack of silenced gunfire chases.

She lands on her back, the coolness of the soil beneath her, the dew soaking her shirt as weeds tickle her arms.

Her head swims, her vision is a giant bright dot. She raises both Sigs, points at the hole in the RV's floor, or at least where she thinks the hole is.

She's mostly blind, mostly deaf. The grenade was a flashbang, designed to blind and deafen, to stun and create easy kills.

The hard thump of boots draws close.

"She's not here?" The voice sounds perplexed. Whoever it is, he looks for her specifically.

Impossible. Simply can't be. Who could know I'm here? The FBI men are probably still handcuffed. Their radios destroyed.

Her vision clears by degrees, becomes shadow spackled with white dots.

The hole above is splintered plywood, jagged.

Something burns.

"Find her." A different voice. "She's here."

A pistol appears above, its tip visible on the hole's edge.

She braces to fire. There's two of them. At least. She'll get this one, then figure out the rest.

Smoke thickens around her, catches in her lungs. She has to run.

Then a growl and a mountain range of sharp, white teeth.

The dog's breath is hot, inches from her face, impedes what little vision she retains. Huge teeth glisten as the dog's mouth lowers, leans close, sniffs.

She angles her gun, brings it in line for a shot.

The dog snaps, clamps the pistol, shakes hard, sends the weapon scuttling into the night.

She twists the other Sig just as the dog leaps away, vanishes again.

She turns to the hole, sees the pistol scanning, moving slowly.

An idea forms. Shoot through the floorboards. She adjusts her aim, squeezes the trigger. Then something white and rusted next to the hole on the camper's underside, covered in dried mud and cobwebs. A propane tank. She releases the trigger. If she hits the tank, it'll be game over.

Only in desperation.

She focuses on the hole, listens through buzzed ears for the dog and the men inside.

Above, the pistol appears, sweeps toward her.

Smoke closes, thick, choking. She stifles a cough, holds her breath.

The pistol circles. Whoever holds it keeps their distance, scouts careful and cautious, looks for a quick kill.

There's a crash from the camper's front. Then, the crunch of footsteps outside.

They're trying to flank her.

She's in trouble. No shot above, partially blind, ears ringing. The Doberman, the propane tank, fire somewhere, two assailants, one Sig gone.

She has to move, can't lay here and wait to be killed.

She levels the Sig at the footsteps, knows death stalks closer with each footfall.

She can get one, but certainly not both, and the Doberman, while staying clear of the inevitable propane explosion.

Ears ring like a mic too close to an amp. Vision sparkles with shadows and lighted specks.

The man outside draws close, perhaps a few steps more, on her right.

She glances under the RV, toward the man outside.

Another man appears in the hole above. "There you are, little rat."

She's made a mistake, lost a second looking for the man on the ground when she should've stayed on the hole and guaranteed herself a single good shot.

She rolls right as far as she can.

The man fires. Dirt explodes as hearing squeals to a sharp whistle.

Something flashes by.

To her right, below the RV's frayed undercarriage, two thick legs appear.

Rhyme fires at them, then turns and fires twice through the hole.

The man outside drops, writhes, grasps his leg, eyes crazed, mouth curled.

He raises his gun.

Sig spits, strikes him in the neck and chest.

He falls, lies still.

Smoke pours through the hole, covers her. Eyes water, burn, lungs scream for a fresh gulp of air.

Move!

She scoots from under the burning camper. Flames sear her face, singe her hair. The tank's gonna blow any second.

From inside, a gunshot. A small hole appears on the wall next to her. Screams rise from the camper, then a feral growl, another shot, more screams.

Rhyme rushes to the entrance.

Smoke pours like a steam train. The door lies dented on the ground; the tin steps, crumpled.

She crouches, angles for any shot, even a blind one.

Flames flicker through shadow, leap from the camper's windows, dance on walls like yellow savages.

From inside the grunts of a struggle.

The dog yelps.

A man bursts through smoke and flame, arms raised over his face, then sprints into the surrounding woods.

She turns to fire. Then, something akin to a jackhammer slams her down. Her spine screams as she drops, struggles to keep Sig leveled and on target.

The Doberman flashes after, takes two long strides, then leaps into the night and disappears.

There's a scuffle. The harried cry of a man. "Sam! Sam!"

Rhyme rises, searches for breath as empty lungs strain; as ears buzz, eyes striving through vision blurred with tears. Coughing, desperate for air, feeling like drowning, she stumbles forward.

Then a gurgling sound like water down a drain.

She squints ahead.

Shadow becomes form.

The Doberman stands on the man's chest, its jaws clamped on his throat.

It releases, turns toward her, bares its teeth, crouches to leap.

"Who's a good boy!"

She has no idea from where the speech comes. Perhaps something subconscious, something she used to say to her dog, Buster, as a little girl.

The dog's stance changes.

It steps from the man's chest, shakes itself with a harsh flap of floppy ears, then pads over and nudges her hip.

Rhyme squats, gets a bloody lick on the mouth. Then, the dog bounds away. There's a rustling, the pat of thick paws. Within seconds, he blooms from the darkness like a specter, the lost Sig clenched in his jaws.

Rhyme bends, pats his head, takes the pistol. "You've got to be kidding."

CHAPTER 10

ISRAEL

At the checkpoint, we show our credentials. A member of the Israeli Defense Force scans our IDs with a thorough eye. Before we'd left the church, I made sure to plunge the needle, and my fix is just checking in for the day.

The soldier's uniform is dirty, but I can't tell if it's stained with blood or just mud. He looks too young to witness such horrors. Early twenties, dark hair, hazel eyes.

"Looks good," he says and motions us along.

"Wait. I'm a reporter. Can you tell me the situation?"

The soldier glides a hand across his face then swipes the sweat on his camouflage uniform. "It isn't pretty. There's still some skirmishes in the mountains to the north. Where are you two heading?"

I glance at Longinus, ever the mute when he's in his elegant form. "Jerusalem," I say. "Are the roads clear?"

He peers at a sullen sky. "I think so, may be a little bumpy where you're heading. There was an attack there. Apparently, a large group of the enemy was embedded with the Jews who relocated to Israel. A clever way of mobilizing a ground force, if you ask me. When the attack started, they mobilized en masse. I'm told they were well-armed and killed every moving thing. Women, children, priests, it made no difference." He glances behind us, where an old blue Fiat with a loud engine slows to a stop. "I saw footage of the guy who destroyed most of the force. Damnedest thing I ever saw, like something from an action movie. Pretty amazing."

The soldier speaks fast, and it takes me a second to process his words. I glance at Longinus and wonder how he'll feel if I tell the soldier that the man of whom he speaks sits right next to me.

"Sounds amazing," I manage, "can't wait to see. Haven't had much luck connecting to the internet. Can't even make a call."

The soldier glances at the Fiat. "We had the same problem, but our engineers worked a fix. We're up and running for now, at least on the military band. I'm not sure you'll have any luck for a while. When you get a chance, take a look. I can tell you, if it wasn't for that guy, Jerusalem would've fallen."

"No doubt," I say. The soldier is talkative; there's nothing a reporter loves more than someone who wants to talk. "Anything else we should worry about?"

He glances at the Fiat, wipes his head again, adjusts his cap. "Yeah," he says. "The bodies. Millions of them. The death toll is… We're taking extra shifts just to try to collect and, um, process them. In a lot of ways, whatever happened up on Mount Tabor is even more impressive than what happened in Jerusalem. The guys think the priests up there did something, invoked God's wrath somehow. You know, like the old testament, God intervened to save His people."

I consider his words, not as quick to process them with my fix on board. "What was it?"

"I don't know," he says. "Lightning, but a million times stronger. All I saw was a bright light from atop the mountain, then a million bolts rolled down and over the plains. It spread like something alive, rained ruin on the invaders. If I hadn't seen it, I wouldn't believe it. Nothing on Earth could've caused that." When he holds my eyes, I hope he doesn't notice my glassy stare. "In a second, the battle was over," he continues. "That lightning, fire—whatever it was—just rolled through them. Cut them down to a man. Planes, tanks, trucks, soldiers. I mean, their guns melted. Their tires melted. It hit everything at once.

All I could do was hide. The planes crashed down, tanks exploded, soldiers dropped dead with giant holes in their chests. It jumped from one soldier to the next, then to a tank, then to other soldiers, then up to a jet. I'm still trying to make sense."

The drugs make everything he says more vivid, like I can see it all. I'd been there, felt the power when Longinus discharged the spear. Felt the energy sizzle, watched the brightness leap forward, hungry for destruction.

But something doesn't add up. I glance at Longinus, who holds the steering wheel, hands at ten and two. His face is blank.

Through my drug addled haze, I have a thought. "There were two defenders of Israel? Two men who saved us?"

"Yep. Separate incidents. One on the mountain, one in Jerusalem. As if God pre-staged our saviors. At first, the higher-ups thought it was part of the invasion, then the footage surfaced from Jerusalem."

"I so wish I could see it," I say. "Have you any way to show me? It's very important."

He glances once more at the Fiat, then pulls a phone from the deep, square pocket of his trousers. "Sat phone," he says. "And you didn't get this from me." I nod, manage a smile, feel a bit bad that I fixed up this morning. The drugs are effecting my concentration.

He pokes a few buttons. "Take a look."

The footage is grainy and hesitant, shot by an amateur. I glance at my own phone, as good as a brick right now. These days, when we lose technology it's like losing a loved one, an empty hole that leaves us wandering and confused.

The screen shows fighting within a hazy cloud, either due to my drugs or the phone's night mode, if I have to guess. My mind slowly catches up to the images. It's a massacre, a third-world country's coup. People scream through the streets, panicked, clutching children and small sacks.

I hear the sharp chatter of gunfire and watch them fall, watch their children try to run before being mowed down by advancing soldiers.

These soldiers kill with glee. Murder innocents without thought or remorse. I try to process it, force my reluctant mind to accept that this isn't a movie at a local theater, not some bootleg copy of the latest hit, *real* life, *real* people.

Horror creeps in. Visions of the massacre I'd witnessed at Sundamir's mansion, too horrible to retain, let alone recount. More and more soldiers appear, an unimaginable number like some Hollywood blockbuster's CGI added thousands to the scene. Guns spit like firecrackers. With each pop, an innocent drops. A person loses their life.

The video shakes but stays on point, films a tempest of wanton death. Whoever filmed it was trembling. A very brave person. I wonder if they're still alive.

The army advances, the harsh cackle of their guns announcing their progress. Civilians topple over, mouths frozen in terror and retreat. The soldiers' faces are grim, determined. They're well-equipped, advancing, murdering.

Then, a single man enters from camera left, directly in the path of the storming invaders.

He raises a twisted stick above his head and the screen fills with such light that one would think the sun exploded.

Then, silence. Exhausted fog drifts away on the wind. The image clears, and I hear rapid breathing, realize it comes from whomever shot the footage.

The camera scrolls right and at first, I can't make out what I'm seeing. But as the image clears, my mind absorbs the horror. Bodies are everywhere. Twisted soldiers line the street, the sidewalk, every conceivable inch. Smoke rises into a green night. Weapons lie like so many sticks; smoking, melted clumps. The dead burn, vehicles smolder on the street. Street signs are melted and droop like noodles. The dead stare, grim faces frozen in death. The video frame jerks, turns to the ground, then goes dark.

I look at the phone in disbelief. My drugs protect me from fully processing the carnage, and I mouth a silent thanks to whatever entity truly exists. I currently lack the faculties to process the amount of death. The power loosed by a man with a stick.

I stare at Longinus, speechless. My mind replays the footage as if it's memorized each frame. My tongue glides over dried lips. The images creep through the drugs. I'm shaking.

I recognize the man carrying the simple stick. I know him on sight and without doubt. Pieces of this impossible puzzle float before me, then crash to the floor and splinter to millions.

"Igneus," I whisper.

Longinus doesn't react. I speak louder. "Igneus is the defender of Jerusalem." The words come as more of a question, although I'm certain what I've seen. It *was* Igneus, the frail Jew.

Longinus remains silent, either not hearing, or just ignoring, my words. His face betrays no emotion as he stares down the road.

Until I see a twitch at the corner of his mouth and a grin appears.

"What do you know?" I ask.

He glances at me, says nothing. I wait, stare at the Roman, think an awkward silence will pry words from his mouth.

Behind us, the Fiat finally toots its horn. The soldier holds up his hand.

I hand the phone back. "Wow."

He waves us forward. "Yeah," he says. "Now, be careful. We don't know how many invaders remain. Stick to the main road as much as you can, that's if you can stand the sight of all the corpses."

"Be well," I say, and Longinus accelerates up the damaged road.

"That was Igneus," I say, looking at my silent companion. "No doubt about it."

The Roman drives on, doesn't seem to notice me.

I decide to remain silent, turn my mind to the video, the reappearance of Igneus, the shattered puzzle before me.

I fight the drugs, reimagine the puzzle, start anew.

What series of events unfolded for Igneus to suddenly appear as Jerusalem's savior? At least part of the mystery is solved. I know where he is now.

But how in the great smoking blazes did he thwart the army? How did he acquire such power? A power akin to what Longinus wielded atop Mount Tabor's church.

Perhaps there are two spears: one for Longinus, the other for Igneus.

I consider the question, discard it as nonsensical. I'm willing to bet neither Cain nor Igneus has an extra relic lying about. Another relic of amazing power. A relic that's never been used or mentioned.

No, has to be something else. Maybe Cain located Igneus and welcomed him back to the fold. Cain had done so with me. It's a logical possibility—an Antichrist's way of getting the band back together after his miraculous resurrection. He finds Igneus, works some magic, then imbues him with power similar to Longinus.

It makes sense. Like any super villain, Cain would certainly empower his trusted henchmen. Hell, he'd probably empower untrusted henchmen, too. Perhaps he and Igneus have made amends, or more likely, Cain found the Jew and intimidated him to do his bidding.

My mind tests puzzle pieces, flips them over, turns them around, sideways, upside down, trying to find a fit. I spend the journey thinking of different scenarios to match the facts. I think of Pappy's words, his warnings, and try to work out how these events are part of that. I think of the spear, laying in the Land Rover's cargo compartment. So easily accessible if anyone knew about it. If anyone but Longinus had the strength to wield it.

We bump over roads pitted with gunfire and grenade bursts. They're a disaster, brim with gigantic holes from bomb and missile. Some places are so damaged we end up going off-road, bouncing through charred fields where splintered stalks rise to the sky. Up goat paths, past burned-out farms and smoking war machines. The Land Rover traverses these obstacles as Longinus guides us through the dead, the charred, the ruined.

Only a few structures remain intact and people use them for shelter, collecting whatever they can find. Death is everywhere, farm creatures, civilians, soldiers. The living form small groups and work to gather the bodies.

We head south as the day becomes afternoon. I notice the piles of corpses growing larger as the day progresses. Civilians work alongside the Defense Force, as if the populous decided that the first order of business is to attend to the dead, loading them in wagons and trucks, delivering them to roadside contingents. Charred machinery is everywhere: the crumpled fuselage of a jet fighter, the hulking, crushed skeleton of a bomber, the smoking remnants of a tank. The area is covered with detritus of every kind. Fenceposts are strewn like toothpicks. Clothing is scattered among common household items, a toaster, an upended armchair, a framed portrait. Strips of jagged metal jut from the ground as bits of yellow insulation take to the breeze and flutter toward black, broken trees. Splintered trunks that rise toward the sun and await rebirth.

Odd things appear in places they shouldn't. A wooden door stands erect in the center of a wide field, impaled as if an inviting entrance to some country home, only without the actual home. Civilians push carts, collect whatever they can find, clothing, shoes, firewood. Others process dead farm beasts, stripping their hides and collecting the meat while it's still somewhat fresh. As we pass, some of them wave, bloodied knives dripping, dirty faces stained with tears.

A young woman holds a baby in her arms and weeps. In front of them is the corpse of a man I assume to be the child's father. The baby has dark eyes and chubby cheeks, doesn't know it's fatherless, doesn't know what this new world brings.

I mourn for them, with them. My heart weeps for their future, this verdant country now wasteland.

I look ahead, close my eyes, let the drugs chase off the images.

The nightmare is just beginning.

CHAPTER 11

JERUSALEM, ISRAEL

Hours later, we enter the city. A gray sky haunts as afternoon yields command to evening. The air swelters, unseasonably hot. Sweat rolls down my forehead as I cast a long glance at Longinus, who's maintained his silence despite all the horrific things we've encountered on our way from Mount Tabor.

Corpses are everywhere, the country, the suburbs, the city. This hive, once bustling, a melting pot of culture and civilizations, has become a wasteland of dead bodies and anguished souls. The living look hypnotized, shuffle catatonic down blood-drenched streets. Shell-shocked children wear horror and disbelief like itchy masks. Fresh wounds abound, eyes drip tears, those black pearls with which I'm so familiar.

Joy has run to far-off places. Only terror remains, only corpses, heaped on sidewalks, strewn on roads, in alleys.

The hidden force was both ruthless and efficient, and as I witness the scene, I realize very few dead soldiers are present, very few of the attacking force.

I feel selfish, sitting in the air-conditioned Land Rover, watching people search the dead, attend to them, flop over them, trembling hands pressed to their heads, mouths contorted while wailing prayers to an uninterested God and shrieking their hopelessness to a steel gray sky.

An old woman kneels next to the body of a young girl. A weathered face bleeds tears from eyes that have seen too much. Younger people surround her, share her tears, place comforting hands on sobbing, sunken shoulders.

From unknown corridors, other cries arrive as people discover the bodies of cherished loved ones. Children slouch on bullet-pocked walls, stare with haunted eyes that see a million miles.

Cain caused this, I think. He and Khalifa have found success in their endeavors.

The surprise attack caught the city unaware, and I'm reminded of the conversation between Khalifa and Cain back in the Devil's Needle. I'm reminded this was part of the plan all along. Relocate the Jews, then exterminate them.

We creep through an intersection. The traffic light is dull and dead, and I realize that nothing electrical is working. Neon signs hang askew, their tubes snuffed. Store fronts are dark caves rimmed with fractured glass. What cars I see move slowly, their driver's focused on corpses, searching for family members of their own. The living look stupefied, stumble along, collect whatever they can find.

We weave through the misery, through this senseless killing field devoid of kindness, charity, or hope. I wonder if those things still exist. I wonder if God's already abandoned us, left us to suffer the antics and whims of Cain.

An old lady walks toward us aided by two children. Dirt streaks their cheeks, lines where tears have cleansed a path. In our world, seems those black pearls never stop.

This is when I look to Longinus, take in his elegant face and focused features. I hope to my core that this new version of the giant possesses some level of compassion.

A poker face hangs from chiseled features, blue eyes look ahead, lack outward emotion as slender hands guide the vehicle among the debris, through the dead, past the hopeless and bereft.

"Where are we going?"

He flicks his eyes ahead.

People stream toward the Temple, and I wonder if they're going for prayer or shelter. Longinus taps the horn a time or two, and the people part without a glance, eyes downcast as they trudge like zombies.

We drift by, are waved through a guarded checkpoint to enter the Temple's grounds.

Longinus exits the vehicle and I follow to a makeshift stage that stands before the Temple proper. In its center is a podium that's survived without harm, and, for some reason, I'm impressed by this. After such a calamity, I expect a podium of boxes and plywood.

To my right a couple of news crews set up, peer through lenses to align their shot, oblivious to the suffering around them. Like me, just here to do a job.

The throng gathers, calls out names and hopes for an answer. Some greet and embrace, share tears of joy and relief, while others collapse in desperation, shrieking, bereaved. Their loved ones haven't returned.

It seems the Temple's become a bastion where people gather to seek the missing. Or to rejoin the living.

I marvel at the courage, the humanity, the spirit of this country. The city has known death from the time of its very birth, and I'm buoyed by its tenacity, by the undeniable courage of the people, the sense of community, the pulsing heart of endurance and victory.

Next to me Longinus speaks, and I turn my head as much from surprise as anything else. He speaks to someone I can't see, and I step forward and discover Cain's arrived.

From where he's appeared is a mystery, or I'm losing my powers of observation.

Or, you know, the drugs, but I'm certain he hadn't been there just a moment ago.

To my further surprise, they're joined by the Israeli PM, Laslo Slabav, whose face tells me he's overwhelmed. I study him, can only describe his expression as one a drowning person wears when they go under for the last time. Calamity, horror, surprise and shock, all scrawled across a square jaw in bold, black Sharpie.

"Laslo," Cain says, nods.

Laslo nods back, says nothing.

"Excellent," Cain says. "Let's proceed."

He passes without a word and the three ascend the stage. Unmatched chairs sit in a line behind the podium, and the three take their seats. Cain whispers something to Slabav, who rises and goes to the podium.

The crowd sees him, turns solemn faces toward their leader.

For some reason I'd expected a cheer and realize what a stupid, non-connected thought that is. These folks have been through too much to cheer. Any semblance of joy or happiness, of energy, youth or animation has been drained. Most have lost someone; many more have lost everything. What can Slabav possibly say to raise their spirits?

I pull my notepad from my pocket but don't press the record button on my iPhone, trying to conserve what little battery power remains.

Generators hum as Slabav starts.

It's hard to pay attention. The day is hot and reeks of death. Sweat rolls down my back and my head throbs. It's a wonder I'm not vomiting. But then, I guess, one can get used to anything.

My thoughts return to my conversation with Pappy. His warning about the next things that will happen. How Cain will usurp authority and claim control of Israel, all its lands, maybe more. I glance at Cain, whose brilliant hair glistens in the sunlight. He seems unaffected by the heat, comfortable even, smiling, nodding as Laslo speaks.

I direct my attention to the PM; briefly wonder why he still lives. I know the answer, though: he's a fish caught in Cain's talons as much as any of us.

The PM drones on. Standard rah-rah stuff. We'll get through this. God is with us. The normal litany of rhetoric. I'm tired, hungry, nauseous and thinking about Rhyme. Cell towers are down, and I haven't been able to reach her. But I wish I was there with her. Wish she wasn't alone; hope she's managing alright without me.

Sunlight twinkles off shattered glass onto items that litter the street. A shoe here, an empty purse, the remnant of a cherished teddy bear, its stuffing spilled from its gut. I relate to the toy, feel gutted in the same way. This is too much, too real, too surreal. What was beautiful and vibrant, has become a war zone. People who were once happy have been drained of all hope, sapped of all joy.

Slabav looks into the cameras and announces the dreaded statistic, the number of dead.

I've always found politicians love statistics as much for disinformation as to bend the figures to their own wants, but when I hear the number my mouth drops.

"It's estimated that almost four million people died in the attack." A frown mars his face as he looks down and wipes an eye. "I'm not sure if that number's correct. If anything, it's conservative. My people tell me there could be more."

He pauses, looks to the sky, then scans the crowd but seems mechanical. "This is a dark day for our nation and a black day for humanity and for those who wish us evil." There's scattered applause as Laslo inhales. "My countrymen, I stand before you today undaunted.

"I stand today, full of hope.

"To my Israeli and Palestinian brothers, I say, we remain that city on a hill as mentioned in scripture. A city that cannot be hid. A city that *will not* be hid. We are a shining light for the world. A beacon for the holy. The downtrodden. The heartbroken." His voice cracks and he pauses, composes himself.

"We remain united and will no longer suffer war." His voice bounds from surrounding buildings, careens off the Temple's facade to fly over the assembled crowd.

"Hear these things, oh persecuted people of Israel!

"I'm told that, even now, other nations size us up, lions who eye the herd for the wounded and weak.

"They think us easy prey.

"They *think* we're beaten, ready to give up, ready to drop our weapons and flee into the wilds, to hide from their onslaught, to give all we can to appease their hatred."

Words echo through broken glass and razed streets.

"People of Israel, hear these things!"

"To those nations who think this an opportunity, I say, if you come, you will be crushed!

"If you seek to destroy what God has built, the peace we've managed, the solidarity we yet retain, then I bid you, come with your jets and bombs and guns.

"Send your armies. Send your tanks. Send your false-tongued messengers but know that God's people will not be cowed!

"Know that any you send will die!

"We *are not* beaten!

"Neither will we compromise our morals, our resources, or our people."

The crowd stirs; despite the heat, a murmur rises.

I'm surprised at the PM's tone. I've never heard him speak with such confidence, such boldness. He's asking Israel's enemies to attack, and this strikes me as foolhardy. The heaps of the dead serve testament to the danger of his words. I wonder if he's lost his mind. Then I look to Cain, who nods and smiles as Laslo continues.

"As we investigate the nations responsible for this attack, we can take heart. God was, indeed, with us. As in days of old, God protected us.

"It sounds fantastical even as I say it, but I'm told eighty percent of the Russian coalition was destroyed.

"I'm told what allies they had, were also destroyed.

"I'm told it will take years to overcome this carnage and rebuild our country."

He lowers his voice, eyes now focused and alert. "Take heart, blessed Israel, for God is with us and has His arms fully around us. He has saved us from this evil purge and from those forces that would see our ruin.

"Take heart! We've re-established our connections with the world and they mourn with us. Many tales abound, rumors, intent on discord and deceit. But today I speak openly, giving all the facts I know.

"As communication returns, I'm sure many of you have seen the video of a single man defending Jerusalem with God-like power.

Footage of a lone saint, crushing these invaders. Likewise, many of you have heard of a different man protecting the Church of the Transfiguration on Mount Tabor. Another lone prophet who annihilated this army, again with God-like power.

"Never before has the world seen such a thing.

"Never before has an attack of this magnitude been witnessed.

"But God provided us His power, and I'm certain, even now, our enemies ponder this with spinning heads and stilled tongues.

"I'm certain these two men prevent our enemies from attacking again and again. Until we are destroyed.

"Today, I confirm the truth of these rumors. The truth that these two men did, *indeed,* save us from annihilation. That these tools of God were sent to rain ruin on those who wish us ill."

All eyes regard the PM, heads raised, mouths open, eyes focused and brightening.

"Today, I can confirm that Israel holds absolute power and *cannot* be defeated by any force on the Earth.

"God protects us, and we are stronger than ever before.

"So, I say to you and the world, woe to those who come against us!"

A smattering of cheers rises, smiles actually bloom on a few faces. More people have joined, all listening with rapt attention to Slabav's speech of strength and victory.

"To those nations who prowl like thieves in darkness, I give this warning.

"Do not test our capabilities!

"Do not doubt our resolve!

"Do not question our unity!"

The crowd erupts, animates, cheers.

Laslo clears his throat and adjusts his glasses.

"On this horrible day, we'd be remiss if we didn't give thanks. You see, we have one man to thank for our salvation, and that man is among us, sharing our tears, our grief, our misery.

"He wishes to address you, and so he shall. Ladies and gentlemen of the world, I give you Cain, the Savior of Israel."

Cain rises, smile flaming, hair white and writhing as he runs a hand over his suit.

He moves to the podium and looks into the cameras.

I've watched him enough to know his shtick, and today he's spot-on, affecting a look of genuine concern.

He takes in the crowd but remains silent. A tried-and-true technique, something about not speaking when people expect speech causes them to divert all their attention to him. Cain knows this, has mastered it. So, he waits.

Next to me, Longinus beams. Elegant features display confidence and, dare I say, real joy. He looks as resplendent as Cain, sits with one knee propped on the other, seems to hang on Cain's next words, or certainly plays the part.

My nerves tingle. I feel tense, taut, confused by this departure from the norms of this group. Usually, Longinus is out doing something dastardly while Cain uses his eloquence and charm to ensnare whoever crosses his reticle. I scan the crowd, hope to catch a glimpse of Igneus, wonder if the frail man will make an appearance, wonder if he's rejoined Cain.

"My friends," Cain starts, bowing his head. There's a gleam in his eye as his hair glitters above Jerusalem's ravaged streets. He scans the crowd, holds a single person's attention before moving to the next.

"May all goodness shine upon you forevermore."

Scattered blessings waft in response.

"I'm humbled to be among you. Humbled by this festival of courage and spirit.

"My friends, my countrymen, peace was our only wish. To live our lives and raise our families, to endure life's torments and live in peace was our only hope. Our birthright even. Our destiny."

All lift their heads and fall for his charms.

"Yet, it seems hope has been ripped from our grasp.

"It seems avarice has triumphed.

"It seems evil doers beset us on all sides.

"It seems the powers of darkness gather on our doorstep like drooling wolves hungry for the feast.

"It seems we're beaten.

"It seems we're broken. Maimed and hobbled.

"Alas," he says, turning his face toward the muted sun. *It seems* hope has fled.

"As we bury our dead, and burn the corpses of our enemies, it seems foul darkness has turned to fetid night.

"That the light of goodness has been extinguished by the rancid waters of war.

"It seems we live in times without hope.

"That sorrow rains from Heaven to stain the faces of the Just.

"It seems the world has crumbled.

"Some say we'll never recover.

"They say our days are numbered.

"They say we are defeated.

"They say there's no hope."

He pauses here, searches the crowd's filthy faces. Piercing blue eyes rivet those in attendance, demand the focus of the whole world as he drips honey in their ears.

Then, he whispers. "But I beg to differ."

The crowd stirs.

"It seems They don't know us very well.

"It seems They don't believe the indomitable power of our spirit.

"They doubt our strength. Our resolve. All we've endured. All we've overcome.

"Mister Slabav has given me credit for saving this land." He nods to Laslo, displays that gleaming smile. "He's bestowed an honor of which I am not worthy.

"Mister Slabav says drastic times require drastic measures and has asked me to stay with you through all of this. To help guide and defend this nation as we forge our way through a dark and deadly wilderness, not so unlike our ancestors.

"Yet, so unlike our ancestors.

"As Thaddeus Drake, I was murdered before the eyes of the world.

"Assassinated, in order to be silenced.

"But the Father has other plans, and today I'll share them in the hope that you take heart and know we cannot be overcome. That we cannot be defeated. That God has come and walks among us. That He protects us and loves us.

"After I was murdered, I was transported to the heavens where the one God told me of the troubling times ahead. He told me of days that will test the resolve and commitment of all people on Earth.

"On that day, God spoke with me, commanded me to return to my works of peace and charity.

"Many of you wonder what befell me and how it is that I came to return.

"Many of you noticed the changes in my appearance and have inquired as to my intentions.

"Many others have asked how I came to perform such miracles as have been done in these last days."

Cain's hair glows like a halo, louder by the second. His voice increases in timber and pitch, becomes that of a vast choir, millions of voices rising as one, all speaking the same words.

"Oh, ye faithful, do not be troubled."

I push to the front and see his face perfectly.

His eyes are open, but unfocused. Glowing in perfect, calm aqua below a glistening mane of blinding alabaster. His voice isn't his own but sounds like a heavenly host, endless, harmonic, hypnotic, gorgeous. It resounds, gains volume but doesn't hurt my ears. I struggle against the trance as he enwraps my soul. I feel filled with power, with purpose, with a clarity of mission I've never known before.

His words continue as if flowing without his knowledge, spreading to caress the very face of Israel, to shake the Earth's deepest foundations, as if he speaks for God himself.

My knees quiver, and I look to the gathered crowd who seem hypnotized. They hold each other for strength, eyes glassed over as Cain plies his gifts.

Words flow, passionate. Impossible to ignore. Echoing, heavenly, otherworldly.

"Are ye so blinded that ye cannot see?

"Have ye so few with vision?

"Oh yea, have ye so few who see the hand of God?

"I have risen from the grave.

"I have ascended to rest my gaze upon the plains of heaven.

"I have viewed the holy hosts, rising in glory, surrounded by angels, commanding mc to be born anew.

"Throw down evil, they bade.

"Overcome darkness, they pled.

"A peaceable kingdom, they sang.

"Rejoice, oh ye righteous!

"Lament, oh ye minions of evil!

"I send you my son, in whom I am well pleased.

"He has drunk of my power, and to him have I given dominion.

"Obey him as you would me, for he will lead My flock through treacherous forests and set your feet upon paths of glory.

"He will go on. He will abide, as I told you from the start. Cannot ye see?

"Oh, people here me, and come with open hearts.

"My son has returned so that ye may know grace through the coming season.

"This is he who threw down the gates of Hell.

"This is he who smote the serpent.

"Let those with eyes, see. Those with ears, listen.

"His temptations have ended. His purgatory has ceased.

"He will see My kingdom rebuilt in righteousness.

"And woe to those who conspire against him.

"Woe to those who ignore his words.

"He will see Israel remade. Strong, proud, and beautiful.

"The righteous shall rise, and by his hand, the wicked perish.

"My people! Walk with him, unafraid and glorious, in the light of day.

"For he will save you, and by his hand shall it be made so."

Cain's head drops as if he hasn't the strength to hold it further. A tear glitters as it falls from a piercing blue eye. He wavers, holds the podium for balance. His face is pale, his forehead soaked in sweat. He looks into the cameras, expression more serious than I've ever seen. More driven, more solemn, filled with a power both palpable and undeniable.

"I am that I am," he says.

"I am the Messiah. Returned to you."

"So sayeth the Father."

CHAPTER 12

SEDEROT, ISRAEL

Years earlier

"They're in there."

"Roger, proceed as planned."

Jonas peers down the empty street; the M4 rifle feels cold in his hands as the steel claims the night's frost. He adjusts his helmet, then speaks into the throat mic and attached earpiece. "At least three hostages, maybe as many as seven."

"Roger. Hamas doing its thing."

"Stay frosty. Slow is smooth."

"Roger."

He squeezes hands to fists, focuses his thoughts. This conflict will never end. So much death, so little thought as to strategy. Politicians speaking strength without a clue.

He shivers, glances up the dark street. It's no time to think of politics. Stay on task; keep everyone safe; free the people; dispatch the enemy.

Easy steps make an easy day.

He glances to the roof across the street. Sees Anan, barely visible, the tip of his sniper rifle resting on the roof's ledge.

"Position?" Jonas says.

"Ready in back." This is Zeb, the team's youngest member. A man who shows his youth by acting without thought. He's come a long way in six months, Jonas thinks. Besides, Benny's with him, should be able to keep him focused and on task.

The windows on the first floor of the shabby two-story splay small strips of light on the darkened sidewalk. A mom-and-pop store. The business on the ground floor, living area on the second. The entire store front is glass, making for easy sight lines.

"Your walk home should be easy tonight, Jonas." This is Eitan, the team's demo expert. Jonas glances down the street. Six blocks, two left turns, and he'll be home with his wife and son. Jonas starts to reply, wants to joke, knows he needs to focus on the mission. If he gets distracted, or lets his men get distracted, people will die.

"Stay focused. Get in position."

"Already there, Captain," Benny says.

Jonas imagines the smug look on his best friend's face, then grins. Benny's a pro, can handle himself, knows where to be and where not to be. Jonas moves forward, squats behind an old Mercedes where he leans around and sees Eitan in place at the building's far corner.

He reviews the plan. "Anan, cover with the sniper rifle. Can you see everything?"

"Roger. Full view, but second floor windows have curtains pulled."

"Me and Eitan will breach from the front, while Benny and Zeb breach the back. After that, clear the ground floor, regroup at the base of the stairs to the second floor. I'm not a betting man, but I expect the hostages there. Questions?"

No response.

Good, he thinks; the team's ready.

"Any update on the number of hostages?" Eitan asks.

"Police said at least three. Could be more. And the bad guys will be expecting us." He checks his Casio. "We're a go. Stay alert and check your fire. No civilian damage if possible. Police have cordoned the area, so if anyone gets past us, they should pick them up. Let's *not* let that happen. It endangers the community and the police. This is our job, fellas. Watch for surprises, stay on your toes, let's do what we do."

"Movement up top," the sniper, Anan, says. "Only a sliver but looks like someone crossed the window. Dammit. Curtains are pulled. I have limited vision."

Jonas surveys the windows, assures no one's taking aim at them. "Standing order. If you have a shot, take it. Just be damn certain it's a bad guy."

"Roger that."

Jonas inhales, grips his M4. "Are we clear?"

"Clear," Anan says. "Doesn't look like anyone's watching, but they probably are, and I just can't see them. If they show their face, I'll part their hair."

Jonas moves from the Fiat to the building's eastern edge. On the western side, Eitan slides around the corner, then approaches and places a charge on the door's glass.

"Breach in five, four…"

Jonas moves close, still counting.

"Three, two, one."

There's a sizzle, then a shower of broken glass. Jonas moves through, kneels just inside, sweeps with his rifle. Eitan enters, sweeps to the left.

The shop is small, consistent with the pre-mission briefing. To Jonas's right is a wire shelf stocked with chips and candy. Past that, a check-out counter. Before him, four long aisles run the store's length toward the back.

Eitan moves left, sweeps each aisle as he crosses. Kneeling by the first endcap, he peers down the aisle. "Clear left."

Jonas glides to the checkout counter, slides over, levels his rifle toward the lone door at the building's rear. "Clear front," he whispers.

He remembers the building's layout. The door leads to a small room with a storage area and bathroom. Past that, the building's rear entrance. He listens, hears nothing. No sound is good, means Benny and Zeb entered without incident and are clearing the area. They should appear any moment.

The radio crackles. "Clear back, proceeding." It's Benny, performing his task with usual proficiency. The door cracks and Zeb's head appears. He enters and moves right, kneels near the glass door of a walk-in cooler. Benny enters, moves left, rifle aligned on the building's single flight of stairs.

Jonas moves around the check-out counter, down the aisle closest the stairs. Eitan moves left, down the aisle on the far side of the store.

Zeb turns from the cooler, takes cover behind a tall shelf.

"Is the walk-in clear?" Jonas asks. Walk-ins are a priority for clearance.

"Roger," Zeb replies.

"Eitan?"

"Clear here, moving up."

Benny slides against the wall at the stair's bottom. "Two flights," he says, peering up. "A landing in the middle."

"Zeb, move up."

Zeb crosses to position opposite Benny.

Eitan passes the cooler, kneels by the door at the rear of the room.

"Okay, guys, be precise. The stairs are the single limfac here—"

"Limfac?" Zeb asks.

"We've been over this. Limiting Factor."

"Roger."

"Don't get bottlenecked."

"Roger," Zeb says. "I'll—"

Gunfire erupts as Benny fires up the stairs. Precise bursts. "Contact. Stairs."

"Eitan, behind you!"

Breath whooshes through the earpiece.

Zeb falls, limp.

A man steps from the cooler, rifle blazing.

Jonas pitches forward, fires a three-shot burst.

The man flies through fractured glass, lies limp on the cooler's floor.

"I'm hit," Eitan wheezes.

Jonas twists right, sees another man enter through the rear just beside Eitan.

Benny and Zeb cleared that area. How could they miss someone?

The rifle spits. The attacker crumples. Then, behind him, another steps in, fires twice. Jonas's arm sizzles as a round strikes and spins him off balance.

He falls flat and fires.

The man droops. A second later sliding down the wall, rifle clattering to the floor.

Jonas crawls to Eitan. "You okay?"

Eitan's face says it all. Eyes wide, staring, lifeless.

"Shit."

"Benny, you got the stairs?"

"Roger."

Jonas moves to the cooler. Boots crunch on broken glass. It's empty.

"Cooler's clear," he says. "Thought you cleared it, Zeb?"

There's no response.

Then Benny, "Kid's dead."

Jonas kneels, cuts away a strip of the dead man's pants, ties it tight around the wound on his arm.

Gunfire squeals in Jonas's earpiece. "Contact. Stairs," Benny says.

Jonas exits the cooler, assesses the stairs. Two of his team down in less than a minute. Evac and regroup, he thinks. Call in support, cut your losses. "Stay on the stairs. I'll check the back," he says. "Got it?"

"Roger," Benny says. "I'll be right here."

Jonas stays low, forces the pain from his mind. With a glance right, he hurries to the open door of the storage room, senses attuned to every sound. He steps through, sees mops and buckets, stacks of paper towels, boxes of product.

He sweeps, sees a shadowed square in the floor's center. An open hatch rests against the boxes.

"Shit," he says. "Found a space beneath the floor. That's where they came from. I have to clear it. You good?"

"I've got it."

"Anan, you there?"

"Roger. Want me to join?"

"No, I want you right there. Cover those windows. If you have a shot, take it."

"Roger that."

Jonas draws his Glock, leans over the square hole. The flashbang clatters as he drops it in.

The instant it fires, he drops through and spins in a tight circle.

The dugout's about four feet deep and four feet square.

It's empty.

"Clear back," he says. "Moving up."

"Roger."

The pain in his arm intensifies, throbs like a warning beacon as he moves from the back room.

He steps over Eitan, past the body of Zeb; joins Benny at the base of the stairs.

"Anan, get the medics in here ASAP. Two down, first floor. Moving up."

"We should abort," Anan replies.

Benny's eyes meet his, then a subtle shake of the head. His face is focused, eyes alert, rifle pointed up the stairs. If anything moves, he'll kill it.

"Negative. Continue as planned."

"You alright?" Benny says.

"Got hit. I'll get by."

"What now?"

"The kid half-assed his job and got Eitan killed in the process. Thought you cleared that."

"We did, the kid went to the cooler and I came to the stairs. I wasn't watching him, but never dreamed he'd blow off the cooler. We trained him better."

"I'm a little pissed." Jonas says.

"What's the plan?"

"Good old burst and bash."

"Roger."

"Don't hit the hostages."

"Roger. I'll hit everything else."

Jonas peers up the stairs, to a landing that turns one hundred and eighty degrees. Past that, another short flight will open to the second floor.

Benny moves up, reaches the landing, steps over two dead terrorists. He fires a short burst, and Jonas hears a thump.

"Contact. Down," Benny says, pulling a flashbang and tossing it up.

They hear the pop and sizzle, then race forward.

The room's a large square. Directly across from them is a small kitchen with bedroom doors on either side; to their left a living area with a rumpled red couch and brown recliner.

Four doors open into this room. One to their immediate right, next to the stairs. Two on either side of the kitchen, and one at the building's front, to the far left of their current position.

Benny moves right, kicks the door open.

Jonas moves left, the room's front corner.

"Bathroom. Clear," Benny says.

Jonas moves along the wall, alert, gun ready. This is the building's front, and he knows Anan watches from across the street.

He opens each curtain as he moves then crouches to cover the door before him.

"Can you see, Anan?"

"Affirmative," the sniper says. "Did you open all the curtains?"

"Affirmative."

"There's another window with the curtains drawn. In the room right in front of you."

Jonas regards the door, instinctively looks for traps or wired explosives. "Do you see anything in there?"

"Just a crack. Looks like a man, maybe two hostages. He keeps leaning forward, but not enough for me to get the shot."

"I'm going in. If you get the shot, take it."

"Roger."

Jonas hears a thud, some rustling. "Contact. Down. Clear." Benny says. He's cleared the room to the kitchen's right. "There's a couple hostages here," he says. "Have to secure them. You good?"

"I am. I'll wait and cover out here."

Two more rooms, Jonas thinks. Benny will quickly zip-tie the hostages and instruct them to lay still on the floor.

A minute later Benny appears and moves through the kitchen to crouch before the door on its left. "Ready," he says.

"In tandem," Jonas says. "Let's finish this."

"I'm so gonna kill these fucking guys."

Jonas opens the door before him, tosses a flashbang, presses against the outer wall.

The flashbang pops.

Jonas enters, sweeps.

The room is small, cramped. A man sits dazed on a tiny bed, back pressed to the wall, facing the door. In front of him, like shields, are a woman and child. All look dazzled, blinded.

The man leans forward, screams something.

"Acquired." The sniper's voice in the earpiece.

The child holds a candy bar.

The lady's mouth is open.

Jonas knows her. Loves her.

The man shows a grenade.

"Daddy!" the boy screams.

Jonas freezes. "Anan! No!"

Anan fires.

The grenade falls.

Chapter 13

Jerusalem, Israel

Present day

News vans surround the apartment building as reporters huddle and sip from Styrofoam cups.

Inside, Igneus faces Jonas from a threadbare recliner, then hefts a steaming mug and does his best to ignore the reporters' clatter.

Drawn Venetians cast his friend in dark shadows that mimic his own expression; smoldering features etched with bristles and spikes.

Jonas lowers his head, eyes glittering and far away. "It was my fault."

"How could you have known?"

"I should've," Jonas says. "Everything just went to shit so fast. I guess I was shook by the loss of two of my team, then simply stunned when I saw my wife and son. Seems the terrorists planned to kill the hostages the whole time. To take as many of us with them as they could. They knew we were coming, counted on the fact we'd storm the place. Glory by suicide, killing as many innocents as possible." His gaze is far off, as if talking to no one but himself. "The sniper took the shot, and the grenade fell between the terrorist and my family."

"There was nothing you could do," Igneus says.

Jonas looks to the floor, head shaking. "There's always something you can do. Always a way. Everyone in there was my responsibility. Everyone."

"But you can't…"

"*My* responsibility. *My* wife and son. *My* best friend, Benny. *My* team, Zeb, Eitan."

"Benny died?"

Jonas's eyes are wet, his body slumped. "Yep, Benny too. Died saving me. After he cleared his final room, he came to back me up, found me frozen in the doorway staring at my family. He read the situation and pulled me out just as the grenade went off. The shrapnel killed everyone except me. Left me with this." He opens his shirt to reveal a myriad of scars, more scars than Igneus can imagine, more than even Longinus. As if Jonas sprinted shirtless through a patch of cacti.

Jonas holds his hand over his chest. "Those I love are here."

Igneus nods, abashed. "Yes, always in your heart."

A tear slides down Jonas's cheek. "No, in these scars. Bits of bone. The doctors said too many to count, too many to remove. They said I'd be infected, that the surgery would take hours." He wipes his eye, exhales. "But they never got infected, just healed over. A mix of my family, my best friend, and the terrorist that killed them." Jonas glances up, manages a smile. "You should close your mouth."

Igneus startles, realizes he's staring with his mouth open and snaps it shut, then places a hand on Jonas's shoulder. "I'm so very sorry."

"Me too," Jonas says. "Me too."

Silence hangs over them for many seconds, then Jonas continues. "After that I felt nothing, had nothing. I took responsibility for the entire thing. Then I left the service and found work at the parking garage. I spend my time taking care of Ishmael, taking care of the garage, but not much else. Can never really think clearly, can't think of it without breaking down.

"If it weren't for Ishmael, I'd probably be on the streets. It's been many years, but the wounds are fresh, the scars a constant reminder." He rubs his chest. "I can feel them, you know. The fragments beneath my skin. Little sharp shards. I've spent hours wondering which fragments belong to who. Which are my wife's? My son's? Benny's? I've convinced myself that none of them belong to the terrorist. That my body rejected those with extreme prejudice." He looks at Igneus, holds his eyes. "What really messes with me, though, is why they didn't get infected. Why they didn't dislodge themselves. The doctors were certain they'd find their way out and told me so all the time. But they never did, they've never moved." His laugh is nervous here, strained. "I've decided it's my family. That Benny takes care of them now and that they all wait for me. That these scars are them refusing to leave, reminding me we're always together, no matter what comes." He looks down, wipes another tear. "Ah, but enough of that," he says. "We have things to do."

Jonas crosses to the small kitchen. Outside, reporters gaggle near news vans; umbrellas and plastic bags protect their heads from a relentless rain.

"You want some coffee?" Jonas says.

Igneus feels dumbfounded. He nods absently, leans back into the sofa, glances at the room where Sebastian sleeps. He can't imagine the man's loss, can't imagine the weight he carries, blaming himself for the deaths of his wife and child. He leans his head back, closes his eyes. Tries to imagine the scene, Jonas's feelings, Jonas's terror, his heartbreak. If anything ever happened to Sebastian, Igneus isn't sure he'd be able to continue in any meaningful way. The boy's brought such joy to his life, has made his entire miserable existence worth living. Worth living again, he thinks, but realizes, in the centuries prior to Sebastian, he'd never really lived a worthwhile day. Before Cain, he'd spent his days attracting wealth: an estate, servants, the ears of Roman Senators. He'd had it all. After Cain, he'd found himself enduring miserable centuries performing the madman's bidding, knowing escape wasn't possible. Ever.

When all had finally been revealed, Igneus felt it like a rough hand gripping his shoulder. Relief like a breeze on a hot day, like food in a starving belly, like air to suffocation. How things have changed. He never imagined he'd have a son, that he'd be granted the formidable opportunity to guide a young man through his formative years and forge the person he'd become.

Jonas sets the coffee in front of him and moves off into the apartment. Igneus watches him go, broad shoulders carrying so much weight. So much horror.

Sometimes memory is the heaviest thing.

Sebastian looks up to Jonas, reacts to him and his masculinity on an instinctual level. Not that Jonas wears machismo on his person like a tattooed drunk, but rather carries it with effortless precision. As if he's just comfortable with his being, with his person, with the qualities that make him a man. Not brooding or petty or overpowering, but something internal, something that animates his psyche, his movements, his demeanor.

Jonas returns at another knock on the door. He doesn't answer it but assumes a seat across from Igneus. His look is stern, serious. "What now?"

Igneus isn't ready for the question. He stares for a second, buys some time reaching for his coffee and taking a long sip. It's hot and bitter and warms his insides.

"Well," he starts, "I think I should face the press and make some statements. I think I should use this notoriety to our advantage. It's time to tell the world the true nature of Cain and his plans. I think the reporters will offer that platform—the question is whether my words will ever reach an audience. X'chasei controls the airwaves, controls more than anyone could possibly imagine. And at the head of the serpent is Cain, not an unworthy adversary."

"Well, let's go," Jonas says, rising.

"No, Jonas. This isn't your fight. You've done too much already. The garage is ruined; your country, piled with corpses. I can't ask you to help. This is something I need to attend on my own."

Jonas stops cold, scans the emaciated frame. "You know, I'd like to tell you just how insulting those words are. They make me feel like lashing out at you for being so selfish and closed-minded." Dark eyes never waver. "I'd like to remind you of your own journey here and your choices along the way. But I can't, or rather, I won't, because I know where you're coming from." He pauses, eyes locked on Igneus. "I realize your intent isn't to insult, but to save. And I think that comes from a pure place. My mother always told me, 'If your intent is pure, you shall not fail.' I've found that to be sage advice. Coincidence doesn't exist, it's just something we make up so we feel like we have control of our own destiny. Especially when it doesn't go the way we intend."

He steps close, eyes locked. "Igneus, hear me, and hear me well. I'll no sooner leave you, than I'd leave Ishmael. What I think doesn't matter. What you think doesn't matter. What matters is that we're family, and families stick together. A family doesn't buy or barter their love. It just is. Blood doesn't make a family. Do you know that? Know what makes a family? Intent. That's it. Plain and simple. Intent to do no harm, intent to hold someone else's best interests at heart. Intent to give, to love, knowing it'll be returned in the same manner. Given freely, gained freely. The simplest of concepts, really, but most people don't get it and treat their families with contempt and ill-will, which, by the way, is usually well-deserved. But here's the thing, they all know better. Every one of them know better but continue on like they don't.

"I want you to know this. *I* am not them. *Ishmael* is not them. You're our family now, for good or ill, and if you can't see that, you're not the man I thought you were."

Jonas stares as if he expects an answer. Igneus considers the words like inspecting a diamond for its qualities. Jonas isn't incorrect, isn't even close to wrong. Is it that I've been through so many centuries without a real family, I've forgotten how to behave? I've never had children, never even thought about them. What makes a family, and what do family members owe each other? He looks at the dark man standing before him, sees the answer clearly defined on his face. Nothing is owed, only given. Nothing is counted, only gained. The cornerstone of family is trust. A bond that says no matter what comes, no matter what riches tempt or where twisted paths lead, our family will weather the storms together and gain strength from our bonds.

Igneus smiles, stands, and embraces Jonas. "You teach me much, my brother."

Jonas grins, gives Igneus a painful slug on the arm. "Don't make a big thing out of it." His smile is huge, genuine, dark eyes twinkling.

"You know Cain will kill you?"

"Yes."

"And?"

Jonas considers his words, coffee mug steaming in his hand. "The only thing I've ever regretted was not doing the right thing when I knew I should. Death doesn't scare me, Igneus. I await it. My family waits for me there. Benny waits for me. Death is an escape I long for." He places a hand on Igneus's shoulder. "But, until that time, I'll endeavor to show my quality in all I do. Death surrounds us, yet we live. It's senseless to question why that is. What matters is how we go forward, our intent, here and now. When I die, my people will remember how I lived."

They hold each other's eyes.

Finally, Igneus nods. "So be it," he says. "Let's wake the others. We'll start this crusade at the Temple."

Jonas grins. "Aye, aye, Captain."

CHAPTER 14

JERUSALEM, ISRAEL

The apple turns from luscious red to black and rotten within seconds.

Cain doesn't notice and takes huge bites, consuming the fruit like a first meal after a long fast. Nausea squeezes my stomach as I watch.

Longinus retrieves a napkin from the limo's well-stocked bar. Cain nods a thanks, then dabs at the corners of his mouth. I regard the Roman, notice he doesn't hold a drink. Odd considering if there's a bar present, Longinus will be drinking it dry.

"That took a lot out of me," Cain says.

After his speech, his proclamation of himself as God, as the Messiah returned, Cain needed assistance departing the stage. Longinus, of course, had been at hand to help. Still, he hadn't forgotten me, even then. "Dear Emery," he said, suddenly fastening his gaze upon me, "won't you join us?"

Minutes later, I find myself in the limo, wondering if all Cain said is true and if his powers extend to an ability to read my mind. I try to cleanse my thoughts as I look out the windows at the masses of the dead, at the living, who, I have to admit, seem more animated after Cain's speech, less sorrowful, as if Cain's gifts have somehow been magnified to cast a spell over the entire populous.

I hear the whir of servos as the black privacy screen separating the passenger's compartment from the driver's cabin lowers. "A call for you, Mr. Cain."

Longinus interjects. "Hold all calls, Jeremy."

"It's the US President, says it's urgent."

Longinus moves to Cain, kneels beside. "You don't have to take it. You've endured much today."

Cain waves a hand. "Nonsense." Then to the driver. "Send it along, dear Jeremy."

A red light blinks on the armrest, below a phone cradled in black plastic. Cain smiles at me. "You should be recording."

I hit the proper icon, then nod.

Cain presses the flashing button. "President Carpenter, what a lovely surprise."

The president's voice sounds detached as the hum of the connection fills the limo. "The pleasure is mine," he says. "And I guess congratulations are in order. You've managed to ruin the world in only a few days."

Cain laughs, his eyes gleeful. Something about the president's statement has tickled him. "Dearest Tom, sometimes a world needs remade," he says. "But I'm afraid I can't take all the credit for such grand accomplishments. Laslo's team has done a fine job. I merely provided a bit of extra security."

"Is that what you're calling it? Your super soldiers. Your super weapons. You have everyone here on edge, Mr. Cain, and that makes for nervous trigger fingers. I've done nothing today but reassure world leaders that the US has firm control of the situation and is sending troops, ships, and other resources to help you rebuild and maintain peace."

"And to secure the oil."

"What?" the president says.

"To secure the oil. Please, my dear friend, don't try and appease me with your words. We both know what concerns you. Can we not speak bluntly?"

Another pause, then a sound as if the president covers the phone with his hand. A second later he speaks. "Very well, then, let's be frank. We're very concerned about recent events. You've basically run a coup d'état in Israel, now you occupy the entire region. You've become cause for great concern around here, and other world leaders agree you must answer as to your intentions. Normally we'd do this through diplomatic channels, for the press and the people, so to speak, but things are moving with such speed that the face of the Earth is changing by the hour. We cannot tolerate you to continue unbridled and without any sort of restraint. So, I'm calling to offer you a chance to explain yourself."

Cain's voice is pure elation, like a child gaining attention from a favored parent. "You've forgotten the destruction of the Russian force?"

"And that!" The president's voice oozes stress, a crack amplified, hardly presidential. "Explain yourself."

Cain looks at his right hand, the mark softly glowing in the limo's confines, a barely perceptible hue on the limo's ceiling. "Dear President Carpenter, I don't answer to any power on the Earth and thought I made myself quite clear during my speech. I aim to cleanse the world. To recreate a kingdom of peace and harmony, a kingdom of plenty, a world without need or want. All will rejoice under my reign, so sayeth the Father."

There's another pause and I imagine the president trying to collect himself. Cain's always enjoyed popping people's party balloons. There's an audible sigh. "Do you know you sound like a nut job?" Carpenter says. "Like a maniac intent on world domination."

"I'm sure I do, but I'm neither of those. One cannot dispute my results, and unfortunately, my mind is set by a higher power. I'm afraid I can be of no use to you, nor will I suffer your questions or explain my actions."

"We had a deal, Cain. It wouldn't be wise to cross me."

Cain smiles, sounds pleasant. "Of what deal do you speak?"

"Do I need remind you? I agreed to support you in exchange for a share of the region's resources. Perhaps some military bases, a few diplomats, extra security, and the like. We can help protect the oil fields; we can help transport those resources out of the country."

"Oh, yes," Cain says, raising a finger. "I remember. I believe the words you used were *no military support.*" He pauses, looks at the ceiling, sighs. "My dear friend, in the interest of clarity, let me explain the situation. My country doesn't consider you friend or ally, but rather only a self-interested enemy. Prowling capitalists who covet only wealth and comfort. Your history is rife with how helpful your nation can be to those it encounters. Tales of exploitation and theft abound. These days it would be unwise to employ the same tactics, the same threats. You've ruled poorly and the time of reckoning is nigh. A wiser choice would be to surrender the United States to my authority. Join us and show your fealty. Repent and accept divine rule. I'll say this just once: your country is an abomination. Its destruction was prophesied long ago. You've turned your face from God, from that which is holy, from that which is blessed. Your people bleed in the streets, pressed by the heels of tycoons. Yet you desire only enrichment, only idolatry, only vice. My kingdom cannot suffer such a plague. The time is short, repent your ways and submit, or be judged and destroyed. The choice is yours, so sayeth the Father."

I'm amazed watching Cain act so like a god. He's so convincing, I wonder for a second if he's for real, dwelling among the holy trinity, talking with God the Father.

The phone goes silent again, and I find myself hoping the president will agree and surrender. I consider the lives at stake, the culture. Then I consider all of which Cain is capable. I've no idea if he can back the threats, but I've seen enough not to doubt him. I want to scream at the president, beg him to accept the terms, which for Cain's part, are quite generous.

"You're threatening us?" The president's voice is clear and confident. "The grandest power the Earth has ever seen? This is terrorism. *You* are a terrorist. We don't negotiate with terrorists."

"A shame, that," Cain says.

"We'll see you soon," the president says, then the line goes dead.

Cain holds me with steel blue eyes, watches for so long it becomes unnerving. The harder I try and clear my mind, the more I think he sees my every thought. For Longinus's part, and true to form, he remains silent.

"Well, that went well," Cain says with a frown, seems genuinely disappointed. He looks to Longinus. "Is everything ready?"

Longinus is eager to answer. "Yes, my lord, in a matter of days our plans shall bear fruit. The meeting is set."

Cain's hair seems normal now, doesn't bristle or glow atop his head. There's something here, I think. Like the perfectly kept mane telegraphs his intentions, rising and glowing at times of power, subdued and normal at others. I glance at his mark; the light has gone, leaving only a puckered scar on his right hand.

"Good news," Cain says, "and what of the Russians?"

"All goes as planned, my lord. President Ming has started his invasion, tells me they're unopposed. Very soon they'll have complete control of that nation. Seems the Russians placed their eggs in one basket. With their army destroyed, it should be easy work for the Chinese."

"And the missiles?"

"First thing over which we took control, Highness. They are ours without question and we can do with them as we wish."

Longinus continues to surprise. He's like a clone of Cain these days. Perfect speech, perfect dress, perfectly put together. He wears a tailored suit of dark maroon with gray speckled tie, perfectly knotted. His hair is short, slicked back above blue eyes that have replaced the dark orbs of the original Roman. But it's the honorifics that undo me, and I can't restrain my expression as I stare. This new Longinus is an enigma, changing forms at times, speaking with eloquence, a trusted and elegant advisor to the self-appointed Messiah.

"And the virus?"

Longinus's grin grows wide. "Released."

Cain smiles. "You serve me well, dear Longinus."

Longinus's expression becomes that of a dog scratched behind the ear. My mouth falls open. He's indeed changed, has become Cain's lap hound.

The Roman beams, then continues. "You know the president will go after your wife. He seems rather outraged. They'll send troops, organize a coalition to come against us."

"Yes, my dear friend, wait and watch. It should be a grand show."

Chapter 15

Jerusalem, Israel

Sent to find Igneus and return him to the fold, Emery shuffles toward the Temple.

Longsuffering, that one, but not too smart.

Cain thinks of sheep. Thinks of loyalty. Thinks of Rhyme.

The two deserve each other.

When they find out the truth, they're going to be poleaxed. Perhaps their little minds will start to grasp the fact that their resistance is futile, their life together lost.

That's *if* dear Emery survives.

And if he dies? Well, no big loss. Simply choose another biographer from the throng of minions.

As part of their deal, Rhyme made him promise Emery's safety. Done, and done in spades, he thinks, then frowns and bristles. She still loves Emery, he knows, but does she have to act like a fool? Act like most sheep when they're under love's spell?

"Patience," a voice whispers. "Before long she'll accept you without question. Then, together you'll rule the world."

Longinus interrupts his thoughts. "What of Igneus?"

The limo pulls off as Cain turns his attention to the Roman. He's been a faithful servant and deserves such rewards as Cain can give. Women, money, drugs, all his for the asking.

"Tell the Americans that the source of my power flows from the Jew. Do this in such a way as to make them believe that, should they destroy him, they'll render me powerless. Do this discretely."

Longinus's grin shows he realizes the implications. This new Longinus is quite a bit brighter than the other oaf.

Longinus retrieves his phone and speaks. After a few minutes, he ends the call. "Done," he says.

"Why, dear Longinus, you made quick work of that."

Longinus revels in the praise, a broad smile spreads over his face. "The Americans are coming," he says. "Their covert operatives are already activated." His face forms a question his mouth won't ask.

"Perfect," Cain says. "Just as I expected." He pulls a Treasurer from a tin as Longinus offers a lighter, its flame burning yellow and weak.

Cain inhales as his thoughts turn to his true home.

After his work is finished, he'll return to the only place he's ever felt comfortable. To the only place he's ever felt at home. Reminiscing has never been his style, but he finds his thoughts traveling to that place of torment and fire, to that place of desperation and agony. His mouth waters and he swallows hard. He's of a mind for mischief.

The limo slows and pulls to the curb. Longinus opens the door, and three women climb in. Dressed like party girls, each wears a sequined gown, adorned with diamonds and rubies, coated in intoxicating fragrances, fruit with a hint of vanilla.

"Fresh from X'chasei's stables," Longinus says. "They exist only to provide pleasure."

Cain inflames, feels saliva collect in his mouth. He doesn't know it, but his eyes have become red slits; his face, a dusky hue.

"We've earned a break," he says, then turns to the ladies. "Who do you serve?"

"X'chasei," they say in unison.

"And from where flows your pleasure?"

"From the one true God."

Cain's heart bounds in his chest, his erection throbs. It's been a long time, he thinks, but the master commands and has bestowed this boon as a reward.

Two women slide next to him. One lowers her head to his lap as the other kisses him deeply and starts to unbutton his shirt.

The feeling is exquisite. The aroma, intoxicating, tempting the nose and numbing the mind. These servants, so talented.

He closes his eyes, lays his head back, accepts all the pleasures.

He simply *must* remember to dispose of their bodies when he's done. A good task for Jeremy, the driver.

A smile blooms. I'll see these ladies again, he thinks, just as soon as I get home.

CHAPTER 16

JERUSALEM, ISRAEL

Glass crunches beneath my shoes as I pass burnt-out cars and demolished store fronts. Smoke burns my nostrils and mixes with the acrid scent of burning corpses. I wonder how the bodies burn in the endless rain.

I pull my jacket close and wish for an umbrella. In the city, the puddles are brown and reflect the smudges of leaded clouds. I wish the color was only dirt, but know it's the runoff of body fluids and blood.

The smell is horrific. I quicken my pace.

The Temple looms ahead as I'm joined by others.

I hear the voice before I get close.

"Cain's a liar. A thief."

It's amplified, familiar. I hasten through the growing crowd, breathe courtesies as I push past. "Excuse me." "I'm sorry." "Pardon me."

The speaker continues. "I've walked with him, was a trusted ally, participated in crimes from genocide to human trafficking, from murder to manipulation of currencies. I've started wars, then stood back and watched as he snuffed the lives of so many people."

I stand on tiptoe to peer over the hundreds before me.

Then, I see the emaciated frame, the drawn cheeks. It's Igneus the Jew.

"I was evil," he continues, "convinced by lies. You see, Cain hypnotizes. He wields special powers that allow him to dupe and lead astray. This is what happened to me.

"Until God showed me the truth. Until He gave me the means to save Israel. I stand before you today, a conduit of God. Sent to dispel Cain's myths and expose his lies.

"Cain is a madman. Cain seeks only destruction. Seeks to throw asunder goodness and wrest control of the entire Earth. He seeks only to offer us all as sacrificial lambs, so that he might attain something God refuses to give. Forgiveness. He's been cast out, rejected, doomed. The attack on Israel was his fault. Ordained… arranged, by him and no other. Now, he holds the ear of your prime minister where he serves as a trusted ally. He wants you to think he serves Israel, that he's a servant of God and is anointed with His powers.

"Hear me, oh people! You're being duped! Slandered! Led to the slaughter!

"Resist, I say. Overcome! Open your eyes! See Cain for the devil he is!

"Have you witnessed his miracles? His arrival on Easter upon a white horse like an errant knight returned to his kingdom?

"Deny him! Overthrow him! Scripture says what's to come, and you must believe in order to reap the splendors of Heaven.

"God has sent us to tell you, to warn you. The end races toward us unless we act!" He motions to his left and I see the boy, Sebastian, standing next to him. I remember the kid from the compound of the Children of the Rocks. The boy with a penchant for fried chicken. And lots of gravy, as I think about it.

He's grown, looks healthy and loved.

I push forward, ignore the protests of those around me.

Igneus continues. "Here may you find shelter and food. Here we offer warmth and aid. Here we speak truth and dispel lies. Step forward! Join us! Together we can overcome this enemy in our midst!" Igneus motions to his right, and I see a table with a young man sitting behind it. "We have a doctor, and more are coming. We will help you, nourish you. Heal your wounds and raise our voices in prayer. Do not be sheep! Do not be swayed by words that drip like honey! They are poison! Join us! Time is short!"

As I strain to see, a man limps forward wearing a tattered tweed jacket beneath a week of straggly beard. Blood-stained trousers complete the picture, and he cradles his right arm against his chest.

Igneus steps from the makeshift podium. The young doctor moves from the table and speaks to the man, his expression genuine, eyes kind. Too young to be a doctor, I think.

Then Sebastian steps forward, circles the man a single time and places his hand on his arm. I see the glow of soft blue light, then the man steps back, astonishment plastered on his features, lips quivering at the corners. I can't tell if he's going to laugh or cry.

He stretches his hand above his head. Looks like an Olympic torch bearer without the flame. His face is jubilant, his arm healed.

Sebastian kneels, touches his leg. I see the same faint glow and watch as the man wavers, almost falls. He looks at the lad, eyes drenched with shock, then leaps in the air and does a jig worthy of an old seafarer.

Around me, the crowd sighs and presses forward. They make a line behind the dancing man.

I squeeze left, circle to approach Igneus.

He sees me as I draw close. "Emery!" He grabs me up in a bear hug. "I thought I'd never see you again. I've missed you. Did you escape Cain? I have to admit, I'm amazed to see you alive, but praise be to God, your presence makes me so incredibly happy!"

I return the hug, like hugging a skeleton. "It's good to see you," I say, laughing. "You've been busy."

He looks around with an expression of humility. "Oh, Emery, how I wish I could take credit. It seems God works in mysterious ways. Can you believe it? Cain builds a Temple, and it becomes a shining light in a dark tempest? Ah, but enough of that." He waves a hand. "How are you? Where's Cain? And Longinus? Can't imagine the dastardly things they're up to, but then…" He stops, regards me with a quizzical smile.

"Look at me prattle. Plenty of time for that later. Are you hungry? Injured? God has certainly provided. We have healing and nourishment here."

I grin at the little man who seems so animated. Despite his frailty, he exudes an aura of power, of boldness. "I'm doing pretty well, all things considered. But since you ask, I was wondering if you could tell me what happened after the Temple? After Cain disappeared and Longinus burned? I have no recollection, and my mind won't let it go."

"Always the journalist," he says. "I sure missed you, Emery." He looks around, lowers his head. "Walk with me."

We push through the line in front of Sebastian as a man approaches wearing a puzzled expression. He looks fit and capable, military if I had to guess. "Ah, Jonas," Igneus says. "Meet my old friend Emery."

He shakes my hand with a firm grip. "Pleased to meet you."

"You, as well," I say.

"Jonas, join us." Igneus turns his eyes toward the angry sky. "More rain's coming. Let's go to the apartment and catch up. Do you have time to visit, Emery?"

I nod. "Absolutely." I then add, "I have much to tell."

Jonas glances at the line of the sick and injured. His eyes rest on the young doctor. "I think Sebastian will be okay here. Ishmael will keep an eye. Looks like they'll be busy for a while, anyway."

We move through the crowd, stopping only for Igneus to exchange brief words with some burly, tattered men. "Keep a watchful eye," he says. "I don't think there'll be trouble, but stay alert. We won't be too long."

"Friends?" I ask as we move along.

Igneus laughs. "Yes. New friends. We're using the Temple and its grounds to help people. They're doing the same over at the Dome of the Rock: giving aid, services, food, medicine." He smiles here. "We've become a sort of focal point for those in need."

I glance at the child. "Is he *healing* people?"

Igneus chuckles. "It appears so, but I don't know when or how he developed that particular skill. God does indeed work in mysterious ways." He raises a hand. "One second." He cocks his head as if he's listening to something. I look at his ears, search for an earpiece, but see none. I glance at the boy, who appears busy with his work.

Around me people laugh and hug, smiles bloom despite the rain, the odors, the corpses, the misery. They're joyous despite all they've endured. I'm reminded of Seuss's *Whoville* and its inhabitants who, despite having their Christmas stolen, still gather in joy and harmony.

Of course, what's gone on here is leagues worse than anything Seuss would dare imagine. Body collectors work around the clock. People live in what's left of their homes. Funerals abound and take place on the streets. City parks and fields have become cemeteries. But what's most interesting, and through it all, the people have banded together. Muslim, Christian, Jew, all faiths, all religions, with one purpose. I wonder at the thought, think of Cain's plans and how, even through his evil deeds, goodness rises like a phoenix from the ashes.

"Okay, let's go," Igneus says. "Sebastian says he'll be fine."

The child kneels about fifty feet away, attends to a middle-aged man who points at his ear. Next to him, Ishmael, the young doctor, tends to a girl's wounded arm, deftly spinning a bandage and smiling the entire time.

Igneus reads my expression. "Don't look so confused, Emery. We have much to share with each other."

CHAPTER 17

JERUSALEM, ISRAEL

Ten minutes later, I sit in a small apartment on a small couch. This is certainly not the luxury Cain affords, and I wonder how Igneus found himself here.

Jonas offers a steaming cup and I accept. "Thank you."

"Always a pleasure to meet a new friend," he says.

I hear the front door open and a rush of shouting. Igneus enters. "The press," he says, hiking a thumb toward the door. "They're rather relentless, which amazes me because the city's in such disarray. You'd think they'd have better things to do."

"Power's coming back in some places," Jonas says. "We'll get through this and be stronger for it."

Jonas looks like a man who knows something about tenacity through hard times, grit in the face of hopelessness. I get the feeling his story, like mine, is full of heartbreak and loss. He assumes a threadbare recliner as Igneus sits next to me on the couch, a wooden staff leans on his leg. "Emery, Emery," Igneus says, smiling. "So good to see you, I can hardly believe God's wonders."

"I'm not sure God had much to do with it. You wouldn't believe what's happened since I saw you last."

He leans forward. "Have you seen Rhyme?"

I frown. "I have. Not the happiest of reunions, truth be told."

Igneus nods. "I imagine not, how are you handling it?"

"That she's Cain's wife?"

"Yes. I didn't want to say it aloud, if by chance you didn't know."

"Unfortunately, I do know. Although I wish I didn't."

"I don't know if you remember but, in the Temple, when you were on the verge of death, I tried to tell you she was still alive. Do you remember any of that?"

"I remember you saying her name," I say. "Then I woke in heaven with John showing me a war between angels. I'm pretty sure it was a dream, but seemed real enough, more real than a dream actually. Unfortunately, I didn't learn about Rhyme until the hospital discharged me. It may have been the worst moment of my life, seeing her, seeing Cain with his arms wrapped around her, her lipstick smudged on his lips." I shudder, force myself to think of the good.

"This isn't a normal situation, Emery. People do things they wouldn't ordinarily do. I don't know Rhyme well, but I get the impression she married Cain for reasons other than love."

I hold his eyes, look at my shoes, lean back on the couch, press the mug to my lips. A reason other than love, I think. "And what reason would that be?"

"I don't know," he says and waggles his head a bit. "But there's lots I don't know these days."

"Well, I think there's still hope for she and I," I say, grinning. "Which is always dangerous."

"Indeed, my friend. Hope, like truth, is a sword with razor edges."

I sip my coffee and tell my tale since leaving the hospital. The trip to D.C., meeting Bill, Rhyme and Longinus, his sword and spear. When I mention the relic, Igneus animates, leans forward, then tilts his head like hearing a dog whistle.

"What?" I say.

"That's it. The relic. I remember it from the old days. Remember everyone's dismay when it wasn't the superior weapon for which they'd hoped."

"Now it is," I say. "I saw it with my own eyes, felt its power, its energy. The thing almost killed Longinus, almost killed us both. I'm still healing."

"Where is it?"

"No idea. Longinus keeps it somewhere."

"And where is Longinus?"

"Cain sent him to prepare for a meeting of some kind. Says it's to raise awareness of Israel's plight. Seems odd, having such a thing with Israel in disarray. Selfish, to say the least."

Igneus looks at me in such a way that I think about what I've just said. Then we both burst into laughter. Cain is to selfishness like Longinus is to brutality.

"Do you think you can get it?" he asks.

"The spear?" Surprised, I shake my head. "I can't imagine how I could. Longinus is pretty tight-lipped as to its whereabouts."

"When is this meeting?"

"Two days, I think. Cain's given only a few details. I know it's in Israel and the spear will be there but don't know much more."

Igneus rubs his chin, thinking. "This can change everything. *If* we can get our hands on it."

I chuckle. "Yeah, let's pick a fight with Longinus, that worked out so well last time. After we kick his ass, we'll just take it."

"You said he was smaller now. Maybe we can do just that."

"Perhaps I misspoke. Even with his new appearance, he retains his former density. It's like the *big* Longinus was compressed into a smaller, more elegant form. Then, when he used the spear, he became the giant we all know and love. I doubt we can win a fight against him, and if he uses the spear, there's just no way."

I sip my coffee as Igneus tells Jonas about all of this. About Longinus and his metamorphosis, about his immortality and penchant for devilry, about the spear and its power. Jonas listens attentively, nods occasionally. "Sounds like a super weapon," he says. "But won't do us any good."

"Why?" Igneus asks.

"Who can wield it?"

"Perhaps I can." He hefts his staff. "Perhaps the power is similar. Perhaps God will empower me as Longinus was empowered."

Jonas runs a hand through dark hair. "Perhaps. But perhaps not. We can't have you getting killed trying to find out. You're the only thing keeping Cain at bay right now."

"I saw the video," I say. "You're a sort of folk hero now."

Igneus frowns. "No, no. Don't canonize me yet. No one's indispensable. If I fall, God will raise another. Perhaps Sebastian can wield it?"

"You and he are about the same size. I'm sure the child wouldn't have a problem with a super relic," I say.

Igneus knows I'm teasing, smiles at me as Jonas chuckles. "A long shot," Igneus says, "but we have to try."

"To?" I say.

"To get the spear. Even if we *can't* wield it, we can still *deny* their use of it," Jonas says.

"So, you're just going to go to the meeting and steal the spear? How are you going to get there? They'll see you coming miles off. You don't even know where it's being held? The security arrangements? It's suicide."

"Oh, I'm not going, Emery," Igneus says. "Jonas is."

Jonas wears an expression like a thief caught in a spotlight. "Me? No way. No, no, no."

"Yes," Igneus says. "It makes perfect sense. You know how to do things like this. How to survey a building, gain entry, slip away unnoticed. It has to be you."

Jonas's head shakes like a bobble-head doll. "I can't even begin…" he says. "I'd need blueprints, equipment, transport, support personnel, weapons…"

"Uh huh," Igneus says. "You'll have none of those."

Jonas's stare is almost comical, the equivalent of asking him to cure cancer in the next hour. "It's impossible," he says, "even with a full team and a month to plan, it would be difficult. The security will be astounding. How on earth can I even gain entry to some event of Cain's, let alone get the relic and escape?"

"I don't know," Igneus says.

"I've no time for surveillance, no intelligence as to the building, the grounds, entry points, lights, security…"

"Correct."

Jonas stops, stares at Igneus.

"If we can get the relic, it will change everything," Igneus says. "You can do this."

"No, I can't."

"My father used to say, 'Can't never could'," I say.

Igneus tilts his head, again listening through that invisible earpiece. "Good news. Ishmael's going with you."

Jonas stands. "The hell he is! I don't even want him to know about this."

Igneus frowns. "I'm afraid it's too late, Sebastian already told him."

Jonas collapses into the chair with a sigh and look of hopelessness.

"How did Sebastian know?" I ask.

"We share our thoughts," Igneus says.

"How?"

"God."

I'm flabbergasted. "God? Are you kidding right now?" He nods solemnly. "Well, that's great!" I say. "He can get the relic for us. Or just do us a real solid and destroy the thing, saving us the trouble of trying to get it."

Jonas leans forward. "Now that's a good plan."

"That's not how it works," Igneus says.

"Not how what works?"

"God."

"How does He work then?"

"In mysterious ways."

I collapse on the couch as Jonas collapsed on the recliner. Our faces must mirror each other because his expression reflects my feelings perfectly. Dismay, disillusionment, confusion, even fear.

Jonas rolls his eyes. "How do I get out of this chicken shit outfit?"

CHAPTER 18

WEST VIRGINIA, UNITED STATES

Smoke sears her lungs.

Tears stream down her face.

The old RV blazes.

Her skin tingles, starts to singe.

She grasps the clamp, glances to the shadowed woods. Engines rev in the distance, close fast with a foreboding hum, bounce lighted shafts, long, broad, glaring, through the picket of surrounding forest.

More coming. More attackers.

She does the calculations.

If she's lucky, she has about sixty seconds. If not, less than thirty.

She grabs the rusty clamp that holds the burning camper to the Bronco's hitch, heaves upward. *No time for this, have to go!*

Flames devour the RV as she strains against the hitch the farmer stomped in place when he'd secured it to the Bronco.

Surrounding woods become cackling specters; ghostly orange, dusky yellow. Approaching headlamps bound through shaded foliage. Flames leap high, turning the leaves above black with heat and smoke.

They're close, maybe twenty seconds.

So much for luck.

She ignores the pain, heaves with all her will, rusted iron gouging her fingers.

A gunshot ricochets next to her.

She cringes, drops to a knee, adjusts her grip and pries with both hands. She can't afford another fire fight, too much exposure, too much risk. Who knows how many more?

She pours her strength into the iron, rages through intense heat, ignores the pain. Then standing, placing a foot on the rusted hinge, she turns her back to the raging inferno and pulls with as much strength as she can muster.

Bullets sizzle past, send dirt and gravel over her arms and face.

They're shooting blind.

But not for long.

When they burst through the poplars, she'll be an obvious target, alit by the camper's flickering flames.

She glances at the bouncing shafts, heaves again.

The clamp pops with a grating squeal, then flips open and smashes her finger.

Gunshots explode around her, shrieking as they bounce from the hitch.

She dives left, sprints for the driver's seat. Her right hand aches, her middle finger feels fractured.

Two SUVs roar into the campsite, glossy black reflects fire and shadow. They skid to a stop as agents exit and race toward her.

Her hand throbs, aches, howls as she turns the ignition. The finger isn't working right. She glances, sees it bent askew and out of place.

She hunkers down, stays low, hammers the key again, swallows the cry in her throat, stomps the gas.

The Bronco hesitates, then bursts to life as the driver's window shatters; as more rounds impact its body work.

She hunches low, glances for the Doberman, leans on the accelerator.

Shots pepper the Bronco with metallic pops.

Keeping low, peeping over the dash, she takes in a menagerie of headlight, fire, and whistling rounds.

How'd they find her? How'd they know?

Tires spin. The truck jolts forward, circles the burning camper as she aims for a narrow path at the campsite's rear. Leaving the front way isn't an option. Have to move, to disappear, become a ghost.

Are these Feds? How many? Where's the dog?

A ball of flame washes the windshield as the RV explodes. She squints against sudden blindness, night vision toasted, flames leaping in to singe her hair.

She smells smoke, slaps auburn locks as the odor of gunpowder mixes with the cool woodland.

This *isn't* going to happen. I *won't* be taken. Still too much to know, too much still to do.

The V8 roars like a pouncing tiger, narrowly slides between two thick trees.

The side mirror shatters as thick limbs pummel.

The rear window explodes. A round zips past, pops a hole in the truck's ancient radio. Agents fire with abandon, seem to enjoy the freedom to shoot without care for collateral damage.

She twists the wheel left, glances at her middle finger, cockeyed and twisted, dislocated. The Bronco shimmies, lurches sideways, bounces over a ditch to fly four feet before landing on a dirt road a bit wider than the trail she just abandoned. Tires spin gravel in a rocky rooster tail as she wrenches the wheel right and stomps the accelerator to speed down this new trail.

Behind, a black SUV fishtails, straightens, gives chase, guns chattering.

Sig appears in her hand. She suppresses a shriek, forces her mangled finger to grip the pistol.

Teeth clenched, skin burnt, night vision barely returning, she yanks the wheel to its full extent, feels the Bronco skid, tip up on two wheels, before crashing back to all four with a thud and harsh grating sound.

Slamming the brakes, she leaps from the driver's seat, sprints toward the oncoming SUV. Agents fire with wanton lust, hungry for the kill.

Sig feels natural in her hand, a part of her, a deadly appendage, part of her flesh, her DNA. She fires twice, then dives from the path of the speeding SUV, barely clearing the bumper, tumbling through a summersault, then standing in twinkling starlight.

The SUV flows past, angles into the brush on the trail's edge.

Rhyme speeds forward, squints through the darkness, vision obscured by blazing crimson brake lights.

Then, the bright flame of a pistol shot. A bullet howls past, close enough to hear, too close by far.

Sig belches its steely payload, once, twice, three times.

The SUV bumps to a stop against a broad oak.

Sig ejects his clip, snaps another in place. The other Sig appears, matches its mate, steady, ready.

At the SUV, the driver slumps sideways over the center console. The passenger stares at the forest with empty eyes.

Then, a cacophony of steel and tree and brush as a second SUV ruptures the forest behind her. Must've been another trail close. An attempt to flank, to hem her in.

Blindly, instinctively, she fires, then falls and low crawls under the first vehicle.

The second SUV streaks past, bathes the forest with the blood of brake lights.

Two agents jump out, use the truck as cover, guns leveled, searching, sweeping.

They don't know where I am.

Advantages: surprise, confusion, darkness, twin Sigs.

Disadvantages: Outnumbered. Trained enemy. Dislocated finger, obscured night vision, more agents coming.

She rolls left.

Twig and gravel abrade her arms.

Sig pops.

An agent yelps, drops, lies still.

She rolls again, back the way she came.

Millimeters from her head, the ground erupts, sends rock and earth over her face, into the vehicle's undercarriage.

The remaining agent takes no chances. Fires two pistols, moves constantly, keeps her pinned in place.

Rhyme squints through spinning vision and blinding taillight, through dusky gun smoke and choking dust.

Metal sparks, then tufts of gravel, bite her face.

She stops, rolls the other way, a duck in a shooting gallery, seeking advantage, a single opening.

Then the crackle of leaves, the harsh snap of branches.

She spins, levels both Sigs. Needs only one good shot.

A shadow, slick, dark, blazing black, soars through the air.

The agent screams as razor teeth clamp his arm.

Houdini leaps away.

Rhyme fires twice.

CHAPTER 19

MOUNT TABOR, ISRAEL

"Did you speak with Igneus?"

I look down. "He wasn't interested."

Cain stares with icy eyes. Then, turns his attention elsewhere.

I wonder if he knows I'm lying, knows that I never asked Igneus about rejoining our sordid group of madmen.

We buffet and I test my seatbelt, pull it a bit tighter. I've always liked helicopters but never rode in one.

Can't say it's my favorite.

I glance out the window, at the brown and black squares of scalded Earth, some of it still smoking. The chopper bounces and a wave of nausea grips me.

As helicopters go, this isn't bad for one's first ride. The presidential helicopter, well-appointed with soft, airplane-style seats and a large interior. Laslo Slabav sits next to me and, despite my efforts at conversation, has been pretty quiet, casting occasional glances at Cain, then quickly lowering his head. He looks as if he's aged in the last week. A square jaw hangs like a weathered rock. I can only imagine what he thinks of recent events and how Cain's taken charge.

Across the aisle sits Cain, nodding his head. I glance to Longinus, who also nods from time to time. They're somehow conversing, a level of telepathy of which I'm unfamiliar.

I wonder at the power they wield. Wonder at the changes to both. Cain's hair is subdued, an off-white, looks somewhat normal even for a super model. I remember the tunnel that ran through his head when we'd retrieved him from the morgue. Then, my stomach seizes even as the helicopter descends and pushes it to the back of my throat. My ears throb with the sensation.

Longinus and Sima have their hands clasped like teenagers at a movie. She wears a black jumpsuit that looks tactical and hugs her form, leaving very little to the imagination. With Longinus's current form, they seem perfectly suited, and I wonder if she's seen him as the hulking Roman. I also wonder if she knows the psychopath he is, and, if she does, what she thinks about it.

I pull my notebook, jot a few questions to ask her when I have a chance.

For some reason I can't take my eyes off their hands, specifically can't stop myself from examining her delicate fingers and remembering the music she'd played in her father's mansion on the day Longinus came to call. I can't figure out how she survived and, although I'd asked Longinus, he'd only replied with a lovelorn, "'Twas meant to be." Not much by way of explanation, but the way he said it caused me to drop the subject, or at least try and pick it up when I get the woman alone.

She leans back, rests her head on his shoulder. He smiles and drops his head on hers, gives her a smooch on the forehead. They have all the trappings of love, all the outward signs of genuine affection.

And this makes no sense to me, none of it. This is a centurion of the Roman Legion. A legend for exploits both real and imagined. I wonder at Cain's tapestry, at the billions of tiny details he's strung together in his quest to get here.

I tap the Percs in my suit pocket and congratulate myself for having the insight to load a syringe prior to leaving Jerusalem. As soon as we land, I'll find a place to hide and plunge the needle so I can be as numb as possible for whatever the day might bring.

I glance at Longinus's arms, his eyes. There are no needle marks, no glaze darkens his orbs. Just, and this sounds dumb if you know Longinus, love, as he looks on Sima and appears awash in her presence.

His spear sits beside him, appears as a simple stage prop designed by some celebrity prop master. Gleaming gold, etched lines subdued and dark. I think to cross the aisle and examine it more closely. Perhaps if I'm bold enough, Longinus will let me. I'll tell him I need a detailed description for Cain's biography. With Cain present, I might have a shot. Rhyme thinks the relic's of the utmost importance, as do Pappy and Igneus, and I'm sure any details I collect can help join some of these jagged puzzle pieces.

I glance out the window to see the ground come closer. We hover, then slowly descend over a parking lot. The helicopter rotates in such a way that as we land, the Church of the Transfiguration comes in view.

I remember the adventure we had just a few days ago. Longinus and I, standing on the roof, wrestling the spear's enormous power, besieged by helicopters and fighter jets, whipped by wind, beaten by rain, seared by the relic's energy, surrounded by an army so vast, that even now it seems like a bad dream.

Cain exits first, followed by Longinus and Sima, Slabav, then me. I immediately look for a place to go and fix up. That's a junkie term for injecting drugs. I absently tap my Perc-pocket.

The day is cloudy, cooler than what it's been the last few days. Pappy appears and waves us toward the walkway as a harsh wind rushes over. I hear thunder, realize more choppers are circling, even more approaching from a distance.

"Mr. Cain, a pleasure as always," Pappy says.

Cain smiles his hypnotic smile, shakes the friar's hand. "The pleasure is mine, dear Brother Papadopoulos. I trust the funds I sent helped get things on track."

Pappy looks abashed. "I'm afraid I've given most of it away. It seems my parishioners were in dire straits after recent events."

Cain affects a look of concern. "Of course, of course, people come first, as always. I'll send more, and you can use it as you see fit."

They walk up the broad path toward the church, Slabav and I in tow. I glance around, notice Longinus and Sima have got off to somewhere.

"I think it's gonna rain," I venture to the PM.

"Uh huh," he replies.

I get the impression I can say anything, and he'll just say, *Uh huh.* He looks a bit shellshocked, as if the weight of all that's transpired slowly crushes him.

I shut my mouth, follow Cain and Pappy through the church to Pappy's office as Laslo shuffles behind.

"I'm sorry I don't have more chairs," Pappy says. "I rarely get visitors and never those so highly regarded."

Cain takes the chair at Pappy's desk as Slabav and I face him. Pappy stands under the window, hands clasped before him. The ever-present sticky notes have been removed, leaving only ancient stone walls of gray. It seems Pappy's cleaned things up, and I wonder how he came to know of Cain's visit. I only learned of this trip a few hours ago.

"Everything's set for your meeting," Pappy says.

I butt in. "What's the meeting for?" Aside from the location, I'd been told nothing. I did, however, have the presence of mind to send a note to Igneus.

Cain turns his head and smiles in silhouette. "My kings, dear Emery, leaders of the Middle East. I've invited them here so that we can all gain the same understanding."

I know what Cain means by *understanding*. It's his way of getting them all together and letting them know who runs things.

I glance at Pappy, remember his theories: Cain as Antichrist, the fulfillment of prophecy, the crown prophecy and things yet to come.

The friar avoids my stare and smiles pleasantly.

"Why here?" I ask.

Cain gives me the stupid-question look, and I feel my face heat. "You've seen the rest of Israel," he says, "hardly suitable to host such important men. Thanks to the efforts of our dear Longinus and, of course, you, there remains one place unmolested and intact. A place of historical significance and legend. What better place for these things to transpire?"

I feel a familiar tingle as I tap my syringe. I can easily duck out and fix up but to do so would mean I'd have to do it in the church, which for some reason fills me with dread and fear. As if the sacrilege wouldn't go unnoticed by God and would be swiftly punished. If you're reading this, you're probably thinking how stupid that sounds, fearing punishment from an apparition for which we have no evidence. But I have to admit, and I think you'll agree, after all I've seen, the one thing I can take for flat, undisputable fact is that God deals His wrath in ways best avoided. So, why take stupid chances?

I inhale, swallow, squeeze my fists. The monkey cackles, my sweet tooth aches for nectar, panic starts to squeeze as sweat beads on my forehead. I feel cold, clammy, hollow. Perhaps I can sneak a Perc and down it dry. Perhaps I can say I have to pee, and down a few in the bathroom, if this place has one.

Then, another friar pokes his head in. "Everyone's ready."

Cain rises. "This shouldn't take too long," he says, then turns to Laslo. "Are you ready?"

Laslo returns a nervous grin. "I am."

Chapter 20

Mount Tabor, Israel

In the church, the benches are crowded. Cleaned up since I'd seen it last, it lacks signs of dust or rubble from the attack. Overhead, long rafters add shadow to the darkness of the day and the church's interior.

I move to the back of the room and find a seat on the outer aisle. Kings, I think; I'm rubbing shoulders with kings. I glance around, notice the leaders of all Mid-east countries are present. Around them, security men look me over as they hover near their respective charges. I smile, try to appear non-threatening. They remain expressionless. It seems an olive branch has been extended from these nations in support of Israel and I'm certain Cain's gifts have brought this meeting about.

Cain takes a seat in the front row. As he surveys the room, I tap two Percs into my hand and slide them to my mouth. I swallow hard, feel them stick for a second before continuing down. I sigh, close my eyes, count the seconds until they work their magic. My mouth fills with saliva as I finger the syringe in my suit. I can go outside and fix up, I think, but then I'll miss the meeting and won't have information to share with Igneus.

I inhale deep, distract myself by checking off the countries and leaders represented.

Seventeen are in attendance today, and of that number, seven are kings. I'm suddenly star struck at the realization and wonder what being a king is like. Do they have limits to their authority? Do they have peons and serfs like days of old? Harems? Knights? Ladies-in-waiting? I'm too ignorant of the region and the customs of all these countries but have no delusion about Cain's knowledge of the same.

I wonder if he controls them, then suppress a chuckle. How else are Muslim nations going to throw support behind Israel? It's unwise to think Cain's hand isn't at work. All serve at the gloved man's pleasure despite the fact the gloves are gone.

Upper and lower altars serve as backdrop as Laslo moves to the front and faces those gathered. The lower altar gleams but isn't half as impressive as the upper one. A dome of gold shines over him, a fresco of Jesus rising from the Earth surrounded by prophets. Below the fresco, the words ET TRANSFIGURATUS EST ANTE EOS. Latin I think, and try to translate its meaning.

"And he was transfigured before them." Brother Pappy wears a smile cut from a magazine, taped-together in the way of a TV ransom note.

"How'd you know?" I ask.

He slides next to me, flutters his robes a bit, crosses one leg over the other. "Through the years I've seen many people stare at those words with the same expression. It's become habit to translate it for them."

"I appreciate it," I say, retrieving my notepad and jotting the words.

A noise behind us demands our attention and we turn to see a security detail of ten enter. Two reporters follow behind, and after them, two cameramen with large cameras propped on their shoulders.

"This is to be broadcast?"

"Cain's idea, to enlist worldwide support," the friar says. "Remember the prophecy. This should get interesting."

In front, Laslo waits for the newcomers to settle.

The detail moves forward, then splits, half moving to one side of the church's broad, arched columns, and half to the other. The reporters hold their place in the rear, as the camera guys get in position.

When all is quiet, Laslo speaks.

"My friends," he says. "My brothers." He nods solemnly, looks overwhelmed with gratitude. "Let me start by extending my thanks. I'm sure you all know the devastation of recent events, and I can't say how much it means to me, my government, and my people that you aid us in our time of need."

Kings and leaders sit in stone-faced silence. I glance around and see nothing out of the ordinary, but have a feeling something isn't right.

Then, another man enters and moves boldly up the main aisle as security nears the stage from both sides. I know the man but can't remember his name. His image spawns a memory, though. I search my opiate fog and struggle to recall.

Pappy whispers. "Israeli Defense Minister Bernard Rugari. Shouldn't be here, but is."

Laslo smiles nervously, looks confused. "Bernie?"

Bernie steps forward, hands in his pockets. I'm impressed at his nonchalance. "Laslo Slabav, you're under arrest."

Slabav's mouth drops, his hands fall to his sides. "Surely you're joking," he chuckles. "I've done nothing, and you haven't the authority."

"I'm afraid I do," Bernie says. "Times have changed."

The defense minister motions, and security roughly twists Laslo's arms behind his back. The unmistakable sound of handcuffs rolls over ancient stone and rises into the rafters.

Slabav's face goes magenta. "On what grounds?"

Bernie doesn't look like he's enjoying this.

I look around the room. Those gathered nod and smile, as if we're at some stage production of *A Comedy of Errors*.

It's a set up, that's pretty obvious, and I look at Pappy, whose smile has turned to consternation.

"You're under arrest for the murder of Otho Usmani and Pavel Sundamir," Bernie says. "Also, for the murders of Mr. Sundamir's family and associates. Add to that treason against the State of Israel and conspiring mass genocide with Oshi Khalifa, who remains at large and is presumably in hiding."

Slabav stammers, struggles a bit. "That's preposterous!" Spittle flies in tiny splotches. "You need to look at Drake, or, um, Cain. He's the mastermind, he's the one you want. Unhand me this instant!"

Bernie shakes his head, places a hand on Slabav's shoulder. "We have, Laslo. Cain and his associates have been cleared of any wrongdoing. He's been completely cooperative with our investigation. The intelligence he provided led us to you." Bernie pauses here. "How could you, Laslo?"

Slabav sputters something unintelligible.

Cain stands, shows that movie-star smile, then steps forward as Slabav is dragged off. His protests echo through the darkened church.

"Laslo," Cain says, "do take care."

Slabav struggles in security's grasp, digs in his heels, gets dragged out the door. Those assembled watch like it's a new reality show. Openly smiling, they shake their heads as if the whole thing's a surprising shame.

"Help!" Slabav screams, voice fading as he disappears from view. "It's a set up! I'm being framed!"

Cain smiles, clasps his hands as if praying. "Peace be with you," he says with a curt bow and to murmured responses from those gathered. He gives the reporters a nod, and they quickly pack up and leave. Then, he nods to the gathered security, who exit the church.

"Alone at last," Cain says to scattered chuckles. Only heads of state, the friar, and I remain.

The men in the room seem energized by the spectacle, relishing the sight of Slabav humiliated. I wonder what they're thinking even as I try to find a reason Cain would arrest him.

Cain's hair glows now, flows opalescent as crystal eyes dazzle. "I must apologize for that unpleasantness. If I'm to get this house in order, I'm afraid some unpleasantness is necessary. It seems our Laslo's been a naughty boy."

Everyone laughs.

"Shall we get to business?" he says. "We have much to do, and I have only *an hour*." He chuckles here for some reason. I lean forward, and Cain winks at me. I look to Pappy, whose face tells me he understands the reference.

"Nations shall come to your light, and kings to the brightness of your dawn," Cain says. "I stand humbled today in your presence but find myself equally embarrassed as I gaze on leaders muted and paralyzed by sleeping giants.

"Where once men of vision roamed these lands and bade their will to eternal supplicants, now fat oafs lie bleating like lazy camels, bawling their needs to a host of servants."

I glance around, see grins disappear, replaced by open mouths at Cain's sudden audacity.

"Where once wise men ruled with leadership and foresight, they now find contentment with only what they're *given* by those with the biggest weapons.

"Here and now, I see gathered before me, leaders who lack the will to take what's theirs and restore true greatness to the terms king, minister, and leader."

He pauses, looks at the floor. "The greatest leaders of an age, stymied by somnolent juggernauts and meaningless postures. Leaders who lack the will to rise, to vanquish and conquer, to restore their birthright, their heritage and their future."

Gleaming teeth flash as he looks around the sanctuary. "Surprise shadows your faces. Oh, how your cheeks glow as my words ravage your wretched hearts.

"Have you forgotten?

"Have you been so surrounded by those who nod and agree, that you cannot bear the truth?

"Has vision abandoned you?

"Have the voices of your line grown silent?

"Or just been ignored?"

Murmurs rise, but none speak openly.

Cain strolls up the aisle, crystal gaze resting on each man. I marvel at his boldness, then think, if one can't die, boldness comes easy.

Footsteps click like a metronome. His voice lowers. "I *did not* come here to preach hope or stroke egos.

"I was sent to inflame bloated hearts and loose silenced tongues.

"I came to fan the faltering embers that smolder in your breasts.

"Those embers have meaning." He traces his gaze over them. "They are cinders of destiny. They are fractions of greatness. They are kernels of will, long dormant. Perhaps even forgotten.

"Today, I came to remind you exactly who you are—who *we* are—and to discuss that which is truly important.

"Where once roamed men of vision, now tread the hollow hearts of those to whom sacrifice is foreign.

"Where truly great kings once ruled from golden thrones and bade their will without explanation or second thought, now sit bloated beasts who want for nothing but still bawl displeasure.

"Vision has fled. Will is forsaken. Sands of complacency have strangled your breath and obscured your vision even as this desert becomes a tomb.

"But I've come to see this greatness restored. Yea, I have come to remake this nation.

"I've been reborn to guide your steps, to raise you to the lofty heights where kings stroll in majesty without care for inanity, avarice, or invader.

"I hold the power to destroy any force under the sun and will defeat all who come against me.

"All who come against us." He pauses here, looks them over.

"Together we'll no longer suffer discord from our countrymen or inferiors. Neither shall we suffer interference or threats.

"No more shall we hide!

"*We* keep our own counsel!

"And loose our wrath on those who speak with twisted tongues!"

Heads start to nod as others lean forward, mesmerized by Cain's eloquence.

"All will join us or perish.

"And I will smite, with terrible vengeance, any who oppose me!

"I will lay low, with horrible savagery, any who come against me!

"I *will* reforge this land and restore its place upon this Earth!

"The world has changed, my friends, and I've come to remake it in ways of goodness and peace. No longer shall we repel invaders. No longer shall we be split by faction or religion or skin. No longer shall we suffer lies meant to deceive and separate. No longer shall we yield as larger forces make of us a mockery.

"I stand before you and say, these forces will be thrown down! Decimated so entirely their memory shall never again stain our lands or our tongues.

"Hear me! I am merciful and will grant all a chance to join a bounty of peace and brotherhood.

"As ordained from the first! As true from the day of my birth long ago! I've taken my rightful place and shall rule in mercy and fairness! From this day to the last, I shall rule!"

He stops, turns toward them, smooths his suit and offers that smile.

"You are *my* blessed kings, and I, your beloved emperor.

"My rule requires no changes to currency or religion, no treatise on government or politics, no oath of money or blood.

"It requires only supplication. Only loyalty. And my justice will swarm upon any who seek to undermine or lay low.

"You saw what happened in Jerusalem. The overwhelming force, invaders intent on plunder and destruction." Eyes blaze, his words quicken. "You witnessed the power I set loose and the carnage that followed. You witnessed the might I command and bestowed on those I chose to wield it.

"Be it known, even the strongest force on the Earth is paltry compared to the power of *our* kingdom.

"I've no wish for war. No wish for battle, or famine, or disease. Even now, as has always been, I desire only peace. For our lands and our people.

"Long ago we had a saying, as true today as it was then. *Si vis pacem para bellum. If you want peace, prepare for war.*

"Today, I say, *si vis pacem fac bellum. If you want peace, make war!* Hear me, my kings, and know that those who fail to heed my words will not see the sun set on another day.

"Hear me, my kings! For even now they eye our country like stock masters at auction.

"Hear me, my kings! For even now plans are being laid for our destruction.

"They come as false friends, then abduct our wives, steal our fortunes and ply us with poison fruit."

He smiles, adjusts his tie. His hair blazes, writhes above bright, steely eyes. "But we are not fooled.

"As they lay their plans and shine their weapons.

"As they aim their missiles and prepare their armies.

"The choice is yours, my kings, bow to me and live your lives. Rule as you see fit. Raise your families. Extend the lineage of courage and kinship, of bounty and joy.

"For today is a day of great joy. A day that will shake the very foundations of the Earth."

His eyes dart among us, gleaming in aqua, hair bristling, excited, full of energy and power.

"Today we create the nation of *Imperium!* A nation that will eclipse any before it and prosper until the end of time itself."

More nod, more lean forward, grand smiles appear. "Together we *will* subdue this Earth and unite all nations under one authority.

"My authority." He pauses, waits, I guess, to see if any listening will speak against him.

I watch their faces, their glazed eyes, their grand smiles as thoughts for wealth, for absolute power, flow from their hearts to display on their countenance.

Cain's gifts have ensnared them, and they know not what they do.

I swallow with a dry mouth, tap my syringe absently, think how I can down more Percs.

Next to me, Pappy looks pale as a bleached sheet. His ability to divine the future from Revelation's prose has failed to steel him against this reality.

"Times ahead will try us," Cain says. "Will test our metal *and* our loyalty to our new kingdom. But I say to you, stand fiercely in adversity's face. Fill your hearts with courage. Trust in the wisdom of Imperium's Emperor and, for your efforts, gain peace among your countries and harmony among your houses.

"All will want for nothing. All will have plenty."

He pauses, hands clasped before him.

None speak.

"My first decree is that all countries within Imperium become kingdoms.

"You, gathered here, do you not know? Bow to me and inherit your kingdom. Supplicate, and together we will destroy any who lay word or sword against us.

"Rejoice with those who join us, decimate those who resist.

"The time has come for this land to rise, and even as the Temple and the Mosque share common ground, so shalt we share history."

The church echoes with his voice. Those gathered seem hypnotized.

My mind runs with questions.

"Come," he says, "approach your emperor. Offer fealty in open view of the world. Then, together, we'll announce Imperium has come."

Those gathered look as if they've snuck a hit from my syringe. A cameraman quietly enters, kneels, and starts to film.

One by one, they move forward and kneel before him, grasping his hand, offering oaths.

By the time the hour ends, all have sworn their allegiance to Cain.

Thus, the Kingdom of Imperium is born.

CHAPTER 21

WEST VIRGINIA, UNITED STATES

Houdini's kiss is cold in the night air. Rhyme stares at her crooked finger like a broken antenna. She inhales deep, glances at the backtrail, holds her breath.

With a crunch it snaps in place.

Dizziness rises, nausea ratchets. She exhales, stares at spinning stars, collects herself.

Lucky, lucky.

Houdini nudges, gives her injured finger a quick smooch.

"Who's a good boy?" She kneels, grasps the dog's enormous head and floppy ears. "Who's the best boy?"

The dog pants, lifts his head, nuzzles her face, eyes closed. Bristled fur relaxes at her touch. She examines him head to paw but sees no injuries. "Such a brave boy!"

The animal's saved her twice in as many days. "I'm keeping you." She nuzzles a wet nose. "No doubt about it. Who's the best boy?"

Houdini responds with a lick and another nudge at her hand.

"No fella, we have to go."

Crickets serenade the night. Bullfrogs preach a chorus to the darkness. Must be a pond or lake close. Glancing back, she hears no engines, sees no signs of other threats.

A search of the dead yields little by way of identification, but she finds a map labeled: GEORGE WASHINGTON NATIONAL FOREST.

Is this Octavio? X'chasei? Maybe Mossad, or the FBI?

So many, so suddenly. Too many. Hiding is complete folly, absolute futility. They're tracking her, will never stop coming.

Not until she's dead.

Voices echo from down the trail, bound through tree and leaf and darkness from the direction of the burning camper, maybe a mile.

Then, the sound of engines.

At the Bronco, she grabs a four-foot length of 550 cord, then moves to the agent's SUV.

She pries the gas cover with her knife, unscrews the gas cap, glances back at the approaching sounds.

The cord all but disappears into the gas nozzle. She fishes it out, reverses it, then feeds the dry end back in.

It reeks of gasoline. She'll have to be fast.

She coils the cord around the gray gas nozzle, leaves two inches protruding.

The dog's muscles ripple in shimmering black, making him all but invisible as he focuses down the trail, hackles raised.

"Mount up!"

Houdini takes two long strides and leaps through the shattered driver's window. Whoever trained him knew what they were doing.

The engine turns, sluggish, then starts. Seems crashing through the forest isn't the best thing you can do for a vehicle.

She drives as close as possible to the agent's SUV, then leans out the Bronco's window. The flare sizzles to life, a bright flame on its tip. She shoves its base into the nozzle, assures it's set and sturdy even as sparks fall and pinch her skin.

Dangerous. So dangerous. But should buy a few minutes.

She starts forward, glances at the smoldering flare.

Then another thought.

Ambush.

This is a perfect place to lie in wait. When they arrive, she'll deal with them, then finish her business without further harassment. The surrounding forest provides great cover, especially at night, and reminds her of a forest in Carter's Glen, New York, of the Giggleshmertz Institute, of lessons in fighting, and cover, and survival.

The flare casts sparks above a dripping wick as she considers advantage and disadvantage. They've appeared so rapidly; have to assume more are on the way.

Crispy'd say: "Ambushes are risky. Everything has to be perfect or it all goes to shit. Only do it as a last stand."

Houdini curls in the passenger's seat, then props his thick snout on the center console. His look says: "Are we gonna sit here all night?"

Headlights pierce the darkness. More vehicles approach.

Flipping the Bronco's lights off, she moves further into the wilderness, caresses the dog's nose. "Such a smart boy."

Houdini's chest rises and falls with a contented groan. He closes his eyes.

The night fills with flame as the SUV explodes, squelching the song of cricket and bullfrog.

She doesn't waste a second, hammers the accelerator, flips on the headlights.

This moment is critical. They'll never see her due to the explosion, the flaming blaze. Gives her precious seconds to get far away.

A million trails in the Washington Forest. May take them a century to find me. Need to hole up, need to think.

She presses the accelerator, moves as fast as she dares down the dark trail, turning every second trail, alternating left and right. Random actions, impossible to reason or plan, impossible to follow. By the looks of it, they've sent everyone, and when they find four of their own dead, it'll quickly become personal.

How'd they find me?

The nape of her neck tingles, says she controls none of this, that she's become prey.

The only option left: go to ground; survive; travel by night; conceal everything.

Five bumpy miles later, she turns down a fire road. Three miles after that, a right onto a wide rocky trail. The view blooms here; rising verdant hills, a blanket of treetops like bunched broccoli, small rivulets dribbling down the mountain toward the distant valley, toward the river.

A thought seizes. *Might be perfect.*

Lightning splits the sky. Houdini startles as rain pounds the Bronco's roof. Thunder peels, rolling through darkness, rumbling toward a silent horizon.

When the sun rises, they'll be all over the place.

Have to get far. Have to get clear.

Lightning sizzles in ragged lines, leaps across the sky and into the valley.

A river. Perfect.

With a snap of her hand, the map opens. Flashlight in her mouth, she traces squiggled lines, looks for the fastest route to the river, to escape.

A logging road in another mile, perhaps a little farther.

She checks the rearview, angles the Bronco down the treacherous trail.

Get to the river before daylight. With luck, the rain will continue, perhaps fall even harder. Even better. This might actually work.

She caresses Houdini's snout, squints through jagged streams flowing down the windshield. The rain will slow the agents as much as her and she's probably far enough away, can rely on some small measure of safety based on distance.

Nevertheless, she presses the Bronco as fast as she dares, keeps a sharp eye out for the trail to the river.

Once she gets there, no one will find her.

CHAPTER 22

MOUNT TABOR, ISRAEL

Christ ascends on rays of glory as Cain stands before us beaming. His eyes shine like a Caribbean pool. I turn away, afraid of falling under the spell like those around me.

It seems only Pappy and I have been spared, and for Pappy's part, I can't say that for certain. He looks gaunt, worse by the second. A bead of sweat trickles down his forehead and into his eye. He swats at it, as if the intrusion has blinded him for too long.

I'm afraid if he stands, he'll collapse from anger or, perhaps, the sheer weight of this verification of his read on prophecy. Fists are clenched on his knees, knuckles blanched from the strain. If my thoughts on the man are correct, it's all he can do to endure Cain's proclamation and say nothing. If my read on the man's correct, intelligence alone keeps his bottom pressed to the hard bench, his lips squeezed tight beneath his nose.

I lean over and whisper. "You alright?" He looks at me like I'm an apparition, not seeing me but looking through me.

My head throbs. The Percs sing a siren song. The syringe nestles in my pocket, waits to push demons in my veins. I welcome the thought, glance around to see if I have a chance to duck outside. I consider this an option. Outside the day is dark and cloudy as rain continues sporadically as it's done for the past few weeks. Behind me, the church is bathed in shadow as if someone's pulled a shroud over the entire structure. Up front, Cain's hair is the brightest thing in the room, gleaming, shimmering, silver snakes in a tidal pool.

I lick my lips, glance to the exit. The demons will bring peace. I might get soaked, but at least I'll get fixed up.

I hate to admit it, but my mind can't comprehend the depth of Cain's plan. Perhaps the demon's call clouds my thoughts. Perhaps I've come to the limits of my intelligence, attained my maximum level of competence on a ladder I can climb no further, a steep and treacherous path to which I can no longer hold.

I sense movement next to me and find Sima. Her black bodysuit reflects the beams from Cain's coif. She slides next to me, grasps my hand, whispers, "What did I miss?"

I stare like a dumb ass, ill prepared to recount all that's happened in her absence. She gives my hand a squeeze even as a delicate mouth forms a smile. She's kind, I think, and wonder how being Longinus's main squeeze will destroy that quality.

She leans close and her scent strikes me: burnt oak with a hint of something sweet and smooth, like a flower's nectar. "Watch this," she says.

Longinus sweeps by, gliding down the aisle like it's a catwalk, lithe form cutting a silhouette more suited to boardroom than church. Beside him, the spear gleams, seems to writhe as I watch, to struggle as it did on the church's roof.

He strides forward, confidence oozing.

Cain nods and steps aside as Longinus lifts the spear, then pops the floor a single time.

Golden beams splay broad rays that assault my eyes and demand careful observation.

The relic rises, floats. Red and blue lasers sizzle along its length.

Longinus releases and it moves higher, about fifteen feet, then begins a light show both wondrous and magnificent. Deep, pulsing maroon and crisp, icy blue mix with shimmering gold to fill the space with vibrant light that climbs to the rafters in a kaleidoscope of color and tumbling triangles. The spear hovers, tip pointed at the ceiling, spinning on its axis like a top, showering all in neon lines and radiant glory.

Longinus raises his arms. "Behold the standard of Imperium," he says with a distinctly non-Longinus eloquence.

He closes his eyes, raises his chin toward the relic as the tenor of his voice echoes.

> *Blessed beacon.*
> *Holy lance.*
> *Let all who see, find solace in your shelter.*
> *Let no man with goodness fear and no man with*
>   *evil endure.*
> *In aqua, show us the vastness of Heaven and the*
>   *speed of our lives.*
> *In flame, show us the embers from which we're*
>   *spawned and to where we shall yet return.*
> *Let golden rays give succor, and ever-reflect our*
>   *kingdom's glory.*
> *Fly, great staff, from the banners of the faithful,*
>   *so that the world may know,*
> *Imperium.*
> *From this, to the end of days, and always, and*
>   *forever.*

Silence fills the room as the spear spins above us.

I'm reminded of the X'chasei meeting held in the catacombs before Cain entered the Temple. Of his mark coming alive, filling with such despair and misery I barely withstood the assault.

But this is different.

No visions flood my core. No feeling of evil or hopelessness or despair.

If anything, joy fills me. A flame ignites my soul, gives me a reason to live, to sacrifice, to trust in Cain's will. Has he compressed his gifts in the relic? I glance at the others, who look stymied and mystified. Grins lie on their faces as eyes gaze at the spinning lance.

"Told you," Sima whispers. Blue and red trace her face and embolden her features. She's beautiful, exotic, and with something else that tells me to keep my distance. Like seeing a lion up close, certainly gorgeous, but instinct warns of grave danger.

Around us, all focus on the relic. I glance at Pappy, who seems as mesmerized as everyone else. Then, Cain steps forward and gives the Roman a hearty handshake. Longinus beams, and I'm struck by how the two appear as twins just now.

Cain's hair absorbs the dancing blues and reds, the flickering gold, then makes them disappear such that no lines or pattern can be seen. His eyes gleam a darker shade of crystal as portions of malice glisten.

"Bear witness, my kings," he says, "to the wielder of the spear and the power I've imbued. This is Longinus, my general, my *legatus legionis,* who takes direction from me alone. It will be wise to heed his words, as you heed mine. To do otherwise will invite death upon your house and lineage."

He looks at them with an air of complete authority.

They nod in unison; some even slide from their bench and drop to their knees.

"Longinus has instructions for you all and will outline the boons I've decided to gift. Rejoice in what we've done today, and what we shall do tomorrow." Longinus steps forward, hands raised, as Cain steps from the altar and exits the ancient church.

Chapter 23

Mount Tabor, Israel

G ET TO TABOR. SPEAR IS THERE.

A note delivered by a weathered old man in a rusty blue truck. Written by Emery.

They'd left immediately after receiving it, hurried to the mountain for no other reason than to wait.

The underbrush is thick and wet as Jonas surveys the parking lot. He shivers, pulls his jacket close, glances at Ishmael, who lies dozing within a small copse of scraggly trees.

Interesting things are happening, and Jonas has spent the day trying to figure them out.

First, the closing of the road from the base of the mountain, the only way up to this church except for forgotten foot paths known only to locals. All traffic has been diverted and the area cordoned to allow for the arrival of a constant stream of helicopters which landed one by one in the church's small parking lot.

He'd seen heads of state off-loaded, then security posted, and patrols set in motion that had almost caught them a time or two as the afternoon wore on.

Most amazing was Cain's arrival with his entourage: Emery,

Longinus, some young woman, and Israel's Prime Minister, Laslo Slabav.

For the PM's part, he hadn't stayed long, having been dragged to a waiting chopper while handcuffed and protesting at volume. An hour or so later, all the other visitors had departed as well.

Is this a coup? No more perfect time for a little insurrection, a blatant power grab. With Israel in disarray, it doesn't take a genius to assume other countries will see it as ripe pickings, even despite how Slabav handled the crisis with some aplomb.

It seems Igneus's warnings have been sound. Cain's consolidating his power. What else explains the appearance of the region's leaders? What else explains Slabav being led off in cuffs?

He hunkers down, blows into thin gloves, adjusts the Kalashnikov assault rifle.

Rifles have become easy to come by since the invasion, and Jonas is glad for the weapon. Perhaps the only thing to level the playing field when he goes after the spear.

The day's cool and cloudy, raining off and on, and as night falls, it's going to get cold and more treacherous, stealing body heat and increasing misery by exponents.

He starts the chant, a little mantra he's made up to pass the time.

Get the spear and disappear.

Get the spear and disappear.

Get the spear and disappear.

He creeps to the very edge of the parking area serving as helipad, scans the area for residual security as shadows grow long and better conceal his position. He knows shadows can hide other positions and scours the area now void of traffic from street or sky.

He's close, knows the spear is his if he has the will to get to it.

Earlier, as he sat in the thicket shivering, he watched the man, Longinus, walk toward the church gripping the spear.

But the Roman wasn't as Igneus described: hulking, brimming with muscle, a ruffian from the streets. Here was a man tastefully dressed with a suave demeanor. A man who treated his lady with respect and kindness. Emery said the man could become a giant, but Jonas has trouble imagining that. Longinus looks like a mere businessman, nothing a trained soldier would consider a threat.

Still, one mustn't take unnecessary chances, especially with one's non-military brother in tow. We've got one shot to get the relic; if that gets ruined, the element of surprise will fly away forever. If we're found out, if we fail in this task, the spear will become virtually untouchable, every measure taken to keep it safe.

Their downfall is pride. A certainty: they suffer no natural predators. A belief beyond doubt: they're above attack. Immortal like Igneus, they can't even *entertain* the thought someone could steal from them.

Jonas knows his advantages: darkness, surprise, pride. With Ishmael as spotter, they may just have a chance of getting this thing, of putting a considerable dent in Cain's plans, especially if Igneus or Sebastian are able to wield it. If nothing else, Cain will no longer have it, and that has to be worth something.

He starts to move, then hears the rush of rotors as a broad dark shadow drifts overhead like an inkblot. He reclaims his hiding spot, motions Ishmael to stay put. The chopper shakes the trees around him as it lands.

He tries to control his breathing, to keep it light and measured. The night's cooled to the point where his breath causes foggy plumes. A certain way to surrender stealth if someone happens to be watching.

Six armed agents debark and set up a loose perimeter. Then four more exit, flanking another man, a VIP of some sort. The interplay between shadow and light makes it hard to discern the man's features as he stays low, coat pulled over his face to protect from the rotor blast.

They scurry up the walk toward the church.

Jonas presses against a rough tree trunk, looks at Ishmael, shakes his head. This visitor will delay things.

He slides down the path, using darkness as cover, staying close to the bushes and trees that line it. Ishmael follows and soon they're moving down the mountain to circle east and approach the church by another path.

He glances at Ishmael, dressed in black pants, boots and jacket, dark gloves with matching knit watch cap. He blends well, seems to disappear in the darkness. Precisely the reason Jonas dressed him this way.

"Radio check," Jonas whispers into his earpiece.

Ishmael raises a hand to his ear, presses his own earpiece in place. "Check."

"Take your hand from your ear."

"What?"

"Put your hand down. It's a giveaway you're using a radio."

"Oh," Ishmael says, dropping his hand. Teeth flash through the darkness and Jonas knows he's grinning. That grin, toothy, broad, so like their father's. Jonas thinks of a million times that grin has stopped him in his tracks, baited him to agree with something he normally wouldn't. Ishmael is his weak spot, the grin a hidden joy that always brightens the day.

"Stop grinning," he whispers, then sees the flash of teeth grow broad. "Clown," he says.

"Hooligan," is the response.

Hooligan, a running joke about Irish soccer fans and their passion for beer. There are soccer hooligans, Guinness hooligans, army hooligans. There are hooligans in hats and mittens. Hooligans in cars driving like old ladies. Hooligans who don't do the dishes or take out the garbage. He's been called all of these by his brother at some point, and if he has to guess, he's now a shadow hooligan. Jonas can't help but grin, then hears, "Stop grinning." A few seconds later, "Ya, hooligan."

Jonas almost laughs, has to shake his head and focus. This is no time for messing around, which has always been the brother's strong point. Ishmael is magic, has the ability to make Jonas laugh without trying. The very definition of effortlessness. He can smile a certain way, or look at something with a certain expression, or make an off-hand comment about a stranger, and Jonas is set off in peals of laughter.

Jonas hunkers down, looks to the church, ignores the *hooligan* comment for fear of cracking up then and there.

"Get the spear and disappear," the earpiece crackles.

Jonas glances at his brother. The grin's gone. Ishmael nods, tries to look stern. It still looks comical.

About fifty yards away, the Church of the Transfiguration looms into the black sky to meld with the darkness. Jonas imagines lightning flashing behind it as maniacal screams emanate from within. It looks part haunted castle, part medieval fortress. Dark, solid, ancient, like a bastion from a war movie.

Colors bound from within and ruin the war motif. Like a gothic mansion turned disco club, the church's few windows dance with light, flash red and blue with occasional bursts of yellow. It looks oddly out of place, the colors brighter in contrast to the darkness of the night and their surroundings.

"You got your glasses?" Jonas asks.

"Yep."

"Keep watch, I'm moving up. Stay low and quiet. If you see something, say something. If anyone comes close, click the mic button three times and I'll come back to you. Got it?"

"Yep."

"Remember our mission?"

"Get the spear and disappear."

"Roger that."

CHAPTER 24

MOUNT TABOR, ISRAEL

Pappy moves about, lighting candles. It seems he's not so particular about matching size or shapes and uses the candles only for light. They flicker to a glow, then cast the room in buttery tones.

Cain sits with his feet propped on Pappy's desk. He wears an absent expression as he looks at his mark. "I understand you think I'm the Antichrist?"

Pappy freezes, half bent, lit match in hand.

Then straightens, brow glistening sweat.

Blue eyes focus on Cain, then dart to the floor. He seems to have an inner dialogue because his posture changes, becomes stolid and bold. "I'm afraid I do. Your methods aren't subtle."

Cain chuckles, feet still propped, still staring at his mark which appears wrinkled and engulfed in shadow. "You're very perceptive, friar. Smarter than most, possessed with an intelligence above that of a holy man." Cold eyes regard the friar, hold him for many seconds. "I'd like to offer you a job as my Chief Religious Advisor."

"No."

Cain startles a bit, blinks twice. "Dear Brother—. Is it Pappy they call you?"

Pappy nods, Adam's apple bobbing as he swallows.

"Now, now, dear Pappy, don't be so quick to refuse when you haven't even heard the offer or its details. Perhaps haste isn't your ally just now. I need a high priest, a man of God. Someone to give credibility to my kingdom and supervise all its religions."

"Not a chance," Pappy says. "I'm a follower of the true God and won't see my life's work made a sham by serving Satan's minion."

I press my back against the wall. Cain won't tolerate being called a minion, and his wrath can be swift.

Cain becomes introspective. "Do you know, through my millennia, how many *so-called* men of God I've thrown asunder? How many fell while clinging to the belief that God will save them? It's been wondrous really, men with such deep convictions that even torture and death can't dissuade them from their service." He sighs here, removes his feet from the desk. "In the end I wonder if they received their just rewards or merely discovered they were playthings for a childish and testy Savior. I often wondered, when I dispatched them, when they lifted their eyes to Heaven, searched for godly assistance, when I watched the light fade, watched them realize that God deserted them, I often wondered, if in that final second, they realized His true nature. The full truth of His preference for blood. A life wasted serving a cretin."

His eyes illuminate, swirl in a mix of flickering candlelight and steely blue. "Sometimes I'd see the realization in those last seconds. Read their final thought as an understanding they'd been wrong and sacrificed their lives for nothing at all."

He stands, steps close to the friar, focuses on his eyes. "It all comes due in the final sum, dear Pappy, and I do applaud you for seeing through it with such vision. Very astute, very perceptive, a combination of gathered knowledge, endless study, and an intellect to connect dots others don't see."

A drop of sweat trickles down Pappy's forehead. He returns Cain's gaze, stands bold, refuses to be intimidated. He looks like a man staring into Satan's face as flames lick his heels and lap his fingers. An expression of hopelessness, like a man who's realized there's no saving grace, no *thing* to look forward to, save fear, misery, and endless eons of suffering.

But Pappy stands tall within that dark gaze.

I will myself to step forward, afraid Cain might kill him here and now.

"Relax, dear Emery. I promised you he'd come to no harm, and I intend to keep that promise. After all, you've earned it."

Pappy looks at me with an expression of betrayal. As if I've just burst through the door wearing an Antichrist baseball jersey and waving a pennant that says Go Satan!

Cain waves a hand. "You're no threat to me or my plans. My power can't be subdued by the likes of you." His sneer is obvious, a hint of redness shadows his face. Then, he tips his head back as if listening to something through headphones. He nods a single time, says, "It seems we have a surprise visitor. How excellent. Emery, you'll come with me. Friar, stay put."

Pappy steps aside and Cain exits. I regard the friar, search for something to say so he knows my true allegiance and can appreciate the complexity of my predicament.

Then, Cain re-enters. "Dear Brother Pappy, I forgot to inform you that this church is now Imperium's property and will fly its banner proudly. See to that, won't you?"

Pappy's face betrays his rage. Lips part as he steps forward.

I grab his arm, stop him before he can speak. "It's not the time," I whisper. "Patience, Pappy. Don't get yourself killed in a moment of righteousness."

Pappy stares at me, and I can't imagine the calculations in his mind. Then, he nods, steps behind his desk and drops into the chair.

From the church's interior, I hear, "Emery, come."

Shocked eyes stare at clenched fists as Pappy sits lonely, surrounded by ancient stone and darkness.

I leave him to his thoughts, leave him to make the decisions with which we've all wrestled.

CHAPTER 25

MOUNT TABOR, ISRAEL

"Dearest Tom, what a surprise. To what do I owe the honor?"

President Carpenter stands in the center aisle staring at the spinning kaleidoscope from Longinus's relic. "Nice fixture. Get it at HomeGoods?"

"Not at all," Cain chuckles. "Seems dear Longinus found it at a yard sale."

The president glances at me, then his eyes drop to my hand which fingers the bottle of Percs in my pocket. I stop, having no idea I was even pawing them.

I affect a pleasant expression as monkeys claw my back. Too much reality in too short a time. I think of Pappy, think of his expression as I abandoned him to obey Cain's call. I slide my hand over the syringe as it burns a hole in my thoughts. I don't *need* this, but it sure would be nice.

"All junkies say that," Lenny says, and I'm surprised to hear the voice absent for so long.

"Right you are," Vince answers.

"Mr. Merrick, I see you're still keeping questionable company?"

I move beside Cain.

"And how's the wife?" the president continues.

I glance at Cain, then say, "I'm divorced."

Carpenter smiles, tips his head in an exaggerated nod. "Oh yes, she abandoned you for this man if my intel is correct."

He's baiting me, baiting us. For what purpose? Is he trying to rouse Cain's anger? A bad idea, I think, but then remember I have vastly more experience with the Antichrist than he.

Cain flashes that smile, waves his hand. "I'm afraid that's none of your concern, dearest Tom." He steps forward, flicks his gaze to the relic. "To what do we owe the honor of your visit?"

Carpenter doesn't miss a beat. "I felt a bit uneasy after our phone call. You seemed, well, not yourself. And when you said those very nasty things about us being enemies, I thought a visit in order."

"How very kind of you," Cain says. "I suppose you're taking the opportunity for some press releases as you tour the ravaged lands of Israel?"

Carpenter nods his assent. "One must seize opportunities as they present."

"Indeed," Cain says, "and what opportunities do you see to *seize* here?"

Carpenter reaches for the spear, too high for him to grasp. He holds his hand as if gauging its temperature and energy. The relic spins with astonishing speed. Seems to have increased incrementally since Longinus tapped the floor and sent it toward the rafters.

"I offer only friendship," Carpenter says. "I've always felt if something is worth saying, it's worth saying in person. Don't you agree?"

Cain doesn't respond.

"Perhaps I was too zealous with my words before," Carpenter continues. "Long day and all that. This job can get to you if you let it."

Cain nods, smile undiminished.

"I'll be frank," Carpenter says. "You've upset the world balance. The balance of power, you see? The balance of peace. China's invaded Russia unopposed. Russia is decimated, as are all the countries of the coalition that attacked Israel. I suppose you had a hand in that?"

"Let's say their surprise attack wasn't much of a surprise. They played into my hands, which isn't so impressive if you think about it. One need only follow the slimy trails of greed and power to their end points. On that path, intent becomes glaring."

"Of course," Carpenter says, "and very perceptive."

I see movement in the rear of the church and notice four secret service agents in a wide perimeter, hands clasped before them. Carpenter isn't a normal president, and for that I like the man. A hands-on guy, he seems to move about more freely than his predecessors and likes to look people in the eye when he speaks to them.

Then again, what do I know? Maybe presidents do this sort of thing all the time. Perhaps it's common knowledge that they go where they want and do what they will. X'chasei has controlled the media for so long, I've learned that nothing reported can be counted for truth, only for manipulation.

A man rises from a bench near the door, and I realize it's Longinus. He stands stoic as the Secret Service men tense.

It's quite a risk Carpenter takes, being here with two psychopathic immortals. If they knew the truth, he'd be whisked to the presidential bunker for all-eternity's safekeeping.

As in Pappy's office, I glance at Cain and find myself hoping he doesn't kill the man.

For Cain's part, he flicks his gaze to Longinus, then back to Carpenter, who continues to speak, his tone more solemn now. "What exactly are your intentions?" he says. "I'd like to part as friends, and you should know I'm having trouble keeping our allies from invading Israel in the name of peace and order."

Cain grins. "UN peacekeepers? Is it to that you're referring?"

"Something like that. Let's just say I'd like to avoid any further unpleasantness. The world has seen enough destruction for a while, although there always seems to be more." Carpenter takes a seat on a wooden bench in the front row, then props one leg on the knee of the other. "We have no wish to occupy Israel—for Israel's own safety, of course—and seek only assurances that we can work together and rebuild this great nation."

Cain nods, seems unimpressed. "Of course," he says, "our friends rush to our aid."

Carpenter nods. "Exactly. That's how we'll portray it anyway. Of course, you'll have to cede power and allow us to…appoint a steward…until such time as things can calm and return to normal."

"How very gracious of you."

Tom grins. "The least we can do."

Cain steps forward and sits next to the president.

Here it comes, I think. In the time it'll take Cain to kill him, Longinus will easily subdue the Secret Service guys and leave me again staring at lifeless bodies, filled with familiar sensations of horror and nausea.

I squeeze the syringe in my pocket.

"Tell me, dear Tom, what help do you offer that we cannot attain ourselves? We needed no help repelling the attack. We needed no help decimating the armies. We required no aid to invade a defenseless Russia, and we needed no aid in creating the Kingdom of Imperium. So, tell me, how can you help us?"

"Imperium?"

"Oh, yes, how silly of me," Cain says, beaming. "I've united all the countries in the region under one banner. Of course, you wouldn't know about it because we finalized everything today. Gone are individual nations, united is the Kingdom of Imperium under one rule." He turns, crystal eyes boring into Carpenter's. "My rule. For, you see, I am now supreme emperor of this vast new kingdom and each country's leader has sworn fealty to me. Everyone is quite ecstatic about these new changes, this new world order, if you will. With the exception of you and your allies, which consist of—what?—most of Europe, Canada, a few others?"

"That's preposterous," Tom says. "Where's Slabav? You can't subvert the authority of a duly elected prime minister."

Cain tsk's. "I'm afraid Laslo's been arrested by the defense minister. It seems he's implicated in numerous murders. The word *genocide* was even bandied about. I've no idea of the particulars of the charges, but I'm sure justice will win the day as it always does. The truth has a way of finding its own light."

Tom's face is red. "You can't just take over like that. I know Laslo, he'd never be involved in murder, much less genocide." Carpenter stands, looms over Cain. "This is the coup we're concerned about. This overthrow cannot stand."

Cain laughs here, affects an air of nonchalance. "Have you seen Israel? We can hardly be described as prosperous just now." He rises as well, stands inches from Carpenter's face. "Your points are valid, however, and I accept them. Perhaps in a year or two we'll have an election that I'll win. Would that appease you and the allies?"

Tom's thick jaw juts forward as he levels a finger at Cain. "No, it won't. You've usurped a nation's sovereignty."

"Region," Cain says.

Tom blinks at the comment. "Yes, region. You're behind the invasion of Russia, and God only knows what's become of their weaponry. We're very concerned their nuclear arsenal will fall into the wrong hands."

Cain nods. "I see your concern," he says, "but I'm afraid you'll have to talk to the Chinese about that."

Carpenter throws his hands in the air. His breath escapes in a rush. "You're saying you have nothing to do with that?"

"How could I? My duties keep me busy here."

"I see," Tom says, collecting himself. An agent steps forward and whispers in his ear. Tom smiles, offers a hand. "It seems I'm needed elsewhere, but I do appreciate your time. I'll be in touch and perhaps we can find a way through this quagmire together."

Cain shakes his hand. "Mr. President, safe travels."

Carpenter stalks from the church, Secret Service agents in tow.

Longinus's voice falls on stone walls in a thin echo. He stretches his arm, and the spear flies to his hand. "It seems he didn't care for your words."

Cain giggles like a schoolgirl, fast and high-pitched.

"You know they'll come, right? You know they'll not let this alone?" I say.

Cain gives me the stupid-question look. "O dear Emery, ye of little faith."

CHAPTER 26

MOUNT TABOR, ISRAEL

Imperium? New world order? Russia invaded?

And was that the US president?

Confusion clouds his mind as he crouches against a high stone wall on the church's southern side. Above him, a small window flashes dizzying hues of gold, red and blue.

He pulls a small mirror, holds it angled just beneath the window, slowly raises until he can see inside. The spear spins like it's powered by a nuclear reactor, then abruptly flies to the Roman's hand.

Cain, Longinus, and Emery stand talking. Longinus spins the spear absently.

"Carpenter should be gone now," Cain says, "and I believe I'll retire myself. We've accomplished much today and should be proud. Emery, can you give my regards to Brother Pappy? I'll see you both in Jerusalem."

The three move up the aisle, Cain in the lead. Jonas angles the mirror, looks for others, specifically for the woman Longinus arrived with. But with their departure, the church is empty. He scrambles along the outer wall, watches them walk down the path toward the parking lot to the west.

He whispers for Ishmael to move west, cautions him to move quietly up the dirt trail that leads to the parking area.

Glancing toward the sky, he expects the shadow of a chopper to circle, then land. Instead, a sleek, black limousine pulls up, and Cain gets in as new rain begins to fall.

Jonas covers the distance silently, draws close to the lot as the limo disappears into the night.

Emery and Longinus exchange a few words, then Longinus starts back toward the church.

No time like the present, Jonas thinks, then levels the Kalashnikov.

We exit the church to a drizzle from a cold sky. I follow Cain and Longinus and wonder why they bother to speak out loud at all when they share thoughts without words. Efficient, magical, supernatural. ESP on full display.

In the parking lot, a stretch limo sits idling.

"It seems your night isn't over just yet, dear Longinus. Uninvited guests will arrive shortly." Cain closes his eyes and speaks softly. "Oh, how I wish I could watch." He turns to us. "Have a wonderful evening, but don't dally. We have much to do in Jerusalem."

"Aye," Longinus says.

The limo makes a wide arc and leaves the parking area to head back down the mountain.

"What was that about?"

Longinus turns toward me. "In time, dear Emery," he says and stalks off toward the church, golden relic swinging at his side.

CHAPTER 27

BASE OF MOUNT TABOR, ISRAEL

The passenger's wiper squeaks across the windshield as the driver's wiper quivers in place. Igneus squints through the rain into the darkness.

He'd thought the mountain empty with the departure of the last helicopter and ventured from his hiding place along the dirt road on Mount Tabor's south side. He needs to be in position until he hears from which direction Jonas and Ishmael are descending.

He backs the old truck between two trees on the side of the road.

Then he waits.

Everything rides on this attempt to defang the viper. This effort to remove the bull's horns. "Not much of a plan," Jonas said, but with the pace of everything these days, they'd had to accept *doable* over *perfect*.

The small truck, rusted, formerly blue with bald tires and filthy interior, is a loaner from a man Sebastian healed at the Temple. Igneus exits the vehicle as rain pelts his face. It feels good, and he pauses to inhale the slick freshness of the night and surrounding meadow. In the distance, a cow bellows as he moves to the rear of the truck and relieves himself. It's been a long day, and an even longer evening mostly watching helicopters arrive and depart. Now, it seems, traffic has stopped.

Why did Cain call the meeting? What's he up to? Hopefully Emery will fill him in when next they meet. For now, though, wait for Jonas and Ishmael, get the spear, defang the beast.

As he zips his pants, he's blinded by the harsh glare of headlights not twenty feet ahead. The vehicle has come from the church, emerged from a mountain road Igneus thought deserted.

He freezes, knows if he runs, he'll be found out for sure. Act nonchalant. Probably an Israeli Defense Force vehicle leaving the mountain, work completed for the day.

The vehicle approaches, then the lights go out. It's a stretch limo, sleek, shiny, rain glistening in beads on a black exterior.

It creeps past; the rear window lowers.

"Dear Igneus! How lovely to see you! And in such an unusual place."

Igneus tenses, realizes he's left his walking stick in the truck's rusty bed.

"What do you want?"

"Is it so offensive to say good evening to an old friend?" A gleaming smile splits the night. The rain picks up. "An old friend who stands in darkness, dousing the tires of a rusty truck with fresh urine? An odd place to find oneself, it seems. If I didn't know better, I'd say you're up to something."

Igneus moves close, leans toward the gleaming crease. There's no reason to fear Cain. A point made clear outside Slabav's office.

"I *am* up to something, devil. I'm destroying your plans and undoing all you've done."

Cain laughs, actually guffaws and slaps his knee. "Marvelous, simply marvelous," he says. "I do appreciate your tenacity. You and I have become great foils to each other, and I find it delightful. I, as evil agent; you, the Almighty's sharpened arrow. Who could've predicted it?"

Igneus crosses his arms, steps toward the rusty truck. "I'll be seeing you."

"Of course," Cain says, "and do take care." The window starts to rise, then stops abruptly and lowers. "Oh! Dear Igneus, excuse my forgetfulness, I've had so much to manage lately. I did mean to ask though, if the two men up there are with you?"

Icy shards spike Igneus's veins. He tries to keep his face clear of panic, tries not to betray concern.

"Relax," Cain says. "They're unharmed. For now, anyway, but Longinus plans to dispatch them soon." Steel blue eyes look toward the sky as he thinks. "Perhaps if you hurry, you can still help them. I'm certain Longinus will be overjoyed to see you again after so long. Do you have your stick? I ask because…"

Igneus dives into the old truck, listens to the engine grind, then halt. He cranks the key, once, twice, three times.

Cain's laughter swarms his ears as sweat mixes with the rain on his face. He's suddenly hot, suddenly desperate, twists the key harder, stomps on the gas.

The engine whines as if turning over is too much for the old thing. Igneus breathes a prayer, wrenches the ignition again. The truck shudders, then finally clunks to life.

He slams it in drive, stomps the accelerator.

Bald tires spin on wet grass and the truck ambles forward.

Cain's laughter chases as Igneus fishtails onto the road and presses the truck up the mountain.

Chapter 28

Mount Tabor, Israel

They say you never hear the shot that kills you. As if death spares one the harsh crack that signals their demise.

But I hear the shot.

Followed immediately by another.

Longinus lurches, staggers, then falls like a deer in a meadow.

I hear the footsteps before I see the man.

Jonas sprints past, black rifle attached to his extremity as if it's been there as long as memory.

He grabs the spear from the inert Roman, then sprints back toward the underbrush.

I know where he's going, although I didn't know the plan was to assassinate Longinus.

Then a shadow zips by, huge, a rock monster come to life, bolting after the relic's thief.

I can't believe the speed at which he moves.

Longinus is back in original form, chasing Jonas, who's just steps away from the brush on the lot's perimeter, rifle in one hand, spear in the other.

Longinus is a step behind as Jonas dives, then, horizontal and airborne, manages to flip over, belly to the sky.

Longinus lands on him and I hear a cry, deep, hoarse, and agonizing.

The Roman staggers to his feet.

The golden spear juts from his chest as jagged lightning slices the sky behind him.

Jonas somehow knew he wouldn't make it to the brush. Had managed to spin in midair and skewer the Roman with his own weapon. I replay the movement in my mind. His situational awareness is off the charts, and I can't discern how he sized up the Roman's speed and position so perfectly. He moves with an agility that decries his age, ripping the spear from Longinus's chest, then sprinting for the bushes and the safety of the trails beyond.

Then, like a cobra, Longinus wraps a thick hand in Jonas's shirt. With a twist and shake of a bulging right arm, Jonas flies back into the parking lot, slides through gathered puddles like a tire made for drenched roads.

He gains his feet in an instant and faces the giant. His eyes are dark, yet bright, crinkled, focused, deadly. In his hand, the golden relic gleams.

"You fancy me pike?" Longinus stalks forward, undaunted by the death stare.

Lightning flashes, shows three dark and bloody wounds in Longinus's chest.

He's unphased, curled fists and bulging muscle. Rage sparks from darkened orbs.

Jonas circles, thrusts the spear at the Roman's gut.

The spear slices his shirt but misses its mark.

Longinus grabs the relic with both hands and starts to spin like an Olympic hammer thrower.

Jonas's face shows surprise as he holds as best he can.

In seconds, centrifugal forces best him and he flies across the parking lot, leaves a wake like a cruise ship.

Longinus is on him before he can move, lifts him in the air, intent on slamming him to the asphalt as he'd slammed the Apostle outside the Temple.

But Jonas isn't the Apostle, and as Longinus lifts, Jonas sinks both hands into the giant's hair. Longinus adjusts immediately, drops to one knee, lines up the other beneath Jonas's wriggling body.

I hear the grunt, the rush of wind as Jonas crashes down on the giant appendage and rolls across the lot.

Longinus stomps after, a precocious child splashing in puddles.

But Jonas outpaces him, spins, kneels, raises the rifle. How he's managed to hold onto it is beyond me, and I chalk it up to training. I've always heard soldiers are trained to be with their weapons twenty-four-seven, heard stories about naming rifles after women, doting on them as if they're alive and can reciprocate affection.

Flame leaps from the barrel.

Longinus reels, but the shot does little to stop his advance.

He grabs the rifle, pulls, moves Jonas so fast his head snaps back. Jonas slides across the asphalt as Longinus stomps with a huge foot.

Jonas avoids the blow by a fraction but doesn't get up. Then, I see he's attached to the weapon by a dark sling.

Longinus stamps like an irritated toddler.

Jonas rolls, slides, scurries—does whatever he can to keep his distance. Somehow, he frees himself from the sling, then rolls across the parking lot, throwing water like a pinwheel.

The man is agile, fast as a viper. He manages his feet, ducks three massive punches, then steps between the giant's arms and goes to work.

The blows sound like punches on a frozen side of beef, wet, harsh, powerful.

The Roman grunts as each finds its mark, steps back with each impact, tries to drive his arms down and enwrap Jonas as the rifle skitters into the brush.

But Jonas expects this, ducks under huge arms, circles, rains blow after blow on the Roman's abdomen and back.

Longinus spins in a blind strike, catches Jonas with a glancing blow, enough to back him a few steps, giving the giant time to reset.

A massive chest bulges as lightning shreds, as raindrops grow and gather in splotched puddles.

I can't believe Jonas has lasted this long. He's certainly brave, certainly a skilled combatant. Perhaps fear drives him, a sense of pure survival, panic prodding speed and agility. He dances backwards, dodges blows, calculates his next move.

I scan the lot, see the spear lying gold and lonely in a puddle twenty feet away.

How does he hope to get the spear and escape, when the best he can hope for is to render the Roman unconscious? He'd shot the man thrice, skewered him with the relic, yet Longinus moves forward, seems no worse for wear.

A shadow catches my eye. Then, the young doctor sprints from the brush.

Their plan becomes as obvious as a water balloon to the face.

Jonas distracts, moves to keep the Roman's back toward Ishmael as the doctor rushes for the spear.

Jonas is betting his life, wagering he'll live long enough to distract the Roman. After Ishmael disappears, he'll need enough strength and speed to bound into the brush and race off.

I realize the point isn't to best the Roman, but to deceive him. They've felt confident enough in Jonas's abilities to pit him against the centurion in single combat.

Ishmael flies past, grabs the spear from the puddle, sprints for the underbrush.

I glance to Longinus, who has no idea what's occurring behind him.

The Roman leaps forward, attempts to grasp Jonas in a bear hug.

In a flash, Jonas slides under a huge arm, then leaps on the Roman's back. Muscled arms wrap the giant's throat as his face wears the strain of staying atop the huge centurion, squeezing with all his might. He keeps his head low, keeps it directly behind Longinus's broad neck. Longinus reaches over his shoulder but can't quite grasp the man.

Then, I see the ploy.

Jonas uses the Roman's thick muscles against him. Uses the sheer bulk of the Roman's arms to keep him from reaching over his head.

Longinus struggles, tries to reach as huge biceps block his arm from fully bending, fully reaching their target.

The Roman spins like a dervish, arms flail, reach, his face turns a deep magenta that glares through the darkness.

Jonas rides, a cowboy on a prized bull, holding for all he's worth, straining to maintain his grasp, face taut and stretched.

Longinus drops to a knee, reaches desperately behind.

He's done it! In a few seconds, Longinus will be unconscious, and Jonas and Ishmael can escape with the spear.

Then, from the edge of the parking lot behind me, I hear another voice. A strange voice, lilting, teasing, feminine.

"Oh, bo-oys."

I look to Sima, who stands on the lot's edge, a dagger pressed to Ishmael's throat.

Chapter 29

Mount Tabor, Israel

Damn rain, damn old truck, damn bald tires!

Driving like a lunatic, Igneus barely keeps the vehicle between the edges of the slick road. The truck fishtails, then stutters like it's out of gas. He grips the wheel, turns it hard, slides around a switchback, fights to keep it from spinning out of control.

The rain falls harder, rends the darkness in slick sheets. Wind blows debris across the road as a bolt hits close, the flash momentarily blinds. He doubles his efforts, leans into the steering, presses the gas to its limit, balances urgency with control, panic with sheer determination.

The night blooms with the bright ghost of lightning's impact, a jolt that sears its memory on his retina. He pushes, undaunted.

Then, the old truck shudders, lifts its front tires as a huge branch crashes on its back half. A second slower and it would've landed on the two-seat driver's cabin.

Igneus breathes a prayer, wrenches the steering through another switchback, then stomps the pedal to the floor.

The truck shimmies, seems to come alive. He glances in the rear view, sees the big branch fall away. He presses further, hydroplanes, barely controls the jalopy.

He's almost there, a few seconds more.

Lightning rends the sky in sizzling strokes. Rain pounds the rusted metal roof. Water flies in thin spirals from bald tires as he leans forward, fingers clenched, blanched.

The parking lot appears.

He slams the gas, pours his entire body into the turn.

The truck tips, slides sideways, right, then spins out of control.

Images flash.

Jonas, atop Longinus, arms wrapped around his throat.

Longinus's eyes popping, face dark and red for want of air.

Rain pelts the roof like hail on tin.

Then, Ishmael, still as stone, eyes wide, lips parted.

Then a flash of something, a glint of steel.

Lightning flashes, and for a brief second the full scene becomes apparent.

A woman stands behind the doctor, dagger raised, lightning dancing from her blade.

Ishmael's eyes bulge, his face loses expression.

Then, he falls, a jeweled dagger jutting from his neck.

Chapter 30

Mount Tabor, Israel

Rage and anguish fill the cabin as Igneus howls.

The truck skids to a stop.

Sima steps aside, looks pleased with herself as she glances at the young doctor. She notices Igneus and sticks her tongue out.

The truck leaps as Igneus hammers the gas, directly at her.

She tumbles left, sprints past.

He wrenches the wheel, slides sideways. Tires spin, scream after her.

Longinus steps forward, Sima slides behind.

Jonas blazes past, slides across the vehicle's hood and races for Ishmael.

Broad hands crunch potholes in rusted metal as the truck slams the Roman.

Igneus leaps out, reaches in the bed, searches crushed metal for the staff.

Longinus looms. A grin twists his features. "Ye should non have come."

Igneus flicks his eyes to the bed, then to the raging Roman.

Huge hands clasp, then hammer down.

Igneus drops, sees the truck's bed collapse under Longinus's fury.

He rolls, races to the truck's other side and leaps fully in the bed.

Something clamps his ankle, pulls hard.

Hands scramble, search discarded wire, dirty hay, greasy rags. A menacing puzzle that hides his staff.

Longinus lifts. Igneus writhes, twists, grasps crushed metal and holds tight.

The stick is there, inches away. Dark wood blends with the bed's detritus, tucked under a section of crinkled metal.

The giant wrenches him free.

Slippery hands fumble as he becomes weightless, raised by the heel, suspended like a piñata.

Then, rain sizzles with white flame.

The Roman sails to crash through the trees beyond.

Igneus raises the staff, hones on the slight girl, then sees Jonas on the ground, cradling his brother's head. A shadowed face splashes tears as huge raindrops plop. His mouth rages, eyes squeezed, face raised to Heaven.

The storm drowns him out.

I glance to where Longinus flew, wait for him to reappear.

Igneus bolts for Jonas.

"This is getting good," Lenny says.

"Watch and learn," says Vince. Then to me, "Shouldn't you be doing something?"

I glance around. I want to help, but stand frozen instead, unsure.

Igneus screams at Jonas. "Put him in the truck! We'll get to Sebastian!"

Jonas's eyes are glassed, far off, not registering words.

"Jonas move!"

Jonas jolts, then wraps up his brother and makes for the pickup.

I hear the sound before I see him, a monstrous seal splashing in surf.

I turn, venture a step as Longinus blazes through torrential rain. He's a linebacker, a raging wrath, a bulldozer at max speed.

He takes Jonas broadside, sends Ishmael sprawling like a discarded teddy bear. Huge arms rise as hands clasp above the Roman's head.

Muscles ripple in a sizzling descent designed to smash Jonas into oblivion.

The sky ignites.

Igneus steps in, pins his staff beneath the giant's arm, then twists in a subtle but fluid motion.

Longinus flies head over heels, an elephant on a trapeze hitting soaked asphalt with a whoosh and wet smack.

Igneus levels the staff, grins as lightning rails behind.

Then, Sima appears, golden spear in hand. She rears, launches like a Spartan warrior. I'm stunned by the force, that such a slight girl can achieve such power.

It whistles as it flies, a high-pitched song of death.

Igneus raises his stick, but too late. The spear's too close, too fast.

Then Jonas snatches it mid-flight, spinning to fire it back at twice the speed.

I hear the cry as the spear hits home. See her eyes bloom in surprise, then darken as she drops.

Rain pops in puddles around her.

Thunder rolls.

The Roman's wail is loud, primordial. A howl of anguish, of pure despair.

He rushes to her, scoops her up, spear and all.

Jonas slides in the truck, drags Ishmael over his lap.

The doctor's skin is gray, his tongue lolls from his mouth.

"Hurry!" Jonas screams.

The rain falls sideways now, furious gales trail lightning like a jagged kite.

Tires spin slick as Igneus mashes the accelerator. With a metallic clunk, the truck catches and skids out of the lot to disappear down the mountain.

Longinus cradles his woman. Presses his forehead to hers.

He produces a radio and speaks rapidly.

Vince and Lenny call me names as I stand dumbstruck.

I'm drenched on the outside. Barren and dry within.

CHAPTER 31

MOUNT TABOR, ISRAEL

Igneus slides through tight arcs as wind buffets. A rain-drenched road tosses hazards everywhere.

He skids left, slams the wheel right, then spins left again just before they fishtail.

Beside him Jonas whispers. "Hurry, hurry, hurry! Hold on, Izzy. Hold on, clown."

Gravity helps *and* hinders as they race down the mountain. Igneus thinks only of Cain. Has he set this in motion? He'd obviously known of the men waiting to take the spear.

The drive to Jerusalem will take a couple of hours, far too long for Ishmael.

He slams the brake, slides to a stop in the middle of the road, leaps from the vehicle and crosses to the passenger's side.

Jonas stares ahead, eyes soaked in disbelief, drenched like the surrounding road.

Igneus kneels, places hands on Ishmael's wound.

The dagger protrudes at a sharp angle, plunged where neck meets clavicle.

"Father," Igneus says, "through your grace let this man be whole."

He presses the wound, then slides the dagger free and drops it on the wet road.

Wind whips the truck's door, makes it bounce on his backside.

Broad bolts stream across the heavens. Bruised clouds move west toward the sea.

Igneus doubles his efforts, focuses, concentrates on all that empowers, all that fills him.

Need whips his heart. Tears brim over his cheeks.

"Jonas, do you see it?" Ishmael whispers.

"Hold on, Izzy. You're gonna be okay."

Ishmael squeezes his brother's hand, gives a weak smile. "I'll miss you, hooligan."

"Don't talk like that…"

Ishmael's hand drops. His smile drifts as breath flows away on howling winds.

"NO!" Pure anguish chases the storm, shrieking grief, sheer sorrow. "Ishmael! Please! Please!" His voice lowers, whispers. "Please, don't leave. Don't leave me alone. *Please, please,* don't go."

Igneus stares at Ishmael's lifeless eyes.

Jonas's face is deadpan, hair dripping black drops. "He's gone, Igneus," he says. "My sweet Izzy. He's gone."

Silent spasms wrack his body. He pulls Ishmael close, presses lips to his forehead. "Ishmael," he whispers, "Ishmael. Ishmael."

Igneus drops in the road's center, rivulets flow past in dark streams.

Jonas pours sobs, silent but deafening.

He holds Ishmael gently, speaks to him in kind tones, tones of guilt, of loss, of misery. He spills his grief, his disbelief, cheek pressed to forehead, eyes squeezed, body heaving.

Thunder punctuates his anguish. Night engulfs, offers neither condolence nor consolation.

Igneus places a hand on Jonas's arm, feels powerless against the throbbing ribbons of his shredded heart.

He's been too late.

They're beaten.

Ishmael's dead.
The spear, gone.

CHAPTER 32

Maryland, United States

Knife is life.

Crispy's survival axiom.

Joined by: *Ration sweat not water. Never kneel in the dirt. Don't survive, thrive.*

The blade beads with rain, makes quick work of a clutch of branches. Rhyme tucks them under her arm, moves to the Bronco as water flows from a lead-heavy sky. How long's it been raining now? Twelve hours? Fifteen? *Gotta move if I'll have any chance.*

She rifles through her gear, pulls a dry bag, starts to stuff.

Just the minimum, have to travel light, move quick, stay dry. Hypothermia is death as surely as meeting a mamma bear. Her mind seizes the word as a shiver rolls through her body. She's close now, can hear running water as morning sun threatens the eastern horizon.

Around the bend, the river waits.

I get one chance at this, need portions of luck and gall to survive, to escape.

She closes the dry bag, presses out the air and rolls it shut. Then, thinking again, opens the bag and lets the air back in. If it needs to float, now it has a fighting chance. May just save my life. She trims a ten-foot section of 550 cord, ties it around her waist, then under the dry bag's straps.

Houdini watches from under a broad tree. Drenched and shivering, he wears his misery on his long dark face. Doberman's aren't water dogs, and his disquiet presses her to move faster.

"I know, I know. I'm hurrying."

She dresses the bundle of branches by wrapping her jacket around them, zipping it closed, then pulling the hood over the remainder where she pulls the strings tight.

From the bunch, she pulls a single branch, long and thin, then measures it with her eyes, bends it slightly with both hands. "This should do."

Houdini shivers, stands, shakes rain from his fur. "Stay," she says.

At the Bronco, she turns the key, whispers a prayer, then heads for the river. Despite the rain, the banks are still visible, not yet overrun. Effects of the past month's relentless heat, the river at historic lows, buying her time. The storm will go a long way toward refilling reservoirs, nourishing crops and people—helping fugitives escape.

She inhales deep, then eases the Bronco's nose into the flowing water. Not too deep, she thinks, but just deep enough. She glances through the shattered driver's window, downriver to a narrow strait. A perfect bottleneck.

The risk she's taking would make Crispy declare her officially daft. She doesn't know the place, has no idea if the river has soft spots, hidden gullies, even how deep it is.

She swallows hard, presses the Bronco ever deeper, angles toward the river's center. In the passenger's seat, jacketed branches look ahead with frightened eyes. She chuckles at herself. "Project much, Rhyme? Jesus."

The Bronco bumps over the river bottom. It's too deep to cross. Too cold to swim.

But that was never the plan.

The Bronco lifts, slides sideways, starts to float.

Pressing the gas, she wedges the thin branch between the pedal and the driver's seat. Then, she grabs the bundle, opens the Bronco's door and splashes onto the truck's running board. She closes the door, props the dummy of sticks in the driver's seat; she pulls the seat belt to hold them upright and in place.

The engine roars as the SUV floats toward the river's center, the deep water.

She has only seconds.

Heaving the dry bag, she leaps into the waist-deep current, struggles her way to shore, dry bag floating behind, secured to her waist with 550 cord. On the river's edge, she hurries along the bank, watches the Bronco drift down stream, propelled whenever spinning tires impact something solid. It bumps, shudders, then slides to a stop in the river's middle.

Caught on something. Good enough.

Unstrapping a Sig, she points at the sky and fires twice. Then, after a few seconds, three more times. She casts a final look at the wavering Bronco, feels a sense of loss at letting her favorite vehicle die this way.

She races into the brush, up the muddy trail, back to the waiting dog.

CHAPTER 33

GEORGE WASHINGTON NATIONAL FOREST, WEST VIRGINIA

What's she doing? Why ditch the truck?

She's either brilliant or stupid. Has no idea she's being tracked.

Below, the woman fills the scope's sight picture. She jogs up the trail, disappears in the brush. He sweeps to the floating SUV, suspended in the water, riding the current, bouncing yet unmoving, starting to sink.

No idea, he thinks. Losing the truck accomplishes nothing other than making her more vulnerable. Looks like she propped a dummy in the driver's seat as well. He snorts a laugh. The dummy will fool exactly nobody. If she wanted a dummy in there, she should've stayed herself.

He scans the bank, traces the direction she went, tries to think where she's headed. On foot, she'll be even easier to catch.

Dumb! Dumb! Dumb!

Panic. That's the only explanation. The hunger, the elements, the cold, injuries, must've overwhelmed her logic. Maybe hypothermia's set in. People make bad decisions when embraced by cold's deadly fingers.

He trains the rifle across the river, up the surrounding slopes.

He knows she'll reappear, just doesn't know where.

A glint of light startles him, causes him to simultaneously hunker down and start to move. His heart bounds as sweat appears, mixes with falling rain. He stops, stills his mind, suppresses the demons, ghostly images of horror and war, of living and dying, at random, fate decided by the narrowest whims of luck.

He grips a tree, grounds himself, realizes he's not in *that* fight, that deadly desert and its hidden enemies. The flash hadn't come from enemy sniper fire. He swallows hard, eyes closed, suppresses memories, ghouls of death, harbingers of unadulterated fear. A shaky hand slides over his face, reaches out to wipe the scope instinctively. Pursed lips exhale as heart rate slows. Reality comes in view. He reacquires.

And there she is, binoculars held to eyes, watching the SUV bob in the river below. She's gotten higher than he expected, and in so short a time. She's in good shape.

The woman lies flat, pulls surrounding branch and leaf over her body, then lies very still, watching. She's made another rookie mistake.

He would've never seen her if she'd taken the time to conceal herself before using the binoculars.

He judges the distance, considers the wind, the terrain, the rain. All have certain effects on the shot, best managed or avoided. Trained fingers spin the silencer onto the rifle.

Above, a helicopter speeds through a wide circle, then hovers above the Bronco.

The radio squawks.

"Gemhunter, we found her. Have eyes on a vehicle matching the description. It's lodged in the river. Looks like the subject's still inside. Must've gotten trapped trying to cross. Over."

"Roger that, Amethyst, ground enforcements en route. Maintain visual. Over."

"Roger. Roger."

The helicopter buffets in the wind but hovers easily. Then: sirens from her side of the bank and the flash of emergency lights racing toward the river.

This side of the river lights up as well. The trail fills with wailing SUVs and barking dogs, descending as one.

He looks to her position.

She's still as stone, binoculars glued to her eyes.

She's trapped now, can't move without being seen by the responders who comb over the mountain.

"Rookie mistakes gonna get you killed."

Chapter 34

Jerusalem, Israel

Sima's lips are pale. Sweat beads on her delicate forehead.

Longinus holds her tiny hand in a giant palm. He whispers to her, but the helicopter drowns him out.

She hasn't opened her eyes or said a word since leaving Mount Tabor.

"We're landing near the Temple," I tell him. "Pilot said that's the best place to seek care, hospitals are overrun. Says it's our best chance."

A giant head nods but doesn't look at me, just leans close to Sima and surprises me as he kisses her forehead.

We buffet, rotate; then a hard bump signals we've landed.

Longinus sweeps her up. He's in his suave form, clothing tattered and flapping, so I'm surprised he lifts her so easily.

I've never seen him like this, so gentle, caring, so delicate.

We step off the helo through rain, toward a smattering of tents large and small. People move about us, strained faces mixing raindrops with anguish.

Longinus bellows, "Help! We need help!"

A few people turn, surprised by the Roman's volume. A man steps from the crowd. "This way," he says. He looks at Sima, places a hand on her neck, produces a pair of thick scissors and, with a few quick snips, exposes her upper chest.

Jonas's aim was true, the spear found its mark in her left upper thorax.

"Missed her heart," he says. "Whatever it was, it was sharp. May have caught a lung, though." A stethoscope appears and he places the bell beneath the wound.

I see no blood from the wound, no signs of life from the woman.

"We should…" Longinus starts but gets silenced by a harsh "Shush!" and a raised finger. After a few seconds, the man looks at the Roman. "It doesn't look good. I don't hear any breath sounds. Come with me and hurry."

We push through the crowd, past a hodgepodge of tables holding remnants of food, ponchos, and big, yellow coolers.

The man moves fast, shouts occasionally to clear the way. Then we're in a tent filled on both sides with makeshift stretchers. The injured and sick lie atop them, some moaning, others quiet as night.

Longinus ducks under the entrance flap, follows the man who motions him to lay Sima atop a litter of khaki green.

"We need help," he says. "Who's in charge?"

A woman appears and swipes Sima's arm with an alcohol pad. Then, with extreme precision, pokes a needle into her vein and attaches a bag of clear liquid.

"More, Nora," the man says, "as many as you can start."

The woman wastes no time, moves to Sima's other side, repeats the procedure. Then she surprises me by moving to her foot and removing her boot and sock. There, she places another IV.

"She needs surgery."

"Then get the surgeon," Longinus says. His voice is shaky, barely holding it together. "Where's he at?"

The man frowns. "We don't have one."

"Who does?"

"Maybe the hospital, but it's hard to say. There's so many wounded, any available surgeon has probably been in the OR since the attack."

Longinus moves to lift her. "We'll go there."

"She'll never make it."

"She has to." He looks at Sima, frowns, then glances at the man I assume is a doctor. Longinus's eyes water, and I wonder if he'll cry. Wouldn't that be something, I think. A wonder to end all wonders. Then, his eyes brighten. "You do it."

"What?" The man looks perplexed, shocked.

"You do it."

The man wags his head. "I've no idea where to start. I'm not trained as a surgeon, just a general practitioner."

"Are you a doctor?"

"Yes."

"Then what's the problem?"

"I'm not a surgeon. Never been trained."

Longinus leans an inch from the man's face. Lips twist on elegant features. "Ye best *become* a surgeon in the next few seconds."

The man steps back, eyes darting back and forth. "I can't... Listen, we..."

A hand appears on Longinus's arm. "I'll help." It's a child's voice.

Sebastian steps between them, places a rickety step stool and climbs atop. He leans close, his ear a centimeter from Sima's mouth. "I think I can help," he says more to himself than to us.

Longinus steps forward, eyes crazed. I step in front of him. "Longinus, calm down. This is Sebastian. He can do wonderful things."

"He's a child!"

"I know, but what do you have to lose?"

The Roman's eyes flare with grief, rage, and, surprisingly, helplessness. He hesitates, looks at the boy, then steps back. "Somebody best be doin' something, or you'll all pay hell."

The boy holds his hands over the wound.

"No pulse," the doctor says. "Begin CPR." The nurse rushes to the stretcher's other side.

"Wait." Sebastian says. "No one do anything."

Longinus steps forward, and I place a hand on his arm. He stops abruptly, and I think for a second he might scramble my brain with a right cross.

But he doesn't, just glances at me, then back to Sima as worry clouds his elegance.

Sebastian presses the wound. A thin blue hue appears beneath his hands as he leans close, stands atop the rickety stool on tiptoes.

I don't understand the subtle blue light or the words he whispers, another language, flowing and beautiful. Something pure, if such a descriptor can describe language.

Sima jolts awake, sits straight up, eyes darting, soaked with fear and confusion.

Longinus leaps past and sweeps her up. He beams pure glee. "Oh Sima, my Sima. You worried me so."

She rests her head on his shoulder. Her face, a picture of contentment.

Then something amazing happens.

A tear rolls down his face.

Sebastian stands smiling as the doctor and nurse stare.

"Good as new," the boy says. "Go and be blessed by God and His glory."

Longinus turns, lowers Sima to stand next to him.

"My thanks to you, lad. What can I do to repay this kindness?"

Sebastian doesn't miss a beat. "You can renounce evil and follow the path of the righteous."

Longinus grins and seems unsurprised at the suggestion. "Fat chance," he says, reaching into a filthy, shredded suit. A wad of cash appears, and he tosses it on the gurney. Then, he turns to Sima. "How do you feel?"

She wraps her naked chest with a nearby blanket, then retrieves her boot and puts it on. "I could use some food."

Longinus smiles like a stud in a perfume commercial. "Right away." Then, without a word or whistle, he stomps off, spear clenched in one hand as the other wraps Sima's slim waist. She walks on her own, looking healthy and fit. The rest of us watch like we're hypnotized.

"Mr. Emery, right?"

I tear my gaze from the lovers and settle on the child. "Hello, Sebastian. I'm surprised you remember me."

"I remember much," he says. "Do you still serve the dark one?"

"I don't serve him," I say. "I'm writing his biography. He's my employer."

Sebastian nods, seems wiser than his features. "You should find a new line of work."

Anger rears in my heart, and I start to tell the child exactly what I think of his advice. He's poked a tender spot, focused my misgivings on the single fact I work for Cain. As if to suggest if I quit the job, things will go pleasantly back to normal. I think of Rhyme, think of what she's doing, think of what normal means. Her and I heading to dinner, sharing the Sunday crossword, taking strolls hand in hand through the park.

I think of Cain, of what it means to *serve* him.

Then Pappy's words come, nothing wise or special, more of a gesture and phrase. "Uh huh."

Sebastian's smile is pleasant, innocent, without malice. "Dad should be back anytime. Would you like to wait with me? I can find some food and we can discuss things."

I almost laugh.

The boy sounds so big, assuming the role of sage while I fill my usual role of dumbass.

I have to admit, as my anger fades, as I stare into his cherubic features, the boy's right. I serve Cain as surely as any servant, bound as tight as a dog on a leash. I chafe at the words; at the expression of knowledge and certainty he gives.

He leans close, whispers. "Did we get the spear?"

He doesn't know about Ishmael. Doesn't know, even now, the young doctor fights for his life. "About that," I say, "things didn't go well. Ishmael was badly injured."

As soon as the words leave my mouth, his head shoots up. Color drains from his face. Eyes turn from competent contentment to pure panic.

I remember how they communicate, he and Igneus, and surmise the boy's just received news of Ishmael's injury.

"He's dead," Sebastian says, tears glittering. "I have to go."

He sweeps by, exits the tent, and breaks into a sprint to weave through the crowd as only a child can.

The doctor and nurse move off to attend other patients, and I find myself, again, standing like a dumbass by an empty stretcher thinking of Rhyme while trying to suppress the full meaning, the full warning of Sebastian's words.

As soon as Rhyme and I are together again, I just *may* find a new line of work.

CHAPTER 35

UNDISCLOSED LOCATION

The bank of TV screens, twelve in all, spill an eerie glow on the conference room's speckled brown carpet.

"I'm afraid we have a situation," Tom Carpenter says. "I've just left Israel, just spoke with that idiot Cain. He seems to have united the region under a new umbrella he calls *Imperium*. I don't need to go into the strategic details here. You all know the threats. To the region, to the world economy, to the world itself."

An aide steps forward, whispers in his ear.

Tom raises a hand, listens intently. "We're going to pipe this through to everyone. Apparently, Cain's holding a press conference from somewhere in Israel."

The TVs flicker static, then Cain's face fills the screen. His smile is comforting, genuine as he looks in the camera and speaks.

"I'd like to start by extending my thanks to all who could join us for this grand announcement. As many of you know, the nation of Israel has come under attack from a coalition of countries headed by Russia." He frowns, looks solemn. "It seems a coup was attempted, our national sovereignty threatened. Our losses are devastating.

"Fortunately, we were able to take quick action to repel this threat and decimate these armies. I've been granted universal authority to

195

aid Israel in its time of need. As such, the nations of the Middle East," he stares into the camera here, icy blue eyes that don't blink, "have banded together and ratified a new nation. The Kingdom of Imperium. They've elected me as this nation's emperor. I've received numerous phone calls from various world leaders expressing their concern and displeasure, not at the blatant and brutal attack on our sovereignty, but at the fact we've joined under an umbrella of peace to create our kingdom and assure harmony for decades, even centuries, to come.

"I've received a visit from the president of the United States, who personally expressed his concerns about our new nation and its threat to the world. He told me we're ripe for another invasion. He told me he didn't think he could stop other nations from attacking in the name of, quote, peace and order. They wish to occupy us under a guise of international aid. They wish to send troops, ships, and aircraft to, quote, secure the oil.

"Although I appreciate the sincerity, I see their words as no more than threats to Imperium's sovereignty. As they've done so many times before, they approach with good intentions only to deceive and manipulate for their own ends.

"I wish to be very clear. The Kingdom of Imperium will not tolerate an incursion on our soil. We will not tolerate an invasion disguised as international aid. The world order is changing, and we will not be stamped out, bullied, or intimidated into surrendering our birthright, our sovereignty, or our homes.

"I'm reminded of the words of a good friend. Former Israeli Prime Minister, Laslo Slabav. He liked to say, 'Beware the bearer of gifts for a dagger they may conceal'. I feel his words are appropriate today. The coalition of which the president spoke does not wish to render aid or to help rebuild. They wish only to secure resources and set up a puppet government. They wish only to destroy our kingdom and keep the region in a constant state of warfare, terror, and barbarity.

"I say to you, to the world, to those waiting in the night to rob and pillage, to them I say, this will not be tolerated. Imperium will not suffer another invasion. We wish to rebuild, in peace, and thereby restore harmony and balance to a region that for centuries has been filled with violence and upheaval.

"I've met with all Imperium's kings, and I speak for all kingdoms within Imperium.

"Do not test us.

"We have the means to defend ourselves and will utterly destroy all who come against us. Imperium is a sovereign nation and will defend itself by any means necessary.

"We do not wish war, but if war falls, neither will we shy away. We destroyed the invading force and will do the same to any others.

"In short, do not try us. From this day to the end of days, and always and forever. Thank you."

The TVs blink and return to the images of the leaders in attendance. France, United Kingdom, Italy, Germany, Canada, others. They look astonished.

"Imperium?" This is the German president, Hans Steiner. "First I've heard of it."

"Yes," Carpenter says, "Imperium. I thought Cain mounted a coup in Israel, but I was off. He mounted a coup of the entire region. Imperium makes up seventeen nations, all of which are now kingdoms. He's also set himself up as the emperor, no less, and states he has supreme authority." He shakes his head. "I don't know how he pulled it off under our noses, but this threat cannot stand. Russia's been invaded by the Chinese, which aids us in some ways, but upsets the balance of power in others. One less threat to deal with becomes one giant threat, with China controlling a huge percentage of the Earth. Not to mention the impact on resources, trade, economics. I've spoken to the secretary general of the United Nations and asked for an emergency meeting, but honestly, I don't think we have time for that. With every second, Cain consolidates power."

Prime Minister Reginald Barxley of the United Kingdom speaks. "What do you suggest? War? An invasion?"

Carpenter laughs, sets his jaw in an expression of defiance and confidence, an expression that's served him well during his rise to power. "No, no. Nothing like that, but I think it would be prudent to mount an incursion. I don't think we can laugh away Cain's words, and an international response will send a message to the rest of the world that Imperium is not a threat—that we have the situation contained. I'd like to emphasize: we're not starting a war but assuring peace and security. A balance, if you will, to the changing world landscape. I don't believe we can watch and wait for things to develop. Israel's in disarray. I was there personally. Saw the carnage with my own eyes. Although they beat back the coalition, their losses were devastating. They're not even rebuilding yet, just burying the dead and trying to get basic services up and running. I think we should occupy them for a short time…"

Italy's leader interrupts, followed by Germany and France, all speaking at once. Carpenter speaks fast and loud. "To say they're in disarray is an understatement. This occupation will actually *help* them whether they believe it or not. They haven't the means to mount a defense, and it will be our chance to prove to the world that we have only their best interests at heart." He leans back, takes them in. "I think it's our only option."

The Italian president, Giuseppe Montalvo, an older man with bushy eyebrows and a sharp nose, pipes in. "I disagree," he says. "I saw the video and my experts can't explain what happened with the two men and their weapons of great power. That invasion should've been easy for Russia and their friends. Instead, they were completely destroyed. I know, Tom, you think these are parlor tricks of a sort. But I don't share that sentiment and won't send a single troop to be destroyed."

Carpenter nods as other world leaders echo the same opinion. "I know," he says, "I get it. My best people have been on it since the videos surfaced. We don't think these are new weapon systems. Just a new version of weapons already in existence. You must remember, Cain is actually Thaddeus Drake, a billionaire with long reach. We've identified numerous facilities belonging to Drake. Of course, they're all buried in mounds of corporate filings, but fortunately, my people are tenacious and can prove ties without doubt. These facilities have been implicated in the creation of chemical weapons, arms deals, and extensive R and D of top-of-the-line systems. And on top of that, we believe Drake was instrumental in the rebuilding of the Temple in Jerusalem. We believe he's responsible for the murders of his Muslim counterparts. We believe he replaced them with his own, hand-picked successors. It may surprise you to know, Laslo Slabav has been arrested in Israel and now sits in prison awaiting trial for murder and treason. We know this Cain, formerly Drake, enjoys theatrics. Do you not remember his arrival at the treaty signing in Jerusalem? You were all there and saw what happened. He's positioned himself perfectly to take over the region. Who can say what's next?"

"You prove my point," Giuseppe says.

"Allow me to finish, my friend. We've studied the video and surveyed all our satellite imagery. The source of the power was two men. One Longinus, no last name given or found. And one Igneus, again no last name." He chuckles. "Maybe Cain has a penchant for naming his folks like James Bond villains." Scattered laughter. "But we've discovered these two men wield these weapons. We've received intel suggesting the man, Igneus, is the power's true source—"

"One man is the source?" Steiner sounds astonished. "Just what are we dealing with?"

Carpenter rubs his eyes. "Yes, amazing if true. But try to see this through logical terms, through lenses that are sane. We know the supernatural doesn't exist. Only weak minds grasp such concepts. It's *our* business to apply science and reason."

"But what if it's true?" Steiner speaks with a thick German accent.

"It can't be," Carpenter says. "Plain and simple, those things don't exist, can't exist." Others start to speak, and Carpenter raises his voice above them. "Listen! It doesn't matter either way. Yes, Cain's done some amazing things and we've had no luck figuring out how. But despite all that, the plan is to subdue both this Igneus and this Longinus and render them inert. That will end this nonsense once and for all and rebalance the world order."

He takes them in, pauses for effect, for control. "In that ilk, I propose a surgical strike from our combined special forces with the goal of disabling, specifically, these two men and retrieving the weapons for further study. A way to defang the serpent, so to speak.

Intel assures me this is doable and that if the weapons are captured, Israel, or Imperium, hasn't the means to mount any sort of robust defense. In a way, Russia did us a favor by attacking. It softened them up a bit."

"What if you're wrong?" the UK PM asks. "Our intel doesn't support your theory of only two weapons. What if Cain has more? What if, when we arrive, we're decimated as Russia was? It seems too big a risk, Tom."

"Risk comes with the territory, Reginald. Do you think I want to deal with this? If I had my way, things would never have changed. But they have, leaving us to deal with everything else. This is a strategic threat. If Imperium is allowed to grow and flourish, knowing the history of the region, how long do you think before they invade Europe? How long do you think it will take for their armies to equal our own? If we wait, we lose strategic advantage. If we move, again a surgical strike on two targets, designed to disable their defense systems, then we can provide aid to their people and show the international community we care." He scans the faces on the screens. "I should mention I'm prepared to authorize this mission unilaterally using American forces, but if I do that, I'll not give credit to any member here today, nor will I share resources with any of you. If the United States does this alone, we alone will control the region until such time as it's ready to assume its own leadership."

"You mean, you'll put your own leaders in place. A coup in its own right." This is the French president, Jean-René Beauchamp, a small man with shifty eyes.

"Nonsense," Carpenter says. "We believe in sovereign nations, but we also believe in stamping out threats. I believe, Mr. Beauchamp, that accusing us of launching a coup is insensitive and foolhardy. We'll merely secure a friend and ally, the state of Israel, and dissolve Imperium. In the process we'll share new technology and resources and bolster the region by adding some military bases and defending our combined strategic interests. When the time comes, we'll present a solution to the UN, and power will be peacefully and fully transferred to a duly elected prime minister. Perhaps even returned to Slabav. He's always sensible and easy to work with, not to mention his heart's in the right place."

The German president speaks up. "I agree with President Carpenter. The threat is too great. If Imperium is allowed to flourish it becomes a direct threat, not just to a single nation, but to the entire world. Our intel matches the US, and I too believe a precision strike with exacting goals is the best option. Germany stands with the US."

"Agree," says Giuseppe.

"As do we," says Reginald, the UK leader.

"Jean?" Carpenter asks.

France's president sits back, shifty eyes blinking. He sighs, leans forward and tugs at his tie. "France will support this."

Carpenter can't hide his smile. "Excellent, my friends. My commanders have already made a plan. I'll have them contact your defense ministers and we'll get this moving. When it's over, Cain will be imprisoned for treason, and we'll assure he won't bother anyone again. After this is finished, I'd like all of us to announce what we've done, together. You all understand, a better way to control the narrative."

The leaders nod and state their assent.

"Well, that does it," Tom says. "I'll see you on the other side."

CHAPTER 36

JERUSALEM, ISRAEL

They buried Ishmael at the base of a broad oak in a simple pine box.

Jonas bathed his brother as best he could, then dressed him in a long, white garment and placed him in the coffin.

They dug with an old pick and shovel while trying to ignore the sounds of other mourners: the cries of weeping mothers, of wailing wives and sisters. The smog of grief, a pollution of despair.

The entire nation, it seems, has become cemetery, and they aren't the only ones burying a loved one today.

To the west, the sun dips below the sea, casting wide rays of orange and pink over calm waters.

Jonas sits weeping as Igneus gathers fresh daisies.

"I'm sorry," he says, placing a hand on Jonas's shoulder. "I forced you to go. If I hadn't, Ishmael would be alive."

Jonas stares at the freshly turned earth, his thoughts elsewhere.

After a minute, Igneus turns toward the rusty, old pickup truck.

Then, Jonas speaks quietly, as if to himself. "I've lost so many. My wife, my son, my best friend. Now my brother." He glances at the oak's bare branches, then whispers a quiet prayer. "So much suffering," he says. "So much loss. Especially here, as if the very desert yearns for blood, and we feed its cravings daily." He wipes his eyes with a shaky hand. "I don't know how to go on. Don't know why I should. What's left for me? What purpose remains?"

Igneus feels his loss like a hollow ache in his gut. Ishmael, the young doctor, the man who'd treated he and Sebastian without thought of payment or personal gain.

A fresh wave of sorrow washes over Jonas, and his shoulders shake as he silently sobs. The man is bereft, lost in deepest despair. Igneus remembers the feeling, foreign after so many centuries.

"I wish I had something to say to relieve your pain," Igneus says. "I wish I could mend your heart and reverse time so we could make different decisions."

"That's nonsense and serves no one. Every soldier knows the price, the cost. The risk. My brother knew, he just wouldn't listen."

"But he wasn't a soldier."

"He still knew."

"He wouldn't leave you. Couldn't leave you."

Jonas remembers their days at the orphanage, Ishmael always by his side. They'd said he had *attachment issues* due to the sudden loss of their parents. Ishmael became reserved, nose always in a book, speaking to no one but Jonas for the better part of a year. A constant wave of child psychologists tried to get him to venture from his brother's side. They never could.

He remembers Ishmael's tiny hand sliding into his as they walked to school or to the park to kick the football. At night, huddled under threadbare blankets, reading stolen comics and pretending Mom would call supper any minute. He felt the impact of their parents loss even more acutely than Jonas. Had absorbed the pain of another dark secret known only to them.

"He insisted," Jonas says. "I told him not to come, but he insisted."

"He loved you. Love trumps logic."

Jonas rises, and Igneus hands him the daisies. "You should say a few words."

Jonas looks to the darkening sky. A silver tear slides down his cheek. "What's there to say? That he was the best brother?

"That he was the smartest of us, the kindest, the most innocent?

"That the best part of our DNA coursed through *his* veins? That his heart was enormous? That he loved freely and without thought?

"There are no words, Igneus. No bandage for this wound.

"I guess, all I can say, is that I wish I'd spoken my love to him. For some reason, I thought it more masculine to hold in those feelings, as if he knew them by default or just stupid luck."

His lips quiver. Fresh tears fall.

"I LOVE YOU, ISHMAEL!" The words tear through the oak's branches to flow across the meadow and race toward the timeless sea.

"I love you," he sighs. "My dear, sweet brother. You were the best of me," he says. "The best of us."

A gentle wind tussles his hair as he places the daisies on the grave. "I'll never be the same, sweet Ishmael, and I'll race to my end hoping only to join you soon."

Spasms shake his body as he grieves in silence.

Tears drop from Igneus's eyes to the cool green grass.

Jonas inhales, deep, stuttering, then paces toward the truck.

Igneus follows, wishing he could change the past.

The apartment feels as empty as Jonas's heart.

He lies soaked in sweat, head swimming, blankets bunched at his side.

He can't shake the image. The dagger, the blood, Ishmael's final words. *I'll miss you, hooligan.*

Light streams from the bathroom in a long rectangle to spill across the worn carpet. They'd never had much, but for what they had, they'd been happy. Jonas rises, heads to Ishmael's room, lies on the bed and pulls the pillow close.

It smells of him. Cedar with a hint of tea tree.

Tears flow as Jonas closes his eyes, takes deep, measured breaths.

He's afraid. Afraid he'll forget. Afraid Ishmael's memory has no meaning. That his sweet brother's life will be forgotten by the world around them.

Anger surges, hot and sticky, coats his soul, inflames his grief.

In the next room, he hears the boy's sobs. Ishmael's death has affected Sebastian almost as profoundly as Jonas. Fresh tears spill; he thinks to go to the boy.

Igneus is with him, best to have this time to myself.

Restless sleep casts its shroud as the rigors of the day overwhelm grief and strength.

Visions flash.

Burning flame, reaching, licking, never consuming.

A branch floats in unquenchable fire.

Jonas reaches for it.

An asp appears, strikes with slender, pointed fangs. It wraps around the branch, scales black and red, then regards him with beady eyes. "Levi," it hisses. "Jacob," it spits. "Come to me, firstborn."

It becomes vague, turns to smoke and shadow as it fades away.

He's standing in a courtyard, something ancient, covered with dirt and small rocks. In the distance, fields flow to the horizon, long furrows of harvest just sown, waiting for rain.

The branch sticks from the ground now. Appears as a pole fashioned to suspend new growth above the soil. It's stout and strong, reaches for the sky as if planted with great care.

Small green leaves appear, grow large as seconds tick. Lush, wet, healthy leaves bloom and flower. Then almond pods, pocked, tan, hanging in clusters as the branch becomes tree.

Ishmael approaches and Jonas calls to him.

He doesn't notice, moving forward, bucket in hand, gently watering the tree's base.

Jonas screams, races to stand in his brother's face.

Ishmael continues his task, spreading small trickles in the soil, humming a little song. His neck bears a scar, raised, purple, the size of a coin. Then he reaches up and grabs a thick, gnarled branch and breaks it cleanly from the tree.

He swings it through the air, shakes away almonds that fall and roll through the dirt. Then, he runs his hand across the rough bark.

He swishes it like a sword. Like a light saber from his favorite movie. Then, he offers it to Jonas. "Levi?" he says. "Jacob?"

"It's Jonas!" Jonas screams, waving his hands.

He has a feeling it's been centuries since he's seen his brother. Feels as if his brother died long, long ago.

Ishmael holds the branch before him, waits for Jonas to grab it.

Then, Igneus is there, taking the branch and tracing his fingers over its surface.

Red letters ignite, burning for only an instant.

Igneus turns, smiles, offers the branch. "Aaron."

Symbols appear, veiled, hard to read, flaring in puffs of smoke and spark.

Darkness falls, thickens, surrounds. The branch flames through sudden night, then the symbol. Shadow.

Light erases the darkness as rain extinguishes the flame.

The branch hangs motionless before him. Another symbol appears. Water.

Ishmael becomes an adolescent and tries to climb the tree. Child.

His nose runs with green phlegm. Virus.

Rain becomes snow and covers the ground, ankle deep. Ice.

The ice melts, then bubbles with steam. Boil.

Shoots of green poke through the water's rolling surface. Snowy ground becomes pleasant meadow. Crickets chirp and hop. A frog burps its call, then snatches a cricket with a flick of a long tongue. More symbols appear. Cricket. Frog.

A bird zips past, lands on the branch, sings in a high warble. Fly.

A dog, fluffy, spotted, tongue hanging from its mouth as it chases a butterfly, suddenly stops to scratch behind its ear. Flea.

The words burn in Jonas's mind but make no sense. Ishmael looks him in the eye, a sly grin on his face. Then, he turns and walks into the meadow, whistles a song both happy and energetic.

Igneus strolls past, stops to pet the dog, then moves off toward a wilderness of scraggly trees and thick undergrowth.

Jonas calls after, tries to chase but can't move.

A breeze favors him.

The dog moves beside, holds the branch in its mouth.

Jonas reaches for it.

It's smooth now, slim, carved, old.

Symbols burn, then fade into the branch. Frog. Shadow. Water. Child. Virus. Ice. Boil. Cricket. Fly. Flea.

He awakes to muffled sobs and embers of shadow.

CHAPTER 37

JERUSALEM, ISRAEL

"Who's Aaron?"

"I thought you'd know."

"And Levi?"

"The same, I was hoping you'd know."

Igneus shakes his head. "I'm sorry but I don't."

"Who would?"

"You mean who can interpret your dream?"

"Yes."

"Maybe Sebastian would have some insight, but he left early to get to the Temple."

"How's he doing?"

"Well, he's full of surprises. He didn't handle Ishmael's death very well, but this morning he raced out of here intent on doing as much good as possible."

Jonas raises a cup to his lips. The coffee is strong and bitter, an apt description of his attitude. Demons claw at his heart and constantly remind of Ishmael. As if their intent is to never let him forget his anguish, not the beauty that was his brother, but the searing grief that grips him. He thinks of the rest of his family, shredded in his skin, then forces the thoughts away. "That kid is something."

Igneus wears an expression Jonas can't calculate. Eyes focused downward, corners of his mouth stretched and white.

"What is it?" Jonas asks.

"Nothing."

"Nonsense. Something's hounding you."

"I'm just so full of guilt over Ishmael's death. Bereaved, baffled by my choices, at the way events played out. At the fact I was unable to heal him as Sebastian does. It seems we share the same gifts, but I'm starting to realize mine are different than his. Perhaps it's because he's a child, perhaps because he's more innocent. Has less blood on his hands." He sighs, raises his coffee but doesn't drink. "Had I allowed him to come along, he could've saved your brother."

Jonas regards the thin Jew, wonders that he's taken responsibility for Ishmael's choices. "We talked about this at his grave," he says. "Ishmael made his own choice. What happened, happened. We knew the risks. He knew the risks."

Igneus says nothing, traces a thin strip of light with his finger. "I have more news," he says. "News that's not going to improve your mood."

"I'm not sure I can feel worse."

"Last night Sebastian saved the woman who killed Ishmael."

Jonas feels his face heat. "What?"

Igneus nods, focuses on the floor. "He says they came to the Temple by helicopter. Says she was on the verge of death. Says he healed her because he didn't have it in him *not* to heal her."

Jonas's chest tightens, his breath comes short and thin. "That bitch should've died," he says. "If I ever see her again, I'll kill her myself."

Igneus's face shows worry, genuine concern for the man who speaks in such blunt nouns.

"So, you're the one who decides who lives and dies?"

"Don't start that, Igneus. If you knew what I'm going through… I'm on the edge, doing everything I can to hold myself back from hunting her down and finishing her. Then, doing the same to that giant, immortal or not."

"It's rage, Jonas. It's darkness tempting you as Christ was tempted in the wilderness."

Jonas places his tongue between his lips and blows a loud, long raspberry.

Igneus blinks at the intrusion, full of childishness, regret, and blistering rage. "In time you'll see you're stronger than this. Your wounds will heal. Do you think Ishmael would approve of you acting like this?"

Jonas stands, moves to the blinds and peers through. Outside, the normal news vans and throng of reporters. He says nothing as his mind turns to his dream. To the names, the symbols. Then, a thought: *The symbols.*

"Your stick was in my dream," he says. "Had symbols on it. Ten of them."

"Symbols of what?"

"Weird stuff. Crickets, frogs, water. That sort of thing."

The staff stands propped in the corner. Igneus hefts it, feels its smoothness in his palm. "Can you remember what they were? All of them?"

"Maybe." Jonas takes a chair, leans forward, closes his eyes, searches his thoughts. He sees Ishmael as a child scampering around the dream's tree. Sees the phlegm flowing from his nose. "Virus was one," he says. "The staff became a tree, then Ishmael watered it and snapped a branch from it. The branch was your stick. Then you came and added the symbols."

"Think, Jonas. What were they?"

Jonas focuses, pushes away thoughts of that woman and the slow death she's earned. He subdues his rage, buries his grief deep down even as fists clench on the table before him. He feels a need for violence. A need to purge his thoughts, and his soul, by exacting great harm.

The feeling isn't foreign despite the fact it's been years since he'd had it. It's a Jekyll and Hyde thing. On the surface he's a normal man, yet in his mind lies a lunatic held by the thinnest of screens. That man is capable of anything, unstoppable. A killing force, a force that never quits. A force that can take anything and dole it back double. Only Ishmael ever knew this side existed, was the only person Jonas trusted enough to share such a powerful, hateful emotion.

With a great force of will, he suppresses the wild man. Focuses his thoughts to relive the dream.

He's surprised it isn't that hard. Surprised when the symbols flare through darkness and pain to shine, flaming and suspended in his mind.

He rattles them off. "FrogShadowWaterChildVirusIceBoil-CricketFlyFlea."

"What?" Igneus stands. "Can you say it again?"

"FrogShadowWaterChildVirusIceBoilCricketFlyFlea."

"Wait, wait, let me write this…" Igneus stops short, stares at his staff. "Where did you get this?"

"The stick? Um, it was our father's. Stayed in a closet for decades both while he lived and after he died. I injured my ankle once playing football and used it to help me walk. I remember my father did the same. It was the family crutch. Just always with us. I have no idea where it came from."

Igneus holds it an inch from his nose, examines it closely. "Looks like it's lacquered. Did you do that?"

"No. Maybe Dad did?"

"Hmm." Igneus places the stick on the couch then goes into the small kitchen. After some rustling and the metallic clink of silverware, he returns with a steak knife.

He moves to the staff, presses the knife to the wood, and stops. "In your dream, where were the symbols?"

"Near the top, flowing in a straight line down the length."

Igneus places the staff over his knees, then scrapes the wood with the knife. Thin, dark shavings fall to the floor around him, then turn a lighter shade as Igneus scrapes through the lacquer.

He stops suddenly, looks up at Jonas. His face is pale, eyes, darting back and forth as if reading invisible script. "I know what this is," he says scraping with haste as wood shavings fly. "And thou shalt take this rod in thine hands, wherewith thou shalt do signs."

"Does it say that?"

"No, just something that came into my head this second. I don't know why, or what it means." With a puff, the dust and shavings fly away. "Are these the symbols you saw?"

Jonas leans over Igneus's shoulder. His eyes widen, his mouth suddenly becomes parched. "How can it be?" he says. "You're playing a game to raise my spirits."

Igneus shakes his head, holds the staff close. "No game," he says. "No trick. These symbols have always been here, but I think your translation is a bit off." He hands the staff to Jonas, then flops back in the chair where he stares at the ceiling, far away in a second.

"I know what it is," Igneus says. "It just doesn't make sense."

CHAPTER 38

JERUSALEM, ISRAEL

I move past the throng of reporters, ignoring their questions. The clamor is harsh; yelling, snapping pictures. Had I known, I would've found a different way. Fortunately, Igneus answers the door quickly, and soon I'm safely inside.

"How's Jonas?"

Igneus frowns and glances over his shoulder. "A little worse for wear. He's dealing with a lot, and I'm just trying to lend support. I think he's particularly vulnerable right now, saying some crazy things. Try not to ask too many questions…if you're capable of that." He grins at me and I grin back. He's become attuned to my nature. Knows I can hardly stop being inquisitive once the bug bites.

We move through the kitchen and into the living room. Jonas sits holding Igneus's walking stick. Staring as if it might impart some profound knowledge from within its dark lacquer.

"I'm so sorry about Ishmael," I say. "He was a good and gracious man."

Jonas's eyes blaze. "What do you know about it?" He stands, squares up.

I take a pace back, glance at Igneus.

"Do you still work for them? Still work for the people that killed Ishmael?"

I swallow hard. "Yes."

"Good. Tell them I'm coming and I'm bringing hell with me."

"They might've beat you to the punch," I say. "They seem well acquainted with hell."

"The better for them."

I'm speechless, searching for soothing words and finding none. "Maybe I should come back another time."

I turn to leave when my arm is gripped in iron. Jonas spins me toward him and leans close. "I consider *you* one of them," he says. "Don't ever show your face around here again. *This* was your freebie. The next time I see you, I *will* kill you."

I gulp and it's audible.

Igneus steps between us. "Maybe you should go, Emery. He doesn't know what he's saying, doesn't know you very well. Come to the Temple in a few days and we'll talk."

I stare at Jonas, not in an effort to gauge his emotional state, but because I'm too afraid to avert my eyes. I've seen what he can do, the speed and agility he possesses. I know if he has a mind, he can snap my neck before Igneus has a chance to stop him.

There's a knock at the door. I keep my eyes on Jonas as Igneus says, "Emery, on your way out, would you mind answering the door and telling them we're not available."

I step back, eye Jonas cautiously. "My pleasure. They were a hard bunch to get through."

I move through the kitchen, pull the front door open. "I'm sorry, but they…"

I stare down the barrel of a short, black rifle, my words choked. The man holding it wears a dark helmet and flak vest, dressed completely in black, a balaclava covering his features. I'm pulled through the door and pushed to the ground. Then, they zip-tie my hands behind my back.

Four large, square vehicles, like modified tanks, line the street. The reporters are nowhere to be seen. Four soldiers scramble over me, and I hear yells and sounds of a struggle from the apartment. Then I'm hefted to my feet and dragged back inside.

Jonas and Igneus sit on the couch, hands behind their backs, zip-tied as well.

I'm thrust next to them.

Four rifles point at us as one of the soldiers speaks into a radio. "Package secured, ready for exfil."

I hear, "Roger," followed by the whir of helicopter blades.

"We're taking a ride, boys," the soldier says. "I hope you packed fresh underwear." He moves to the window, bends the Venetian slats and peers through.

I glance at Igneus, just as Jonas lunges forward.

The first soldier falls with a flash of steel, blood pouring from his throat.

The soldier at the window turns, too late as Jonas slams the steak knife through his eye. Before he can fall though, Jonas pulls him close and spins.

The other two instantly fire.

Rifle exhaust fills the air.

My ears ring.

But the noise and smoke barely effect Jonas, who thrusts the man he's holding into the soldier closest to him. The soldier becomes tangled as he tries to get around his comrade.

Jonas moves to the other with blinding speed.

I hear a grunt, see Jonas drive the steak knife through the man's Adam's apple. The other soldier fires wild, tries to shoot around the man Jonas pushed into him.

Plaster falls as bullets hit the ceiling.

The room fills with a fine dust that mixes with the rifle's smoke.

Jonas flies forward, slips behind the last soldier with dizzying speed.

The soldier's eyes go wide. His limbs jut out, freeze, then twitch.

The rifle drops, then he falls, steak knife protruding from the base of his skull.

Jonas pulls it, cuts us loose, collects the rifles, then relieves the soldiers of their sidearms.

"Put this in your pants," he says, handing me a pistol.

I glance at it, instinctively shake my head.

"Do it! More are coming!"

I try to slide it in my front pocket. "It won't fit."

"He needs a holster, Len," Vince says.

"Probably wouldn't know how to use it," Lenny says.

"Are you a moron?" Jonas says.

"I don't think so," I say, blinking through floating dust, coughing as my eyes water. I don't know why, or really what, the question has to do with anything at all.

"Tuck it in your belt," he says, then thrusts a rifle in my hands. "Do you know how to work this?"

"No."

He pulls something that responds with a neat *shnick*. A bullet flies out. "It's loaded and ready." He points to the side of the weapon. "Safety is here. You'll use that later, after we kill all these fuckers."

I start to argue but realize I have no words. I'm completely unprepared for a discussion on weapons and the killing of fuckers. I do have a thought about his use of *we*, as if *we* indicates *we're both* ready to kill or be killed. As if *we* means he and I have joined forces.

I look for a way out, see nothing.

Then Igneus steps forward, stick in hand.

The wall behind him disintegrates, launches him across the room to impact the far wall and crumple to the floor.

Gunfire erupts around us.

Jonas shoves me behind the couch. "Stay!" Then he moves forward, eyes crazed, rifle tucked to his shoulder and at eye level.

I hear the impact as the rifle barks. A body falls, then the guttural sounds of someone's death.

I venture a peek over the couch, see at least four soldiers peer around the kitchen door.

A hail of shrapnel shreds the couch's cheap fabric.

The small glass table shatters, holes appear in the wall next to Igneus.

I move to the Jew, crawling, yelling, "Cover me," as I go. I hope Jonas knows what that means. I've only heard it on TV but believe it apt for situations like this.

Jonas moves right, gunfire follows.

He's looking for a better angle, simultaneously drawing fire away from me and Igneus.

Igneus lies unconscious. I'd say dead, but I know he can't die. A trickle of blood rolls from his mouth.

Then, he sits forward, gasping and coughing like an old tractor. His eyes roll back. Out again.

I lift his thin body, hustle up the hall toward the back bedroom.

He wakes. "Emery, what are you doing?"

"We're being attacked," I say as fast as I'm able. "We, specifically, are being attacked."

"Cain?"

"Maybe, but I don't think so. These guys are pros. I saw three flags: US, German, and French."

"Where's my staff?"

I look around. "I don't know. Jesus, does it matter? We need to get out of here. Is there a back way?"

He rubs his chest and grimaces. "Not that I know of."

"A window?"

Jonas sprints in, flings a mattress against the open door. I notice this bedroom has no door, just an opening. "These fucking guys, man," he says, muttering, crazed. "They picked the wrong day." He yells down the hall. "You picked the wrong day, assholes! Come in here and see what I've got."

I look to see what he's got, but see only the rifle, another slung on his back, two pistols jutting from his waistband. "What do we have?"

He holds my eyes for a second. "Shut up," he says, "and get down."

I hunker down, pull Igneus close. "I'm alright, Emery," the Jew says. "I need my staff."

"Are you crazy? We need to get out of here. We can come back for the stick."

"No," he says, "we can't. We don't have a chance without it."

Jonas points the rifle over the mattress, sprays a volley of bullets down the hall.

Then, things go quiet.

I feel a sense of hope. "I think you got 'em," I say. "Good shot."

As the words leave my mouth, an explosion rocks the building.

Plaster caves in as the whole place goes to shit.

Then, the ceiling collapses, rains furniture from upstairs in an odd sort of hail. A desk, small gray divan, matching ottoman, plaster, wood, an end table; all crash and splinter around us.

Igneus stands. "I need the staff," he says, stumbling toward the door.

He's wavering, off-balance.

"Your bell's rung," I say. "Sit."

"Where's your rifle?" Jonas asks.

I nod toward the living room. "Out there."

He tosses me the one he's holding. "Remember what I showed you?"

"Yes. Is it ready to fire?"

"Just aim and squeeze the trigger," he says, "and I wouldn't spend too much time aiming. Just don't shoot us."

I nod, swallow hard, think of Rhyme and how scared she'd be if she were here. I must survive, if for no other reason than to tell her the story of my heroics.

I stand, twist my face to a snarl that fails to buoy my mood.

I'm no soldier, no killer.

I'm a journalist. Maybe I can disarm them with questions. "Let's get the stick," I say.

I feel like a tough guy.

"He's an idiot," says Lenny.

"Right you are!" says Vince.

Jonas kicks some rubble, heaves aside the furniture. "Help me clear this. More are coming."

I move to help. "How many?"

"Like I know? Just stay alert. If we can get the stick, Igneus will do the rest."

"Okay," I say, feeling the farthest from okay as I throw debris from our path.

Jonas peers around the door. "I think this is going to get ugly."

I stare at him, think of the man knifed in the eye, the one knifed in the throat. How can it get uglier?

"You go first," Jonas says. "Stay low and I'll shoot anything that moves. If you stand too tall, that'll include you."

"Okay," I say, feeling less okay by the second.

I move into the hall and expect to be mowed down.

But no fire comes. *Bruce Willis*, DIE HARD *shit,* I think, *yippee ki yay!*

Jonas prods me and I step forward. "Faster," he whispers, and I move quickly into the living room, keeping as low as possible.

Broken glass, shards of plaster, and various furniture items are all piled, barely discernible within the fog of dust and rifle smoke.

I step over fallen soldiers and gag a little. "I don't see it."

Jonas moves past, focused on the kitchen. "Find it. We don't have time."

I drop to my knees, crawl around like a child. It has to be on the floor, I reason, or under one of these piles. Then a thought hits me. "Maybe they took it."

Jonas stays focused on the kitchen. "Doubtful," he says. "I killed them all. It's here. Find it."

I double my efforts, throw debris like a dog digging a hole.

Then I see the tip sticking from under the upturned couch. I scramble to it, pull it loose. "Got it!"

"Great. Get going."

I rush to the back room, notice other rooms are completely caved in.

Jonas says, "Contact," and I hear his rifle chatter.

I'm scampering now, on hands and knees, keeping low, dragging the stick along.

I enter the room where we left Igneus and hold up the stick like I've caught a prize catfish.

Igneus smiles, raises his hand, tries to stand.

Another wall disintegrates.

The concussion strikes me like being drop kicked by Zeus himself. I rocket through the door, slam into the hallway to splat like a bug on a windshield.

Breath vanishes.

My neck and back sizzle.

My legs feel swarmed by bees.

A warm liquid runs down my back, and I know it's my own blood.

Vision wavers.

Jonas steps in view, fires up the hall, talks shit the whole time. "Jerk-offs! Want some of this? How about this?" He's even with the door from which I just flew, pulls two pistols, fires both like a B-movie gunslinger, toward the kitchen and into the room where Igneus sits.

I try to stand but can't move my arms. Try to yell, but my throat refuses.

Where's Igneus? Did he survive the blast?

Jonas keeps firing. His eyes blaze with rage. "This is for Ishmael," he says. "And this is for Emery."

Uh oh, he thinks I'm dead.

Do I look that bad?

I try to raise my hand, but my head falls on my chest instead. I lack the strength to lift it, realize I can't feel anything below my nipples.

I stare at the worn carpet, at littered shell casings, at other people's furniture and shards of debris. Rhyme comes to me with emerald eyes and an expression of pure radiance. I realize I'm dying.

I try to channel the magic of Igneus and Sebastian. My message has to be clear. Has to be strong. I scream, "I love you, Rhyme," but the only sound is from the depths of my soul, the shadows of my thoughts.

I focus hard, paralyzed, terrified, using the Force. I've become Jasper the idiot Jedi, too weak to lift my head, using a fictional energy to bid farewell to my life's love.

"We'll tell her," Vince says.

"Yeah, Em, least we can do."

CHAPTER 39

JERUSALEM, ISRAEL

Longinus hears the choppers but doesn't see them.

Sima lies next to him, nude, sweating, breathless. "You're so delicious."

He rises, moves fully nude to the window of the small apartment.

Silhouettes are dark against the rising sun.

No helicopters should be flying right now, certainly not anything from Israel's arsenal.

"Get dressed, love. I smell trouble."

He slides on a pair of sweatpants, grabs his spear, goes outside in bare feet.

The helos move in a wide circle, as if combing the area, searching.

Across the street, a helicopter rises above a yellow, three-story building.

A smoky plume bursts from its underside.

Longinus dives sideways as a missile obliterates the ground where he stood. The force adds speed to his motion, causes him to roll until he gains his feet.

He sprints to the building, meets Sima entering the hallway. "What's going on?"

"Stay put. I'll be back."

"Not on your life."

He pauses mid stride. "What?"

"If you're going, so am I."

He glances down the short alcove into the street. Two helos land and troops pour out. "Stay put."

"Never."

Anger rears, is quickly subdued by his emotions for her. "Can you at least wait until I come back with a weapon?"

She smiles, steps forward to press her bare breasts against him. "I guess so," she says. "But don't be too long."

He steps from the building and levels his spear.

Jagged lightning streams. The chopper explodes to flaming rubble.

The sound deafens.

Longinus laughs.

People race by, desperate, running like chickens from a fox.

He turns to another helo, raises his spear.

Bullets impact around him, some find their mark and steal his breath. From the right, soldiers approach, fire, move, and seek cover. He levels the spear and lightning flies.

The screams are gorgeous.

Seventeen soldiers on the ground with two more helos somewhere.

Shouldn't take long, he thinks, not with this weapon.

Golden hues turn the smoke a bright yellow. He sprints through a small courtyard and into the apartment's parking lot, away from Sima.

Before him two helicopters surprise, swooping low and firing their cannons.

He drops. His chest burns. He tries to stand, but one leg doesn't work and the other's a bloody mess.

Ignoring the pain, he presses erect.

Gunfire swarms. Slams him back down.

Fingers claw asphalt as he drags himself behind the concrete base of a tall light pole.

The spear rises, shakes in his grasp, as lightning jolts from its gleaming tip.

He feels weak, shaky, watches the spear fall from a hand that refuses to grip it further.

Bullets ricochet, spark in glinting gold as the relic skitters across the lot.

The shooting stops.

Helos cruise over with a whir and rush of wind.

Blackness surrounds, engulfs, consumes.

CHAPTER 40

UNDISCLOSED LOCATION

"We got him, sir. The spear's in our custody."

People whoop and slap backs. The president stares at infrared monitors.

A man lies still as stone, glows shades of red and orange at the base of a light pole in the parking lot's center.

Others approach, and Tom knows them to be friendlies. "Job well done, everyone. My thanks to all on behalf of a grateful nation." The troops love that line. He grins, looks to his aide. "What about the other guy? The one we really want."

A smoldering building appears on the other monitor. "We've had a few friendly casualties here," the aide says. "I'm not sure what went wrong, but we had to take down almost the whole building. We've been watching for a while, keeping our troops back, but we've seen no movement and presume our target dead."

"Excellent," Carpenter says. "Did they get the weapon?"

"Not yet, sir. Waiting for the fire to calm."

"Get them in there! There's nothing more important and there's no time to waste." Frustration rises but he tamps it down. Patience, he thinks. Let the strategy do the work, let the soldiers do their job. Stick to the strategy.

"Just gave the order," the aide says, "shouldn't be a minute."

Carpenter nods, looks at a screen blazing harsh yellow and orange, the heat signature of approaching soldiers. No, this shouldn't take long at all, and when it's done, they'll have not one, but two, powerful new weapons. *Then what, Cain?*

Suddenly the screen goes white, washes out the entire picture.

"What's going on?"

"I don't know, sir. Checking now, perhaps a technical…"

Her words trail off as she raises a hand to her earpiece. She nods, turns to the president.

"Something just blew up."

"What did?"

"Um, a helicopter, sir. It seems a helicopter. Still waiting for a sitrep from the ground."

The whiteness on the monitor fades as Tom leans in.

Slowly, the picture takes shape.

The building isn't on fire anymore, but half of it's gone.

Helicopters burn in the road, bodies lie in the street.

Along the street, sitting cockeyed, Mine Resistant Ambush Protected vehicles burn as well. Called MRAPs by the troops, these are known to take tremendous damage and still function.

"What's going on?" he says. "I need a situation report."

"I don't know, sir. We've lost comms."

"Impossible, we have the best equipment, the best force, the best everything."

The aide says nothing, jabs at the keyboard. "Maybe a glitch. We'll get them back."

Tom looks to the other screen, the force sent to capture Longinus. "At least that went smooth…" Then, the words catch in his throat. The man who'd been lying inert only a few moments earlier is gone, replaced by unmoving bodies.

"What's this?" Carpenter asks. "What happened?"

"Stand by."

Tom feels the first drop of sweat run down his back as seconds pass. "Someone turn up the AC!"

"They're gone, sir. All our operatives are down. I'm unsure if they're dead or alive, but I'm getting no response of any kind."

Tom trades his stare between the screens.

This is horrible.

Impossible.

They couldn't have known we were coming, and even if they did, the operatives are so specialized, so skilled, two men, even heavily armed, wouldn't be much of a problem for the teams.

The heat in his armpits trace its way to his core. A bead of sweat breaks over his brow. This is going to be a political mess and will certainly ruin his chances at re-election. He *has* to bring it back, *has* to get it in order and save the mission.

Only one thing to do, he thinks. A gamble, but worth it if he can save face.

He turns to the aide, leans close. "Executive order," he says. "Send all assets."

"All of them, sir?"

"Did I stutter?"

CHAPTER 41

JERUSALEM, ISRAEL

Igneus steps through the rubble, through a gaping hole big enough to fit a jet liner. The street is silent, filled with smoke, littered with debris and the odor of burning things.

Jonas changes magazines, slaps the side of the rifle. *Kachink.* "More coming."

"From where? I don't…" The sky fills with choppers. Then, from down the street, bursting through a cloud of wafting smoke, three more MRAPs appear, behind them other trucks in khaki green. They skid to a stop and a line of soldiers pour out, more than Igneus can count.

Jonas presses against the dilapidated building's wall. "I'm guessing from that direction," he says. "Where's your stick?"

Igneus looks to the hole they just came through. "In there. I lost it."

"Are you any good without it?"

"Don't know, probably not." He nods at the rifle. "I've never fired one of those."

"Follow me and don't fall behind. I don't think we're going to last long." Jonas turns to re-enter the building.

"Looks like it's going to fall on our heads."

Jonas glances up. "Maybe. I hope it doesn't, but maybe. There's a reason these guys are here. They want something, probably your stick if I have to guess. I doubt they'll use any more hard ordnance because it'll decrease the possibility of getting the thing. If the building collapses, they'll have virtually no chance of finding it. I'll mount a defense here—you go get the damn staff!"

Igneus peers into what's left of the building.

Fires burn where fires shouldn't, most of the structure has collapsed.

"Where's Emery?" Igneus asks.

The response is short, clipped. "Dead. Blowed up."

Igneus blinks, looks into the building, into Emery's tomb as grief stabs his heart. "We have to go to the Temple."

"You're kidding."

"No, it's all that makes sense. Sebastian is there and might need our help. The staff is lost."

Jonas leans around jagged concrete, fires a quick burst. "You want to take all this," he motions around, "there?"

"It's all I can think of. Maybe we can get Emery—Sebastian can heal him."

"I told you he's dead, but even if he isn't, we're not going back to get him. But getting to Sebastian is something I can get behind. Follow me."

Jonas races across a grassy area to the next building. Igneus follows, runs fast, ignores the surrounding force. He feels useless without his staff.

Gunfire chases. Helicopters circle. Then an aircraft bolts overhead with a deafening roar. Gunfire blisters the ground around them: *burrrt.*

"Great," Jonas says, "A-10s."

"What's that?"

He peers at the sky. "More than we can handle."

Chapter 42

Undisclosed Location

The monitor wobbles as Carpenter taps the screen. "Here! This guy! Get this guy!"

"On it, sir." The aide speaks into her mouthpiece, "Two subjects left the building moving north. Priority targets. Dead or alive. Repeat, priority targets."

She nods. "Done."

Carpenter leans back, mind racing. It's going sideways, going to shoveled shit, as his grandfather liked to say. Options flood his mind, fear grips his soul. If this isn't handled soon, he'll not be able to explain it away. Not to allies, nor the Congress or the Senate, nor the American people. And in an election year. He stares at the screen, whips his mind for other options, something outside the box.

A figure moves in infrared, small, running.

Tom squints. "Is that a child?"

The aide pauses, leans close. "I think so. Probably scared and looking for a place to hide. I'll tell the assets to avoid the building."

"Nonsense," Carpenter says, "if that kid ain't smart enough to be out of there, he gets what he gets. Continue as planned."

"But sir…"

"He's a combatant until proven otherwise. Our diplomats will handle the rest. Do as I say."

The aide looks down, sighs quietly. "Roger that."

I open my eyes to cherubic features. Sebastian's smile, eyes alive with youth and excitement. "How do you feel?"

It takes me a moment to answer as I survey my broken body.

I ask my legs to move, and they do. I lift my head easily; see the blood-soaked shirt I wear. Sebastian helps me stand, and to my surprise I feel energized and strong.

"I feel good, Sebastian. Thank you."

"Where's Dad?"

"I don't know. I was knocked out, maybe even dead. Was I dead?"

"I don't think so, maybe close, but I don't think you died. I don't think I can help the dead."

"Well, that's comforting."

Vince and Lenny cheer as Sebastian's smile brightens my day. "We'll head to the Temple. If Dad went anywhere, it's there."

"Can't you do your mind reading thing and ask?"

He shakes his head. "Tried it and nothing. Is he injured, do you know? Maybe if he's unconscious, it doesn't work."

"I don't know," I say, trying to sound like the adult in the conversation. "Seems like the Temple is a dangerous place to go, especially if they're being hunted. We should hideout here and wait. You know they'll come back for us."

Bullets strike the wall beside me. I knock Sebastian down as I dive for cover.

Up the hallway, shadowed figures move through debris and furniture and flame.

"On second thought, let's go to the Temple."

Sebastian's eyes light up, then he rolls to his left, rummages in a pile of debris.

He pulls the staff free and beams. "We have to even the odds. Let's go."

We sprint from the building, gunfire harsh and cackling behind. Jets, loud and large, fly by, scare the shit out of me with each pass. I can't hear them approach and don't know if it's because of the low altitude or the speed at which they move. They have a shark's face painted on their noses and are simply terrifying.

The ground shakes, dirt flies through clotted air.

I lead the way, hug the building as I go, round a corner to see Igneus and Jonas sprint through a courtyard and disappear behind another apartment building.

"There," Sebastian points. I yell after them but can't wait for a response as explosions rattle the ground, rattle my head, shred my nerves.

To our left, soldiers sprint toward us.

Behind us, more soldiers pick their way through toppled furniture and caved plaster.

"We have to move," I say, pointing. "Run to that building as fast as you can. Your dad and Jonas went that way."

Before I can say anything else, Sebastian sprints away, runs in a crazy zig zag pattern that appears comical but seems effective.

Bullets whiz past, strike the ground, careen from brick walls. Either he's extremely lucky or extremely smart.

I sprint forward, zigging as he zigged, zagging as he zagged. Bullets ricochet, whistle past. To my right, a topiary explodes; to my left, a parking lot with smoking black holes.

Then I'm at the building, breathing hard, not in the shape I thought I was.

Sebastian pokes his head from an alcove. "I don't see them."

"Keep going."

He sprints forward, stays close to the building as jets scream overhead, belching their payload with terrifying efficiency. *Burrrt.*

I realize they're not shooting at us, but at Jonas and Igneus.

"Sebastian! Follow the jets! They'll lead to your dad!" Then, I have a thought. "Can you use the stick?"

"What?"

I nod to the staff he holds. "The stick? Can you use it like your dad does?"

"No such luck."

"How do you know? Have you tried?"

He gives me a frustrated look. "I know, Mr. Emery."

He sprints away, crooked staff at his side, occasionally looking to the sky and adjusting his course. The kid is fast, and I have trouble catching him.

Then a helicopter appears like an angry black hornet.

"Sebastian!"

It opens fire.

Sebastian skids to his right, disappears inside the building as rounds hit the wall and send a hail of stone and mortar.

Seconds later, I enter the complex but don't see him. I'm in a reception area of sorts, three long halls going off in different directions. I hear chasing soldiers, know I have only seconds.

"Mr. Emery, this way!"

I sprint toward the voice as a hurricane of gunfire shreds the well-appointed lobby.

He waits at the end of the hall, peers through a double glass door.

"They're after *us* now," I say.

"How do you know?"

Gunfire shatters the glass door.

"Just a guess."

Undisclosed Location

"The child has the weapon, sir. Seems they're making a run somewhere. There's a man with him."

Carpenter stares at the screen, watches the two disappear into a building as an A-10 streaks by.

"Can you pan out?"

"Roger."

The view widens and Tom smiles. Soldiers approach from every direction. "We've got them," he says. "Finally." He turns to the aide. "Secure the relic and dispatch the kid and the man."

"Dispatch, sir?"

"Oh, I'm sorry to use such big words. How's this? *Kill. Them.* Does that clear it up?"

"Yes sir. What about the other guy?"

Tom glances at the other monitor, the one where Longinus has disappeared. "Find them. Kill them. Get the weapon. No loose ends. End this."

The aide frowns. "Roger that, sir."

Chapter 43

Darkness throbs as flickering embers dance on stone walls. The cave is huge, brims with fear. Despair grips in a frigid embrace.

He's in a cavern thousands of feet tall. Stalactites, as large as mountains, hang from the stone above to stretch to the ground.

For the second time in his long life, he feels small. "Hello!" Thundering bass resounds from surrounding rock, bounds into the distance, then fades away.

He steps forward, starts to jog. *Must be an end to this, must be some way out.*

His skin prickles. Sweat blooms as his face flushes.

He removes his suit jacket, tosses it aside.

A thin glimmer appears, dances, grows bright as he closes.

Then he's there, stepping out, high above the landscape, thousands of feet in the air.

His breath catches, awed by pure wonder, glorious magnificence.

Mountains rise, break a dark horizon to sharp points beneath a sky of streaking flame and smoldering shadow.

He peers over the edge.

A sword appears in his hand.

He holds it before him, watches his hands grow, feels his suit tighten, stretch, then tear away in billowing fabric.

Armor clamps in gleaming gold. A thick breastplate subdues the heat as a helmet closes over his head, stretches as if made of liquid gold to send a thin strip over his nose. Two strips grow from the helmet's side, become shields that cover his jaw.

He raises the sword, smiles broadly as flames leap, bustle, glow and shimmer.

Then he grows, so large, so fast, he has to bend to stay within the space on the cliff's edge.

He is Longinus of Misthli. Longinus, the Giant. Longinus, Centurion of Rome. Longinus, the Barbaric.

He leaps into the abyss. Falls, unafraid, streams toward the chasm's floor like a meteor, streaking for minutes toward the ground as the landscape becomes blistered blurs and smoking tendrils. Flames trail from his feet as if the speed of descent has ignited him.

Leathery birds with vast wings veer toward him. Perhaps twenty of them, bigger than him by hundreds of yards.

Angled wings dive in a blistering descent. A large beak opens and snaps. Razor teeth drip blood as eyes like hollow ash never waver.

He raises the sword, swings through an easy arc.

The squawk is deafening, ear-splitting. Its echo, answered by hundreds of other creatures.

The bird goes limp, head sliced crossways and falling separately.

Below, lakes of fire ripple and rage. Blood and lava flow from rocky precipice, stain ragged heights with strips of molten crimson. Billions of people cower, wail in darkness and flame within the smoking, heartless inferno.

On his feet, stout boots appear in gold. He realizes he's unafraid as he blazes toward the expanse's floor.

He lands in a sizzling cloud of flame.

The ground splinters as the impact squelches sounds of horror and misery.

He steps forward.

Billions scatter, scream, trample.

He likes the feeling, the hysteria.

"Ah, dear Longinus," a voice says. "Won't you join us?"

A man appears in a perfect red suit. He sits in a large chair whose back towers above in razor points. His feet rest on a stool of skulls. His face is bearded, gray, as sharp eyes beckon.

To his left, a woman kneels like a dog, a chain of fire flows from the man to a tether around her neck. She rises and smiles. "Join us, love."

Her hair is black, glowing and alive.

The tether disappears.

She wears a red corset now. Her skirt is short, plaid, in red and green, above fishnet stockings that rise to mid-thigh, attached by garters. Spikes appear on her shoulders as a flaming dagger forms in her hand. Stiletto heels click as she walks toward him. She is languid, oozes sexuality and passion's vibrance.

It's Sima.

A delicate hand traces the outline of a nipple on his breastplate.

She leans in and takes him in a long kiss.

Muscles bulge as he scoops her in his arms where she cuddles and coos.

He turns to the man. "And who might ye be?"

The man bows, spritely for someone so aged. "I, dear Longinus, am the giver of gifts." He pauses, holds the Roman's eyes. "I am the wielder of sacrilege. The liberator of blasphemous tongues." He chuckles, presses a fist to his lips. "I am that *thing* feared in the night. Although, I should be equally feared in the day." A closed fist absorbs his laughter. He straightens, tugs at his lapel, returns a smile, kind and wise. "For you, I'll serve as a guide of sorts. Long have I watched and yearned for this meeting."

"'Tis a merry way to greet an ally," Longinus says. Sima nuzzles, purrs into his chest.

"Indeed, it is, my prince, and a fraction of what you've earned. As you are feared in life, so shall you be feared in death."

Longinus steps forward. "Anon and agin, I can non die."

"Tut, tut, of course you can. You're human, aren't you? Most certainly, you can die. It's just been suspended for now. Postponed, if you will. Perhaps you'll never die, perhaps someday you will. The future is unwritten. Your fate, undecided."

He rises, moves close, flicks his head.

Sima disappears.

Longinus leaps back, raises his sword. "Battle?"

The man chuckles again. "Nonsense, lad." He waves a hand. "It's true no force on Earth can subdue you and your relic. But here, I am the master, and you, my faithful servant. Perhaps you should ask Cain. He serves me, as you serve him. Take heart, my menacing Roman, my colossal general, you're a crown prince soon to take the throne. An heir to greatness, a harbinger of doom. The face of hysteria, of chaos, of malice, is called Longinus." He snickers again and tugs at his tie.

"And ye be?"

His eyes grow with surprise. "Oh! How very rude of me. I enjoy these theatrics so much; I sometimes forget my manners." He sweeps an arm in grand style. "I am Lucifer," he says. "Iblis. Satan. And I am very glad to meet you."

He chuckles as he strolls through a river of lava to emerge uninjured on the other side. "Come."

Longinus glances at the river, then wades in. It tickles, sends a pleasant sensation through his groin. He falls in pace with Lucifer as the sword disappears, as gleaming armor becomes a suit of the finest weave, thin pinstripes in subdued red on a background of darkest maroon.

"I'm giving you Sima as a gift. She's quite attached to you, you know. But she comes with a warning." He raises a finger, glances at the Roman. "She's not all she appears. You should've seen her when I found her. Alone, terrified, suffering long nights of torment, shrieking to an uncaring God, begging release from the clutches and inclinations of her dastardly father. Poor thing.

"It was then I sent one to assist. She was utterly alone, you see. Her mother knew but rendered no aid. Her sisters knew but were too glad they'd outgrown him to help her."

"Sundamir," Longinus says.

"Yes, a guest of ours now. He's being treated to some of our finest, let's say, frustrations. Sometimes, Aesma, your Sima, returns to participate. It seems for Sundamir, there are some sins for which you never stop paying."

Longinus's laugh is long and joyous. "I'be keen to fill me eye with that."

"Of course you would, but one must be careful with Aesma. Her lust is unquenchable. Her wrath, without bounds of mercy or temperance. Nor is it diminished by the tempests of time." He stops, seems to turn at random, then points into mists of flickering shadow. "Watch."

The landscape disappears as Longinus looks on his own form, bleeding, helpless, unconscious at the base of the parking lot's light pole.

Twenty soldiers surround. "Find the spear," one says. Then, suddenly, it appears in his chest.

He grasps the shaft, drops to his knees, topples sideways.

The rest turn, raise their rifles.

Sima faces them with eyes of fire, dagger in hand. "Step. Away. From. Him."

They open fire instead.

She moves like elegant flame, red mist trailing, swirling behind. Then, she's among them, dagger spinning, tumbling, slicing. A whirlwind of razor steel and molten rage.

The dead lay at her feet as a helicopter bears down and angles for a shot.

Sima leaps thirty feet, catches a landing skid, then flips up and into the aircraft.

The helicopter skittles, dives, then rears abruptly and gains altitude. Then, it rotates in a slow hover, gradually gains speed, spins like a top until it falls.

Sima leaps from it, lands with the elegance of a ballerina as it crashes to the ground in a rolling ball of flame and smoke.

Longinus stares, awed, mouth watering. She's pure grace, pure wrath.

She kneels next to his body, lays a hand on his chest, kisses him gently. "Longinus, my love, come back to me. I'm waiting."

Longinus turns to Lucifer.

"Treat her well, but with caution," Lucifer says, then fades to darkness.

<hr>

His eyes pop open at Sima's kiss.

He pulls her close, devours her mouth, feels her body relax, her passions inflame. He grasps both sides of her head, holds her an inch away, stares into her eyes, whispers. "I love you, little demon."

She beams, collapses onto him. "And I, you."

CHAPTER 44

JERUSALEM, ISRAEL

Igneus skids to a halt, tilts his head in a peculiar way.

"Why'd you stop?" Jonas asks.

"Sebastian isn't at the Temple."

He sprints back the way they'd come.

Jonas pops the magazine from the rifle, checks his ammo. Half a clip here, one mag left after this. Need more ammo.

He straps the weapon over his back, pulls two revolvers from his waistband, and races after Igneus.

Igneus rounds a corner and stops dead in his tracks. Before him, a scene of flying lead and roaring aircraft.

Sebastian huddles next to a dried-up fountain. Beside him, Emery stares at the sky, cringes with every gunshot, shirt covered in blood.

Helicopters circle but hold their fire as jets scream their wrath to the day.

Soldiers approach from all sides.

They're surrounded, he and the boy, pinned down. It's just a matter of time.

Jonas flies past, pistols blazing as he races to the courtyard.

Soldiers fall, others scatter for cover.

Igneus bolts for Sebastian.

Bullets whiz with a keen whine as helicopters circle and close. Then his leg fills with fire. He stumbles, falls headlong to roll through the grass.

He tries to stand, but legs refuse. He crawls, calls to Sebastian.

Then Jonas is over him, pouring fire, it seems, in every direction. The man's a machine, moves with fluid grace and balance. An artist, changing clips, firing with precision, war as his medium.

He kneels, pushes Igneus's head down. "You're hit! Stay down! I've got this!"

<hr>

The scene clears. The kid and the man trapped behind a low wall next to a fountain. The others have doubled back and now one of them is hit. The child has the relic.

"This is it," Carpenter says, "concentrate all firepower on that area. Kill all of them, get the relic, and get out of there before it gets worse."

"Yes, sir," the aide says, then repeats the order into her mouthpiece.

Carpenter calls for a cup of coffee, then leans back and clasps his hands behind his head. It's done, we got the important one and can take our time getting the other.

Then the screen goes white again.

He jolts forward.

The aide squints at the screen. "Sir," she says, "I think it just got worse."

<hr>

I pull Sebastian close, then hunker as the world fills with bullets and blistering sound. Wind rushes over as jets scream by. Whining shrapnel splinters the low wall around us.

"You should split." It's Lenny.

"A stunning treatise on the obvious, Em," Vince says. "Better get going."

I peek over, see at least fifty soldiers, all firing, moving toward us.

Rotors buffet like a hurricane as a helicopter hovers not twenty feet before me. I wish for Longinus, for his protective purple haze.

But today, I've no such savior.

The helo floats in blackness, an enraged wasp. I see turrets, pods of missiles, find myself wondering which they'll use to end us. I wonder if I'll hear the one that kills me.

Sebastian wriggles beneath me. "Stay down, Sebastian," I say. "I'll handle this."

I have no idea how to handle this. No idea what to do. I raise my hands but stay crouched near the wall as rotor wash threatens to send me tumbling like a weed.

On the ground, the soldiers sprint toward us, rifles raised, bullets popping.

"They're not trying to capture us," Sebastian screams. "They're trying to *kill us!*"

I lean close, grab the stick, heft it in his face. "Only *this* will save us, and only *you* have a chance to make it work. Concentrate or whatever, but get this thing working."

He nods, then his eyes go wide.

He pops up, surrounded by flying metal, raises the stick, then throws it with all his strength.

Oh God! He thinks throwing the thing away will convince the soldiers to let us live.

My insides plunge as I follow the staff's trajectory.

"Why did..." I scream.

Then, everything changes.

CHAPTER 45

JERUSALEM, ISRAEL

I follow the trajectory, see the staff pinwheel through the grass.

Then my eyes refocus, and my brain absorbs the full sight.

Jonas stands over Igneus, arms spread, firing dual pistols.

Igneus sees the stick twenty feet from him, lying between us. He, injured, crawls toward it, scrapes forward inch by inch.

Sebastian drops beside me, screams, "Dad! Get it!"

Fire spits from Jonas's pistols, then he drops them and flips the rifle from his back.

Soldiers approach from all sides, some fall as others advance.

Above me, the helicopter sweeps its turrets toward my friends. Then, six more join and surround us in a hovering circle.

Sebastian wriggles from my grip, sprints across the grass to slide next to the staff like he just stole second base.

A bullet grazes my chest and I cry out.

Sebastian stands, levels the staff.

Jonas takes a knee, fiddles with the rifle.

Igneus struggles forward, looks gaunter than ever as blood soaks his pants.

The heat blisters as one of the helicopters explodes in a massive fireball.

I look to Sebastian, who stands stunned in the middle of the lawn.

The bolt didn't come from the staff he holds.

Jonas pops up, rifle unjammed, fires at the enemy. Empty casings spin through the air and fall to the ground.

Sebastian raises his arms, levels the staff again.

Igneus has found his feet, tries to run. "Sebastian!"

From behind a jet bears down.

I yell, but there's no time.

Igneus turns as if sensing the danger, but too late. The shark-nosed craft has him in its sights.

I watch the turrets spin, wait to see him pulverized, to hear the *burrt* of his annihilation. I wonder how long it takes for an immortal to puzzle their parts back together.

Then, a bolt of lightning sizzles to send the craft flaming to Earth.

Igneus looks perplexed, turns toward the lightning's source.

The Roman appears, golden spear held high, wafting the slightest tendrils of smoke.

Behind him, Sima holds a bloody dagger, wears a broad smile.

Jonas levels his weapon, fires, but his rounds are spent.

He drops the rifle and sprints toward Longinus.

A sizzling bolt sends him tumbling across the lawn.

Sebastian holds the staff aloft, faces the onslaught as Igneus limps toward him.

Angelic features twist to a snarl.

Longinus smirks and levels his spear.

All wasps rotate, then expel their ordnance on Sebastian and Igneus.

The sound invades my ears, rattles my teeth, makes me cower as low as possible.

An A-10 fires at Longinus.

I watch him fly, then turn to see clotted smoke where Igneus and Sebastian stood.

My ears ring, dirt and grass freckle my face and arms.

Longinus lies motionless, smoke rising like steam from a kettle.

Then he stands, rubs his chest. Eyes blaze as muscles bulge.

He raises the spear.

The wasps continue the downpour of missile and shrapnel.

Thick smoke streams from giant hands as the spear sizzles, as muscles grow taut, quiver, bulge. His face is a mix of rage and concentration.

A swift wind cuts war's fog.

Igneus stands as lightning streams from Longinus's spear.

The world comes crashing down.

Whistling fire, bullets, missile, earth, in all directions.

Six helicopters explode in unison, raining debris, twisted metal and burning corpses.

Approaching soldiers glow, then fly, some knocked from their very boots.

Longinus turns to Igneus as lightning flows from the spear.

Igneus takes it head on, one hand outstretched, the other clasped with Sebastian.

He glows blinding white, courses with power as beams shoot from his head, from his eyes, from his mouth and nose, absorbing the energy, holding it, channeling.

Fire sizzles from his staff, sends Longinus rolling to smash against the pocked brick of a nearby building.

Then, silence filled with only the whining pitch in my ears.

Jonas lies unmoving.

Igneus collapses as if overcome by the effort.

Sebastian kneels beside, tugs his shirt, gauges his consciousness.

Behind them I see a shadow, a being of some sort.

Sima appears and sprints for Sebastian.

I jolt forward, try to reach him first.

Then she changes direction and tackles me broadside.

I tumble away as she gains her feet like a panther then blazes past.

I reach out and catch her foot.

She goes sprawling. I leap atop.

With a flash of steel, the dagger penetrates my chest.

Breath runs. I can't inhale fully.

She grins as if enjoying my struggle, then licks her lips, rises and stalks toward the boy.

"No!" I rasp, leaping forward. I'll not let her kill him, not let her destroy the one innocent thing left on the planet. I'm fed up with death. Have had enough of fear and helplessness.

As long as I *can* breathe, even a molecule, I'll fight.

I tackle her, use my weight to pin her down.

"He's gonna get his ass kicked by a girl."

"She's a real spark plug, Lenny!"

Sima struggles like a crazy person, writhing, slippery, arms lashing at any target, my eyes, my throat, my gut. I feel the dagger bite, feel my skin split as it slashes.

I duck the next few blows, manage to catch her wrists and pull her arms apart.

My head throbs, my body screams for just a single breath.

We're at an impasse, her struggling, as I hold as best I can.

Strength and breath diminish, vision starts to fade. I can't keep her much longer.

I rear back and smash my forehead into her nose.

She goes limp, drops the dagger, unconscious.

I topple sideways, straining for air, blood running over my face and down my arms. I plead for strength as small fires burn around me, as the wind howls in moaning petulance.

Then, Longinus stands over me, spear raised, framed by blue sky. He's a mountain range. His neck, a tree trunk. His arms, twin V-8 engines humming with strength. Eyes burn as teeth flash through snarled lips, and inexplicably, I wonder how many have seen this same portrait in their last seconds.

"You're in trouble now!"

"Em, I think he's pissed."

"I told ye to non be meddlin'," Longinus says.

Now, I've seen the Roman angry, but this expression holds a far greater emotion. One of sorrow, pity, even love.

The spear sparks, writhes in his grasp as smoke foams through thick fingers.

I can't raise my arms, can't roll sideways, can't draw a breath.

My vision fills with the buzzing lights of a million fireflies.

I accept my fate, my coming doom.

It's over.

I close my eyes and wait for the relic to end me. I feel only gratitude, a gladness to leave this cast of psychopaths and depart this malicious stage.

Burnt ozone invades my senses.

A flash so bright, it blinds despite closed eyes. The heat so intense my face blisters as I cover my head and strive to breathe.

When I open my eyes, Longinus lays smoldering beside me.

Other aircraft appear; other soldiers pop from hidden positions. With Longinus down, they're emboldened, firing as one, doubling their efforts on Igneus and sparing no bullet to destroy him utterly and completely.

It lasts for minutes. All the aircraft, all the soldiers pouring their wrath onto Igneus and Sebastian.

Then, I hear a voice. Not that of a child, but a prophet. A bearded sage on mountain's peak facing the wicked tempest.

"I am a *witness* of the Father and shall not be harmed!"

The ground shakes. The Earth trembles.

Fire rolls as screams shred the buzzing whine in my ears.

Vision becomes a tunnel. My breathing, harsh, shallow, inadequate, rapid, gasping.

I gape like a fish. Feel my muscles contract, try to grab air, try to force my lungs full.

Then, I simply can't draw another breath. The tunnel becomes bright, a focused pinpoint down a long, shimmering shaft.

The world closes.

Hazy smoke glides over me.

Then Igneus is there.

Sebastian appears, places his hands on my chest as his eyes roll upward.

His features turn serene, angelic like my dream.

Then, Jonas limps past, regards me for a single second, then raises his rifle and points it at Sima's head.

He fires but no shot comes.

He flips the weapon, holds it by the barrel, raises it like a club.

"Jonas, no!" Sebastian cries.

Lightning jolts from Igneus's staff, sizzles brilliant through my fog and coming doom.

I try to speak, to beg healing from Sebastian.

The bolt strikes Jonas a millisecond before he renders the killing blow.

He slides across the lawn and doesn't get up.

Sebastian kneels next to me. His smile is wonderful, innocence and youth mixed with a zest only the young understand and the old have long forgotten.

He works his magic, and I inhale in a rush, vision restored, body whole.

They help me stand and I look around.

The sight is incredible, dead bodies and blazing aircraft, crumpled earth and burning, ravaged buildings. Fire burns everywhere, licking the corpses, changing verdant courtyard to ashen hellscape.

Igneus places a hand on my shoulder. Holds my eyes. "Emery, are you okay?"

I grin like a fool. "How many times can someone be healed before it causes brain damage?"

Sebastian laughs.

Igneus doesn't, just paces to Jonas. "Help me, Emery."

I move to help and together we carry him off.

Sebastian runs to a smoldering black truck that seems the least damaged. He scampers inside. "Keys are here, come on!"

I glance over my shoulder, see Longinus struggle to standing. See him stoop, topple over, get back up and level his spear again. Its gold is subdued now, its etchings still. Perhaps it was damaged. Perhaps we no longer need to concern ourselves with it.

He staggers toward us, levels the relic as Igneus slams the accelerator and we launch forward.

Lightning sizzles around us, past us, but the truck continues.

We screech through a left turn and fly down the street.

"Damn!" Igneus yells, pounding his fist on the dash. "None of us got the spear while the oaf was out."

I stare at him, think to say we had plenty to occupy us. Instead, I lean back, then feel Sebastian's hand reach from the back seat and settle on my shoulder. "You're a good friend, Emery."

I glance to Jonas, unconscious but breathing. "Are you gonna heal him?"

"Yes, of course, when we get to the Temple. Otherwise, I'm afraid he'll return to kill that woman."

"He's not going to be happy," I say.

"Sometimes," Igneus says, "it's not the bite of the wound, but the depths of the scar."

CHAPTER 46

JERUSALEM, ISRAEL

His entire body hurts. His face is bruised, swollen, throbbing. Blood drips from his left ear, echoes like a metronome from the cell's barren walls.

Moscovia Detention Center. Known for its brutality. Decried by rabbis, priests, reporters, and the international community for its barbaric methods.

This is where Israel keeps its enemies. The place they're interrogated.

For three days, he's been without food, water, or a change of clothes. He's too weak to rise, has suffered bouts from hysterical to hallucinogenic.

He can barely speak.

Through swollen lips, he breathes a prayer. Not for himself, but for his son, Israel. He prays for safety, for God's protection, for luck. Perhaps friends have spirited the boy away. Perhaps there's no need for prayer.

Running blood tickles his face as the odor of his own urine stings his nose.

Cain has prevailed, completely overwhelmed and taken over. Has managed to unite the region, whether Islamic, Jewish or Christian.

The Kingdom of Imperium.

Should've saw it coming? So focused on a rebuilt Temple I was blinded to everything else?

Then, the sound of keys in the thick iron door.

Two guards enter. His interrogators, broad, unfeeling, without compassion.

One munches a health bar and Laslo's stomach churns, tries to leap for the food. With a moan, he begs them to leave. Begs for an end to the torture.

He doesn't know how much more he can take.

He does know, however, that they mean to kill him.

A guard approaches and Laslo cries out, somehow musters the energy to lift his arms. Rough hands heft him to his feet.

Head spins as legs threaten collapse. He swoons, is shoved to standing.

"Why?" he rasps.

"Oh, just for fun, I guess."

He's pushed to the door; knows he's going to the room with the chipped metal chair and pocked gray walls. A chair with straps to bind hands and feet, near a table of aluminum that holds the instruments of torture.

He thinks of Israel, breathes another prayer, then steels himself for the coming assault, prays from a sense of sheer panic, a desperate need for God's intervention.

Then, the explosions start.

The structure shakes as a jet shrieks past.

The guards look at each other, then race to the cell's small window.

Laslo pushes against the wall, takes a second to find balance, then steps close and looks over their shoulders.

Smoke rises. Explosions shake the ground. The cell rattles again as another jet screams by. The roar is thunderous, abrupt. He hears the sound, *burrrt*, is reminded of a display of A-10 fighters he'd attended as prime minister.

Can't be Israeli, he thinks, Israel doesn't keep A-10s.

A guard casts a glance.

Slabav lowers his head, steps back a pace, braces for the fist.

"You may as well watch," the guard says. "Might be the last thing you ever see."

Laslo rasps his gratitude, ventures a step closer.

Who seeks to capitalize on Israel's weakness by attacking?

Whoever's the source will pay dearly, doesn't know that Cain's always a step ahead.

Laslo knows this as surely as he knows Cain's motives. Power and control. A coup had been launched, underhanded and covert, in league with that snake Khalifa. May God judge him based on his works.

Another jet screams as lightning streaks an angry sky.

Maybe the thin man's out there. Perhaps Cain's leveraged all available firepower to destroy the man and squelch all thoughts of revolt.

The A-10 circles above a fogged horizon, then races back. A cloud of smoke hangs on its nose as it sings its familiar song. *Burrt.*

Lightning flies, sizzles, strikes.

Flames burst from the fuselage as the jet spins a single time, trails fire like a comet.

"Incoming!" the guard screams, then turns and sprints, knocking Laslo to the filthy floor.

Fire surrounds, engulfs, both guards are muted by a hail of brick and mortar.

Laslo blinks at the rubble, crawls to cower at the base of a sticky wall.

Smoke fills the room in a choking cloud.

Then silence. Serenity even. Odd for this place. No noise from outside. No alarms or shuffle of boots. No cries from other inmates.

Blurred images float, congeal, then separate without apparent pattern: thick smoke, dancing orange flames, inert gray concrete, the bloodied toes of his own feet.

He closes his eyes, waits for the sensation to pass.

Then, he pushes himself upright, stumbles forward, almost

collapses on the rubble covering his tormentors. The health bar lies partially covered in stone and dust, squished from the hand of the guard who held it.

He drops to the floor and devours it in three bites.

Almost instantly, his vision clears. A surge of energy, as if God provided mana in his time of need.

Laslo chews, blinks around, stares at the hole made by the crashing plane, at the bright contrast between dingy cell and glorious freedom.

Voices rise.

"Run!" some say.

"Halt!" say others.

Two prisoners race by the jagged hole and are immediately gunned down.

Two others appear, walking backwards, hands raised.

A guard appears, smirks, guns them down too.

He turns, coiled smoke floating from the rifle, then notices Laslo.

Laslo cringes, braces for the shot, fills his mind with memories of his Israel. The chubby baby he'd been; the awkward, curious youth; now a teenager approaching manhood.

"Oh, look what they've done?" the guard says. He lowers the rifle, waves a hand. "Hurry," he whispers, "the fence is down. You can make it."

A trick, Laslo thinks, so he can be shot while trying to escape.

He stares, sees no deception on the guard's features.

Choices get simple: wait to be tortured or run off and trust God.

He wipes his face, leaves bloody handprints on the wall as he moves.

The path before him is about fifty yards through a grassy common area, surrounded by a fence designed to keep the prisoners in.

Perhaps the fence still stands, perhaps it doesn't.

"Hurry, Prime Minister," whispers the guard, "you have only seconds." He steps in, looks right then left. "Others are coming. You must go. Go!"

Laslo stumbles forward, cringes at the sound of a gunshot as he steps outside.

Sun shines on mangled earth, shines for the first time in a month, maybe longer.

Maybe it's a sign.

Laslo sprints forward as best he can. Flaming wreckage splits the yard in two sections, toward the prison or away. A simple fifty-fifty.

He glances at the guard, then takes the path closest to the prison. He's acting on instinct, a hunch this is the safer path.

Smoke pours over the crash, pops with small explosions. Flames surge forth, singe his skin, prod him forward.

Behind, gunshots occur with frequency. Screams rise but are quickly muted.

He doesn't dare look but concentrates on his pace, ignoring the heat, choking back smoke, moving ever forward, ever closer to freedom, toward a whisper of a chance that he might still be able to reach his son.

He lurches, gains speed, emboldened, hopeful.

Another prisoner races by, then skids to a stop and takes Laslo in.

With a deafening crack, he's shot dead.

Laslo stumbles closer to the flaming wreck. He's running now, cringing as each bullet whistles past.

It's all or nothing, freedom or death.

Behind him, guards sound the alarm. They're chasing, drawing close.

Another bullet screams past as other voices join.

Thick smoke snags his breath, swirls in the deepest of gelatinous vapor.

Then a small breeze clears it for an instant and shows the way forward.

Fifty feet away, the fence lies in a twisted heap of chain link and razor wire.

He presses on, gasping, limping.

He knows he won't escape. He's too beaten, too weak.

"No!" he cries. Then, with an effort of will, raises his head and gauges the distance.

So far away. So close, yet so very far.

Above the horizon, a bevy of helicopters expel their payload toward some unseen target.

Energy sizzles, surrounds, electrifies, makes his hair stand on end as it washes over him.

Then, everything explodes.

The impact is deafening. The concussion knocks him to the ground, rattles his teeth.

Shouts cease as he struggles to stand, then stumbles ahead, eyes locked on the mangled fence. He veers, puts the wreckage between himself and whatever guards are chasing. If they've no line of sight, they can't shoot. With a little luck, maybe they'll think he's dead.

He reaches the fence and stumbles through biting razor wire. Chain link chinks, collects his blood, tries to trip him up.

Then he's through, blinking left and right, staggering forward, head spinning, weaker with each second.

He has to get far away. He'll be easy to spot on the street, easy to recapture once the guards get in their vehicles and start to look in earnest.

And they'll bring dogs, lots of dogs.

He has to do something about his scent. He'd read once that an onion can do the trick but has no idea if that's accurate or where to get one.

He hobbles up a barren street, veers right down an alley.

He'll push as far as he can, as far as his broken body will go, then trust God for the rest.

A large green dumpster comes in view. He rushes forward, demands legs to pump, lungs to find oxygen, energy to last just a few seconds more.

He limps close, tries to climb in, hasn't the strength to lift himself.

He grasps the edge and holds himself upright. Scanning the area, he sees crinkled boxes, some overstuffed trash bags, the remnants of a broken chair. He wavers, inhales, slides the chair close.

Legs quiver as he climbs, then topples into a mound of rotting garbage and plastic trash bags.

He offers thanks. God's heard his prayers.

The lid clangs as it falls, encloses him in fetid darkness and overwhelming stench.

Eyes flutter, then snap shut.

CHAPTER 47

GEORGE WASHINGTON NATIONAL FOREST, WEST VIRGINIA

Rhyme peers through binoculars, watches the flooded Bronco and the helicopter rotating above, unaffected by the storm.

SUVs stream past her hiding spot, dogs bark from within. Emergency vehicles fill both banks, rescuers in orange neon attempt to string a wading line across the river.

Wait for it, she thinks, just wait for it.

She lowers the binocs, stretches her neck a bit. Next to her, Houdini stiffens, then bounds down the trail beyond her sight.

Then, the noise for which she's been waiting. Unmistakable, like thunder in a cave.

Emergency personnel yell warnings, then scramble away from the bank.

A twenty-foot wall of water appears in a quaking torrent of tree and rock and debris.

All that rain in so short a time made a flash flood inevitable.

The river swells, overflows. A raging tsunami of water, tree, earth, and rock smash the Bronco broadside, roll it over like a kayak, then sweep it downstream, tires up, to the narrow strait she'd spotted earlier.

It'll take them hours, perhaps days, to realize she isn't in there. With luck someone saw the dummy propped in the driver's seat. When it's all said and done, she'll be presumed dead and can go about her business.

Now to get out of here.

She slides from the ledge, careful not to send anything toward the river below. A sure-fire way to give up her position, being sloppy, foolhardy. Crispy wouldn't approve.

When she's far enough back, she pushes to all fours, then leans back on her haunches. With everyone heading to the river, her route should be clear.

"Houdini." She calls with a low, calm voice. Can't get too loud, not out of this yet.

Behind her the sound of a snapping branch, then Houdini appears, panting, eyes alert.

"Good boy," she says, "let's get—"

By the time she hears the engine, turns to see the agent leaning from the window, three shots zip past.

She ducks, dives for the brush she just deserted.

The SUV roars by, skids sideways through a trough of mud.

A grinning agent leans from the passenger's window, the hollow tunnel of his pistol pointed at her head.

Twin Sigs fill her hands, sweep toward the SUV and its two G-men.

Then, something tickles her left ear, the whine of a mosquito.

The agent's gun falls as he's hurled hard across the SUV into the driver.

The driver fumbles, reaches for his weapon, then slumps forward as another mosquito buzzes and a bullet takes his temple.

Rhyme dives for cover, slides into the brush, holsters the Sigs.

Sniper! A sniper, for Christ's sake!

This changes everything. Mangles the calculus of advantage and disadvantage.

How many?

Where?

Can't get pinned down.

Acting on instinct, she scrambles into the SUV, keeps low, throws open the driver's door and pushes the men from the vehicle to splat in the mud.

"Houdini!"

The dog leaps in, dashes to the back.

She guns the engine. Tires spin. A whale tail of mud jolts the truck forward and up the trail.

A hail of glass pelts as the back window explodes.

Houdini yelps, leaps into the passenger's seat as two more shots pepper the vehicle. Snipers taking pot shots, hoping for luck.

She presses her advantage—gambles safety for speed as she skids over the trail, wrangles a tight and muddy turn.

At the first road she skids right, then slams the brakes.

Jumping over the front seat into the back, she does a quick search, finds a small tool kit, a tarp, a single black ball cap emblazoned FBI.

Squeezing auburn locks in a bunch, she presses the cap on her head, then exits and grabs a handful of mud. Back inside, she lightly coats her face, then checks her disguise in the rearview.

Thin. Weak. Never work.

Houdini's thick head appears next to her.

Have to try, no other option.

She checks the Sigs, gives the hound a quick pat. "Too far gone now. Let's see how we do."

In the center console lies a paper with her image and name. The words APPROACH WITH CAUTION, EXTREMELY DANGEROUS written in thick block letters. She scans it, sighs, disgusted as she reads her own vital statistics. "One hundred and fifty pounds, my ass. I'm one thirty soaking wet."

Tossing the paper aside, she finds an old pair of shooter's glasses, thick with yellow lenses.

Any port in a storm, she thinks and slides them on her face.

Houdini gives a lick, warns her to stop screwing around.

"Here we go. It's gonna be a long day."

CHAPTER 48

VIRGINIA, UNITED STATES

Hours later, on foot, the SUV stashed and deserted, Rhyme looks down on a roadside eatery. RANDY'S RIBS, blue neon, blinding against a backdrop of bruised cloud. Glancing east, the freeway buzzes with traffic heading for D.C.

The airfield's our only hope, she thinks, fatigued by long shots and slim chances. This luck can't last, never does. She needs to embrace *the Crispy* a bit better, remembers the old adage: "Old warriors don't get old by accident."

From now on, we'll play it straight, safe. Clean, dry and serviceable: my new watch words.

Forty minutes later, she approaches the eatery from the back, legs aching, drenched, a blister on her right heel. Houdini pads next to her, looks tired but doesn't ease up.

Three vehicles sit in a cracked, potholed parking lot: a Chevy Volt, a ramshackle station wagon, and a Jeep Grand Cherokee. She slides a single thread from the inner threads of a length of 550 cord, then ties a slip knot in the center. She glances up, feels beaten, needs sleep. The trick will only work on the station wagon, she thinks. An image of Clark Griswold and his Family Truckster fill her mind.

She approaches, glances around, alone. Holding the thread at the

271

upper rear corner of the driver's door, she slides it in, then shimmies it until the center of the thread is inside the car and the ends are held in either hand outside the vehicle. Sawing the thread back and forth, she eases it lower until the knot hangs just above the small peg of the door's lock. Deftly, gently, she guides the knot over the peg, then pulls both ends of the string hard.

The knot tightens over the lock. *Good!*

She raises the end of the string so it's directly above the peg, then pulls upward with a sharp yank. The lock pops and she opens the door. Houdini jumps in like a seasoned car thief.

Another of Crispy's tricks. The disadvantage: it only works on older vehicles. Like her mentor, it's old school.

She reaches under the dash, fiddles for the wires. A spark and ten seconds, the old woody stutters to a start.

She eases the shifter to reverse and backs out.

In the rearview, an elderly woman hobbles her way, screams, "Police! Police!"

Rhyme laughs despite her anxiety. Was there really a day when one could just yell "Police!" and they'd show up?

She gives the woman a wide berth as she passes, then turns onto the freeway's access road.

The old lady offers a salute with a shaky middle finger.

Advantages: No longer on foot, airfield an hour or so away, Houdini, Sigs.

Disadvantages: Rain, old lady calling the police, airfield an hour or so away.

The wagon shimmies and clunks as she presses onto the freeway. With luck, she'll be there before the cops respond to the theft. With luck, she and Houdini will be long gone.

***

An hour later, she realizes luck's fled.

Eight squad cars give chase.

She looks at the speedo. Sixty-five, as fast as the thing will go.

Accelerator held to the floor, she races on, trailed by flashing lights and sirens. She thinks of the Aston, how easy she'd lose them if she had that.

At the next exit, she doesn't slow, almost loses control as she takes a right at the end of the off-ramp. Can't afford to slow down. Can't afford to give them a chance to use their Pursuit Intervention Technique, or PIT, as the cops say, where they'll intentionally strike the rear corner of her vehicle and cause it to slide out of control.

Rocketing through a left turn, she presses the vehicle down the two-lane.

What she sees fills her with glee and dismay at the same time.

The airfield yawns on her right, three beige hangars, desolate under a pouring sky.

In front of it, two police cars span the road, just enough space between them for the wagon to fit through.

She knows what's coming, sees an officer squat, then slide something across the road between the patrol cars.

"Spike strip!" She yells, frantically searching for a way to avoid the trap.

Her plan's gone to shit. Can't steal a plane. Can't evade the spikes, or the line of cops behind.

Sharpened steel glistens from the road as she speeds forward.

She laughs when she notices the trap's set just *past* the airfield's entrance.

Doesn't change much though. No way I can get in, leap out, and just steal a plane.

Still, bought a few more seconds.

The wagon tips, almost spins out, as she jams the wheel through a hard right and flies through the airfield's open gate. Behind, the police aren't so rambunctious, content in the knowledge they have her trapped. She slams the accelerator, rockets past the hangar farthest right and circles to its rear.

She slams the brakes, barely misses a parked bulldozer near a partially built building.

"Houdini! Go!"

The dog hunkers as if being disciplined.

"Now! Get! Shoo!" She leans across, throws the passenger's door open. "Go! Get!"

Houdini looks wounded, but reluctantly exits.

As soon as he's clear, Rhyme pushes the wagon through a hard left, then races between two hangars back toward the main gate.

Police vehicles block the way, twenty officers, guns drawn and trained, leaning over their hoods.

She stops. Searches for her phone, dials the number.

One ring.

She exits the wagon.

Second ring.

She raises one hand, presses the phone to her ear with the other.

Third ring.

"Answer, Emery. Answer."

Fourth ring.

Two black SUVs enter. The G-men have come.

Fifth ring.

"Hello?"

CHAPTER 49

UNDISCLOSED LOCATION

President Carpenter stands, yells at the monitor. "No! God dammit!" He turns to the aide. "Send in the rest, get them in there!"

"That *was* the rest, sir. All our operatives in the area, unless you want to mobilize the army."

He drops to a chair.

There's no way to explain this away, an attack on the already beleaguered and defenseless nation of Israel. An attack on the new Kingdom of Imperium.

"Sir, you have multiple calls. The German president, the prime minister of the UK, another calling himself Giuseppe, and a guy named Cain."

Carpenter grimaces, then squeezes hands to fists. "Goddammit! Put Cain through."

Cain's voice is dipped in honey. "Dear Tom, rough day?"

"You knew we were coming."

"Now, how could I have known about your covert operation? Did you encounter an army? Air defenses? We both know no one will ever believe that somehow the sovereign Kingdom of Imperium threatened to attack you. This was pre-coordinated, and I am extremely cross. You heard my words, my warning. I wasn't subtle, dear Tom, and unfortunately, an example will have to be made. I do apologize, but it seems you're a victim of your own actions."

The president sighs, listens, hasn't much else to say. So many things going through his mind. Does Imperium have the ability to retaliate? Doubtful. Do I have to sit here and eat shit from this idiot? Probable. Best course now is strategy; besides, there's still one other option.

"I don't suppose sorry will cut it?" Carpenter says.

Cain's laugh is hearty, yet light. "Dearest Tom, I do appreciate your words of remorse. Seems you'll be saying them more when the truth gets out. I imagine you'll be saying them a lot to the families of the fallen soldiers. By the way, I meant to ask, how would you like them back, airmail or cargo ship? Seems we have more than enough corpses here and simply can't be bothered with more."

The words slice his heart to fine strips. He turns from the aide, cups the phone close. "Listen, Cain, we can work this out. What if we publicly recognize Imperium and legitimize it. That would certainly help your new country. We'll let bygones be bygones and cooperate to each other's advantage. What d'ya say?"

The pause is filled with only the hum of the connection.

"Our legitimacy comes from a higher power, Tom. I keep telling you that, yet your mind is as closed as your ears. I'm afraid there will be no such bargain, although my offer to accept the United States' complete surrender remains on the table. Later, I'll be asking your pals in NATO if they'd like to surrender as well. So, you'll not be alone. What d'ya say?"

Carpenter lowers the phone, hands it to the aide, and leaves the room.

CHAPTER 50

JERUSALEM, ISRAEL

We approach the Temple at speed, then Igneus slams the brakes and we skid to a stop in the middle of the road.

"What?" I say.

He points a finger.

Ahead, the road is blocked by military vehicles in camouflage.

"Cain's assumed control of the Israeli Defense Force."

I squint ahead, see men, well-armed in khaki green. "It's a checkpoint. They won't stop us. Why would they?"

"You're sure of that?"

I pause. "No, can't be sure at all."

Sebastian leans over the seat, peers up the road. "They mean us harm. Cain controls the Temple. We're not safe."

A soldier moves toward us, raises a radio and speaks. Around him, other soldiers appear, stalking forward, rifles raised.

"I think he's right," I start, but before I complete the sentence, Igneus slams the truck in reverse and we race backwards up the street. He spins the wheel hard and we fly sideways, tires screeching through a J-turn. He slams it in drive, and we jolt forward.

The rear window explodes in a shower of glass.

"They're shooting," Sebastian says.

"Get down," Igneus yells. "Stay low."

He takes the next turn at speed, then a quarter mile later, we fly through another.

"Where are we going?" I ask. "You know they're going to chase us."

"I know, I know. Let me think."

I look behind, see no one following. Yet.

The truck reels as we skid through another turn. "I think I know a place," Igneus says.

I pull the shattered syringe from my pocket.

I hope they have drugs.

Igneus pulls into an alley off the main road, then slams the accelerator and launches us down the long, narrow tunnel. Buildings loom so close, I'm afraid he'll wreck us. Then the mirror flies off with a grating sound.

I grab the dash, glance over my shoulder, tell Sebastian to buckle up.

"Roger, roger," he says, then leans over to brush glass off Jonas.

Just then Jonas sits up, swings a punch that barely misses the youth.

Sebastian presses against the rear door, eyes wide.

Jonas blinks into his surroundings. "What happened?"

He doesn't look great. His face is swollen and bruised as eyes struggle to see clearly.

"Are you alright?" Sebastian says.

Jonas rustles his hair. "Fine, kid. Got my bell rung is all. What happened?"

Sebastian shakes his head. "I'm not sure what happened, I was busy…" Then realization dawns in his eyes. "Oh," he says, "I remember. Dad had to sizzle you."

Jonas's eyes fill with rage. He glances at Igneus's reflection in the rear view. "Let me out."

"Jonas, you were gonna kill that woman. I can't condone murder, and I think when your head clears…"

"Right. Fucking. Now."

"If we drop you here, you'll be dead," I say. "The Temple…"

"Shut your mouth, Emery. Igneus stop the car."

"I won't," Igneus says. "Too dangerous. It's not going to hurt you to ride with us, and when we get where we're going, you can do what you want."

Jonas's mouth snaps shut, his eyes shift back and forth. Then, he glances around and says, "Fine."

Sebastian leans back, creeps a few inches farther away.

Jonas looks ahead and says nothing.

Igneus glides up another alley, then slows to push a dumpster from our path using the truck as a bulldozer.

We race ahead, turn up another alley where he slows and stops. "Hope this works," he says.

I exit to an alley littered with debris, cardboard boxes, and a few dumpsters. Farther up, the alley turns to the right.

"I remember this," Sebastian says.

I look around, see green doors about every forty feet.

Igneus paces to a door with faded and scratched lettering: LEE'S CHINESE.

"Are you hungry?" I ask as he knocks.

There's the clink of metal from the other side, a lot of metal, then an Asian man sticks his head out. "Who is it?"

"Mr. Lee, it's Igneus and Sebastian. We need your help."

The door slams shut, and I hear the scrape of more metal chains. Then it opens fully to reveal a man, bald and grinning. "Mr. Igneus, come in, come in. Been long time."

Igneus nods and enters, walks without pain. Seems his injury has already healed.

Sebastian leaps forward, grabs Mr. Lee in an embrace. His words are older than his age. "God saves many blessings for you."

"Oh yeah," Lee says, "when they start? I wear my good robe."

I laugh and offer my hand. "Mr. Lee, I'm Emery Merrick. A friend. Thank you so much."

He shakes my hand quickly, waves me inside, and closes the door behind us, attaching the many locks and chains.

"Wait," I say. "Where's Jonas?"

Sebastian shrugs as Igneus moves to the door. "Can you open this again?"

Mr. Lee must be a hell of a nice man, because he reverses the procedure and undoes the many locks.

We step into the alley, Sebastian calling, "Jonas! Jonas!"

There's no answer.

Igneus points to the end of the alley. "Emery, go look up there. It goes to the right, then becomes a dead end. I'll look up here, and we'll see if we can find him."

Sebastian joins me as I walk to the alley's end to see nothing but scraps of wood, a rusted and bent refrigerator, and a cardboard box. No sign of Jonas.

"We used to live around here," Sebastian says. "I miss it."

I chuckle. "You miss living in an alley?"

"Well," he says, smiling, "it's better than all of this." He looks down, frowns. "Ishmael's dead. Jonas just ran off. Seems me and Dad can just come back here, and we'll do fine."

I stare at the boy for a second, then turn and move off. He scampers beside me. "I sure hope we find him."

We approach Lee's, and I stop dead. Sebastian starts to speak, but I shush him. "Listen."

The sound is odd, a scraping.

"It's in there," he says. "In the dumpster."

"Probably an alley cat or a rat."

Sebastian climbs on a rickety chair, opens the lid, and peers inside. "It's a man," he says. "Probably homeless. He's bleeding, Mr. Emery. I think he's dead."

I grip a greasy edge and peer over.

The man lies in piles of waste. The smell is horrific, and I wonder how he can stand it for even a second.

He opens his eyes, dried blood obscures his features, gaunt as a newly bleached shell. "Emery?"

I look close, recognize the face despite the caked blood, black eyes, swollen lips, and matted hair. "Laslo?"

"Who's Laslo?" Sebastian says.

"An old friend." I call for Igneus, and together we enter the fetid filth and free Slabav of his confines.

"He's barely conscious," I say. "Laslo?" I call, shaking him. "Laslo, you okay?"

His eyes flutter but stay closed.

I press my ear to his chest. I'm no doctor, but what I hear is reassuring, a beating heart and breath moving through lungs.

"Isn't that the prime minister?" Igneus asks.

I nod. "Or was, anyway. Let's get him inside."

"Did you find Jonas?"

"No, didn't see a thing. You?"

Igneus glances toward the alley's entrance. "Saw nothing." Concern clouds his features. It's obvious he cares about Jonas.

Long shadows cast the alley in relative darkness. "Come on," I say. "We've done all we can. We'll look again tomorrow."

Igneus pauses, watches the alley's entrance as if Jonas will appear any second.

I tug his arm. "Igneus, he's a grown man, and very capable. I'm sure he'll be fine."

Igneus nods absently, breathes what seems like a prayer. "I hope so, Emery. Ishmael's death hit him hard."

I glance at Sebastian, then Slabav. Igneus lifts his feet as I reach under his shoulders.

Mr. Lee holds the door as we enter and lay him on the linoleum.

"Sebastian," I say, "would you mind?"

Sebastian kneels beside him, speaks words I don't understand. Silky words, full of beauty.

Laslo gasps as his eyes pop fully open.

I smile down on him. "Laslo, you're safe."

Eyes flutter. He groans a single word. "Israel."

Chapter 51

Over the Atlantic Ocean

The surrounding luxury is no balm for his worried mind.

Carpenter sits alone at his desk on Air Force One and contemplates his options.

He picks up the phone and dials the number.

When it's answered, he asks a simple question. "The wife?"

"A matter of time, sir. Closing in as we speak."

"Excellent, keep it quiet and keep her secure. I'll meet you there when I return."

He hangs up, smiles.

Cain. What a fool. Soon the tables will turn, and Imperium will fall.

An assistant sticks her head in. "Sorry to bother you, Mr. President, but I have numerous people holding. What should I do?"

He props his feet on the desk, leans back, hands clasped behind his head. "First, bring me a drink. Then, tell them I'm indisposed."

"Of course," she says and disappears.

He thought he bested me. Thought he had me beat—and I have to admit, he's been a worthy adversary. But I'm better. And smarter. Not about to take more shit from that idiot. I'm the goddamn President of the United States, and that still means something. Very soon, the tables will turn in a wonderful way.

He pulls a legal pad from the desk, starts to make a list of demands. A little Christmas list. Things with which Cain will have to agree to save his beloved.

A shame it's come to this, really. We could've done great things together, and I so hate bringing innocent people into such nasty business.

Chapter 52

Jerusalem, Israel

"You must return to Cain," Igneus says.

"Why?"

"Because he's the only one who can save you from Longinus. Do you think the giant is going to forget what you did to his woman?"

I stand, place my hands on the table. "She tried to kill me! Would've succeeded if not for you two."

"You think that matters to Longinus?"

I think of the giant Roman and our love-hate relationship. I don't dislike the man despite his barbaric ways and neanderthal methods. But now he's super powerful, his spear living up to its reputation.

I stare at the food before us as Mr. Lee pushes through double doors to place a bowl of steaming rice.

"What about Israel?" This is Laslo, talking about his son, not his country. "We need to find him. We need to get to him." He speaks fast, eyes darting around the table. Mr. Lee approaches with a green teapot adorned in Chinese symbols. He fills Laslo's cup, then disappears into the kitchen.

"Yes, Laslo, we do," Igneus says. "Do you know where he is?"

Laslo stares at the plate before him. "I don't. I don't even remember the last few days. I was close to death, I think, and the only thing that kept me going were thoughts of him."

"What about Jonas?" Sebastian says. "Are we gonna stop looking for him?"

Igneus shakes his head. "No, son. I'm not prepared to give up on him."

"So, we forget about Israel?" Slabav says.

"Absolutely not," I say. "Israel must be found, as does Jonas, but how are we going to do it? We have to assume Cain searches for us, and God only knows what's going on at the Temple. I mean, why the security, and why did they shoot at us when we approached? And now you want me to return to Cain? For what purpose? So he can kill me? Or let Longinus kill me? We have to be smart here. And careful."

"I know where Jonas is."

We all turn to Sebastian, who sits smiling beneath blonde locks. "He's at Ishmael's grave. I don't know how I know, but I know."

Igneus rises. "That's good enough for me."

Laslo places a hand on Sebastian's arm. "Son, can you tell me where Israel is?"

Sebastian frowns. "I can't," he says. "I don't know."

Laslo leans back, tosses his napkin on the plate before him. "That's great. We rush to find this Jonas, but leave Israel to fend for himself?"

"No one said that, Laslo," I say. "We'll find Israel. Let's just stay calm and think things through."

The front of Lee's restaurant is covered with plywood, makes the interior dark and somewhat menacing. Night must be falling, I think; as we've been here for a few hours or more.

From the kitchen, I hear Mr. Lee singing in Chinese. The man seems unflappable. Seems to take things in stride and not worry too much. He's been a great host as well, piling food before us in steaming bowls, refilling cups, replenishing plates when they're low. I owe him a *big* tip.

I sit back, ignore the food, consider our options and problems. As much as I hate to say it, Igneus is right. I have to return to Cain, for better or worse. I need to see him, assess what he knows about

Rhyme's whereabouts and how she's doing. My stomach rolls a bit, and I feel a tang of tension. Without Rhyme here to stop Cain, or more accurately stop Longinus *through* Cain, I may be walking into a death trap.

"I'll go to Cain directly," I say, almost to myself.

Igneus pipes up. "I'll go talk to Jonas, then we'll look for Israel. How does that sound?" He's looking at Slabav, who returns an expression of impatience and exasperation.

"It doesn't," Slabav says. "Seems this Jonas can take care of himself, where Israel needs our help."

"Yes, but we know where Jonas is. Believe me, he's a handy guy to have around."

"I disagree. I want to look for Israel first."

"Laslo," I say, "I know you're concerned, even scared. We all are, but Igneus is right. Jonas is an incredible asset and a friend. If we know his whereabouts, we need to go to him first. It shouldn't take too long; he'll either return with us, or tell us to pound salt. I expect either answer will come fast, and then Israel becomes the priority."

Laslo nods slowly, seems to battle logic and emotion. "Forgive me, gentleman. I haven't been myself. I owe you my thanks and will help any way I can."

"We understand," Igneus says. "Good thing we stumbled upon you when we did."

Laslo continues to nod. "Yes, good thing," he says, then adds quietly, "it has to be."

"I leave you as knights to your quest," I say, rising. "If I'm going to face Cain, I may as well get it over with."

Igneus stands and shakes my hand. "Be careful, return here if you have problems. Is that okay, Mr. Lee?"

Lee nods, smiles. "Of course, of course. No business now anyway. Employee went. Just me left."

"I'll return when I can, or when I have to." I give him a shaky smile, false but hopeful.

"We'll get to Jonas, then look for Israel."

"Got it," I say, "and good luck."

Laslo rises. "Thanks, Emery, for helping. I'm sure I'll see you soon."

Sebastian wraps me in a hug, then stands before me and models the boy I'd first met in the sterile chambers of the Children of the Rocks. "Bless Mr. Emery," he says. "This day and always."

I tussle his hair. "Would you mind a shout out for Rhyme?"

"Is she your girlfriend?" he says, teasing.

"Sort of."

He bows his head, whispers a prayer I can't hear. "That was a special one," he says. "Just for her."

"Thanks, Sebastian."

Mr. Lee steps up, bows, then hands me something. "Don't forget fortune cookie."

I accept the gift. There's something calming about him that I like very much.

He unlocks the front door and I step into darkened streets, half-expecting to be shot on the spot.

It's deserted, quiet, even serene.

A gentle breeze brushes my back, encourages movement. I step off toward the PM's building, my mind filled with thoughts of Jonas, Sebastian, Lee, and Igneus. I unwrap the fortune cookie and break it open, nibbling while reading the prize inside.

THE LONGEST JOURNEY BEGINS WITH A SINGLE STEP.

Chapter 53

Jerusalem, Israel

The PM's office buzzes with activity. Light shines from every window and gives the appearance of a department store. Outside, sit four parked limousines, engines running. Further out, a perimeter of military vehicles with soldiers scurrying about and shouting orders to one another.

It's taken me about thirty minutes to get here, walking through Jerusalem's deserted streets, thinking of the lies I'll tell when Cain asks the inevitable questions. The weather is cool, but the rain has held, despite the fact storm clouds have become a staple of Israel's skies.

I step forward, then hear the word. "Halt!"

A soldier approaches as two others step from the shadows.

"Um, my name is Emery Merrick. I'm here to see Thadd…" I stop short, shake my head, restart. "My name is Emery Merrick, and I'm here to see Cain. I'm his biographer."

It's obvious the man doesn't speak English. He says something I don't understand, then twists my arms behind my back where zip ties clamp my wrists. "Ouch! Easy there."

I'm pushed forward as the others fall in step behind. I don't look, but somehow know their rifles are pointed at my back.

Feel fortunate they didn't kill you on the spot, I think. My thoughts turn to Rhyme and I pray she's safe and well. I tried calling her during my stroll but got only the message *your call cannot be completed at this time...*

We enter the PM's building, and I squint against the light. People are everywhere. Soldiers flank the entry, and I'm hurried through a metal detector and into a side room, glaring white with four chairs. In one sits a child of perhaps thirteen. His face is dirty, his clothes torn and worn. He looks up, then quickly lowers his head as I'm pushed onto the chair across from him.

The soldiers says something in Hebrew. Something that sounds nasty, but what do I know. They exit, and I hear keys clatter and a distinct click from the door's lock.

I sigh. The kid raises his head.

"Whatcha in for?"

He smiles, but doesn't understand.

"How long have you been here?"

Nothing.

"Do your parents know where you are?"

Nothing but brown eyes and a pleasant smile.

The door opens and a woman enters. She's beautiful in the way of a girl next door, short-cropped hair, smart blue suit with two-inch heels, black and shined.

"Mr. Merrick?"

"Yes."

She says something in Hebrew and a soldier enters. I tense as he pulls a knife. Then, he raises his hands and offers a pleasant expression. He steps behind me and cuts the binds.

I rub my wrists as I take in the woman. "My name is Marcy," she says. "Cain sent me to collect you. Follow me and we'll go to him." She squats next to the boy and hands him a sandwich. "Eat," she says. "You look like you're starving."

I gulp, try to smile, step after her as she leaves the room. The kid makes a little sound, and I look at him and wink.

The lobby buzzes. A man glides past pushing a wheeled rack loaded with expensive suits. Another, dressed as a chef, appears from a room, moves to a group of boxes stacked against a wall and pops one open. He produces a bottle of wine and examines the label carefully. He shouts something, and a lady appears, opening all the stacked boxes in a semi-panic.

Marcy hustles me past them, through the lobby, past numerous security stations and up the stairs. Seems the elevator isn't working.

"I'm one of Cain's personal assistants, recently arrived from the US." Her smile is pleasant, dainty. She lowers her voice. "It's been a whirlwind. I arrived two hours ago and have been running ever since."

"At least it pays well," I say.

"That it does."

We arrive on the proper floor and exit the stairwell. More people fill the hall. I hear voices from a conference room and look in to see a labarum on the screen. I hear the words, "This is what we're thinking for Imperium, but it's boring. How do we spruce it up?"

I follow Marcy past numerous rooms and numerous people, until we turn into another room where Cain sits at a table filled with flowers and food of all kinds.

"Mr. Cain," Marcy says. "Emery Merrick for you."

Cain stands. "Dear Emery! What has befallen you? Do sit. Are you hungry? That will be all, Marcy."

She nods and leaves.

Cain lowers his voice. "Do you need a place to feed your vice?"

My mouth waters, my ears start to buzz, my skin tingles. I'm Pavlov's dog. A drooling hound waiting for a treat. I nod.

"Of course, of course," he says. "We have much to discuss. I'm so glad you came back. I have a very special task for you."

I swallow, wonder if he's teasing about a place to get my fix.

He seems to pick up on this and waves a hand. "That can all wait. My personal bathroom is just up the hall. You'll be undisturbed. There's a shower in there and a selection of clothes, should you fancy a change. Seems your suit's seen better days."

I glance down, notice my tie is gone, my shoes covered with mud and blood. The torn pants, singed and stained to match my suit jacket, barely conceal a shirt that isn't any better off. Not to mention my socks and underwear and the gruesomeness dwelling there. "I appreciate it."

He winks. "Is an hour enough? I'm currently awaiting another guest and was hoping we could all dine together."

"Of course," I say, but feel like I'm mumbling. All I can think about is the fix, the needle, the escape, the warmth, the numbness and detachment.

He walks to the table, pours a large glass of wine to the rim and hands it to me. "Do take your time, dear Emery. Enjoy the experience. This will help." He hands me the glass and I gulp down half of it.

His laugh is magical, tingling, majestic. "You're a delight, Emery, my favored servant. Please, clean up for dinner and join me back here. Big things are happening," he says. "Imperium flourishes."

His gifts work their magic as I think of Jerusalem, think of Imperium flourishing. I realize the evidence doesn't support the claims. Then, I realize they don't have to. Cain will do that on his own. If he says Imperium flourishes, despite evidence to the contrary, I'm willing to bet it will indeed flourish and rise as a great, united nation under Cain's tutelage.

"I'll return presently," I say and move to the door. Then, I turn back. "Is Longinus around?"

Cain frowns a bit, flashes perfect teeth, snowy hair perfectly coifed. The epitome of style and elegance. "He's quite cross with you." He glances at a splintered chair in the room's corner. "I've sent him on another task. You're safe at present, and I don't expect to see him until tomorrow. But, for the sake of honesty, when he sees you, he may very well kill you and I'm not certain I can stop him."

I gulp the wine, move back to the table, and refill the glass.

"Of course, of course, drink up, be merry. Nothing to fear this evening, and by the time Longinus returns, you should be pleasantly on your way."

"On my way," I say. "On my way where?"

His smile lights up the room. "In time, dear Emery. Shower first, collect yourself. We'll talk at dinner. I think you'll be pleasantly surprised."

I can't think of anything to say, staring at this self-appointed God in Ferragamo shoes. He's a marvel, standing, glowing. Will, power and persona radiate from his every atom. The wine clouds my thoughts, and I stand there for a long time before Cain speaks and interrupts the flow of images. "Your fix, dear Emery, awaits."

I startle a bit, then exit and move toward my chemical master.

I'm a good boy. I've earned this.

CHAPTER 54

JERUSALEM, ISRAEL

Jonas sits on the grass in a drizzle of rain. He looks beaten, broken by Ishmael's death.

Igneus watches, using a flap of cardboard as an umbrella.

What to say? The man's endured a lot and wears those scars on his posture. Slumped, legs crossed, head down, rain dripping from dark locks. He doesn't notice the rain, hasn't looked up in five minutes.

Before him stands a crooked cross, Ishmael's cross, a gravestone in rough wood, name and dates scratched upon it.

Igneus steels himself for rejection, tries to crank up his empathy. Jonas lost his wife, his son, his best friend, now his brother. Seems natural causes don't apply in his circles.

Igneus crosses wet grass, slides beside the broken man, feels a cold wetness seep through his pants to soak his bottom. "I'd apologize, but I'm afraid you won't accept."

Jonas doesn't move, not even a turn of his head.

"What can I do?" Igneus says.

"You can leave me be." The response is clipped, military style.

"If that's your wish, I'll do so. But before I go, I want you to take a second and realize what you have left. All's not lost. You've endured much, too much for any man, really, and I can only imagine the pain that rages within." He pauses, looks to the sky as cold rain falls from the tree above. "But, what we can't— won't— do is stand idle and watch you become something you're not. You're better than this, Jonas. If Ishmael were here, he'd tell you the same. So, I'll ask this one thing: return with us. We need your help, especially now. Everything's changed, and things will only get worse from here. I don't think we can do it alone. You *have* a purpose, remain one of God's children. Something tells me your path's reached a critical juncture, and I fear, if you continue your present course, you'll become a pawn in Cain's game. A powerful pawn, but still a pawn."

Jonas stares with a blank face as rain mists his features. Igneus feels a chill as the wind picks up.

Minutes pass in silence, then Igneus stands. "For what it's worth, I'm sorry I zapped you," he says. "It was nothing personal, but I couldn't let you murder that woman. Even if she deserved it."

"Vengeance rages, calls for recompense. My chance rose before me, and you stole it from my grasp. That woman still lives, as does the giant, and I won't stop until I have her head."

"You're confused, Jonas. Letting grief and anger skew your judgment. This isn't you at all."

The hushed fall of raindrops is the only response.

Igneus stands behind the broken man, out of words. He turns, paces through the grass where Sebastian and Laslo huddle under a broad oak.

"Well?" Sebastian asks.

"He's not coming," Igneus says. "Best to leave him to decide for himself which road he'll travel."

Sebastian looks crestfallen. Stutters a step as if wanting to run to Jonas. He looks confused, doesn't seem to fully understand the moods of adults, the trials, the paths carved, the scars gouged.

"Come, Sebastian. Let's go find Israel."

"I can't," he says. "There has to be something more, has to be something else we can do. We can't just leave him."

"Well, we can't carry him," Laslo says.

"You said we wouldn't desert him, Dad, and now we're walking away?" Earnest eyes shine as blonde locks glimmer with rain. "It doesn't make sense. He's our friend, our family. We can't leave him to sit in the rain and stare at Ishmael's grave."

Igneus searches for something to say, something to tell the lad about relationships and the human condition, about friendship and family. He opens his mouth, then snaps it shut. He needs something wise and powerful, something fatherly to set Sebastian's mind at ease about the ways of grownups.

He comes up with nothing.

Jonas remains unmoving at his brother's side as darkened clouds hover in place, more rain coming. We have to go, Igneus thinks. There's no time to dally when Israel remains to be found. Laslo's held his patience thus far, but any longer is beyond divine providence.

Laslo squats, holds the boy's eyes. "You're correct, Sebastian. One doesn't desert their family. Let us go and share his grief."

Sebastian doesn't hesitate, races through the drizzle to plop by Jonas's side.

Slabav and Igneus join a second later.

"We're here for you, Jonas," the child says. "As you were for us. I just wish I could heal your broken heart."

Jonas moves with a speed both fluid and effortless. So fast it makes Igneus startle. He pulls the boy close, wraps him in a hug as tears stream down his face. "Thank you, Sebastian," he whispers. "A million times, thank you."

Sebastian returns the hug, rests his head on Jonas's shoulder.

"I loved Ishmael," the boy says. He leans back, holds Jonas's eyes. "I love you too, Mr. Jonas, and won't leave you, no matter what."

Jonas stands. He wears an IDF uniform, an officer's uniform. "I'm sorry, everyone," he says. "Just trying to deal with…all of it. I'm not myself. Blinded by rage, by loss." He sighs, wipes a cheek. "Please, forgive me."

"Did you join the defense force?" Sebastian asks.

A look of confusion crosses his face. Sebastian points at the uniform.

"Oh, this," he says, then looks at Igneus. "It seems the IDF is out in force and a curfew's been established. The only way I could be left alone was to wear this uniform. No non-comm will question me, and no higher-ranking officers will be out in this weather. Seemed a safe bet."

"Wow! How'd you get it? I want one."

Jonas's laugh is good to hear, seems Sebastian has some special magic that's managed to bring him around. He ruffles Sebastian's hair. "I'll see what I can do."

Igneus steps forward, embraces Jonas. "We'll get by," he says. "All of us, together."

Jonas glances at Ishmael's grave. "Let's get out of here," he says. "What's the plan?"

The truck moves through empty streets. It seems an officer's uniform wasn't the only thing Jonas managed to secure.

"I have some weapons back there, too," he says. "Kind of hit the jackpot with this truck. We've got a few grenades, some pistols, a couple of rifles."

"Ammo?" Laslo asks.

Jonas frowns. "You never have enough of that, but if we're careful, what we have should last. I'm not expecting a firefight and haven't had any problems getting through checkpoints so far. For now, we'll just lay low and find your son."

Laslo looks relieved, a bit elated. "Let's go by the house, then we'll try Leyada."

Jonas nods, flicks a switch. Windshield wipers squeal across the glass. "That's as good a plan as any. Do you think he's at home?"

"It'd be the safest place. My boy's not dumb. The house is in a gated compound, or was anyway, before my ouster. We should be cautious, but I think it's worth a look. It's not far from here, in any event, another block or two."

Jonas eases the vehicle to the curb. "I'll go ahead on foot. Check things out. You wait here, I shouldn't be long."

"I'm going with you," Laslo says and opens his door.

"You're the most recognizable man in Israel, do you really think that's wise?"

Laslo starts to protest, then stops. "I guess not."

"I'll be back, just gonna look around. I'll leave the keys, and if you even *think* you've been noticed, take off." Jonas shudders, words catching as he speaks. "I'll meet you back at Ishmael's grave."

Chapter 55

Jerusalem, Israel

Cain's personal bathroom is underwhelming. Certainly not the bathroom of an emperor. It's normal and plain, so unlike the man. A porcelain toilet sits in a gray stall on a tiled white floor with green stains in the grout. There's a single sink and mirror, a plastic curtain covers a single shower stall. A wooden stand sits near the sink, appears teak or bamboo. Upon it, a folded hand towel, matching bath towel and washcloth. On these, sit a gleaming hypodermic, a small torch-type lighter, a spoon, tourniquet, and plastic bag filled with my favored demons.

I peel off my shirt, my undershirt, toss them on the floor, then perform my ritual, heating the drug and drooling like Pavlov's pooch. I wonder what its name was. My body tingles and my mind buzzes. I feel giddy, lick my lips nonstop, watch as solid becomes liquid.

Now the good part.

I splash water on my arm, glide some soap over it. One can never be too careful about cleanliness. I'm smiling, anticipation blooms with each motion. My mind races—I simply *must* look up that dog's name —my hands shake. I pause, sip my wine, dry my arm.

Then the plunge, the glorious bite of needle through skin. A quick pull on the hypo's plunger gives a red flash. I think of red flags, the warnings of my ritual. Salivation. I've somehow developed an erection. The darkness of blood as it enters the needle, the bag of demons now smooshed against its cold steel. I'm undaunted, unafraid, willing to give anything, to do anything for these moments. I'm trained like any good dog, like any drooling mongrel.

Now to set endorphins loose, to shoot the demons and wait as they mix with the wine to overcome my mind.

I think of Rhyme, feel ashamed. She's never seen my ritual, and if she did, she may reconsider our love.

Then again, maybe not.

She's weathered much, knows my addictions, my weaknesses, yet, with me, she remains, a solid prop for a tilted life.

Lips quiver as demons invade. Detachment overwhelms. I can't keep my eyes open and become unaware of my surroundings.

Things go red as I stumble, lean on the wall, feel my legs quit.

I slide to the floor, shirtless, struggle for a nanosecond to open my eyes, to focus on something before me.

I hope I didn't take too much.

Yet, I hope I did.

More is good, as close to overdose as possible. Wouldn't it be funny if Cain found me dead, needle askew in my arm? It's sure nice of him to arrange this. What's that damn dog's name? I'll look it up later.

I open my eyes, have no idea how long I've been sitting on the cold tile. As I stand, my head swims.

I toss the needle in the sink, wipe a dribble of blood from the hole in my arm.

The shower is hot, the steam tickles, enhances my mood, sends the demons in a tizzy, prancing through neurons to obscure all that needs obscured. They sing. Howl. Caress with calloused claws and forked tongues.

I exit, dry off, select a gray suit from the rack. I thumb through shirts, select one in red, fire red, adding a bit of sizzle to my look tonight.

I select a pair of shoes from a shelf on the rack's bottom. Black, glossed oxfords. Then, a tie in, what the hell, we'll go with pink. PINK! I'm a devil tonight, an apparition, a ghostly projection of what I once was.

I dial Rhyme, listen to the buzz, pray she answers.

"Your call cannot be completed…"

I finish dressing. Then, load another syringe. Just a tad more, a little boost, a whiff, a taste, a hint, you know, to get me through.

I click as I walk. Expensive shoes call attention to themselves. I return to Cain, my Pavlov, my master, my boogeyman in Gucci and labarum tie clip.

He smiles, nods, welcomes me. Even rises and helps me to sit. So much for acting normal, I think. He's graceful, powerful, and I find myself staring. White hair dances, does the hula on his head. Perhaps it's my wavering vision. A wine glass appears, filled, looks like blood in my hypo. I drink deep, find nourishment from the wine, this metaphor for so many things.

"What's the name of the dog?" I say.

Cain regards me with a small smile. His eyes hold mine, seem to enjoy my waltz with these specters. "Dear Emery, I'd like to introduce you to Israel. You may remember him. I believe the two of you met once. This is Laslo's son."

I nod, stare at the boy's dark hair, contrast it with Cain's. Song lyrics trace my mind, the demons sway with the beat, with each syllable. It's McCartney and Jackson. *"Ebony and Ivory."* I start to hum, sip my wine, wonder how long until I can sneak back and indulge the monsters once more.

Something deep struggles, a memory, a notion. It fights the demons, scrapes the clouds on its way through my subconscious.

"Laslo's son?"

Cain chuckles. "Yes, dear Emery. Do you remember?"

"Maybe," I say. "Maybe not."

I'm sure I remember, yet certain I don't. Who's Laslo? Does he have a dog? Pavlov's assistant maybe? I can't remember, yet I can.

"He's a nice kid," I say. "And how's Rhyme?"

Israel stares at me, seems a bit scared. I lean forward. "I'm a nice guy when you get to know me."

He shies away. Maybe he wants part of my fix.

Suddenly, I despise the boy, wish him dead, see the selfishness bloom on his features as dark eyes hold mine.

What a smart ass. Cocky. A rich kid.

He can find his own fix, I'm not sharing.

"Where's Laslo?" I ask.

Servants appear and fill our plates with meat and potatoes. Mine looks gray, gelatinous. I push the plate away, return my gaze to the little bastard who wants my fix. "Who's Laslo?"

Cain grins, steeples his hands in front of him. "Seems our Emery is a little worse for wear after recent events, dear Israel. I'm sure some food will sort him out."

"I think his question is valid, Mr. Cain. Where is Laslo?"

"Ooo, wow," I say. "Seems our lad is growin' some marbles." I try to sound like my big Roman pal, then a shiver runs through me and I glance around. "Is Longinus here?"

"No, dear Emery, he's indisposed. You're very safe at the moment."

I chuckle, lean back. No longer Stoker's *Harker*. "Good," I say. "I'd hate to kick his ass."

Israel's gaze hasn't turned from Cain. Cain nips a bite of the gray mass on his plate. "Dear Israel, your father asked me to look after you. I assure you, I don't know his whereabouts or what he's up to, but it shouldn't be long until you're reunited."

"We are men of action," I say. "Lies do not become us."

Israel turns toward me. *"The Princess Bride? Is this guy crazy?"* He slides back a bit more.

Cain's laughter rises, a tinkling bell—Tinkerbell—buzzing through fleeing demons. "He may indeed be, dear Israel, but he's a trusted, if unruly, ally. I do ask your patience with him." Cain takes another bite as the gelatinous mass turns to perfectly cooked sea bass. It smells wonderful. My stomach leaps.

I pull my plate close and dig in.

"I've arranged for you to accompany me to the coronation, dear Israel. You'll be a featured guest in your father's stead. A perfect prince of Israel come prince of Imperium. Consider it training for future achievements." Cain fills a glass with wine, offers it to the boy.

"I'm not old enough," Israel says with a head shake. "Father wouldn't approve."

Cain looks about the room rather theatrically. "I don't see him presently, dear Israel. I won't tell if you don't."

Israel glances at me, then back to Cain. He accepts the wine and takes a bigger drink than I expect. I finish my fish, the potatoes beside it, the peas after that. I down my wine and sit back, sated.

My senses start to clear—why am I thinking of dogs? The demons run off, cackling. Do they dissipate, or just sleep in my cells, hide in my ribosomes and mitochondria, wait for their chance to re-emerge?

"You said I was going someplace?" I say. "Care to share?"

Steely blue eyes scan my face, then a smile emerges. "Of course, dear Emery, we need to discuss that. It seems our Rhyme has some trouble coming her way, and I'd like you to take an X'chasei jet and go to the States to collect her for me."

Now we're talking!

I lean forward, heart racing, face flushed. This is a task I can get behind. "I'm your man," I say. "It'd be my pleasure to collect and return her safely." What an idiot he is, I think, loosing the fox in the henhouse.

"Excellent. You'll leave first thing. Time is of the essence."

I feel a chill. "Is she in danger?"

"I'm sure you know our Rhyme can handle herself, but I've deemed it best to get her out of the country as fast as possible. I'd go myself, but I have much to do here." He frowns. "I'm afraid you'll miss my coronation, though."

"Coronation?" I wonder if this has already been discussed and somehow I missed it?

"Yes, I'm to be coronated as Imperium's emperor." His lips turn down, his eyes lose some of their blueness, some of their glint. "I do so hate these formalities, but for the sake of the kingdom and its people, I thought it best to be formally crowned. Pomp and circumstance and all that, you understand."

I nod. I don't understand, and care even less. Rhyme consumes my thoughts. I can't wait to see her, to be near her. "Of course," I say. "It ain't easy being you." I smile, stand, offer a small bow. "If I may be excused, I believe some sleep would be beneficial." And more drugs, I think.

Cain rises, grasps my hand. "Of course, dear Emery. I'll see you in the morning. Find Marcy, and she'll take you to your assigned quarters."

I nod, suppress a giggle. Quarters? How very military.

I exit the room and turn down the hall. I've no intention on finding Marcy. I pass a small information stand, a relic now, holding pamphlets on workplace safety and complaint processes. I nab one and slide it in my pocket.

Farther along I find a security station.

The guard nods at a clipboard on the table before him. It's a sign in/sign out sheet. I scrawl my name and time, then pocket the pen.

Ducking into the stairwell, I write a note on the pamphlet and fold it. Then, scamper down the stairs to the room where I was first held.

The boy starts as I open the door, enter, and kneel beside him. I show him the note, point out the address. At first, he looks confused, then nods, points, and nods again.

"Excellent," I say. "Follow me."

He doesn't move. Doesn't speak my language. I motion him to follow.

We move quickly down the corridor, through the main entrance, and into the night.

A guard stops us, says something in Hebrew I don't understand, then grasps the boy's shirt.

I'm surprised at my reaction.

I swat his hand like a correcting mother, say in a loud and angry voice. "Cain says to let him go. Do you understand? Cain said it. *Cain.*"

The guard doesn't understand but doesn't miss the name drop. He steps away, turns, and moves off.

I walk the boy up the street, out of sight of the building.

I point at the address on the pamphlet.

The boy nods, takes the paper and sprints into the darkness.

CHAPTER 56

Fluorescent lights flicker, then cast the restaurant in a soft-white glow.

"Well, that's a step in the right direction," Jonas says, accepting tea from Mr. Lee. "Power's back on."

Mr. Lee blinks at the brightness, looks around the restaurant. He picks up a broom and starts to sweep, singing a little song to himself.

"That's quite a story, Laslo, and at the risk of sounding like a disbeliever, I must ask, are you sure?"

"As sure as I'm sitting here," Laslo replies. "Cain's taken control of Israel. Taken control of the entire region. Says it's a new kingdom, Imperium. I'm guessing the battle had to do with allies realizing the situation and coming to help." He looks away and mutters. "Not like it did any good."

"Is there anything you can do? I mean, you must have some forces still loyal to you."

Laslo shakes his head. "Probably not. I was the prime minister, not the minister of defense. I didn't know any soldiers or commanders personally, certainly not well enough to ask them to break ranks. At present, my concern is Israel. If Cain threw me in that pit, I can't imagine what he did with my son."

Jonas stands, moves to a counter and leans against it. "Let's see. He wasn't at Leyada. Wasn't at your home. Where else? Does he have any favorite haunts, perhaps friends who would've taken him in?"

Laslo looks downtrodden, the weight of the situation taking its toll. A square jaw hangs from a stubbled face, scratched, bruised, swollen. "None that I know of. He has his own security most of the time, but with the phones not working, I've no way to check."

"And," Igneus says, "we have to assume you're a wanted man. Cain isn't going to be pleased about your escape. We have to lay low."

"We have to get my son. Any risk is worth it."

"You don't know Cain very well."

"I know him well enough to fear him, to fear what he'll do to Israel. Some of the things I witnessed can't be explained. They were supernatural, unworldly. I've been deposed and have to admit, my thoughts dwell more on my boy than the fate of the country. It's the world's problem now."

Igneus considers the statement, agrees with Laslo's assumption. Perhaps the world will notice, perhaps they'll come and help. Had he known the attackers were friendly, perhaps things could've turned out differently. Still, they were after the staff, seemed focused on the relic, and didn't seem to care who they killed. The force treated them, both he and Longinus, as equal threats. He stares at Slabav, wonders if he's getting the full story.

Mr. Lee disappears into the back and returns with a dustpan. He scoops the sweepings and dumps them in the trash.

"Your boy is the priority," Igneus says. "After that, we'll see what happens."

He leans back, sips his tea. *What if it were Sebastian? What would I do?*

The answer's simple: I'd move heaven and earth. "Jonas, how dangerous is it to use the army truck and go out looking? You're wearing the uniform, know the rules and jargon. Might be the edge we need."

Mr. Lee walks past just then, holding a small TV. He sits it on the counter and plugs it in. The picture is snowy, and he fiddles with the aerial. "Power on," he says. "Maybe TV work."

Jonas's brow is furrowed, his eyes downcast. He thinks about the vehicle he stole, now parked in the alley, flanked by overflowing dumpsters, covered with wood and cardboard in an attempt to conceal it. "It'll be dangerous. If I'm asked for credentials, we'll be cooked."

"It's worth the risk, my friends." Slabav says. "The sooner the better."

"Ah ha! There you go. See? TV work." This is Mr. Lee.

They all focus on the picture. It seems regular programming has been pre-empted by a newscast. A man with dark hair and complexion looks into the camera and speaks.

"Is there volume?" Igneus says. "Not too loud though, Sebastian is sleeping."

Mr. Lee fiddles with some knobs and sound comes from tiny speakers.

They listen with rapt attention. News of both attacks, of body count, of efforts to restore utilities, information on shelters and where to get food or medicine, where to bury the dead. Cain's declared a curfew, has assumed control of the country. The broadcaster isn't shy about heaping praise on him. How he rebuffed not one, but two attacks. How he's rallied Mideast nations, set up food banks and medical clinics, how the populous adores him for saving the country from total annihilation, how Imperium will rise to power and restore balance to the world.

"Viewers are asked to remain inside," the announcer says. "If you leave your home, you may be stopped and questioned by Imperium safety patrols."

"Imperium safety patrols?" Igneus scoffs. "Nothing more than martial law from a silver tongue." He looks at Jonas. "Can you get through checkpoints?"

"Maybe?"

"Can you get in government buildings? Maybe we can get supplies and weapons."

Jonas thinks about it. "Doubtful, but again, maybe. It's just hard to say."

Someone pounds on the front door; the OPEN sign flaps out and back with each harsh knock.

"Closed! Go away!" Mr. Lee yells, fiddles with the TV's aerials.

The pounding persists.

Mr. Lee grumbles, then opens the door.

A teenage boy with black hair and shabby clothes bursts in, out of breath. "A note," he pants in Hebrew, hands Lee the paper.

Lee glances at it, then crumples it into a ball. "This rubbish! You go now!"

"Wait," Igneus says, taking the note. "It's hard to read but I think it says: ISRAEL AT PM OFFICE WITH CAIN. HEAVY GUARD."

Laslo leaps to his feet. Jonas peers over Igneus's shoulder.

"The PM's office. Martial law. Means military patrols." Jonas turns to Laslo. "Our chances of getting there are small, our chances of getting Israel, even smaller. I don't think…" He pauses, looks at the TV. "Can you turn it up?"

Mr. Lee obliges, the newscaster's voice comes through waves of static.

"…The coronation is set for the day after tomorrow. Please join us as we welcome our new Emperor and thank him for aiding us in our time of need. Curfews will be temporarily suspended so all may attend."

"Coronation?" Igneus says.

"Day after tomorrow?" Jonas says.

Laslo stares at the screen. Then, Cain comes on camera, starts his typical unity shtick.

Laslo gasps, leans close. Behind Cain, in an expensive suit, stands Israel, a broad smile on his face.

CHAPTER 57

MOUNT TABOR, ISRAEL

With a harsh clap of thunder, the rain starts again. Pappy glances from his book and out the office's small window. He spins in his chair, examines the rainbow of sticky notes on the wall.

Words like *Antichrist, signs, seals, bowls* abound, some scrawled such that he can't read them at all.

He runs a hand over his scalp. Coronation, he thinks.

The crown prophecy, just as predicted. The Antichrist taking control. He chews his fingernail, thinks of the prophecies. The attack came from the Americans, of that he's sure. A superpower trying to shove a smaller country in line.

Seems Cain doesn't care about such things. Is undaunted in his rise to power and absolute control. He thinks about attending the coronation, thinks of the logistics. Can he even get down the mountain? Get to Jerusalem? The land is improving as people try to return to normal. He'll hold regular services this week and try to assure his parishioners that everything will be alright, despite the fact he knows they won't.

He thinks of the reporter, Emery. Wonders if he'll return. Wonders if he's even still alive. Video has surfaced showing the attack, playing nonstop on the only TV station currently on air, and, oddly, without commentary.

What's Cain's next move? After he's crowned Emperor, then what? He considers the options. Obviously, Cain isn't worried about an attack, the video repeatedly shows Longinus using his spear to level a fleet of helicopters. It shows the other man, the skinny one, getting absolutely pulverized by helicopters and surrounding soldiers. Then, that flash of light and the enemy utterly destroyed.

No, Cain's become all-powerful and not just in the sense of a regional warlord but, instead, on the world stage. No one will dare come against Imperium after that display. No one will dare try to subdue the men or their relics.

He stands, feet scratch ancient stone as he paces. "What's next, what could be next?"

The realization hits him like an electric jolt, sizzling through his mind. "Oh no." Suddenly he feels very hot, smoldering even. Sweat breaks over his forehead, his eyes widen.

Cain's next move will be devastating, will cement his power for all time, change the Earth as never before. He thinks of a painting by Vasnetsov, thinks of the pale horse of death.

Time to go to Jerusalem. Time to stop Cain, even if that means his life.

He moves to the stout, dark door and opens it.

A man faces him, the labarum proudly displayed on the left shoulder of a black uniform. "Father Papadopoulos?"

Pappy swallows. "Yes."

"My name is Major Vasili. I'm a commissioned officer in the Legion of Imperium. I've been sent to ask you and your order to vacate these premises by edict of Supreme Emperor, Cain Augustus. This facility is now under state control, and we're here to assist your..." He pauses, considers his words. "Peaceful departure."

The friar stammers, looks past the officer down the short hall. From the sanctuary he hears the sounds of furniture scraping over stone, men's voices, talking, joking, occasional laughter. "This is preposterous. You can't evict us. This is our home. We've devoted our lives—"

Vasili interrupts. "I'm uninterested in your issues, Father."

"Friar," Pappy corrects.

"Excuse me, Friar. I'm uninterested in your issues at present and cannot undermine or change what the Emperor has decreed. To do so is punishable by death." He holds Pappy's eyes, seems to infer he doesn't agree with the decisions of the new management. "For what it's worth, I'm sorry. But you have until sundown to depart. If that doesn't happen, my men will…assist you." He leans close, lowers his voice. "It'd be in your best interest to comply."

Pappy stares, completely numbed by this change of events. "Where will we go? You have to understand…"

"No, Friar, it's you who must understand. This place has strategic importance, and, with the recent attacks, a strategic outpost is needed. Please don't make this hard on yourself or your brothers. Sundown today. No excuses. I'll return then."

He turns sharply and disappears down the short corridor and into the sanctuary.

Pappy stands bewildered, completely blindsided. Where will they go? What shall they do?

Then he jolts forward as he thinks of the real problem: Cain's plan and the horrors associated with it.

First task: tell the brothers of Cain's command. Then, find a way to Jerusalem. Time is short.

―――――――――

Thirty minutes later and message delivered, his brothers stand arguing about their options.

Pappy doesn't listen, doesn't tarry long enough to hear their plans. He heads to his room, packs his few belongings in a small, black duffle. Retrieving a large, black garbage bag, he slides it over his head and pushes each arm through the stretched plastic. Not much of a raincoat, but better than nothing.

He steps into the rain, takes a long look at the grounds, a last look at his beloved and sacred home. He steps off, down the walkway, through the parking lot, and onto the winding road toward the valley below. Squinting into the squall, he asks God to guide his steps.

Things are going to get very bad, very soon.

Cain's power grows. Soon he'll be unstoppable.

When that happens, woe to us all.

CHAPTER 58

JERUSALEM, ISRAEL

The boy hangs on Cain's every word. He smiles, nods, appears jubilant, fully under Cain's spell.

"Israel, oh Israel," Cain says. "Together we'll do mighty things. Impossible things, but first, I need to tell you some news that I fear will trouble you."

Israel's smile remains. He leans close, looks like he's stretching his neck for the guillotine. Cain continues, his expression serene, even caring. "Your father's been arrested for murder and treason. I'm afraid he'll be executed for his crimes, but I promise to do everything in my power to commute that sentence. He's served Israel well, and I think that should be taken into account."

Israel stares, smile unwavering. "Fuck him," he says. "If he broke the law, he should be punished. That's what he taught me, and I think it needs to apply universally."

I realize then how far Israel's fallen.

Cain frowns, slides close to the boy. "Wise words," he says. "Mature words. You're more intelligent than your peers, I'm guessing."

Israel's smile brightens. "Top of my class."

"Of course, you are, dear boy, excellence is in your blood and will serve Imperium well."

Israel beams, seems to fall into a daydream as he looks out the limo's window at the dark sky.

As I stare at the boy, Cain glances at me in such a way I cringe and shift my attention out the window as well. "We're beset on all sides, dear Emery, and the time has come for decisive action. The US and its allies were bold to attack so brazenly, but I fear they don't yet know our true power. President Carpenter will soon realize he matters very little," Cain says. "In a way, by missing my coronation, you'll be front and center for something even more grand."

"Such as?" I say, glancing at the wilted bowl of fruit.

"In time, dear Emery. All in due time."

Marcy, who sits next to me, regards Israel with an expression of compassion and empathy. She looks motherly and caring.

Cain looks out the window, then shifts to me. "Our Rhyme is quite a woman. Wouldn't you agree?"

I nod, say nothing, suppress a smile and hold my joy close. I long for her voice, long to hear her silky tones and tell her all I've learned. The thought crosses my mind that perhaps she knows all that's happened already, that she's been part of it. Perhaps she's in league with Cain and playing me for a patsy.

I push the thoughts away. I have to trust her, have to be true to my love for her.

"I can see you're of two minds regarding all of this," Cain says. "There have been many changes recently, with many more still to come. It's a lot to absorb."

I nod again, mouth suddenly parched. Cain retrieves an apple that begins to turn black at his touch. He takes a giant bite.

Nausea assaults as I watch a bit of fetid juice run down his chin. "I feel a bit overwhelmed," I say.

He dabs his mouth and nods. "To be expected, my boy. Especially from someone without my insight." He leans forward, gives my knee a friendly slap. "Take heart, dear Emery, our time is at hand. You are the most fortunate of my servants. I promised when I became God, you'd be in my favor. Now those prophecies have been fulfilled, and you sit at my right hand with the blessed charge of writing my story, creating a new Bible for the world to embrace."

"And you'll force them to embrace it?" I say this before considering my words. Cain's dangerous now, unpredictable, and I don't know how far I can push. Call it bravado or foolishness, but the reporter in me just can't stop asking questions.

"I won't need to," he says. "Besides, that's why I have Longinus. He's my prophet, my archangel. He knows what to do and shares my thoughts the very moment I have them. Believe me when I say, we'll have no problems with the masses. They'll obey the shepherd with the sharpest prod."

I think of my first meeting with Cain, the day he'd outlined his history. I remember calling *bullshit*, and the word crosses my mind again.

I hold my tongue and consider the evidence.

He's done all he said he'd do. He's died, returned from the grave with supernatural power, has imbued his servants with the same. He's performed the remarkable, the impossible, and if what he says is true—and I have no evidence to tell me it isn't—he now controls the entire Middle East.

He may even control the Chinese, who have invaded Russia and taken control.

Add to that, the power he'd bestowed on Longinus. The changes in his appearance. The confidence he exudes as he talks of his plans. All evidence points to the fact that Cain actually is a god, or the Antichrist, if you consider Pappy's opinion.

I remember Brother Pappy's words, see them playing out before me. Cain's conquered the region, unified the people, taken control of the resources, plans to be coronated as Emperor. My mind tries to refute his claims but can't overcome the man he is, the fact that the silver-haired lunatic gets whatever he wants.

"What's next?" I ask.

Cain's smile calms me, makes me feel warm and comfortable. "Isn't it obvious, dear Emery? Travel to the US and collect Rhyme. It seems Carpenter thinks he can control me, if he can capture her. X'chasei operatives are in place but have had a hard time catching up with her." He glances out the window, then at Marcy's legs. "I expect she'll do something outrageous. That's how she is, you know, wonderful and outrageous. A heart of fire burns in her breast." He regards me here with a grin of pity. "Why she adores you remains a mystery." He shows perfect teeth as he waves a hand. "In the end, it matters not at all. Please go and bring her back. A jet is waiting to take you and will bring you back once you have her. Understand?"

"I do, but how will I find her if your operatives can't?"

He chuckles. "A problem that takes care of itself, I assure you." He winks. "I'd hate to ruin the surprise though. Believe me when I say, you'll find her easily."

I nod. "Okay, and forgive me for asking, but since we're being so honest with one another, do you mean her harm?"

Cain looks astonished, his hair brightens a few degrees. "Dear Emery, do you think me so mad I'd murder my wife?" I think of Constantine the Great, of the story of his murdered wife, Fausta. I don't have the balls to answer. Can't take the chance of invoking his wrath when he's just ordered me to go find the woman I love.

"Just kidding," I say.

He nods, glances at Marcy who appears uncomfortable under the gaze.

"Of course, you're kidding, dear Emery." He crosses to sit beside me. "You've earned a boon. Allow me to do you a favor."

I tense, thinking he plans to choke the life out of me and toss me from the limo to lay bloated and dead in the street.

He places a hand on my head as eyes of crystal turn endless black.

Atop his head, hair roils, shifts, turns black as coal. I see no hint of light from the coif, no shimmer or sheen, as if the mane absorbs all brightness into its depths and holds it hostage never to be seen again.

The words that follow are guttural. A language I've never heard, thick, heavy on consonants. I get the feeling it's ancient, dark like his hair and eyes.

My chest starts to ache, then burns like being branded, like something drug from the chambers of my heart.

My breath is stolen. From somewhere I hear myself gasp. I'm detached now, somehow protected, feeling pain but not *aware* of it, like bells echoing through snow-capped mountains.

Tears run down my face in a warm gush. All my muscles tighten, then seize. I hear a groan, realize it comes from me. My arms flail and I can't control them.

Then, I hear another voice, speaking the same ancient language, answering Cain.

Razor claws tear my innards even as they struggle to resist Cain's will.

They argue, Cain's words come in quick syllables, chastise, command.

My chest tightens. I struggle to inhale, feel like I'm being murdered.

The other voice becomes a screeching wail, a terrible cacophonous harmony of deceit and malice.

"Open your eyes, dear Emery."

I force them open as a being rises from my chest.

It snarls and claws, snaps its jaws an inch from my face. Twisted lips stretch around an overstuffed mouth of razor fangs. It shrieks, smells like sewage, writhes, struggles to re-enter. Eight arms bulge with knotted muscle as they jolt for my neck, as sharp talons graze my flesh, as ten eyes, each as dark and as absent of life as Cain's, reflect back my own horrified image.

Slobber hangs from the thing's mouth, thick and ropy; it stretches to drip on my shirt. I buck and kick, or try to, as the green mucous oozes toward my skin.

The thing snaps mammoth jaws inches from my face. It wails, gropes for my chest, digs claws in, then struggles to pull itself back inside as mucous dangles from its mouth to swing inches above me.

"This is *your* demon, dear Emery," he says, unconcerned, calm, like this is an everyday occurrence. "Addiction," he continues, "one of my favorites, although a cheeky bugger." The demon twists under the spell. He examines it like a scientist, inches from his own face. "This little guy," he says, "slowly consumes everyone. Baits them from all that's good and proper down a path of misery and death."

He pulls it close, looks into its plethora of eyes. "It invades the mind. Attacks reason, you see? Makes you think you can't live another second without your fix. Makes you believe the *fix* is your only hope. You desert your family, your friends. You steal, cheat, lie, until you've nothing left but *it* and its commands. Then, it exploits that pain, promises relief, gets you chasing the addiction, to *need* it like air. When you finally hit the deepest, dismal bottom, it dangles your lost dreams before you, a forgotten family, an abandoned love, all you've done to feed and nurture it. It makes you see these things, to know what you've thrown away, how you've been deceived, all you've lost. It feeds on your misery, becomes stronger with each unquenchable need. And when it's finally done, when it's finally and totally consumed you, when it's taken every possible thing you have, it dumps you in a forgotten cesspool of your own creation."

The demon above me roars, rages, drips, snaps muscular jaws, lunges with a gaping mouth.

Panic invades to overwhelm my logic.

I struggle, consumed by misery, devoured by fear and helplessness. I try and raise my hands but find I'm paralyzed.

Cain's next words are soft, spoken as an afterthought. "It will bother you no more."

Eight muscled arms leap for my throat as dripping fangs lunge.

I hear a whoosh, see a black pinpoint open into the void.

A cacophony rises, fills my ears, clangs in my brain, millions screeching, the tortured torment of hopeless humanity.

Then it's gone, replaced by an odor of acrid flint, the smell of a burning gunshot.

Cain returns to his seat, adjusts his cufflinks, tightens his tie, glances out the window. "I've freed you," he says. "You're addicted no more."

I collapse, panting, soaked in sweat, trade a panicked gaze between

Cain and Israel. Marcy presses against the limo's door, face blanched, hands trembling. A single tear slides down her cheek.

I notice the bowl of apples, all now rotted and black.

Israel shows a small grin with, perhaps a hint of pity, but more one of amusement and amazement.

The limo slows to a stop and the chauffeur opens my door.

We've arrived at the airport.

I vomit onto the asphalt, wipe my mouth with the back of my hand. I try to stand. My legs shake, my heart races.

"Have a safe trip, dear Emery," Cain says, chuckling into his fist. "Do give my love to my wife."

I manage to stay upright as the limo moves through the airfield and into Jerusalem's night.

From inside my suit, my phone rings.

CHAPTER 59

JERUSALEM, ISRAEL

"Emery?"

My heart swells as her voice eases the terror and memory of whatever the hell Cain just tore out of me. She's a drink of water for a parched mouth, a warm blanket on a snowy night. "Rhyme, thank God! Are you okay?"

"I don't have a ton of time to talk. Just *had* to hear your voice before..."

"Before what? Do I hear sirens? What's going on?"

"I've done something rash, taken a gamble. I'm not sure what will happen from here, but you must know that I love you and always have. I have to tell you my reasons for everything. The reason I married Cain."

"Rhyme you're scaring me. I'm getting on a plane right now headed for Washington. I'll be there shortly. You can tell me everything when we're safe."

"There isn't time, Emery, so just listen. I married Cain to save your life. I don't have time to go into the whole story, but suffice it to say that Cain and I battled to a stalemate. One where I was protected and free of him. But then I met you. Cain found out and used you against me. He told me the only way I could save your life was to make a deal with him, and that deal was to be his wife. I didn't want to, Emery. I loathe that man. But he was going to kill you and, well, I just couldn't bear the thought, not after losing our baby. So, I married him, made him guarantee your safety. But he outsmarted me, hired you, kept you close, taunted me with what would happen if I didn't keep my end of the bargain."

Memories fill my head as things start to add up. I feel like I'm going to pass out.

I'd been watched the entire time, from the time Rhyme clocked me and left, until Longinus knocked on my door.

I've been so selfish, so naïve and conceited, thinking Cain's interest stemmed from my superior skills as a reporter. I've failed in almost every instance, have been seduced by the man's power and lifestyle. And with Rhyme suffering all the while, her love for me dangled in front of her as some sort of sick joke. She'd married Cain to protect me while I was off chasing the story and the fix.

My eyes brim with tears. Sorrow sweeps through. I realize the truest measure of Rhyme. She's sacrificed. For me. Given herself to the madman. For *me*, for *my* protection, all because she loves me and never wavers no matter the odds.

I feel weak and foolish, realize I've failed at every turn, used every excuse to wallow in misery of my own design.

I realize why she kept me away. Why she divorced me, issued a restraining order. Why she'd cast me aside.

"Oh, Rhyme," is all I can say.

Sirens blare, grow loud on her end of the line. "Rhyme, what's going on? I have so much to say, so much for which to apologize."

"I have to go," she says. "I love you."

"No, don't go!" I press the phone to my ear, struggle to make out the sounds, the voices.

A man yells. "Freeze! Drop the gun!"

"I love you," she says again. Then, I hear a horrible, hard clunk and the line goes dead.

Chapter 60

Outskirts of Washington, D.C.

Rhyme drops the phone, stomps it to scraps of circuit and plastic. She eyes the men around her. Stares down pistols and assault rifles. The night flashes blue light from the tops of police cars. Sirens wail in the distance as more officers approach.

"Freeze! Put the gun down!"

Sig clatters to the asphalt.

"Now turn around and place your hands on your head."

Rhyme turns, raises her hands then clasps them together.

She hears the footsteps, wary, smooth. This officer is well-practiced.

"She has another gun."

She recognizes the voice: Agent Elroy. He's come to get her, probably with head still throbbing from when she body slammed him. Add to that his wounded pride, and she knows it's going to be a long night.

"On your belly!"

Rhyme complies, lowers to her knees and lays on the ground.

In seconds she's cuffed, her other Sig removed.

They pull her up, turn her to face Elroy.

He maintains his distance as he eyes her and rubs the back of his head.

Rhyme grins. "How's the noggin'?"

Elroy flashes the leather bifold that hold his credentials. "We'll take it from here, officer. National security issue, federal jurisdiction. This is a high priority target. Good work, guys."

The officer's face shows frustration. He's not happy having his arrest pulled from his grasp and stalks off to the other uniforms.

More cars screech onto the tarmac, black SUVs with government plates and tinted windows.

This *is* going to be a long night.

Rhyme's hands are cuffed behind her back, not as loose as she'd like. That officer was no rookie, hadn't eased up on her due to her sex.

Elroy grabs the cuffs, twists her arms up. She yelps. "Easy stud, I'm only a girl."

Elroy wrenches harder, grins as she cries out again. "As if."

She turns toward the SUVs, then Elroy wrenches again. "Whoa there, cowgirl. We're not taking a ride. Seems you've picked a perfect spot for us. How about we take a little walk." He guides her roughly toward one of the airfield's hangars about a hundred yards away.

"What's the idea?" she says. "This seems a bit atypical."

Elroy nods, grins. "You're atypical. Things are atypical. What can I say, it's an atypical time."

The police have barricaded the airfield. Twenty patrol cars and a few black SUVs surround the place. Men patrol with automatic rifles and set up checkpoints.

They enter the hangar, yellow paint, faded and cracked. Elroy pushes her to the middle of a space designed for two small aircraft. He looks up at a second story walkway, a metal grating, painted gray, surrounded by a handrail. It spans both sides of the hangar. On the first floor, various doors lead to other rooms, other offices.

Elroy grabs an old four-legged wooden chair and slides it along behind them. It screeches across the concrete, sounds harsh, designed to get in her head, to inspire fear.

She won't give them the satisfaction.

Elroy wrenches her arms, pushes her roughly to sitting as another agent cuffs each hand to the chair's sides. "Oh, the things that are gonna happen tonight," he says. "You've been a naughty girl. Perhaps I'll give you a spanking before we start."

He straddles her, pulls his pistol, presses it hard under her chin, leans close. His breath smells of onions. "I'm supposed to tell you to hold very still, but I really hope you don't."

"Poor baby boy," she says in baby talk, "is him ego bruised?"

The look Elroy returns isn't pleasant.

He cocks the hammer of the weapon, presses hard, motions with his head. Other agents move forward to secure her legs to the wooden chair's front crossbar.

Elroy grabs her hair, twists her head back as far as it can go. "She did hurt him ego," he whispers in his own rough baby talk. "Now her's gonna be sorry."

Wide hangar doors squeal on their tracks as they open. Six black SUVs pull in.

She watches the doors close, watches blue lights narrow, then disappear.

She counts the agents, seventeen in total.

They move through the hangar, check that no civilians are present. Satisfied they're alone, they form a loose semi-circle and set a defensive perimeter.

There's a lot of firepower here.

An agent pulls two Pelican cases from an SUV, then empties them on the floor and begins to set up. In short order, a camera sits atop a tripod, behind it two spotlights, also on tripods. A switch is flipped, and Rhyme squints into blazing beams.

She's blinded now, a full participant in their head games.

She hears a voice, recognizes the tone, can't quite place to whom it belongs.

"At last we meet, Miss Carter. Or should I say, Mrs. Cain?"

Rhyme squints, tries to see who speaks.

A shadow moves in front and blocks the light.

She looks into the face of President Carpenter.

Chapter 61

Words fly, breathless, trying to say everything at once. "Mr. President, I have information about my husband. I know his secrets. You must know the truth."

Carpenter regards her with a smirk. "Do tell, Mrs. Cain."

Relief washes over her. Once she explains everything, they can overcome her lunatic husband.

"He can't be killed." She speaks quickly, rushed, has to get out as much as possible as fast as possible. "He's immortal, punished by God. He's been alive since the beginning of humanity. That's why he's Cain. He's the real Cain. From the Bible. He can't be killed and never, ever fails. How do you think all this happened? All these world events? He's been planning this for centuries. Using trial and error to improve his methods. He heads an organization that controls every aspect of the world. You have to capture and put him away before it's too late."

Carpenter's expression is dubious. He looks around the hangar, then back at her. "You're telling me I can't kill your husband because he's immortal?" he says. "Nice try, but you'll have to do better than that." He chuckles. "You know, I expected you to say something crazy to save his skin, and incidentally, I like the extra touch of making him a

Bible character, but still, don't you think you're trying a bit too hard to save the man you love?"

"I don't love him," Rhyme blurts. "I married him to protect the man I *do* love. It's a long story."

"I'm sure it is, and probably as full of lies as this one."

"I'm not lying. He's been alive forever, was Constantine the Great, created the Bible, changed it for his own purposes. He's bent on ruling the world and will succeed if you don't listen."

The president looks on. "Uh huh."

"You have to believe me!" she blurts, looks down, inhales, collects herself. "I know it sounds fantastic, but it's true. If you don't act, if you refuse to do *exactly* what I tell you, all will be lost. You can't beat him. No one can beat him. But you *can* capture him. He *can* be neutralized."

The president waves a hand. "I've had enough," he says. "If you want to play games, we can play all night."

"But—"

The slap echoes through the hangar. Tiny lights ripple her vision. "Shut your mouth! You're here by your own devices, your own decisions." Carpenter's voice lowers, sounds thick and scratchy. "You think this is our first rodeo? *We* always win, Miss Carter. That's what we do; get our man and get our way." He motions around the hangar. "Normally, I don't like to be associated with such things, but I *will* know the truth, one way or the other. Your husband's making waves. Has taken control of all the oil in the Middle East and Russia. I must admit, it's impressive the speed at which he's done it." He starts to pace, speaks as if giving a speech. "He's upset the world order and if we can't get it under control, things are going to get very bad, very fast."

He moves close, leans down, glides a hand through her hair in a gentle caress, holds her eyes, caresses her throbbing cheek. "Your husband won't listen to reason and seems hell-bent on his present course. Normally, it'd be enough to just let him know we have you in custody, but, unfortunately, times are such that there really isn't any other option than drastic measures. NATO has been forced to act and make no mistake, we *will* regain control of the region, then we'll convince the Chinese to abandon Russia."

"But you can't! You'll never win. You don't understand…"

His head snaps toward her and she braces for another slap.

Then, he snickers. "I'm afraid this is set in stone and there's really no way to stop it. We don't need Cain captured; we *need* him dead. He's too big a threat for us to sit on our hands while he demands fealty from the world. I'm sure you know he's proclaimed himself God. He's even asked me to surrender the US. Can you believe that? Your husband has quite a pair on him, but I'm sure, of all things, that, you know."

Agent Elroy approaches, whispers in the president's ear.

"Thank you," Carpenter says, then turns back to Rhyme. "I'm told we're all set here." He adjusts his tie. "Mr. Jenkins?"

Another shadow breaks the light and moves to stand by the president. The man is small-framed, short. A pencil mustache sits above thin lips. His hair is combed in such a way as to cover the swathe of baldness atop his head. Beads of sweat appear on his forehead. He peers at her through eyes like a game hen, gives the appearance of one whose life has been only laughter and ridicule.

President Carpenter continues. "We learned something from our Muslim friends," he says. "You know, the terrorists who'd film their captives while doing inhumane things. They taught us terror and, although not official policy, it's a useful tool when time is of the essence. Fortunately, Mr. Jenkins here is very, very good at this sort of thing. He'll start slowly and film everything. Then he'll send snippets to your husband with a polite request to renounce his authority and turn himself in. If Cain refuses, Mr. Jenkins will send more footage. Things will get worse and worse for you tonight, Mrs. Cain. Jenkins here is known for being methodical, exacting. For his, let's say, patience. I believe you'll find him unpleasant and, I want to be very honest here, you'll not survive the process, no matter what Cain does.

"You see, it doesn't really work if we just remove a finger and stop. Or just waterboard you and stop. The pause gives you time to collect yourself, to rest and mentally prepare for the next round. We've found this to be ineffective.

"What *is* effective is doing it all in one go and sending the highlights to the person with whom we're negotiating. In this case, your husband. By the time he does as we wish, you'll be long dead." He grins again. "That's an added bonus, no pesky witnesses running to the press and causing trouble. Not that the press would help, we've controlled them for a long time now. But, as you know, sometimes someone gets through, and we can't allow that to happen."

He stoops, whispers in her ear, smells of expensive cologne. "We're very, very good at this."

He steps away, raises his voice. "Keep up the good work everyone, and please support Mr. Jenkins in any way you can."

He turns to Rhyme. "It's a pleasure to make your acquaintance, Mrs. Cain. I'll give your regards to your husband, just before *he* dies."

Words flow fast, desperate. "Mr. President please, just listen. If you go against him, he'll destroy you. Don't you see? Think of the country, the people. There's another way. Mr. President!"

A fist slams her nose. The chair slides back an inch as her vision blurs with stars and tears. Blood runs from her nostrils to drip on her shirt.

President Carpenter enters an SUV, and two agents climb in with him. They pull off with two other SUVs, one behind, one in front.

Rhyme strains through blurred vision, updates her calculations. Eleven agents now, plus Jenkins. Three SUVs remain.

Jenkins stands before her, shaking his hand. "I don't like to hit women," he says, "but for you I made an exception."

Two agents drag a large Pelican case across the hangar's floor. Mr. Jenkins moves to it and draws a small, steel briefcase. He strolls toward her, swings the case wide, whistles a song from the Broadway show: *A Chorus Line.* He takes his time, consciously places each foot on the concrete so it yields the maximum echo from the hangar's walls.

Then, he kneels, opens the case, and turns it toward her.

Implements shine and shimmer in the beam of the spotlights. The tools inside are sharp, polished to a high sheen, encased in black foam and lovingly cared for. She sees something round, like a gear with sharp teeth. Then something that looks like a saw, about twelve inches long with an etched steel handle. Next to that lies an angled prod of some sort, a large version of a dental scraper. Then, at the top of the case, resting in its own cut out of black foam, is a large, steel phallus. Its end tapers to the shape of an arrow, appears as sharp as a straight razor, about five inches wide.

She gasps, stares at the tools, searches for courage, fights the grip of pure panic.

Jenkins follows her eyes, retrieves the phallus, holds it close to her, turns it slowly so it gleams in his hand. Light rolls over its length to reflect on her face.

"I see you've picked a favorite." He leans close, his whisper sweaty and terrifying. "It's my favorite too. Men *and* women both *love* this one." He eyes it, savors the look and feel. "I'll save it for last. It'll be a highlight for both of us."

An agent places a plastic bucket next to her chair.

She glances toward it, wonders what horrors lie in its depths.

"Thank you, my good sir," Jenkins says, then turns to Rhyme. "I see you're wondering what the bucket's for." He purses his lips, rolls his eyes up. A look of relish, of pure joy, of expectation and craving fusing to a savory flush of fulfilled desire. "Let's say it's for souvenirs. I'll let your imagination fill in the blanks."

He crosses to the camera, pulls a hanky from his pocket and polishes the lens. "The record is three days," he says. "Let's see if you can beat it."

CHAPTER 62

OUTSKIRTS OF WASHINGTON, D.C.

Where's Cain?

What's his weakness?

What's his plan?

Always the same questions, punctuated with slaps and punches.

It won't be long until they get to the implements.

They're softening her up, letting fear and pain mix to a gelatin of lost resolve, a marinade of the juices of suffering.

This will be slow, excruciating.

Her head lags. She wears only bra and panties.

They've undressed her to add a little spice to the marinade. They need her to feel exposed. Terrified. Abandoned. Need her to fill in horrific blanks on a terrifying page.

Blood drips from her face and onto her chest. Splattering her thighs, it runs down bare legs to drip on the floor where smooth concrete absorbs and magnifies, liquid crimson on death gray.

The marinade's working, tenderizing her mind, stripping her resistance to thin shreds.

She knows it won't end until she's dead.

They've been at it for hours, maybe days. When she'd gone unconscious, they'd nursed her back.

She's answered all their questions. But they don't believe her. The facts, too fantastical for anyone to take as truth.

Testing the cuffs that bind her to the chair, she steels her quaking mind. At each punch, it abandons simple calculations of advantage and disadvantage. She simply can't concentrate long enough before the next assault.

Exhaustion overwhelms like swarming ants. She feels sleepy, weak, nauseous.

She thinks of Emery and promises to die with resolve.

Mr. Jenkins rustles around in the Pelican case, his butt in the air, muttering, "Very soon, my dear." He chuckles as a tongue, like a worm, pops from his mouth to crawl over thin lips. "You're tonight's favored course."

He turns, spins the phallus, strolls forward whistling the show tune.

She squints through bright light. The phallus glimmers against the dark backdrop of the hangar's shadows. Seems the other agents have abandoned the area for other places.

He draws near, leans close. "Such pretty eyes," he says. "A perfect emerald." The worm pokes as he looks her up and down, takes a moment to stare at her breasts. He returns to her eyes. "I may add them to my collection. I've never seen their equal."

She turns her head, tries not to vomit through the duct tape over her mouth. A bony hand grasps her chin as the other grabs her hair and wrenches her toward him.

"We've been over this, my dear." He speaks through clenched yellow teeth. "It's rude not to look at someone when they're speaking."

She strains, struggles, finds he's stronger than he looks.

"Yes," he says. "Yes, yes. You have plenty still to give."

He releases her with a snap, looks around the room as if noticing for the first time the agents have gone.

"Alone at last." He raises the phallus and spins it, mesmerized by the razor point. "Seems I'll have to help you undress."

Her mind conjures nightmares as the skeleton grip of panic shreds her composure. She bucks, wails against the duct tape, against the cuffs, eyes wide, crazed.

Jenkins licks his lips as his eyes slide over her bloodied body.

She needs to endure, to think, to clear her head.

A switchblade appears in his hand, Benchmade, tactical.

He thumbs a button, and a thin, silver blade emerges.

He whistles the show tune, runs the blade across her bloody cheek, grazes it over her cleavage.

The worm darts from his lips.

Terror floods, rushes in to clamp like a vice. She knows the look, the expression men wear when overcome by desire.

The knife tingles cold, tracing the form of her breasts, sliding under her bra strap.

Then, a flash of blackness, of muscle, glimmering and slick, of snarling white teeth and powerful jaws.

Houdini slams him to the floor, jaws latched on his arm.

The Benchmade skitters. His scream echoes, thin and pathetic. The dog shakes him like a chew toy as blood squirts, as wails rise with each twist of a powerful head.

He shrieks like a canary in a cat's mouth.

Houdini whips his head, drags him across the floor.

Jenkins kicks him in the snout, snatches his arm free.

Houdini yelps, reattacks immediately.

Ears squeal with a harsh gunshot.

Houdini yipes and falls to the concrete.

Jenkins holds a snub nose revolver, smoke wafts from its barrel.

Her wail is muffled by the duct tape.

Her mind explodes, terror chases reason.

Then, raised voices: agents coming toward the commotion.

She fights her bonds, tries to break them with strength alone.

Her rage knows no bounds, her fire no limit. Blood drips from Jenkins' arm, from a place skin and muscle used to be. She'll kill this man if it's the last thing she ever does. Fueled by rage, by desperation, thoughts become sharp, focused, even as the cuffs tear her struggling flesh, yet remain tight.

Jenkins grins, retrieves the phallus, starts toward her.

An explosion rattles the hangar, rumbles over them followed by gunfire. Not the sound of handheld weapons, but a rifle on full auto, firing non-stop. A big gun, something turret mounted.

Agents fly from rooms along the hangar's periphery, bolt to the hangar's man door. Jenkins steps back. Explosions echo from outside, then the sound of a helicopter roaring past.

This is her chance.

She pulls with all her strength, feels the hard steel of the cuffs gouge her skin as blood trickles over her fingers.

The cuffs *have* to break, either them or the chair.

She pulls hard, focuses on Houdini, refines emotion as fuel. Groaning, cursing, fighting her bonds, she struggles for freedom.

Then, a loud crash and agents leaping for cover.

The man door becomes a gaping hole as a bulldozer plows through, knocks over an SUV, then slides sideways to a stop.

The hangar shimmies. Debris falls in chunks of wood and fiberglass. The roof above threatens collapse.

She squints into the spotlights, tries to see the dozer's driver. Flames leap from a rifle, but the lights are too bright to make out the person.

Agents scatter, returning fire, scrambling for cover. Three run toward her but are downed before they get close.

Two others kneel, thinking it better to address the threat before finding cover. A flurry of bullets makes tidy work, and they fall, guns clattering to the concrete.

The rifle pops, relentless.

She leans forward, positions her body for greater leverage as bullets whistle past.

Then: a thought through the chaos.

She tries to stand, strains against the cuffs, sets her mind to break the chair.

A stray round whistles close, a high, shrieking whine.

She throws herself sideways, lands with a breathless thud, sees Houdini rise from a puddle of blood only to stagger and fall again.

Shots deafen as the rifle fires.

She shimmies toward the seat's front edge. Strains, pulls hard.

But the cuffs hold. The chair, not as old as it looks.

Desperation and panic fuse to a single point of pure resolve, a razor's edge of pure will. Her head fills with pressure as muscles contract. She pulls with everything she has.

"I'm not done with you."

Jenkins moves toward her; crazed eyes betray demonic intent.

He holds the phallus, unconcerned with the raging battle, the flying lead.

She pushes harder, thinks of Emery, of Houdini, pours her terror and will and love into the chair, feels the crossbar shift a bit at her ankles.

Jenkins looms, worm poking, saliva coating lips in frothy bubbles.

He raises the phallus for the killing blow.

The crossbar breaks with a sharp crack, her legs fly free.

She twists, yanks at the cuffs.

The phallus arcs through its final stroke.

The chair splinters.

Her hands break free.

She catches the phallus an inch from her head, diverts it just enough that it lays a gash on her left shoulder.

Jenkins pulls back, slams the phallus again.

Rhyme catches his wrist, twists her body to trap his arm and head between her thighs. "Sailor's delight", Crispy calls it.

Jenkins struggles, rasps, tries to free himself.

She squeezes, wrenches his arm, breathless, fueled by panic, head spinning with blood loss, with fatigue and mental exhaustion.

The phallus flies free.

Then steely gray flashes.

Jenkins has the switchblade.

She braces for the assault, kicks free, rolls toward Houdini.

But Jenkins is quick, leaps on her, blade rising to gleam in the heat of the spotlights.

Gunfire comes in quick bursts.

Men scream as glass shatters around them.

The blade streaks for her throat, the worm pops from his mouth.

She raises her hands, tries to block with the cuffs.

The worm flashes, then disappears as thin lips crinkle to howl.

Houdini has him. Razor teeth sizzle as massive jaws chomp his arm.

The switchblade drops.

Blood flows over her face as gunfire clangs like a demented gong.

Jenkins fights the Doberman. Strives for the phallus inches from his grasp.

The dog's eyes glaze, then he collapses. He's given his last morsel for her defense.

Her rage doubles, quadruples, becomes limitless.

Jenkins leaps upon her.

The phallus flashes a millimeter from her face.

She catches the arm, squeezes tight, sees her own reflection in chicken eyes.

The worm emerges, darts across thin lips.

She's waning, tired, lost a lot of blood. With a groan, she focuses her energy, knows she'll die if she lets up. She twists his arm to an off-angle, turns the phallus against the weakest part of his grip, then pushes with both legs.

The phallus comes loose.

Jenkins flies up, staggers briefly, then leaps again upon her.

Rhyme falls back, offers her neck to the madman.

Hands claw as soulless eyes rage. Thin lips, pencil mustache, worm, he looks orgasmic as he falls upon her, as fingers enwrap her throat.

She uses her knees to support his weight, knows momentum will bring him close, knows her knees will keep him level.

But only for a second.

Bony fingers find purchase, clamp her throat.

Air stops, lungs plead.

The worm drips spit as thin lips curl.

She pushes, finds the strength to bear his weight, to bring him close, to keep him level.

With a sickening crack, she drives the phallus through the top of his skull.

The worm hangs dead as beady eyes stare at nothing.

She dumps him on the floor, scrambles to her knees, rips the duct tape from her mouth.

Racing to Houdini, she runs a hand through bristled fur, moves her face close, feels quivering breath on her cheek. "Please don't die," she pleads. "Please God, don't let him die."

Houdini's eyes close, his tongue hangs from a bloody mouth to rest on the concrete.

Rhyme rises, enraged. Moves to Jenkins, finds the handcuff keys, unlocks and lets them fall.

Bullets fly as she races to the side of the toppled SUV and presses against it.

Tears stream down her face. Houdini, brave Houdini.

Anger becomes a zenith as sharp as the probe in Jenkins' head.

Not out of the woods yet.

The battle rages close to the hangar's gaping man door, fifty feet from her position.

She peeks around, sees a man pinned by the agent's gunfire, pressed against the dozer's rear, assault rifle in one hand, a pistol in the other.

His ploy is cunning, fire indiscriminately with the pistol while using the larger gun for precision shots.

Only one man fights like this.

She races from the SUV as bullets sizzle past, then slides next to the man at the dozer's rear.

"What took you so long?" Crispy says. "I can barely hold them."

"I had to pee. How many left?"

"I don't know. How many did we start with?"

"Eleven."

"Five left then, more coming if we don't hurry."

Rhyme closes her eyes, controls her breathing, listens for the next shot, pinpoints the location. She tugs at the assault rifle. "Do you mind?"

Crispy gives a grin, lopsided and scarred. "Not at all, ma'am. Don't know how much ammo's left though."

Rage swells as hope rekindles. She's been taught to use emotion to her advantage, to embrace simmering bubbles of molten anger without overwhelming reason.

She moves from the dozer, fires at the location she pinpointed.

An agent pokes his head out. She creases it with a bullet.

To her left another moves, and she puts two in his chest.

She's on autopilot, constant movement her ally. If she stops, she'll be pinned and flanked. Crispy's held them at bay and bought her the time to deal with Jenkins.

He'd risked his life for her—again—and will never know just how close she'd come to wasting his efforts.

She feels energized, knows it won't last for long. Muscles move through practiced motions as the rifle chatters in her grasp.

Another agent falls as she directs a three-shot burst his direction.

Two left.

She knows Crispy will be moving along the hangar's right, so she stays left, creates space between them so they can both do their worst.

Then something catches her eye.

She turns toward spotlights still shining where the wooden chair sat, the place she'd been tortured.

Emery stands there, hands raised above his head.

Agent Elroy and his partner approach, guns raised, Emery in their sights.

He thinks he's going to give himself up.

She knows they'll kill him.

She raises the rifle, fires, hears only a click.

Simple math: the agents shoot, and Emery dies.

Emery drops his hands, waves them in front of his chest. "Just hold on a sec…"

Elroy fires.

Emery falls.

Her psyche explodes as a shriek tears her throat. Her mind rejects the scene in the most absolute terms. It's something in her heart, a primal kernel, savage, terrifying, rising to sizzle.

She sprints.

They turn and level their weapons.

Elroy's grin is one of satisfaction as they fire.

Rhyme drops, hears the bullets whine past, sliding on her knees, momentum propelling her the final few feet across the concrete.

They adjust their aim, reacquire.

But she's too close, sliding past, grasping a pant leg of each, then rising to her full height and lifting her arms.

They fly, twin acrobats landing hard on their backs.

Spinning, she slams her fist into the first agent's Adam's apple, feels the crack of his larynx as his eyes bug out.

She pivots to Elroy.

He raises his gun.

Rage fuels speed as she grasps the weapon, then twists to the inside of his grip.

The gun pops free.

Then, a smoking hole appears in his forehead.

She turns, crouched, gun leveled, scans for others who might've entered or been missed.

"Clear!" Crispy yells from across the hangar.

She lowers the weapon, races to Emery.

He stands, shakes his hand like it's on fire, then pries the twisted angel ring from a bloody digit.

He stares like a statue, mouth agape, eyes stunned. His lips move but no words come.

Rhyme faces him in bloodied underwear, smoke rolling from her pistol.

He blinks, stutters. "Jesus, Rhyme."

All at once, every radio in the hangar erupts with a shrill wavering signal.

She stares at the handsome, shocked face of her one true love as a warning blares. "Attack imminent…Attack imminent…Attack imminent."

CHAPTER 63

OUTSKIRTS OF WASHINGTON, D.C.

The dead agent stares with glassed eyes as Rhyme digs through his pockets. In his forehead, a puckered hole dribbles blood as his expression holds an air of stupefaction.

Disgusted, I turn away.

"She's hot!" Lenny says.

"Shut up!" I hiss, then, turning back, I marvel at all she is.

Even in her bloodied state, she looks amazing. She wears only underwear, covered in blood, but still has the effect on me she's always had. *What has she endured and how did she endure it?*

She stands, radio in hand, then bends again to take the agent's earpiece.

"Maybe you should get dressed," I say.

She spins and falls into my arms.

Her lips are soft, her hair, like silk. She feels good against me, and I feel our hearts merge. Like one of those Mizpah necklaces, two hearts, split down the middle until rejoined.

"I've missed you, Mr. Merrick."

I kiss her again. "Ditto," I say. "But it's hard for me to save you when you kick everyone's ass in like four seconds. Where in the hell did that come from?"

347

"Now, now," she says, "didn't mean to spoil your moment, but couldn't wait for you to get your armor and white stallion."

Emerald eyes twinkle as she slices a strip from my shirt and bandages my bleeding finger. Then she bends, retrieves the angel ring and holds it before her. "Guardian angel?"

I stare dumb. Look at the expensive ring, now twisted and crumpled. "The bullet hit the ring?" I wonder about many things, about fate, about providence, about destiny.

She starts to speak, is interrupted.

"You dumb shit, why didn't you hide?"

Crispy appears, his face resembling a topographical map.

"I thought I could help," I say.

"That's what you get for thinking, dumbass."

"I see you've met," Rhyme says.

Crispy hands Rhyme her clothes. "Found these over there." He turns his back as she dresses and speaks over his shoulder. "Who's the guy with the dildo in his head?"

"Someone who tried to get fresh," Rhyme says.

I stand on my toes, cast a glance toward the place where the man lies. A silver phallus juts from his skull like a jaded unicorn.

Rhyme ties her boots, stands and pulls her shirt over her head. She moves to the dead agents and retrieves their guns. "Lost my Sigs," she says. "These will have to do." Lithe fingers make the guns click and come apart, then click and go back together. She nods, slides them in the waistband of black tactical trousers.

"And just who are you again?" I ask.

She grins, frowns, then races to a dead dog. She lifts it, thrusts it toward me. "Be careful with him."

Crispy moves to the hangar door, steps over dead agents and pools of blood. "What's with the helicopter?" she says. "I didn't know you had access to one of those."

"I don't," Crispy says. "Have no idea where it came from. Perfect timing though, allowed me to crash in here with the FNG."

I look at Rhyme. "FNG?"

Her smile blooms and I know the look. It's her *stupid man* look. "Fucking New Guy," she says. "It means he likes you."

She follows him across the room, leaves me standing, holding the dead dog, trying to figure out how the term can possibly be one of friendship.

"Rhyme," I call, then nod at the animal. "I think he's dead."

Her eyes instantly water, reflect dread and heartbreak. "I'll leave you before I leave him," she says, then swallows hard and follows Crispy.

I ignore the comment, heft the dog and move after them. A pistol lies on the floor and I bend to retrieve it.

"No!" Crispy yells. "Best to leave that where it's at, son. Don't want you hurting anyone. Including us."

I wonder how Rhyme can be so fond of this man. He seems like an asshole, but an asshole to whom I owe a big debt. If he hadn't come, Rhyme would be dead, and I'd be left wondering what's become of her. I'd arrived at the airport without a clue of how to find her. Then Crispy showed up, said he placed an electronic tracker in her boot and bade me to accompany him. Somehow, he knew she was in trouble, like a guardian angel but without feathers, an angel who knows how to hotwire a bulldozer.

I leave the gun, remind myself to dig deep, to trust my spouse's judgment.

We approach the giant hole that was the hangar's man-door. The dog's blood drips on my trousers as Rhyme and Crispy press in on either side and peer out at the airfield.

Police cars burn, as do black SUVs. I see jagged holes in the vehicles while smoke floats across the tarmac. There's no sound or sign of the helicopter.

"We don't know what's out there, Emery. We have to be careful." Anguish crosses her face as she glances at the dog.

"I don't hear any sirens," Crispy says, "and that's odd. This place should be filled with police by now. We should be fully surrounded, facing one tough fight." He looks back into the hangar. "Wait here."

Twenty seconds later I hear an engine spring to life, then Crispy pulls up in one of the black SUVs. It's dented, pocked with bullet holes, the glass cracked like a spider web. "Hop in," he says, "this one's no worse for wear."

Rhyme helps me load the dog in the back seat and carefully wraps a seatbelt around the animal. I slide in next to it as she assumes the front passenger's seat.

Tires squeal as we explode through the hole we'd made on our way in.

He peers through the windshield, searching the sky. "If that helicopter shows, we're fucked."

"I don't think it will," Rhyme says.

"Why not?"

"I'm pretty sure my husband sent it." She casts a quick glance at me. "I'm pretty sure he wanted me to escape."

"He's your husband. *Shouldn't* he want that?" I speak before I think and regret my words as soon as they leave my mouth. What an ass I am, ruining this reunion, never happy despite the fact that Rhyme and I are together again.

"I'm sorry, Rhyme," I say. "That was stupid."

She looks straight ahead. "It's okay."

Crispy drives, mutters. "FNG."

The dog has a sharp hole in its side, and I press my hand against it. "Rhyme," I say, "I'm not sure this dog's alive…"

She points a finger. "Don't. Say it." A tear slides down her cheek, rolls over quivering lips. I snap my mouth shut while feeling for the animal's breath.

She faces forward, wipes her cheek, then turns a knob on the radio she lifted from the agent. The tone and warning continue. "Attack imminent…Attack imminent…Attack imminent."

"What's that about?" Crispy says, then pokes a button on the SUV's radio.

The tone for the Emergency Broadcast System fills the interior. I recognize it because I've heard them test the system my whole life. I wonder if it's a test, find myself hoping it's a test. We all wait for the tone to end and the instructions to begin.

The radio reads my mind and starts to speak. "This is *not* a test. Repeat this is *not* a test. Nuclear attack imminent. Repeat, nuclear attack is imminent. Seek shelter immediately. Repeat, seek shelter immediately. This is *not* a test."

"Lenny, what are you doing?"

"I wrote Emery a poem. Wanna hear?"

"A poem, Len? I can hardly wait."

"Ahem."

If, indeed, you find me dead,
a trillion atoms through my head.
Forget the search for super glue.
Or tape or paste, I've bid adieu.
Don't think to breathe or gag a prayer,
you might inhale my derrière.
Go get the broom! Go grab the pan!
Then scoop the dust that was this man,
—And dump him in the rubbish can!

"Why, that's beautiful Lenny."

"Uh thank-ya."

"Oh shit!" Rhyme looks at Crispy. "Do you know where there's a shelter?"

"No, but I know where there's an airplane."

The force presses me to the seat as Crispy stomps the accelerator. We streak from the airfield, toward the airport where the jet waits. It should be about a twenty-minute drive but as we near the city, we find the roads clogged with traffic. All lanes have been diverted to allow people out, not in.

"If we're gonna die, we may as well have some fun," Crispy says. "Hold on!" He veers the vehicle off the road, through a chain link fence and across a suburban backyard. We race between two houses, crash through a barbecue grill and a clothesline. Crispy turns hard left, and I fly across the backseat and bounce off the door.

"Buckle up," he says, "fucking new guy."

"Take care of the dog!" Rhyme screams.

I scramble with the seatbelt as Crispy drives like a maniac.

Rhyme holds the radio, has the agent's earpiece in her ear. She's pale, sweating.

"Are you okay?" I ask. "You don't look good."

She nods, turns to hold my eyes. "They just said impact in twenty minutes. They just said the entire US is targeted. Said they expect as many as fifty warheads." She pauses, stares. "You okay? You look pale."

"I…I…I just can't…" I feel nauseated. We're going to be vaporized. "You know this is Cain," I say. "He sent me to get you so we'd be in the same place when he launched the strike."

Rhyme nods. "I know. He wants us both dead, that's the only answer. Wants us out of his circle."

"Why would he kill you?" I ask. "Beside the fact that you're his wife. I thought you had some sort of deal with him."

"I don't know." She glances at the dog, then frowns. "Perhaps the deal is off. Perhaps he doesn't care anymore about what he covets and I possess."

"My phone hasn't rung, and he knows the number of any phone I've ever had," I say, thinking of the one the Apostle gave me. "Doesn't make sense."

"And why would he send a helicopter to help, only to have us blown up by a nuke?"

We look at each other, share the same expression, puzzled faces trying to solve a mystery.

I press on the Doberman's wound. "I think he's breathing."

"Look!" Crispy points out the windshield.

I lean forward to see three rockets streak from the Earth. "Must be the counterattack," he says. "Who could be attacking? Don't they know this will end the world?"

The words clear my mind. Everything suddenly makes sense. Cain *is* ending the world. Needs to end it so he can control and dominate. Needs to wipe out the powers that be so he can rule unopposed. I wonder if he's thought it through, then chuckle. Of course, he has. He's always one step ahead of everyone, including God, whom I'll meet very soon.

Rhyme sits in the front seat, watching thin streams of smoke blaze across the sky. "We need to get out of here."

I grab my phone, dial the number that connects me to Cain. An X'chasei operator answers, speaks in a calm and clear voice, professional, unconcerned, detached.

I tell her my code and listen as the phone rings.

After seventeen rings it becomes apparent, he isn't going to answer. The first time I've called, and he hasn't picked up. He's given us up, left us for dead.

I feel the betrayal like a knife in my heart.

I wonder if the jet still waits.

I call the number again, say who I am and that I need to be connected to the jet's pilot. The wait seems forever and I half-expect the operator to hang up on me. Half-expect my privileges to have been revoked.

The pilot answers on the second ring. "It's Emery! Are you still at the airport?"

She sounds professional, speaks clearly. "I was just hitting the throttle to get out of here. You know there's nukes coming?"

"Yes, yes!" I say. "We're on our way. Don't leave. I repeat, don't leave."

There's a slight pause, and I almost panic as I think we've been disconnected. My mind moves so fast, each second feels shorter than the one before.

"I'll wait as long as I can. What's your ETA?"

I lean over the front seat. "What's our ETA?"

Crispy crashes through a wooden fence, smoke rolls from under the SUV's hood. "Five minutes, maybe ten." He presses the accelerator, throws me into the back seat. I reach for the seatbelt just as Crispy clips the side of a filthy, green dumpster to send it spinning in a flurry of trash and spark.

"Ten minutes at most," I say.

"You're cutting it close."

"Wait as long as you can, we're coming. Don't leave us here to die. Keep the engines running."

"Roger that," she says.

Crispy crashes over a curb, sends me flying to the SUV's roof. I land with a thud. The phone flies into the back cargo compartment.

I leap over the seat, land hard on two Pelican cases. I search for the phone, hear Crispy yell, "Hold on!" Then I'm flying again, up against the roof to slam back down on the cases.

Rhyme looks back. "Quit screwing around and get back up here. Buckle in."

"Look at this pecker head," Lenny says.

"I'm trying," I yell as Crispy takes a corner so fast, I think we're going to roll over. I slam against the right sidewall of the cargo area. Then I see my phone lying beside me.

I hold it to my ear. The line's dead.

I toss it over the seat and follow, leaping the seatback to land on the floorboards. I rise, scramble for a seat belt, manage to click it in place before another "Hold on!" from Crispy.

I look up, see a huge warehouse ahead of us. Crispy speeds toward it, vision obscured by the windshield's cracked glass, the smoke pouring from the hood.

"Wait!" I say. "You can't go through there. You've no idea what's on the other side of the door!" I fail to match the words raging through my brain, as if my mouth wasn't built to speak as fast as I think.

Crispy mashes the gas and we rocket toward the warehouse's center.

Rhyme looks over her shoulder. She looks serene, accepting of whatever fate lies ahead.

"I love you, Emery."

And, right there, time freezes.

I take it in. The dog's ragged breath, Rhyme looking through bruised eyes, nose swollen, blood crusted on her upper lip, emerald eyes shining bright, filled with love.

My heart bursts with who she is, all she is. I'm filled with her, with the fact she's used her final moments to tell me how she feels.

"I love you, too."

Crispy screams, the SUV bucks as we burst through the warehouse door. The hood flies up, then detaches completely.

Ahead of us is a huge machine, pipes and vents running to it, from it, everywhere.

Crispy yanks the wheel and we drift through a left turn. The space is narrow, perhaps an inch or two wider than the SUV. Crispy seems undaunted, presses the engine to maximum, races down the narrow alley flanked by conveyor belts and big machines.

We lose the right mirror.

"Crispy!"

The left mirror flies away in a flurry of plastic and glass.

Rhyme grips the dash. "Careful, careful!"

"Yep," Crispy says. "We got this. No problem, no problem at all."

The warehouse's rear wall screams toward us. Something blocks it and I squint to see what it is. A forklift sits sideways in front of the door, as if abandoned in a hurry. I look to both sides of the machine, see no way the big SUV is going to make it through.

"Hold on," Crispy yells again. I reach for my seatbelt, grip the seat back in front of me, press the dog into the seat.

Just before we hit the forklift, Crispy takes a hard left, tires screeching.

Our tail end smashes into the machine, which flings us to the left and aligns us perfectly with a loading ramp about the width of a semi-trailer. It's about a hundred feet long, rises to a huge garage-type door. A door that's closed.

I glance at the scarred man, amazed he read the situation in a millisecond and used the forklift to effectively bounce us into perfect position.

We rocket up the ramp, all of us screaming.

I grasp the seat before me, scan the rolling door to surmise of what material it's made.

We smash through, fly to land in a wide parking lot that's clear of obstruction. The SUV bounces on the concrete as we fishtail so hard and so much, I think we're going to roll over and over.

Crispy wrangles control, mashes the accelerator.

I peer through the mangled windshield, see the airport straight ahead.

Smoke pours from the engine and I'm amazed the scarred man can see anything.

He floors it, speeds toward a chain link fence surrounding the airport.

The engine makes a weird sound. A grinding metal that clanks in time with my heartbeat.

We crash through the fence and I feel us yaw horribly to the side.

"Damn!" Crispy yells. "Tire blew."

I recognize the thump of the deflated tire, look ahead to see the jet waiting for us about a half mile away. I look to the sky, expect to see missiles raining, mushroom clouds blooming. I wonder if I'll feel it or just be instantly vaporized, so many atoms neither created nor destroyed.

The thump becomes a squeal as we race over the tarmac. Crispy angles toward the runway, our jet waits on the other side.

I look to my right, see an airliner taking off, huge, speeding toward us.

We're in the ultimate game of chicken.

Everyone knows their life is forfeit, everyone knows, *if* they survive, it will be by the thinnest of margins and a few chin hairs of luck.

"Airplane!" I scream.

"Three o'clock!" Rhyme yells.

"Got it!" Crispy yells.

The airliner gains speed as we race to cross the runway in front of it rather than behind. We're close enough that if we get behind the thing, the force of its engines will roll us down the runway like a child's toy.

The tire goes thump, thump, thump. The engine clanks and squeals. Smoke pours from the front of the vehicle as we three sit wide-eyed, watching the airliner speed toward us. Crispy holds the pedal to the floor. We all hold our breath.

The airliner's front wheel rises, the plane's belly swells above, white and blue, like a diver beneath a sperm whale.

I watch, numb and dumb, as the craft's huge rear tires lift, then rise to strike a glancing blow on the SUV's roof.

We're sent spinning. Crispy desperately wrestles the wheel. His hands are a blur, scarred face wrinkled and determined. We tip sideways on two wheels, then Crispy yanks and the SUV falls with a shudder and a sickening scrape of metal.

We streak forward, cheers flowing, hands raised, joy boundless.

Crispy forces the SUV through the grass to the taxiway's far side.

We screech to a stop as I unbuckle, heft the Doberman and head to the jet.

Crispy pops the cargo area. "Grab one," he says to Rhyme.

"Are you crazy?"

"Probably! Just grab one!"

She pulls a Pelican case from the cargo area and sprints to the jet.

The pilot stands in the doorway. "C'mon, we need to go! Now!"

A man stands next to her. A hippie. A man I know.

It's Bill.

He steps aside as I enter and set the dog in the aisle as gently as possible. Rhyme follows, dumps the case and moves to the dog. She pulls him close, hugs and caresses, whispers gently in his ear. "Please, Houdini," she pleads. "Fight. Don't leave. Hang on. I'm here, we'll get through this." A tear drops on the dog's nose, another onto his face.

I collapse in a plush leather seat. Crispy enters and dumps his case atop the other.

Bill moves to sit in a seat across from me.

The jet whines and we move.

I glance out the window where a line of other aircraft clog the runway, waiting to take off.

I yell to the cockpit. "Are we gonna make it?"

She yells back, "Not if we wait for the fat boys!"

The jet turns through a tight right and enters the taxiway. The force of the engines press me to my seat. They roar, pushed to full throttle.

She's using the taxiway to take off.

I glance at Rhyme, who hovers over Houdini, whispering, tears streaming.

The jet catches air, lifts, angles to the sky. We climb higher and higher, endure an abrupt turn or two. The pilot yells back. "Sorry. Have to dodge the missiles."

I look out the window, see the rocket's impact: a bright flash followed by a burgeoning mushroom cloud and the resonance of shockwave.

I wonder if we're fast enough to outrun the explosion.

Then I feel Bill's hand on my shoulder.

We stare at the horror unfolding below.

Tears cloud my vision as a fiery cloud blooms over the face of my homeland.

Tears stream down Bill's face, shoulders shudder as he spasms. He's despondent, shaking his sorrow into the jet's interior, lost in pure despair, overwhelmed by grief.

I press my head against his, feel Rhyme's press against us both.

We share his burden, feel his sobs, as heavy as our own.

Mushroom clouds explode into the atmosphere around us. Then others come in focus, and still others for as far as we can see.

We fly over the Atlantic, numb, catatonic, forlorn. Utterly and completely destroyed. Our sobs fuse, rise, reach a crescendo that's a poor measure of our pain.

Hope turns to vapor.

Goodness to goo.

Our nation is gone. Our hearts, shattered.

CHAPTER 64

JERUSALEM, ISRAEL

Laslo Slabav slouches near a wall. He wears a thick poncho of waxed cloth and a ball cap pulled close to his eyes. So far, he hasn't been noticed. "Do you see him?" he says.

Igneus takes in the faces, peers through the mass who yell blessings to Cain. The people gathered here, tens of thousands, fill every space, shove and cajole for better position, seem not to notice their ripped and filthy clothes, the dirt on their faces, on their kids' faces.

"I don't see… Oh, wait, there he is."

Laslo stands to tiptoe, peers under the hat's brim, stares at his son.

Security surrounds both Cain and Israel as they take the stage.

"At least fourteen on the ground," Jonas says. "Certainly more near the Temple or in it." He looks around, sizes up the nearby buildings. "Snipers concealed as well. Perhaps this isn't the best time…"

"Nonsense," Laslo interrupts. "Israel is here, and we will have him. There's no other reason to be here save that."

Igneus watches the boy, sees no sign of distress. "Laslo, this is going to be hard to hear."

"No excuses!" Laslo snaps. "Either help me or I'll do it myself."

Jonas surveys the area. "Foolhardy. In public. Near the Temple.

Even if I had a full assault team and air cover, this would be hard." He turns to Laslo. "Today isn't the day."

Laslo's lips tremble as he spits a whisper. "You said yesterday wasn't the day. Then said the coronation would be the place. Now you say it can't happen. Again. Are you even interested in helping? I thought you were a tough guy, a man who defies the odds? If this was your son, what would you do?"

Jonas thinks back to his own boy. Thinks about his curious nature and limitless energy. Thinks of playing soccer with him as he and Sebastian played in the parking garage.

Demons wake as visions change. He sees himself staring at a closed coffin, fists pressed to dark wood, fighting the urge to throw up the lid and embrace his son one last time.

He turns to Laslo. "Listen," he says, leaning close. "I understand your pain better than most, but I won't be party to getting us all killed, and I certainly won't be party to your son watching you die because you're too stupid to bide your time. Look at him. He's well treated, in no apparent distress. And you'll have us rush up there and try to take him back?" He holds Laslo's eyes. "Now's not the time, Laslo. The clever warrior chooses his battlefield, subdues the enemy and obtains his objectives while risking as little as possible. What if we charge up there? What if we fail? Does Cain murder your son to teach you a lesson?" He taps Laslo's forehead with his index finger. "Think! With your mind! Suppress your emotions. The proper time will come, but now is *not* that time."

Laslo's face twists with anger as the two stare at each other, neither averting their gaze.

Igneus steps close, places a hand on his shoulder. "Jonas is right," he says. "It will be folly."

Laslo's eyes brighten. "You can use your staff," he says. "Nothing can withstand that."

Igneus opens his mouth just as Cain and Longinus take the stage. Longinus steps forward, raises his spear overhead, then taps it sharply on the ground.

The staff glows golden, brilliant, slowly rises above the Earth to cast its rays over the gathered thousands. It spins on its axis, points toward the sky, speed growing by exponents. A sizzling hum wafts over those assembled. Then a shower of golden rays explodes from its tip to rise above the Earth thousands of feet. Darkened clouds turn blistering gold, send rays brighter than sunlight to splay on the crowd.

Cries go up. Cheers rise. People leap, crane on tip toes, climb on everything so they can witness the spectacle.

They squint against the light. "I can't, Laslo," Igneus says. "I can't risk a battle in so crowded an environment. We have to live to fight another day."

Laslo's words catch in his throat. He stares at the spinning relic, blue and red lasers flow through its etching, a thick, golden beam rises to spread through the heavens.

The rain stops.

Igneus is asking him to put his country over his son, asking for patience and wisdom, for patriotism and selflessness. He regards the mass, the citizens of Israel, of Imperium. His eyes rest on his son. The boy is handsome, well kept, even happy, standing next to Cain, then sitting, as a priest, a rabbi, and an imam come forward.

Laslo can't pry his eyes away, grips the wall before him to keep himself from sprinting up and spiriting away with his son.

On the stage, the holy men go about a ritual of some sort, open a book, light candles, move with great reverence.

Cain steps forward, kneels before the mass as holy men drip oil on his forehead, then make a show of praying over him.

Israel stands, holds a pillow in deep maroon.

Upon it sits a golden crown that shimmers under the spear's radiance.

The priest lifts it high, moves behind Cain as the other two grasp its edges.

They speak in unison as they lower the crown to his head.

> *Blessed beacon.*
> *Holy lance.*
> *Let all who see, find solace in your shelter.*

Let no man with goodness fear, and no man with
  evil endure.
In aqua, show us the vastness of Heaven and the
  speed of our lives.
In flame, show us the embers from which we're
  spawned and to where we shall yet return.
Let golden rays give succor and ever-reflect our
  kingdom's glory.
Fly, great staff, from the banners of the faithful,
  so that the world may know,
Imperium.
From this, to the end of days, and always, and
  forever.

Cain's hair dazzles, seems to enwrap the crown as its placed on his head. He looks pious, humble, as reverent as the holy men who finish their blessing and move off.

He rises, stands in glory before the gathered population.

Igneus squints against the light. Laslo's eyes stay focused on Israel.

Cain steps forward and stretches his arms to the crowd.

The spear crackles, then flies to his hand.

A flash of perfect teeth. Gleaming white hair dances within, through, and over the golden crown's ring.

Thunder crashes and the crowd gasps.

"Father, bless my people," Cain announces. His voice is an echoed cacophony, overwhelming yet soothing. "Give them warmth."

Clouds part to shine bold rays upon the mass.

"And sustenance."

People move through the crowd, distribute loaves of bread, fruit, dried meats.

"And safety."

The spear sizzles, sends streaks of white light in all directions. It's like a supernova. People shield their eyes, even Laslo tears his gaze from his son.

"By the Father am I crowned, by the people I am bound. Forever to serve, forever to serve."

Light fades as the crowd erupts, as voices rise loud enough to shake the heavens.

The holy men step forward, face Cain, then kneel.

Thousands follow, all kneeling as one, heads down and silent.

"From this day to the end of days," Cain continues. "And always, and forever."

Epilogue

The presidential bunker hums with activity. Tom Carpenter stares at the screen. "Status report!"

The aide sweats openly, cheeks flushed, eyes filled with tears. "They've hit us everywhere. Every…Everything is gone. Comms are down, and we've no way to tell the extent of the damage."

"What about the counterattack?"

She stares at the screen, says nothing, looks panicked and shell shocked as sweat pours down her face.

"Major?" Carpenter says.

"Yes…yes, sir."

"The counterattack? A sit rep, please."

She sighs, straightens in her chair as the room goes quiet, as everyone around them stops and listens.

"There's been a problem," she says. Her voice cracks, her hands tremble. "Seems we've hit all targets in Russia and China, but all the other missiles disappeared." Wiping her brow, she glances at the president. "There was a sudden flash of energy. Originating from somewhere in the Middle East, from Jerusalem, I think. Took out a lot of our missiles, all the ones targeting the Mideast." Eyes crinkle, confused. She shakes her head. "Just doesn't make sense. There's no power that could do that, no nation possesses that kind of capability. It's as if…"

Carpenter rises, doesn't need to hear the rest of the Major's sentence.

He stalks from the room, a single word on his mind.

Cain.

Jerusalem, Israel

I've never seen her this mad.

Eyes blaze fire as auburn hair flows in her wake. She moves like a whirlwind as I follow and try to slow her down.

She bursts through the glass doors of the PM's office building. Two members of the Israeli Defense Force step in front of her.

"Just a minute, ma'am," the first says. "We need to do a quick search."

What follows is like something I've never seen. The guard holds up a single hand. The other sits propped on the butt of his holstered weapon. In a flash, Rhyme grabs and twists in such a way the man spins to land with a crunched thud. A harsh whoosh escapes as breath flees. As he's in the air, Rhyme pulls his gun and levels it at the other surprised guard.

The man freezes as she steps toward him and presses the pistol to his forehead. "Please inform my *husband* I'm coming up."

The man swallows hard, manages a shaky grin, reaches to the side of a long steel desk and gets the phone.

"Are we going to have a problem?" she asks.

He lowers his eyes. "No, ma'am."

She lays the pistol on the desk and walks through the metal detector, which sounds a shrill alarm as she passes.

"Sorry," I say to the guard on the floor. "Sorry," I say to the other guard. "Women, right?"

They stare at me, dumbfounded. The guard on the floor still dazzled by his abrupt impact. The other guard speaks into the phone.

I rush after Rhyme and enter the elevator just before the door closes.

"Jesus, Rhyme," I say. "You could've really hurt that guy."

I know the look she gives, one that says she isn't currently open for discussion. Emerald eyes bristle with wild rage, and I spend the ride wondering just how little I know about this woman.

It takes forever to reach the proper floor, and I'm relieved when the doors slide open.

Rhyme doesn't wait but exits as soon as the gap's wide enough for her to slide through.

Four more guards stand in the lobby, each with pistol in hand but unraised. They stare at the twin pistols in Rhyme's waistband but make no move to stop her.

She passes without a word, flies by so fast I'm not sure she even noticed them.

Down the hall, she reels back and kicks the door in. It crashes open, and I watch her disappear through the threshold.

I race after, and by the time I enter, she has Cain by the tie, pistol pressed against his forehead.

"You son of a bitch!" Her voice quakes. All the things she's seen, all she's endured coalesce to a fine point of focused rage. "I'll tell you what, fucker. You're going to answer my questions, or I'll sit here until the end of my life blowing your head off each time it regrows."

"Rhyme, my dear, how lovely—"

"Shut your stupid face!" She screams so loud it hurts my ears. I glance to the door, which hangs askew, dangles from a single hinge. I expect guards to burst through, expect to find myself in the midst of another firefight. I don't relish the thought, but after what I've seen of Rhyme, I'll place my money on her.

Cain's head tilts back as she presses the pistol.

"Now that I have your attention, do you mind telling me just why in *the fuck* you'd leave me to die?"

Cain raises his hands and I cringe. I know the man's speed, his abilities when it comes to fighting, and I expect he'll try to disarm his wife.

If it comes down to it, it should be an interesting matchup, and again, in Rhyme's current state, I'll place my dollars on her.

"Dearest Rhyme," he says. "Believe it or not, I love you and would never send you into harm's way. If I recall correctly, *you* were the one who failed to follow my instructions. *You* were the one who went off the grid. I'd barely found you when I sent the helicopter. Most of the men you killed were X'chasei associates. You were never in harm's way."

"Bullshit!" she says, pressing the pistol. "That little psychopath beat my ass. He was going to kill me."

Cain interrupts. "Are you saying it was a challenge? I do know how you enjoy those."

"You were testing me? Is that what you're saying?" The muscles in her hand tighten as she squeezes the trigger.

"No, my dear, if you must know, I was using you as bait. What would you have done here? File your nails? Go shopping? Knowing the attack was coming, I couldn't run the risk of you being caught up in a rogue explosion. For that matter, I needed the president busy trying to locate you. I needed him to think he could use you as leverage. I knew you'd enjoy the challenge and that you'd probably enjoy the adventure, not so unlike the old days."

I cringe again, feel his answer isn't going to soothe her in any way.

A moment of doubt crosses her face, her eyes flash as she considers his words.

"Still bullshit," she says, "there's more to it. You didn't go to all the trouble just to give me a little adventure, just to keep me safe."

The pistol moves as Cain nods his head. "You're right, my dear. So astute. Beautiful, cunning, and deadly. How can any man resist you? There is more, and I suppose there's no harm in telling it all."

She leans in. "That would be a good idea, *dear.*"

I almost laugh as she exaggerates the word. I glance to the door. No guards appear.

"I needed the US to destroy Russia, and the Chinese to destroy the US with Russian missiles. With both focused on each other, China was wide open. A perfect target of opportunity. None of them ordered that strike. I did. I've spent decades infiltrating, a fortune gaining the codes to launch the weapons. Now they're all history, and I hold the keys to the biggest stockpile of nuclear weapons the world has ever seen." He flashes his movie-star smile. "All thanks to the Russians, who were so easily baited into attacking a nation they thought defenseless. Don't you see, I've consolidated *our* power. The superpowers have been neutralized and I control most everything else. You've become the marvelous, gorgeous Empress of Imperium, the shining star of my empire. Europe should surrender shortly, and everything will be perfect."

Rhyme lowers the gun; a tear rolls down her face. "You're insane. You killed millions, hundreds of millions. What about the families, the children?"

Cain waves a hand. "If one wishes to make an omelet…" He trails off and my mind finishes the sentence: Then you have to break a few hundred million eggs.

His mark appears inert, puckered and dead, his white hair appears normal atop his head.

Rhyme glances at me, then lowers her head. I know the move. She's thinking. Even after all she's been through, she retains the capacity for strategic thought.

She shakes her head, a little twitch at first, then more robust. She stands defiant before the harbinger of all darkness.

"There's something else," she says. "You're holding back."

Cain sighs, stands. "I wish to be very honest with you from this point forward. Our love is too grand to be spoiled by something as common as mistrust."

He glances at me for the first time. A small grin crosses his face.

"There is something else," he says. "I needed you there so I could test the limits of immortality. So, I'd know for certain what an immortal can withstand. An experiment, if you will. A way to see if an immortal can survive a nuclear blast."

Her voice rises. "You used me as a guinea…" She stops cold, stares at him with a look of horror. "Immortal?"

"Yes, my dear. I needed you in Washington so that when I ordered the attack, Emery would be there. And what easier way than to send him to find you, to save you. Most of the men you killed were X'chasei operatives. That louse Jenkins had served his purpose, and the time had come to dispatch the little toad. I'm sure you enjoyed the challenge and really, my dear, you've been through worse."

He sits, steeples his fingers before him. "The idea was to have you safely back here, while Emery stayed behind looking for you. His devotion being such that there's no way he'd depart the country without you. Then, when the bombs fell, I'd have my answer."

They both look at me.

Rhyme's face betrays shock. She's aghast, mouth hanging, emeralds full of pity and deepest sorrow, deeper even than the desolation they'd held when we'd watched America die.

Cain regards me with a glaring smile and a portion of malice.

The full force of his words swirl as my mind calculates their sum.

He was testing *my* limits.

He was sending *me* to die.

I was the experiment.

A sense of assault floods my core. My hands tremble. My mind becomes a whirlpool of thought, swirls at blinding speed, impossible to catch or to focus. My mouth is suddenly dry, my throat parched and cracked like the barren desert.

"You…" I start, then pause to control my breath. I'm having a panic attack, have finally hit the point where too much is more than enough.

I close my eyes, try to calm my body.

"You…" I stammer. "You made *me* immortal?"

Cain shakes his head, flashes that perfect smile. "No, my dear Emery, I'm afraid I can't take credit for that particular boon." A perfect elegance disappears, becomes confusion tinged with rage. "After my return, I knew of your immortality the second I saw you. That emerald aura, not so unlike my wife's eyes. You're ripe with it, almost blinding."

I stagger, heart thumping, mind running and winded. "Bullshit," I mutter. "There's just no way." I stare at Rhyme, see desperation mix with sadness.

Cain seems to suppress his loss of control. His voice is thin, rattled. A quiver of rage haunts his upper lip. He adjusts his tie, then seems to adjust a glove that's no longer there. He pauses, inhales, glances at Rhyme, then at me.

Then, he paces to the window, places a hand on the glass and looks out at the swollen sky. His voice is strained, even confused. "It seems, dear Emery, that God, indeed, works in mysterious ways."

END

Dear Reader

Thank you for reading *Embers of Shadow,*
Book III of the epic series, *Ages of Malice.*

Please take a moment to leave a quick star review and spread the word
to your fellow readers. By sharing your opinion, you lend credibility to
me as an indie author and generate trust in others that they're getting a
story worthy of their time.

The saga continues with *The Tempests of Time,*
Ages of Malice, Book IV, scheduled 2025.

Join Lloyd to get news and more at:

www.lloydjeffries.com

Turn the Page for an Excerpt

THE TEMPESTS OF TIME

———————————————

AGES OF MALICE, BOOK IV

LLOYD JEFFRIES

THE TEMPESTS OF TIME
AGES OF MALICE, BOOK IV

Chapter 6

Hackles rise. A giant paw scratches Emery's door. Houdini spins, whimpers in a high pitch, circles, paws the door again.

"Shh, let the man rest."

The dog nudges her hand, tries to warn of something.

She presses an ear to the door. Muffled moans seep through.

Her own hackles rise. She turns the knob and tiptoes in. Her prince's shadowed form is sleeping, vulnerable.

Passion devours. Her breath comes fast and shallow. She throbs, fights the urge to join him, to wake him with a special surprise, a flash of deadly desire. If he wakes, she doubts the resolve stretched over her feelings will do much to counter her passion.

She considers the consequences, considers what Cain will do to them if they get caught. Bound by marriage. Bound to the Antichrist.

Does pure evil absolve one of a promise? Does the fact of her husband's treacherous nature erase the vows she'd made? Worry deserts as a beckoning tickle centers in her tummy, then flows to her groin. She inhales a stuttered breath.

"Emery?" She suppresses thoughts like "feeble excuse" and "convenient need".

The room's a large rectangle. To her left stands Emery's bed. Past that, windows, broad and draped, block the muted light. How long's it been? Twelve hours, fifteen? He's never slept that long unless bent on drugs and alcohol.

Shivers trace her spine. He'd said he was cured, said Cain cured him. What if he lied? Or was tricked? What if he doesn't know and just took Cain's word for it? What if he's addicted still and sleeps so long because of the chemicals he ingested or injected?

He moans; arms twitch.

"Emery?"

Eyes adjust to the darkness as instinct nips her neck. Something isn't right.

"Emery?" A singsong voice, like the old days. "Time to get up."

She crosses to the windows, throws the drapes wide, giggles at the thought of his reaction to the sudden burst of gray light.

Then, her jaw drops.

Smoke rises from his body, from skin, head, arms. Thin wisps curl lazy, seem magnified by the gray light. Clad only in a pair of blue Tommy John's, he writhes, moans, small blisters bursting in real time over his torso.

"Emery!" She races forward, grasps his shoulders, shakes. "Emery! Wake up!"

Arms lift, then swat at invisible things. A muted wail rises. Hands tremble, clamp to his jaw.

"Emery!"

Houdini jumps on the bed, yelps, leaps away.

Emery's eyes flutter but remain closed, hand firmly pressed to his chin.

Houdini backs away, hackles raised, crouched. A low rumble rolls from his throat. He glances at Rhyme, gives a look that says, "Um, you coming?"

The familiar returns, instinctual, a warning on full alert, sirens blaring as lights strobe. She feels it but can't define it. An inflammation of sense, of primal instinct.

She races to the bathroom, throws a handful of plush towels in the sink, then turns the water on full. Once saturated, she hurries back, drapes the drenched towels over scalded, blistered skin as thick smoke coils on the ceiling.

Emery whimpers, says something unintelligible as eyes flutter like a kite in a storm.

"Is everything okay?"

She whirls, finds Cain in the doorway, sardonic smile cemented on his lips.

She spits the words. "You know goddamn well everything's *not* okay. What did you do?"

He steps close, peers down at Emery. "Is he ill?"

She stammers, steps forward, blocks his path. "I don't know. Is he?" Great transparent pockets grow on Emery's body, threaten to burst a rush of sanguine fluid as blisters spread, thicken, become grotesque. His hand remains pressed to his jaw, locked there as if granite.

Cain looks puzzled. "Odd," he says, "illness shouldn't befall him. He's immortal."

Rhyme feels the rage, an acid that burns cartoon princess and fluttering birds to pastel ash. "Don't give me that. What did you do?"

Steely blue eyes return her gaze. "I did nothing save attend to pressing matters. I returned so we could talk about a task I need you to perform."

A feeling of calm smears her concern as she stares at icy orbs. She turns her back on him, sits on the bed, places a hand on Emery's forehead. "I'm busy."

Cain tuts. "Emery will be fine, my dear. I'm certain of it. Perhaps he's just experiencing the completion of his transformation from mortal to immortal."

Visions of vampires rise. Emery, pale and white, sallow. Long, yellow fingernails grow to crusted talons; teeth become fangs. "Nonsense," she says. "You're up to something and making Emery suffer."

"My dear," he says, placing a hand on her shoulder. "He cannot die. Anything that's struck him is quite independent of me. Perhaps he's suffering the rigors of casting off his addiction, eh? Withdrawal, perhaps?"

"Do we have any Doritos?" Bill stands in the door, dishwater locks bunched in a huge man bun.

"Bill, get in here," she says. "Something's wrong with Emery. I can't wake him. And…and his skin… it looks like it's burning. Look at the blisters, the smoke."

The joint burns red as he inhales, holds his breath, paces beside Cain. "Yeah, dude. He doesn't look good."

Cain chuckles and the blisters disappear. Wafting vapors hang stale, mix with exhaled dope smoke, then swirl and drift to nothing.

She levels a finger at Cain's shaking head. "You did something?"

"I assure you, my dear, I did not." He sighs, smooths his suit. Anger flashes on his features, but fades just as fast. "In any event, he appears quite well currently. In fact, I can't say for certain what we saw was anything more than a trick of light. Floating dust combined with sunbeams. I'm certain he's fine." His smile dazzles, brightens the room by degrees. "I'm afraid I must leave soon, but was wondering if you'd be so kind as to spare a few seconds for your poor accused," he raises a finger, "but long-suffering, husband? Emery needs his rest and I'll only be a minute."

Bill's expression is vacant and glassed.

"Bill, can you keep an eye on him until I return? I shouldn't be long." She glances at Cain. "And I don't believe for a second that he's *fine.*" She exaggerates the last word, eyes locked on her husband.

Bill presses the weed to his lips and takes a long drag. "Uh, sure, dude," he says, smoke flowing. "Don't be long though, Gibran's *Prophet* awaits." His smile is boyish, innocent. He scratches a scruffy beard, then the butt of faded paisley pajamas.

She follows Cain into the hallway, stares at his back, wishes for a knife, or the twin Sigs hanging in the bedroom closet. "What?"

His smile disarms her. He steps close, places both hands on her hips. "Your country needs you, my dear." He looks like a snake basking on a warm rock. "This afternoon I've arranged for you to take the oath of Imperium. As empress you need to be beloved. An example of faith and loyalty. The most beautiful woman in all the realm, much adored by all our subjects. I've taken the liberty of arranging a wardrobe to be delivered. Not that anything could detract from your radiance, but an empress must be especially ravishing. As *my* empress, you need to reflect my power and glory."

She pushes his hands away and steps back. "I won't do it."

Cain looks surprised, shakes his head almost imperceptibly. "Indeed, my dear, you will. It's your duty both as my wife and to your country."

"My country?" she says, flummoxed. "*My country!* What a stupid thing to say! Perhaps you haven't heard, but *my* country was erased by some power hungry asshole."

Cain's head jolts like she just slapped his smug face. "Of course, of course," he says. "Still grieving. And not incorrect, incidentally. In fact, I'm happy to take the blame. An example had to be made."

"Is that what you're doing with Emery? Making an example? Of what happens when one tries to run away?"

Crystal eyes flicker toward the ceiling as he sighs. "My dearest Rhyme, if only you'd place the smallest amount of trust in your emperor. All I do, I do for us, for you. You're the light of my life. A blessed beacon in treacherous waters. What purpose does harming Emery serve me or Imperium? I need no such tricks and took no such measure." He glances at Houdini. "Like your new hound, Emery serves me well. I've no wish to harm him, only to train him."

"He's not a dog!"

"Isn't he?" A smile shines from a chiseled face, silver hair dances above. He waves a hand. "Let's not quibble, my dear. I must go. I'll see you this afternoon, at two o'clock."

No! The word rattles, scrawls bold lines and thick curls. Instinct says he's lying. Says he has *everything* to do with Emery's distress. *Go to hell,* she thinks. *I'm not taking any oath! Not wearing your stupid gown. Not going to be Imperium's shining fucking empress.*

Bill pokes his head out, clears his throat, drags on the joint. "You guys almost finished?" He peers down at worn slippers shaped like Easter bunnies. Button eyes stare back, looking as stoned as the man who wears them. "Doritos?" he mutters.

Another thought hits her. She's had enough of this, her husband, this evil, this crazy game and all its trappings. *Be smart, Rhyme. Be bold. Keep your own counsel.* "I'll be there," she says in a pleasant tone. "Send a car, won't you?"

Cain showers the room with sparkled elegance and effortless tranquility. A single clap reveals his joy and puckered, inert mark. "Excellent," he says, then gives a peck on the cheek. "Tonight, we celebrate in the grandest of style. I'll see you soon." She glares at his back as he steps away. Then he stops and turns. "If it helps, I'll send a nurse to stay with Emery until we return next week."

Rhyme stutters. "Next week?"

His smile holds her, binds her in a comforting, chilling embrace. "A grand tour awaits, my dear. Imperium's empress, the most radiant beauty the world has ever seen, *must* be displayed. There are rounds to make, uses for your grace and beauty to gain the world's confidence." He chuckles, presses a fist to his mouth. "It's probably hard to believe, but sometimes world politics distills to simple, gracious relationships." The Hollywood smile glares, grips, deceives. "You, my dear Empress, are my secret weapon."

Chapter 7

Stone sizzles as my skin erupts in flame. Something seizes my spine, searches, then plucks each nerve like taut guitar strings.

I grasp this reality, realize this can only be death. My throat seizes. My legs go numb, then shoot out, locked in agonized spasms.

The smell's horrific; molten flesh, charred, flaming. Thick dribbles that vent to filthy steam.

I wail, plead for mercy, grovel, beg.

Cain stands above me, a GQ model with dripping fangs.

Clawed nails, black and filthy, rocket forth and grip my throat.

Then, a blinding light.

All pain ceases.

Then a perfect white tablecloth.

I feel calm. Subdued. A bit sedate, even, detached.

Cain sits across from me, raises a porcelain cup painted with pink flowers.

To my right, an elderly man sits regal. His features give the impression of lengthy sickness. Gaunt, sullen like a vast and spreading cancer.

I swoon. The chair tips as gravity presses.

Then, I'm upright.

The man next to me snickers into his fist. "That was unpleasant. Eh, my boy?"

I'm afraid to take him in. There's something, a klaxon in my brain, flashing red. There's danger here. The feel of a knife plunging, of demons wrenching my tongue, then raising my beating heart before me.

I tremble as the warmth of urine soaks my pants.

The man leans forward, caresses my cheek with fingers like slimy fish. He whispers a single word, eyes half shut. "Serenity."

Something blinks. I inhale a fragrance, vanilla and lilac, think of my Rhyme, her hair burnt, her face charred, spitted above roasting flames.

From somewhere far off, I hear a discussion.

"You must be more careful with your servants."

"How was I to know?" This is Cain.

"Of course, of course. How does one know anything at first?"

Then, "Emery, my boy. Emery, come back to us." The voice is smooth and aged, like a somber trombone. "You are sound, my boy. The horrors are gone." A thin hand grips my shoulder. "Open your eyes, Emery. Look around. Breathe. Breathe. That's it. That's it. Now drink this, it will prop you up."

Porcelain rattles on its fragile saucer.

Trembling hands fumble, then raise it to my lips. The saucer falls to smash on the floor.

Then, a tuxedo. A waiter with broom and dustpan sweeping up

shattered fragments.

"There, there, my boy. You see? Not all bad. Yes?" Before I can respond, he says. "Drink, drink. That's it. Now inhale again. Deeper. Good. Now, deeper still. Hold it in. Feel it cleanse. Search your mind, Emery. Reach for peace."

A moment passes.

"There we are," he says. "Almost good as new. That was quite a snootful, was it not?"

I glance at the man, who looks healthier, less elderly. He catches the cup as it drops from my fingers, then places it on the table.

"You really must be more careful with your servants," he says.

"Are they not mine to do with as I wish?" Cain says.

The man chortles, then presses a ghastly fist to his mouth. "Of course, they are. But within reason. You've yet to realize your true power. Temperance must rule, at least for a time. Now, now, don't look so glum. Am I incorrect in the assumption that Emery is your biographer?"

Cain nods, glances at his plate.

"Well, then, what's the harm in showing him everything?"

Cain remains silent.

The man snickers again, the sound of a strangled bunny. "I must apologize, Emery. You see, this is all new to us."

I muster my strength, aided by the tasteless liquid I choked down, then look the man right in the eyes.

My mind fills with scenes of blood and murder, of molestation and anguish, of hope banished, dreams crushed. Howling faces—

He averts his gaze as I inhale sharply. A tremor returns to my digits.

"Never look me in the eyes," he says, "for there, you'll find the unimaginable."

I reach for the cup but knock it from the table with a shaky hand.

"Oops," he says. "Here we go again." He snicker-squeals. "Breathe, lad. Deep. Slow. That's it." Then to Cain. "You may have been a tad overzealous. I'm not sure our Emery will recover."

Something inside me grows, demands self-control. His words inspire spite. I'll recover if it's the last thing I do.

I concentrate on Rhyme's fragrance, inhale, suppress visions of her torture.

Emerald eyes smile as she reaches, then wraps me up. My head falls on her chest where I weep like no tomorrow. "It's okay," she breathes in my thoughts, "you're made of bigger things, *for* bigger things." Feminine hands glide through my hair, then squeeze me tight, just enough.

I look up. Force my breath calm.

The man hands me another cup and I down what's in it. "Where am I?"

His snicker pops, echoes. "Where are you? Such a direct, succinct query. A supreme query, as one thinks about it. But I'm afraid the answer isn't gained so simply." Thin fingers tug a tie of silken blue, perfectly knotted. "Currently, you're in a sort of limbo. You possess space, but do not define it in the way of a sitting chair or a tossed ball. I suppose the best answer isn't really the best, if you catch my meaning. Let's say that you're in between. A shadow of sorts, but not a ghost or apparition—I mean, you yet retain form and mass—but rather a notion, a cobweb adrift on tempests of time." He props his chin on a pale palm. "Are you familiar with Dickens?"

I swallow hard, try to avert my eyes from that kittenish pose.

"Of course, you are, silly question," he says. "All writers know their Dickens." He clears his throat and suppresses a chuckle. "Are you familiar with his tale of Christmas ghosts?"

I nod as I continue to battle the rigors.

"Well, it's not like that at all. But then, it *is* kind of like that. The difference being that no one cares to change your beliefs or attitudes. No one here cares really, and let's do be honest, about anything you think or feel. I could go so far as to say that no one here really cares about your comforts, pleasures, sufferings, or thoughts." A bony finger rises, wags twice. "But don't mistake my meaning. This isn't singular to you. The same applies for Cain and myself. Where you are now is sort of an unreality, if such a thing makes sense. Had I not intervened, I'm afraid my servant may have done irreparable harm."

Cain speaks up. "I believe my servant—"

"You're dismissed." Iblis speaks without even a glance. I hear a shush, like corduroy rubbed together, and by the time I look, Cain's gone. I glance around as tremors return to my limbs.

Iblis focuses on me with an expression like he gives a damn. "But there now, I've changed your clothes and soothed your mind. I mean, as much as I can effect *that* organ. And I think, as you regain your sanity, you'll have a better understanding of just where you are. You see—"

"Hell!"

Feline eyes flash red for an instant, then chill to aqua blue. "Tsk, tsk, we mustn't blurt, my boy," he says. "Hell is from where I retrieved you mere moments ago. Or at least, the version of Hell most solid in your mind. I feel a bit abashed, if I'm being honest, to have usurped my servant's servant for my own purposes. I'm sure he has plans for you, which most exactly explains why you still live. And he tells me you're immortal, so let me be the first to welcome you to such an exclusive society. Unfortunately, your immortality means nothing here. Nor does mine. Or Cain's." A gaunt waiter appears, golden drink balanced on a serving tray.

The man takes the glass and sips, then waives the waiter away. "Thank you, my boy."

Dark orbs flicker. "It seems I digress. You see, it's hard to tell this tale a bit at a time. But I suppose that's my challenge, and I shall give it my best and explain to you exactly why I intervened.

"I was thinking about Cain's new testament, the one on which you currently endeavor. I was thinking of history, and the bad rap I've truly gotten throughout. It was then I realized I had no chronicle, no *record,* of my own exploits. Certainly, humans have attempted to pen unholy books in my name. But the fact is, they've failed to a person.

"It's clear now I was a bit short sighted throughout my long existence. Telling any one person my full story feels beneath a being like me."

He sips again and sets the glass before him. "In that ilk, I'd like to formerly introduce myself, then show you the story about the true nature of that place from which I pulled you." He glances to where Cain sat, then continues. "I'd like to show you those things you don't know," he says, "and to borrow you such that Cain's biography is made even greater, not because of my exploits, but despite them. Consider what you'll endure as a bit of extra spice in the pot. Eh? Some extra zest for the sauce. See? Some pepper for the stew."

I surprise myself. "You can fuck right off."

He startles, blinks twice, then cackles like a broken harpsichord. "My boy! Language, language! If you'd like to refuse, I suppose it's your right, but no need for the profane. We have quite enough of that here and I find it distasteful. I mean, I certainly can't compel you to perform such a task if you don't wish to."

He stands, seems to creak like an antique chair, then paces a step and turns. "I accept your refusal," he announces to the room. "I mean, what's existence without free will?"

I nod and lift a newly placed porcelain cup to my lips. "Thank you."

"Oh, don't mention it." He steps forward, hands on his chair. "Then again, I'm reminded of that place from whence I retrieved you and think it advisable to remind you of that singular love of your life. Rhyme. Cain's wife, if I'm not mistaken. Yes, yes, Rhyme. Cain's wife. He's been exceedingly patient with both of you. Extremely out of character for one of his station and talents." A thin hand grips the glass. He sips, eyes turned upward, thinking. "I'm reminded of the old adage." His smile warms, his face appears more elderly, more trusting, a loving father with sober advice. "Love is blind. Do temper your choices with wisdom."

Then a burst in my mind, a single-second migraine: Rhyme spitted, roasting, her emeralds holding me as she shrieks.

"I'll do it." The words come before I even notice.

He doesn't miss a beat. "Excellent!" he says, then presses his fist to his mouth. "This will be a grand undertaking, and a story even you won't believe."

I sip and try not to think about whatever trick they're playing.

The old feeling returns. The rock pressing me to the hard place. The age-old damned if you do, damned if you don't. Seems a constant theme: fucked no matter what. "I'll need my phone and a notebook," I say.

"Tut, tut," he says. "That won't be necessary. You'll remember everything quite well."

I set my eyes on the shimmering white tablecloth. "As you wish," I sigh. "Let's be on with it. I generally start with name and occupation. Do you mind sharing yours?"

He appears suddenly spry, blooming mischief as he radiates power. His suit becomes fire red. A top hat appears, as does a stout cane like ebony granite.

With a doff of the hat, he bows with a flourish. "I am Iblis, Lord of the Jinn."

About the Author

Lloyd Jeffries enjoys dark comedies, philosophy, clever turns of phrase, and thought experiments involving the esoteric and legendary. A decorated veteran of numerous conflicts, he served in the U.S. military and has practiced Emergency, Trauma and Wilderness medicine for more than twenty years. He hides out in Florida with his family and Buck the Wonder Dog.

Embers of Shadow is the third book in his award-winning epic series, *Ages of Malice*.

The saga continues with *The Tempests of Time, Ages of Malice*, Book IV, scheduled 2025.

Follow Lloyd to get news and more at:
www.lloydjeffries.com